BLACK HORSE
MOUNTAIN

BLACK HORSE MOUNTAIN

KINLEY ROBY

WHEELER PUBLISHING
A part of Gale, a Cengage Company

GALE
A Cengage Company

Wheeler Publishing Large Print Softcover Western.
The text of this Large Print edition is unabridged.
Other aspects of the book may vary from the original edition.
Set in 16 pt. Plantin.

LIBRARY OF CONGRESS CIP DATA ON FILE.
CATALOGUING IN PUBLICATION FOR THIS BOOK
IS AVAILABLE FROM THE LIBRARY OF CONGRESS.

ISBN-13: 978-1-4328-8725-4 (softcover alk. paper)

Published in 2022 by arrangement with Kinley Roby

Printed in the USA
2 3 4 5 6   28 27 26 25 24

For Mary

CHAPTER 1

Jonathan Wainwright stood in his stirrups to give himself a better look at the Kansas grassland with a creek winding through it, stretched out below him, looking deceptively calm in the morning sun. Since leaving Independence, Missouri, he had learned these plains often gave sudden birth to thunder, lightning, and violent storms that ripped the calm to shreds.

He had been riding a week, his only companions his bay horse, Sam, and the pack horse Chew, a young roan mare with fire in her eye and a taste for tobacco. Jonathan had also learned this wide-open country, with its vast sky and constant wind, took some getting used to. The monotonous expanse of land and sky was only slightly varied by prairie flowers, scattered in the grass like white, red, orange, and blue jewels as far as the eye could see.

On that May morning, the grass-covered

plain immediately below him was also dotted with at least fifty very large wagons, looking larger because of the immense water barrels strapped to their sides. A few smaller wagons, their loads also covered in canvas, were gathered near one another. Clustered near each of the larger wagons were a dozen or more oxen, staked out, grazing. Beyond the wagons was a herd of horses and mules, with another herd close by of cattle and more oxen.

People were moving among the wagons and picketed animals. The women, Jonathan noticed, were tending the fires, and the faint smell of frying meat drifting up to him suggested breakfast was under way.

The scene reminded him that he had set out on a journey with no planned destination. Until this moment, he had been able to keep that fact tightly tethered by the routines of riding and sleeping and watching the country unfold before him without making claims on him. The sight of the wagons suggested that freedom was about to pass, restoring him to life with other people, no matter how unfamiliar.

"Well, I suppose it's better than cutting my throat," he said to Sam and dropped back into his saddle. "Come along, Chew. Let's see what we've gotten ourselves into."

Once among the wagons, he was impressed by their six-foot-high wheels, and, never having worked with oxen, he was equally surprised by the massive size of the animals. He was also puzzled to find that the oxen belonging to each wagon were all matched in color, their coats sleek and shining in the morning sun.

Moving Sam at a walk from one wagon to the next, Jonathan found that no one showed any interest in him, forcing him, finally, to stop a short, fat man bustling past and ask where he might find the wagon master.

"He could be anywhere here," the man said, pushing his wide-brimmed hat back on his head and squinting up at Jonathan's unsmiling face. "He's likely to be at one of the fires" — a rendition of *fires* that sounded to Jonathan like *fars* — "and he probably has cadged some breakfast. He hates cooking. Keep going. You'll find him."

With that, the man resumed his purposeful waddle.

Among the wagons, all with fires, all with people gathering around them, Jonathan was not encouraged, until a large, bearded man carrying a double-barreled shotgun, apparently having seen Jonathan coming, walked away from a fire and planted himself in front of Sam. "Are you Jonathan Wain-wright?" he said.

"I am, and you are?"

"Eli Parker, wagon master of this train. The first thing I'd do, was I you, I'd lose those Union cavalry boots."

"You have a good eye for footwear, Mr. Parker," Jonathan said, dismounting, "but these boots are practically new. Shortly before the shooting stopped, I had a heel shot off one of my previous pair. These are hardly broken in."

Parker grinned through his grizzled beard, his first show of friendliness. Jonathan did not grin back.

"When I got the telegraph from Preston Miles, *jefe* of the Santa Fe Freight Company, of which this outfit is a part," Parker said, "telling me you were coming, I was a mite irritated. I'm a careful man and do not like last minute changes. Also, I took you for a greenhorn. I'm guessing you were an officer in the cavalry?"

"I was," Jonathan said. "I rode with General Philip Sheridan from the Shenandoah Campaign to Appomattox. When it was over, I swore I'd never get on another horse, but, as you can see, I was inaccurate in my prediction."

"You're also an educated man."

"That might be an exaggeration. I am a doctor — at least I was before enlisting. I haven't treated anything but a neighbor's cat since resigning my commission."

"You've got an odd look for a doctor," Parker observed, appearing to have found something troubling about either Jonathan's blue eyes or his manner of speaking.

At that moment, a foghorn voice at Jonathan's back bellowed, "Parker, I want my teams at the head of the line."

Jonathan turned and saw a tall, hard-faced man with a thick, gray mustache, dressed in a dark flannel shirt, string tie, black trousers, and wearing a gun belt with a silver buckle and a bone-handled revolver in a tied-down holster. Two equally hard-looking men flanked the speaker.

"Mr. Callaway," Parker said, quietly but firmly, "the drawing's been held. You drew number twenty. The order of the wagons is settled."

"It's not *settled,*" Callaway said, "until I say it is."

Jonathan had encountered men like this all through the war. Confederate raiders, mostly, robbers and plunderers. He guessed from the man's accent that he was looking at another one. "I was present at the drawing, Mr. Callaway. There were no mistakes,"

11

Jonathan said in a deceptively quiet voice.

"You keep your Yankee mouth shut," Callaway bellowed, "or I'll shut it permanently."

In the next instant, Callaway's hat sailed off his head, with the sound of Jonathan's Navy Colt still ringing in the air, the barrel pointing where the hat used to be. Callaway's two companions reached for their guns, then froze as Jonathan barked, "Stop there or he dies!"

"And this shotgun has two barrels," Parker said.

For a moment, Jonathan thought they might give it a try, but, as close as they were, they had to know a blast from Parker's gun would cut a man in half. They lowered their hands, keeping them spread well away from their bodies.

"This isn't over," Callaway said, his face flushed with rage, his right hand still hovering over his gun.

"It is, Mr. Callaway," Parker said calmly. "You and your wagons will not be with us when we leave tomorrow."

One of the men picked up Callaway's hat and passed it to him.

"There will be a reckoning," Callaway barked. Grasping the hat, he turned and strode away.

"I didn't see you at the drawing," Parker

said to Jonathan, meeting the younger man's eyes and understanding better what had puzzled him about them.

"That's because I wasn't there." Jonathan holstered his gun, still watching Callaway. "Perhaps I overreacted."

Parker gave a short laugh. "You might call shooting Callaway's hat off overreacting. I call it damned quick thinking. Probably stopped me from getting shot. My guess is, Mr. Callaway wanted my job and would not have hesitated a second to kill me for it."

"To what end?" Jonathan asked.

"He's probably got a renegade bunch in back of him. After shouldering his way to the leader's position, he would have led the wagons out into the blue beyond, called in the rest of his men and robbed everyone in the train of their gold and silver, collected their weapons, headed up the horses, and ridden away. The war has left a lot of men like Callaway still above ground. It wouldn't have been the first robbery on the trail by Callaway's kind. They're worse than the Indians."

"I'm glad I was with you," Jonathan said.

"So am I," Parker said. "That was pretty fancy shooting for a doctor. It's not my business, but I'll ask anyway. Why are you joining a wagon train to Santa Fe?"

"I couldn't seem to settle down in Boston," Jonathan replied, falling significantly short of the truth.

Parker gave him a long look. "Whatever has brought you here — and *here* being a hard place, Dr. Wainwright — it's not too late to change your mind."

He forced a small smile. "Jonathan will do, and I'd better finish what I've started. If I can be of any help to you once we're under way, aside from my medical skills, don't hesitate to ask."

"I'll take you up on that, Jonathan, and you might as well call me Eli."

The two men shook hands. Then Parker said, "You heard Callaway. He will be back, and when we least expect it. I've got fifty-three freight and sixteen immigrant wagons in this train, a hundred and thirty-nine men, women, and children by my last count, a little over five hundred head of oxen, a sizeable remuda of horses, and a herd of cows. If you're willing, I could use your eyes and the support of your guns — I see that Spencer in your saddle scabbard. I want you to be my eyes ahead of the train, principally to report on any war parties you see, hopefully before they see us. Don't hesitate to refuse if the job's not to your liking."

"I'll be glad to help," Jonathan said, all

the while hearing a voice somewhere in his head telling him, *this comes of shooting off that Reb's hat.* "But I've got a question."

"Which is?"

"Why have you got so many oxen?"

Parker laughed. "Most of the big wagons have six oxen in their teams. The heavier loaded have eight. The animals are switched out at regular intervals to keep them fit, so we have to have a few more being rested than are pulling the loads. We always lose some from one thing and another."

"And their brands tell you which wagon each animal's attached to?"

"That's right. Now," Parker said, changing the subject, "my wagon's a cut-down Conestoga, carrying only a sleeping compartment and my food and water supplies. You're welcome to bunk with me if that suits you."

"Thank you, Eli, but let me think about that. Are there any provisions made for medical needs on these trains?"

"Take your time," Parker said. "And yes, medical supplies for the animals and the rest of us are in a second wagon, with its own ox teams. There's also another big wagon full of parts for the other wagons and blacksmith stuff, even down to a forge. Horses need to be shod. Also some of the mules, depending on their owners. My mules aren't shod. I find that works best. The need for medicals over our next eight hundred and some miles will be greater than you'd think. It's a close race between oxen and people as to who can get into the most trouble. The oxen, especially, need a lot of looking after. The worst dangers to them are being gored and drinking bad water, but yoke sores and hoof damage are a constant. The largest wagons are loaded with trade goods. The rest carry families, looking for new lives. By the way, can you cook?"

"Not really," Jonathan said. "After eating my cooking for three days, I began to seriously consider starving."

"That's bad news, but I'll ask around. There may be a woman in the train we can hire to do it for us. I'd rather chew sand than cook."

"Couldn't we pay one of those families you mentioned to feed us?"

"You in a position to pay well?"

Jonathan managed not to laugh. "I don't think that will be a problem."

CHAPTER 2

One look and a quick sniff inside Parker's wagon convinced Jonathan he would sleep outside.

"It's probably just as well," Parker said. "I believe I snore. You can pack your gear in here if you want. The canvas keeps the rain out, and being stored out of sight makes it less likely to attract light fingers."

"Is there much theft on a train like this?" Jonathan hadn't thought of being robbed.

Parker shrugged. "Not a whole lot. Probably about the same as you found in your regiment."

"The consequences for stealing run fairly high in cavalry units," Jonathan said. "Military jails are nasty places for thieves that live long enough to find themselves in one."

Parker chuckled while trying to fend off Chew, who was pushing her nose against his pockets. Jonathan had been transferring his packs to the wagon as they talked, and

Parker, sounding concerned, finally asked, "What ails this horse?"

"She's hooked on tobacco," Jonathan said, having put the last pack away. "She may nip you if you're holding out on her."

"I might be able to find a plug in the wagon." Parker grasped the mare's reins and backed his newfound friend off him.

"I wouldn't. If you do, she'll pester you to death."

"Then I won't." Parker stroked Chew's neck. "She's a fine animal. The train will begin leaving by moonlight tomorrow morning. We'll spend the rest of this day getting everyone ready to go."

"Which means what?"

"That you'll ride around with me, meeting the people, getting a hang of how this is going to work, or not, for the better part of the next two or three months, depending."

"Depending on what?"

Parker laughed, but there was no humor in it.

"Weather," he said, "trail conditions, raiders, cholera, renegades, and Indians. The last either want to trade or cut your throat, and it's not always easy to tell which until they're right on you."

"I had a chance to stay in the army and fight Indians," Jonathan said, "but, from what I saw, I found I was more inclined to fight *with* them instead of against them."

"You ever meet the Comanches and the Pawnees?"

"Can't say I have."

"Hold your decision until then. Let's go."

"What about Callaway?"

"When he came to confront me, he had his two wagons hitched up and ready to move to the lead position. He's probably already turned them back toward Junction City. He'll either join the next train forming or he'll gather in his men and give us some lead time, then hit us."

"Your plan to defend against such an attack is . . . ?"

"We've got at least twenty-five men with rifles. More with sidearms, and my second wagon is carrying a good supply of ammunition," Parker said. "The hitch is, we'll need half an hour to circle the wagons and get those men into position."

"Is that where I come in?"

"That's right. You can give the men some training in organizing a defense. I'll arrange for a night watch and give you some backup on point. You'll need to be riding far enough out to see trouble coming soon enough to give us time to get ready for it."

"Were I Callaway," Jonathan said, "I'd

strike at first light while the train is all strung out and the animals are still grazing."

"Makes sense, so we'll pull together at the end of the day, and we'll make a roster for night watching. I'll have a meeting before we go and explain that we're all going to have to keep our guns within reach, especially at night. Everyone with sidearms will wear them during the day, and the rest will keep their rifles where they can grab them."

"What about the men driving the oxen? Will they be available in an attack?"

Parker made a face. "No, at least not quickly. Their first task is to get the wagons into a circle, and trying to hurry an ox team is like trying to make water run uphill."

"Why are oxen and not horses pulling so many of the wagons?" Jonathan asked, his impatience showing.

"There's several reasons," Parker said, clearly on comfortable ground again. "Indians won't try to steal them. They want mules to sell and horses to add to their importance. The grazing's poor along much of the Santa Fe Trail, and an ox can thrive on a diet that would soon wear a horse down. Also, if it's properly cared for and worked wisely, an ox will still be pulling its weight long after a horse is coyote scat."

By four the following morning, the break-fast fires had burned down, and dirt had been kicked over the coals. By the light of a three-quarter moon and the bellowing of oxen being yoked and the shouting of the teamsters, the wagons, creaking and groaning, got under way. "We could use a breeze," Jonathan said, squinting in the dust kicked up by the sudden movement of so many animals.

"Dust is right behind horse flies and mosquitoes for a plague," Parker said. "I've never gotten used to them, but I've long since given up trying to fight them. A little rain and mosquito netting are some help. I'll fit you out with netting. A lot of rain makes mud, which is a misery. What we're going to do now is get the small family wagons up to the head of the line."

"Don't they have numbers?" Jonathan asked, breaking into Eli's litany of woes.

"No." Parker rose in his stirrups to turn more easily and survey the action. "They lead because they can begin the circle more quickly in an Indian attack. Also, they seldom get mired. Were that to happen and they were at the back of the train, they might fall behind the rest."

"And make more likely targets?"

"That's about the size of it. We're not on

a Sunday picnic."

They were approaching a group of smaller wagons, some drawn by horses, others by mules, several of whose owners were pulling down the edges of the canvas covers and tying them to pegs and iron rings set in the wagon beds. All over the field, the oxen were moving, their drivers shouting, the cracking of their whips sounding like small arms fire in the rising clouds of dust. Jonathan thought he might tie a handkerchief around his neck, to pull over his nose and mouth at such moments as these, and noticed many of the men had already done that. Breaking through the other noises were the high-pitched voices of children running and shouting in excitement, hurrying to get the last of their belongings into the wagons, and women calling to one another, snatching clothes spread on the ground for drying, boxing up cooking gear, and gathering in the children who were running everywhere.

"Let's stop here a minute, Jonathan." Parker pulled up beside a medium-sized wagon, all its gear stored. A tall, raw-boned man dressed in black sat up front with the reins in his hands behind a pair of black mules.

Jonathan took him for a minister, but his first glance at the woman seated beside the fellow riveted his attention. She wore a pale-gray dress and matching bonnet, her hands folded in her lap. It was her face, framed by the bonnet, that arrested his attention. By ordinary standards, it was not a remarkable face, although Jonathan had already noticed her dark eyes and thought them lovely. He was also quite certain he had never before seen a face displaying such serenity. It was the serenity, he told himself, that gave her an arresting beauty.

"Mr. Stockbridge, ma'am," Parker said, touching the brim of his hat and leaning forward slightly in his saddle. Such formality from him surprised Jonathan. "I'd like you to meet Dr. Jonathan Wainwright. He has agreed to help me with the train from here to Santa Fe. I warned him it wasn't going to be a hayride, but he stayed with me." Parker swung around in his saddle. "Jonathan, this is Mr. Gideon Stockbridge and his daughter, Miss Patience Stockbridge."

"Dr. Wainwright," the man said in a heavy voice, regarding Jonathan with quiet intensity.

Patience met Jonathan's gaze with a quiet smile. "I'm pleased to meet you, Doctor. You will be very welcome on the train. I think you are the only doctor among us."

Jonathan removed his hat. "It has been some time since I have practiced, Miss Stockbridge."

"My name is Patience," she answered. "I hope that is what you will call me. Father and I tend to dispense with unnecessary ceremony."

"And mine is Jonathan. I would be honored if you would call me that," he said, quickly putting on his hat again.

"Thank you, Jonathan." Again, that quiet smile. "Father and I welcome the informality that indicates no lack of respect or earned esteem."

"Certainly not," Jonathan said, startled into his answer. He'd never before met a young woman who spoke with such frankness. Encouraged by her openness, he said, "May I ask why you are going to Santa Fe?"

Her expression turned sober. "Father and I are Quakers, and it came to the attention of our community that slavery was still being practiced in New Mexico . . . especially in Santa Fe, where the Indians are often enslaved by wealthy Spanish families to this day. *Genizaros,* these unfortunate souls are called."

"And you hope to work towards ending the practice." Jonathan strove not to sound incredulous. What could this young woman and her father do, all alone in a strange city where such things were accepted?

She inclined her head. "That is our intention, in response to our calling."

Parker interrupted the conversation, speaking rapidly and with too much cheer. "We wish you success, don't we Jonathan? And, on another subject, I would like you to lead us off, Mr. Stockbridge."

Stockbridge, scowling at Jonathan, asked Parker to repeat his request. The wagon master did so, and Stockbridge nodded. "Certainly. Someone must," he said, his scowl vanishing.

"Thank you," Parker said, looking relieved. "I'm going to call us together before starting. Once you're under way, keep to this side of the river, and please don't hurry."

As Parker and Jonathan moved away from the Stockbridge wagon, Jonathan said, "I didn't know there was slavery in New Mexico. If there is, have those two lost their minds, butting into it?"

"I expect you was winding up to say something like that to Patience when I cut in." Parker pushed his hat back on his head a little. "As Patience said, they're Quakers, and the old man is stiffer than a crowbar. He usually brings up short any man he judges is taking liberties with his daughter. Had you said what you were going to say, he would have had your scalp."

"Interesting." Jonathan felt mostly amused, but also puzzled. "Are there really slaves in Santa Fe?"

"There are plenty of stories to that effect, but the *Genizaros* live and eat with the families and are pretty well cared for. Or so I hear."

"Where do the Stockbridges come from?"

"Rhode Island, I think," Parker said.

"I thought I recognized the accent. In times past, the Quakers had a bad time in Boston," Jonathan said as the two moved off down the line of wagons. "There was a while in the seventeenth century when Puritan magistrates were cutting the ears off Quakers, until Charles II put an end to it. After that, they had to be satisfied with stripping them to the waist, men and women alike, tying them to the back of a wagon, winter or summer, and whipping them all the way to the state's border. Luckily, Rhode Island welcomed them."

"Sounds about like that outfit," Parker said.

"I'm surprised they have mules pulling their wagon. They looked as though they were well enough off to afford horses."

"Didn't the army use mules for pack animals?"

"Yes, come to think of it."

"If I didn't want to avoid unnecessary attention," Parker replied, "I'd be riding a mule. On average, they're stronger, smarter, longer-lived, and easier to feed than horses. Treat a mule right, and you've got a friend for life. Also, they don't have to be shod."

"I can't imagine a cavalry regiment mounted on mules," Jonathan said, laughing at the thought.

"Triumph of ignorance over reason," Parker said and rode off.

Jonathan was soon too busy sorting out the wagons and choking on dust to think about the Stockbridges or their mules, but, every once in a while, Patience's face would slip into his mind. Each time, conflicting feelings arose about their brief conversation. He had come away from their meeting feeling like he failed at something, but unsure what, exactly. He also wasn't sure whether her buoyancy and forthrightness pleased or offended him. An answer was not forthcoming, and that too annoyed him. He decided he did not want to think about her and tried hard not to. To his further irritation, her quiet smile and pretty dark eyes kept popping up like a slightly condescending jack-in-the-box.

It was late afternoon before the last of the oxen teams had drawn their wagons to the gathering place. Jonathan had spent most of the time riding up and down the train, making himself available to any of the bull whackers having difficulty with their wagons or their oxen. The most common problem was having one of the green oxen get a leg over the tongue chain.

"There's some good news," Parker said when he and Jonathan were together again. "I've got us a cook, and it's not going to break us paying her. She's one of the older girls in the Howard family. They're the ones with that cross-eyed collie named Bailey. The girl's name is Jane. Keep your fingers crossed. She's cooking our supper tonight."

Jane Howard did not annoy Jonathan. She was too pretty and too clearly what she was to offend anyone. Tall and straight backed with wavy, light-brown hair caught back in a red ribbon, she had large green eyes bright with life and good humor.

"I wouldn't ordinarily do this," she told Jonathan, having shaken his hand with a strong enough grip to make him squeeze back a little just to stay even. "The truth is, I'm putting together my hope chest." She laughed, her cheeks flushing slightly, and added, "But you don't have to worry, though. There's precious little in it. How do you like your meat done?"

"I don't want to have to kill it a second time," he told her.

"Sounds right," she said. "I'll get to it."

By the time Jonathan had watered the horses, their dinner was ready. She had even made biscuits.

"There's more of that antelope and drippings in the big pan," she told him and Parker, "and potatoes in the small one. I guess you won't starve. If there's anything wrong with what I've set out here, tell me about it in the morning." She eyed Jonathan. "That Chew horse is a sweetheart. Does she ride as good as she looks?"

"You wouldn't stay on her long enough for me to let go of your foot," Parker said. "She's at least half mustang."

Before Jonathan could say anything, Jane bristled. "If I had half a dollar, I'd bet you I could ride her up and down this train sweet as sugar candy."

"Have you ridden before?" Jonathan asked, concerned she might get hurt. He hadn't shared his views on Chew, but they weren't far off from Eli's.

"I been riding since I could walk. Pa ran a horse farm, and help was scarce. Put a

29

bridle on her and let's see what happens. Don't worry about a saddle. I don't need one."

"I'm not sure this is a good idea," Jonathan said, but nobody was listening to him.

Jane and Parker walked off toward Chew, needling one another as they went. A few minutes later, Jane took the reins in her mouth, pulled up her skirt with her right hand, grasped Chew by her mane and vaulted onto her back. She spat the reins out and grabbed them as soon as she found her seat. "Go!" she said and pressed her heels into the mare's sides.

Chew went off like a rocket. Jane gave a whoop as her hair and her skirts blew out behind her, making Jonathan groan and Eli burst into laughter. "My God!" Jonathan said. "I hope her mother doesn't see her."

"That girl's an Injun," Parker shouted, waving his hat. "She's riding like she was glued to that mare."

Jane took Chew in a wide circle, flying between two wagons and bringing her back at a full gallop that ended in a swirl of dust. Laughing, her eyes shining, she leaped off Chew before the mare had fully stopped and hit the ground running.

"Where's my money?" she said, breathing heavily, her face flushed with laughter and the exertions of the ride.

"Right here." Parker hurried to her, pressed a silver half-dollar into her hand, and closed her fingers around it. "You are one fine rider and an outstanding cook. The man who marries you will have struck gold."

Jane's face flamed red, and for a moment she and Parker didn't seem able to break away from one another.

Grasping the moment, Jonathan joined them. "Miss Howard, you are a very fine horsewoman. I am impressed."

"I guess I made kind of a show, didn't I?" The flush left Jane's face, but she still let Parker hold her hand. "Jumping the tongue of that wagon was drawing attention to myself. Pa would have whopped me for it when I was a kid."

"Well, your pa didn't see it," Parker said, "but if he had, I think he would have swelled up and said, 'That's my daughter. Ain't she a crackerjack rider?' "

Jane's blush came back, but this time she freed her hand and said loudly, "Land sakes, Eli, I was joshing about this money. Here, take it back."

"Not on your life. You won that fair and square. When we get to a store, you can buy yourself something pretty with it. But right now, I'm hungry enough to eat grass. You get on. I'll take care of Chew."

Jonathan watched all this with a wide grin on his face, the first time he'd smiled like that for a very long time. Throughout the evening, whenever he thought of those two, standing together and holding hands, the smile came back. Parker never mentioned the moment and neither did Jonathan, but he was sure Parker and Jane had not forgotten it.

"Lord above," Parker said, pausing to catch his breath. He'd finished one of Jane's antelope steaks and started on a second. "We have found us a treasure. If some enterprising youngster don't run her off, we will be living in clover all the way to Santa Fe. How do you suppose she's managed to stay single?"

"Can't say," Jonathan replied. "One thing I do know, if you're looking for a wife, you could do a lot worse."

"Oh, Lord no!" Parker almost dropped his biscuit. "I'm way past that foolishness. She's more in your age range."

"Thanks, but no thanks," Jonathan said with finality. "I would make a very bad catch. You haven't left your forties. Think it over."

"What's this about your being a bad catch? From what I've seen, I'd think you could just about take your pick."

"Nice of you to say so." The words came out more sharply than Jonathan meant. "Perhaps you didn't notice that I would have killed Callaway and his two sidekicks earlier without a moment's hesitation, even though none of them had done me any harm."

CHAPTER 3

Later that night, Jonathan lay on his ground cloth, his head on his saddle, wrapped in a red- and green-striped Hudson Bay blanket, staring at the night sky. As usual, sleep had been fleeting. The night wind having kept off the mosquitoes, Jonathan had put aside his netting. After picking out the Big Dipper and the North Star and making a brief calculation, he decided it was about midnight. Perhaps he had slept a while without knowing it.

Close by, Chew and Sam were grazing quietly. Above him the Milky Way, surrounded by a darkness with not so much as the flare of a match to dim it, spread across the cloudless sky as if a giant's brush had swept over the vast emptiness, strewing it with stars. It was a sight Jonathan had seen many nights during the war, always drawing some degree of peace from its immensity.

Aside from the sentinels and the men

guarding the herds, the people in the long line of wagons were asleep, but Jonathan's mind, averse to rest, slowly drew him back to the event that had started him on this journey.

"If you go on this way, you will probably kill yourself or someone else." Dr. Amos Pendexter, white-haired and distinguished, had scowled across his desk at Jonathan before slowly unfolding his tall frame from his chair.

"Granted, there are days I would like to burn down the State House," Jonathan heard himself say. "But the problem, Amos, is that, after two years, neither of us appears to know what to do about it."

"I will address that later. I've seen your problem in other men who have come back from the war, their lives in tatters." Amos walked around the desk, pulled a spindle-backed chair closer to Jonathan, and sat down facing his patient. "Unfortunately, you don't have one problem," he said. "You have two."

"I don't know what you mean," Jonathan snapped back.

"Yes, you do. You just won't admit it."

"There's nothing to admit."

"John Hawks died while you were removing a chest abscess. He knew his heart condition made the operation a serious risk. Just as you feared, his heart failed, and you lost him. There isn't a surgeon who hasn't, sometime in his career, lost a patient. Many have lost several and kept on operating. What was your response?"

"I joined the Union Army," Jonathan said, wanting to jump up and run.

Amos changed the subject abruptly. "Two years ago, come April," he said, "you resigned your commission and came back to Boston a changed man. Am I right?"

"I would say so. I was three years older with some white in my hair. It's still there."

"Yes. You were what, thirty-three?"

"Yes."

"How would you describe your life?"

"I don't think about it," Jonathan shot back. "I get up and do whatever's before me."

"Did you sleep well last night? Did you eat a hearty breakfast?"

"Where is this going, Amos?" Jonathan asked, his voice darkening.

"Toward a deeper understanding of your situation, I hope. You did not sleep well, possibly not at all. If you did sleep, you had dreams that roiled your mind and wakened you, terrified or furious, gasping for breath. As for breakfast, you may have drunk some coffee. Has there been a single day this week when you have not found yourself seething with anger over something that should not have upset you at all?"

Jonathan sank back in his chair and shook his head.

"It's getting worse, Amos," he admitted. "That's why I'm here. You're the only one I can tell what living has been like since I came back."

He paused and gave a bitter laugh. "Since I withdrew my offer of marriage from Henrietta — for which she thanked me profusely — people I hardly know keep bringing up the names of young women I might like to meet. What in God's name, Amos, would I do with one of Boston society's cradle offerings?"

"I'll tell you. In less than half an hour, you would scare her half to death."

"I scare myself."

"You can't stay here, Jonathan. You stepped straight out of the war into the buttoned-up world of upper-crust Boston, which you left as one person and returned to as another. Am I right in saying Brahmin Boston is no longer a place where you fit in?"

"Truth be told," Jonathan admitted, "I feel

increasingly as if I'm going to choke to death."

"I'm not surprised. Does Harvard or the hospital need you? Do you need them?"

"No and no."

"Then leave. You're a wealthy man. Your father left you sound for life, am I right?"

"Yes, but Amos, I can't stop working. It's all that's holding me together."

"It's tearing you apart. Are you taking any pleasure from lecturing to medical students?"

"I am not."

"When you stepped down from that horse you were riding — "

"I had two shot out from under me," Jonathan said.

"The last one, then." Amos said, ignoring the interruption. "You went straight into the classroom. It was a serious mistake. You were in no fit condition to undertake such a radical transition or even wrestle with the question of whether or not you wanted to be a college lecturer, to say nothing of practicing medicine."

Jonathan sat silent a moment, thinking about it. "What follows?" he asked.

The older man sighed. "I think you know there's nothing in my training that tells me what to do for you beyond what I've already done. Therefore, what I'm going to say doesn't come from my medical training and draws only on my experience of trying to cope with your problem and that of others in your same situation. Shall I go on?"

"Yes, go ahead. It might even help — although I doubt it."

"I understand, and I give no guarantees. As I see it, you wake every morning to find yourself a stranger in a strange land. Have I come close to describing your situation?"

"I suppose so. I had not thought of it that way. I feel alarmingly detached from everything around me, and what I'm doing day after day seems to me a farce."

Amos nodded. "You wisely stepped back from resuming your profession as a doctor. You're in no state to practice medicine. The people closest to you see someone who isn't there, and the more you pretend to be that person, the worse you feel."

"That is true."

"Henrietta Choate," Amos said, urging him on.

"Her parents are breathing fire, but she's loose from me and staying that way," Jonathan admitted.

"Wise young woman. Was yours a sexual relationship?"

He stared. "Is that a joke?"

"I thought not. You're putting yourself at risk remaining here. I want you to go partway back into the life you left."

"Amos, I resigned my commission. The Union Army doesn't need another colonel, at least not since the South was brought to heel. And I don't want to fight Indians."

"I don't want you to reenlist, but I do want you to leave Boston, for a while at least. Go away, live a footloose life that will free you from conventional commitments. I want your days to be filled with outdoor activity and constantly changing scenery."

Jonathan gave a short bark of bitter laughter. "Am I to leave here and start walking in any direction but east?"

"Shall I answer that or save my breath?" Amos asked.

"Oh, go on. I want to hear what you're going to tell me."

"Do you know anything about New Mexico?"

"I know where it is."

"That's a start."

Jonathan paused, then said, "Hold on, Amos. You're not suggesting I go to New Mexico!"

"I have a connection in Santa Fe," Amos said briskly. "Preston Miles, a nephew. He owns a shipping company that transports goods north and south along the Santa Fe Trail. He also drives cattle, horses, and mules north along the same route. He would be glad to have you accompany one of his southbound wagon trains, leaving from Westport Landing in Kansas."

Jonathan's shoulders sagged, and he looked at Amos as if the man had lost his mind. "I spent most of the three years I was in the cavalry living outdoors, Amos. I have no desire to repeat it."

"Your life is disintegrating, and don't deny it," Amos said. "You came back with no more interest in marrying Henrietta Choate than I had, and even less in teaching medicine at Harvard. Despite your efforts, you're dying inside inch by inch, and one of these fine days you will grow tired of the struggle and either step in front of a runaway team or put a bullet in your head."

"You can't know . . ." Jonathan protested, upset by what he was hearing and the harshness of the doctor's voice.

"Yes, I can, and you know I'm right. The worst part of it is that you've stopped fighting this affliction. You've decided to die. For God's sake, Jonathan, get out of Boston. Give yourself a chance to live."

Forced to confront himself in Amos's description, Jonathan was flooded with sudden rage. He snatched his coat off the chair and strode out of the office, slamming the door behind him. The door had scarcely stopped rattling in its frame when he was struck by a flash of insight that rocketed across his mind like a sliver of lightning. In that instant his anger burned away, and he saw with alarming clarity what Amos had been struggling to make him understand.

He whirled around and walked back into the office. "You're right, Amos. I can't go on this way."

And he hadn't. Jonathan lay for a while longer, staring at the stars, wondering if he had done the right thing. The physical efforts of the day, added to the peace of the night sky, gradually quieted his mind, and he slept.

CHAPTER 4

Jonathan was wakened by Chew, standing over him and nudging him with her nose. It was first light, with the morning star still bright in the eastern sky and a pale-gray glow outlining the horizon.

He pulled the blanket from over his head. Sometime in the night, the wind had died, and the mosquitoes had found him. "Thirsty?" he asked the horse, looking up at her.

Sam was watching Chew, apparently with interest. Both animals were hobbled, and it was a long walk to the river. Chew appeared to be waiting patiently as Jonathan took his bed apart, but, when he bent over to pick up the ground cloth, she shoved her nose under his seat-end and gave him a hoist that landed him on his stomach.

"Hey!" He scrambled up, trying to sound angry, but it didn't work, so he settled for scratching behind her ears, which was what she had wanted.

At this point, Sam hopped over to have his neck stroked, a favorite form of attention for the tall horse.

Jonathan came into camp, leading his horses. Sam was saddled, and Chew was carrying a light load in her packs. "Look what the cat's brought in," Jane said, straightening up from stirring a pot over the breakfast fire.

"I thought we were going to have to drag you over for breakfast," Eli added, filling his cup with coffee.

"What's in the pot? It smells good," Jonathan said, cheered by Jane's smile.

She stood with one hand on her hip, the other brandishing the spoon. With the sun at her back, her pale hair falling around her face and glowing like a halo, Jonathan thought she looked beautiful. He started to say so, then quickly changed his mind.

"It's porridge," she said cheerfully, "but it looks like goose droppings."

Jonathan laughed.

"I heard that," Eli said, "and will keep it in mind when I'm eating it."

"Bacon and eggs to follow." She went back to stirring. "I expect these will be the last eggs we'll see until we reach Santa Fe, although there's a few wagons that brought some laying hens in cages. My opinion is that hens are nasty things. I should know. When I first came to the Howards, it was my job to tend the hens and collect the eggs. When one of them went broody, I had to plunge her into the rain barrel. Lord, what a to-do!"

"Did it work?" Jonathan asked, surprised by what she had said.

"It mostly did. Spoiled the rooster's fun, though," she added, ladling the porridge into their bowls.

Jonathan and Eli looked at one another, neither seeming to know whether to laugh or not. Eli recovered first and ate a bite of porridge. "Jane," he said, "this is very good and would be better with cream. Does the milk come from your cows?"

"That's right. Ma said she wouldn't budge out of where we was if they didn't come along."

While they ate the porridge, Jane finished cooking the bacon and eggs. While she loaded up their plates, she said, "Perch Trailer, one of Pa's nephews, turned up last night. He hangs around me, hoping one of these days I'll throw my legs around his back, but it ain't going to happen. For one thing, he's my cousin and for another he works for that Rand Callaway, who pulled out of here in a hurry. Perch said things might get really lively around the train before long, and Pa was to get the wagon off by itself and sit tight when it started."

"Is Perch the one with a scar on the right side of his face?" Eli asked.

"That's him," she replied. "Got hooked by a steer when he was twelve or thirteen. Tore up his face. Afterward, he got laughed at a lot by some of the kids in town. I think it was that made him mean. Something surely did."

Jonathan caught her eye. "Jane, have you any idea what he meant by what he said? About things 'getting lively'?"

"Well, I don't know what moved Rand Callaway to pull out of the train," she answered, "but I would guess, knowing something about the man, he intended to come back and make some trouble. He's been run out of most of Kansas. Trouble seems to be what he's good at. Now, eat them eggs before they go cold."

After she left them, Eli said, "It's clear as spring water what's coming. That Perch kid confirmed it." When they had finished eating, Eli went to the wagon and came back with a large brass hand bell. "Jonathan, climb onto Sam and go the length of the train, ringing this bell every now and then. They'll gather at the big center wagon. I'll take care of Chew and be there by the time you're back.

"I suppose the kid could be just bragging, to look good in front of Jane," Jonathan said, mounting up.

"How much would you bet on that?" Eli asked, passing him the bell.

"I'll ring the bell," Jonathan said.

Eli had climbed onto the seat of one of the big wagons while Jonathan was bringing out the people now gathered in front of him.

"I got all I could," Jonathan called from his saddle. The noise of the crowd, talking, laughing, and greeting one another, had made it necessary for him to shout.

"Get up here with me," Eli said. "I want them to get a good look at you."

Jonathan climbed up beside him and looked over the backs of the red oxen in the team pulling the wagon. The driver, dressed in leather trousers and jacket stained with wear, was perched on the back of one of the leaders, his long bull whip rolled in one hand. Seeing Jonathan, he raised the whip, and Jonathan returned the greeting.

"Let's have the bell," Eli said. He took it and started swinging it. The voices died

47

away, and Eli began his talk by running through the protocols of what he called wagon train survival, some of which was fairly scatological, which brought a scattering of whistles, shouts, and good-natured laughter, the women laughing along with the men. That startled Jonathan almost as much as Jane's comment about throwing her legs around a man's back.

That part finished, Eli paused for a full minute until the crowd's voices dimmed to silence. Jonathan recalled the cavalry officers were told about that strategy for gaining attention and was caught off guard by an unexpected flood of nostalgia for his cavalry days. The sound of Eli's voice erased it, leaving Jonathan with a trace of longing for something he couldn't name.

"What I'm about to say may decide whether you wish to stay with this train or not," Eli began in a loud voice, riveting his listeners' attention.

He paused to let his words sink in, then continued.

"A man by the name of Rand Callaway started with us. Some of you will know who I'm talking about. He and I had a disagreement as to who was going to be the master of this train. He left but warned me he'd be back. It was clear to Colonel Wainwright and me that he intends to return with armed men, to make his claim stick.

"For those who don't know who the Colonel is, he's standing here beside me. He has agreed to help me get this motley crew to New Mexico. He was in the Union cavalry and rode under General Philip Sheridan from the Shenandoah to Appomattox. Are those qualifications good enough to suit you?"

An explosion of cheers and shouted affirmations answered his question. Jonathan thought he ought to be angry, to be put forward as Eli had done, but, at the same time, he found a sense of pride flickering somewhere in the darkness of his mind, another feeling he had lost somewhere between the Shenandoah and resigning his commission.

"Then that's settled," Eli continued when the shouting ended. "Callaway is a dangerous man. He made one attempt to take my place as wagon master, backed by two men with guns. It failed, thanks to Colonel Wainwright, but Callaway will make another, this time with more men, and he will come shooting. He's a killer and a renegade. We've every reason to believe he intends to strip this train of whatever money we're carrying and drive off the stock."

Eli paused again. Studying the crowd for their reactions, Jonathan saw only grim expressions.

"I'm going to ask any of you willing to form an armed resistance to come forward," Eli said. "But first I want to say that if any of you choose to leave the train and wait for another, I will return your money with no hard feelings. That's your choice. Now, if most of you stay, we have more than enough men in this train to outgun Callaway. If you are willing to fight, come forward. Drivers, I'll talk with you later. The rest of you can go back to your wagons. We'll soon be on our way."

The assembled crowd murmured and shifted. Eli rummaged in a canvas sack between his feet and passed Jonathan one of two clipboards with a piece of paper and a pencil. "We'll get their names and what they've got for guns," he said.

Twenty men signed on, and all had both rifles and hand guns. Eli talked to them for five minutes, and they agreed to gather again following their evening meals.

"A couple of them can't be more than fifteen," Jonathan said as he passed his list to Eli, "but, from their looks and their accents, I'd guess they've been shooting squirrels since they were old enough to lift a pepper gun. Of course, toward the end, General Lee was fighting a war with an army, on the average, not much older than them."

"Whatever we can get," Eli said.

Jonathan thought he had glimpsed a bonnet behind the last line of men, and, now that they were leaving for their wagons, he saw Patience and Gideon Stockbridge sitting in the buggy he had seen tied to the rear of their wagon, apparently waiting to speak with him or Eli. Stockbridge sat stiff but calm, just the way the man had sat in his wagon. Patience was wearing the same gray bonnet, but her dress, he noted, was a pale pink. He did not ask himself why he had retained that information.

"Good morning, Jonathan," she said in her clear, bright voice, her eyes meeting his calmly and steadily.

"Good morning, Patience." It took him a second too long to break away from her gaze and address her father. "Good morning, Mr. Stockbridge. Can I be of any help, sir?"

"I think it's more a case of our helping you," Stockbridge said.

He spoke pleasantly enough, but he was, Jonathan thought, a man short on smiles.

Patience spoke up again. "Father means that, although we will not physically resist

Mr. Callaway's raiders, we are able and willing to set up and staff the closest thing we can manage to a field hospital for the wounded. We would, of course, treat the men from both sides of the encounter. I have spoken with several women who are eager to help. You may be pleased to hear that Jane Howard is one of them." She said this last with a slight smile flickering around her lips. To his great embarrassment, Jonathan felt his face begin to burn.

"I am certain Mr. Parker will be glad to have your help," he said, struggling to regain ground.

"You may find yourself having to make a difficult choice, Jonathan," Mr. Stockbridge said.

"I'm not sure I see your point, Mr. Stockbridge," Jonathan replied," but I think the actual shooting is likely to be over very quickly. In encounters like this, there is usually a mounted attack that will either carry the day or be broken. In the latter case, the surviving attackers will most likely break away and retreat."

"Often leaving the dead and wounded behind them," Patience said. "Father and I did some work in field hospitals during the war. You must have treated hundreds of men during your time in the army."

"No." Her comment disturbed Jonathan. "I served as a colonel in the cavalry, as Mr. Parker said. As I was never seriously injured during my service, I never was hospitalized."

"Was there some tragic event that caused you to abandon being a physician?" Patience asked, a slight frown disturbing the tranquility of her face.

Jonathan hardly knew how to respond. Her inquiry seemed to him to cross all sorts of boundaries and made him extremely uneasy. "You ask difficult questions," he said, floundering. "But, no, I found the cause that had brought us to war was too strong to resist."

"You enlisted to end slavery, not to preserve the Union," Stockbridge said.

"I wished to see both accomplished," Jonathan said firmly.

"How could you not?" Stockbridge sighed. "Now it is ended. The South is crushed, and several hundred thousand men are dead. Do you think, Jonathan, that slavery might have been ended another way?"

"Not in our lifetimes, sir." Jonathan's voice hardened. "They fought to preserve it to the bitter and bloody end. All the Southern prisoners I spoke with believed God had intended the black race to be enslaved. For three years, I saw Southerners in their hundreds risk dying to preserve it."

"It was terrible," Patience said quickly, seeing, perhaps, that Jonathan had begun to think her father was baiting him. "Thank God it is over."

Jonathan came close to saying he doubted God had anything to do with it but shut himself down. He touched his hat and was about to leave when Stockbridge said, "You are the only physician in this train. Do you intend to treat the wounded should we be attacked?"

"You do not know me well enough, Mr. Stockbridge, to ask me that question," Jonathan said, his temper flaring, "and I will not answer it. I must go. Thank you for your offer. I am sure it will be accepted."

"Jonathan." Patience's voice rose in concern. "Father did not wish to insult you. Although you do not practice, you are still a doctor. Isn't that so?"

"You must excuse me, Miss Stockbridge, Mr. Stockbridge. It is a subject I do not wish to discuss." He turned and strode away.

Chapter 5

The sun had lifted above the horizon, the morning wind had begun to stir, a large red-tailed hawk was climbing into the new day on updrafts created by the sun's warmth, but Jonathan scarcely noticed. He was extremely angry, and Stockbridge's question kept rocketing around in his head like a bird on the wrong side of a window.

The cause of his anger was, in part, Stockbridge's having asked him such a personal question. The remainder of the reason, possibly the larger part, was that he had not treated the wounded in the war and at his enlisting had registered as a Harvard Professor of Medicine. After resigning his commission, Jonathan had reluctantly resumed his profession, but he had not allowed himself to question his conviction that his service to the country had been fully as important as working as a doctor.

Jonathan desperately wanted to believe

that he had acted honorably in responding to Patience and her father as he did, but, as he fled their presence, he increasingly felt he had behaved in a shockingly ungentlemanly manner, completely contrary to his upbringing and the image he had fostered of himself. Most alarming, he suddenly realized that he could not have given Stockbridge a coherent answer even had he wished to.

All around him, as he hurried toward Eli's wagon, the wagon train was stirring like a giant reptile. The bellowing of the oxen, the shouts of the drivers, the cracking of their whips, the groaning and creaking of the huge wagon wheels being dragged into motion, the swirls of dust kicked up by the wheels and the animals' hooves, mingled with the women's voices calling to children and the lingering people's hurrying to clamber into their wagons, created an atmosphere of tension and excitement that even Jonathan, disgusted as he was by his own behavior, could not help feeling.

"We only lost half a dozen families, and they all had a passel of kids," Eli shouted as Jonathan made a running mount onto Sam.

"I've got to speak with the Stockbridges," he shouted back. He did not have far to go, and he had no idea what he was going to say to them, but it was very clear in his mind he must say something, and the sooner the better.

The Stockbridges' team was leading the train. Jonathan reached it and brought Sam to a walk beside the front of the wagon where Gideon sat. "If I may, Mr. Stockbridge," he said, "I would like to make amends for my rudeness. I am very sorry for it. If you would prefer not to hear what I have to say, I fully understand."

"It's not necessary," Stockbridge said, in the calm voice Jonathan had come to expect, but somewhat louder to compete with the creaking wagon and the drumming of the horses' hooves in the remuda being driven past at an easy lope. "But if it would make you feel better, my daughter and I will gladly hear you out."

"Oh, yes, very gladly," Patience said — easily enough, but Jonathan noticed the worry line in her normally smooth forehead.

"Thank you," he said. "My reasons for abandoning the practice of medicine are things aside from the manner of my reply to your question. I deeply regret the tone of my response. It was entirely uncalled for. I hope you will allow me, over time, to convince you it is not indicative of who I am, although there is no reason at present for you to believe me."

Stockbridge's bland expression made Jonathan uncertain how his words were being taken. Despite his attempt to concentrate on Stockbridge, he found his gaze darting repeatedly to Patience, to see how she was responding.

She leaned toward him, no longer frowning. "Jonathan, Father and I have no sense of being insulted by your response. We would also like to say how sorry we are for having upset you. Among the people we recently left, we are accustomed to the open frankness with which we addressed you, but we both forgot that you might find it intrusive, even alarming."

Before Jonathan could muster a word, Stockbridge cleared his throat. "Jonathan, I think Mr. Parker is trying to attract your attention."

Turning in his saddle, Jonathan saw Eli, standing on the seat of his wagon, waving at him.

"I am afraid I must go," he said. "Thank you for your kind words."

Stockbridge nodded. "You are more than welcome."

"And do not be a stranger." Patience managed a smile.

"I will not." Jonathan replaced his hat on

his head and urged Sam into a gallop, feeling that a great weight had been lifted off his mind.

Eli looked worried when Jonathan reached him. "Our wrangler tells me we've got a problem," he said.

Wrangler was a word Jonathan knew only as someone who quarrels or a third-year University of Cambridge student who wins a math award. He had no idea what Eli was talking about.

"He's in charge of our remuda," Eli said impatiently. "His name's Morgan. I think he was born on a horse. He won't even go for a piss on foot."

"What's wrong with the horses?"

"Nothing, except two of them are stallions," Eli answered in disgust.

"How did that happen?" Jonathan asked, a bit more sharply than he had intended.

Eli did not appear to notice. "Morgan says the second one came in with the last dozen horses we acquired just after dark last night. They're going to the Becknell Santa Fe Company. Hiram Rodman is their owner, or will be if we get them there. He's dead set on breeding blooded horses. Wants to race them. Will you catch up with Morgan and see what can be done about the situation before he puts the barrel of a gun in the ear of one those stallions and shoots it? He tends to draw a straight line between a problem and its solution."

Jonathan chose not to tell Eli that what he knew about racehorses would not fill a calling card. The prospect of meeting the wrangler and seeing what kind of chaos the stallions were creating in the remuda had braced his spirits, and he gladly rode off to do as Eli asked.

Morgan Baxter was about half a foot shorter than Jonathan, whose first impression was that Baxter had got that way by being shrunk in the sun and turned into rawhide. He didn't appear to have an ounce of fat on him. The weathered skin on his face looked as if it had been painted over the bones. His eyes were a bleached blue, and his hair, tied back in a ponytail, was coal back, despite the fact that he likely wouldn't see sixty again. Shaking his hand was like gripping a knot in a hemp rope.

"You know anything about horses more than which end eats and which end shits?" Baxter asked, in a loud voice much too deep for a man his size.

"I do," Jonathan said, getting into the spirit of the question. "The first man who had anything to do with them invented swearing. I had a jug-headed roan for a while, meek as a lamb while you were looking him, but if you forgot and looked away, he'd kick you into the middle of next week."

"What happened to him?" Baxter asked with a grin, proving whatever his face was made of was limber.

"A minié ball went right through him. He thought I'd done it and died trying to get his teeth into me."

"Cavalry?"

"Yes, with General Philip Sheridan. By the time we got the horses, any good ones had been run off and sold to the other side."

"Ever worked with stallions?"

Before Jonathan could answer, a shrill scream split the air. Horse, not human. Looking over the remuda, Jonathan saw a coal-black animal standing on its hind legs, its mouth opened wide and its front legs flailing.

"I gather that's one of them," he said.

Baxter nodded. "It is. He's a thoroughbred, going to Hiram Rodman, and should never have been sent this way. He's also dangerous as a cornered rattler."

Jonathan had been watching the stallion. "He's big, with hindquarters like a draft horse."

"He's three hands taller than the rest of the horses in this herd," Baxter said, "except

61

for the chestnut quarter horse stallion that's also going to Rodman. The chestnut's almost as heavy but built along stockier lines. There he is on the back side of the herd, chivvying that white mare."

"I've got him," Jonathan said. "Have the stallions tangled yet?"

"Not seriously. They've tested one another a couple of times, but I've managed to break them up."

"Any of the mares in estrus?"

"No, but the way the chestnut is hanging onto that white mare, she's probably on the way. With winter behind us, all the mares in this herd will be coming into estrus soon."

"All hell will break loose when the black horse gets a whiff of her," Jonathan said.

"That's right. Can you work a rope?"

"No."

"I thought not. Can you cut a horse out of the bunch?"

"Yes. What have you got in mind?"

"Well, it's not a perfect solution to this mess," Baxter said, adjusting his hat as he spoke — the only show of emotion he had made since shaking hands with Jonathan. "We'll have to cut the remuda into two bunches."

"One stallion in each?" Jonathan asked, not expecting an answer. "And you're right about it not being perfect. Those two will be trying to steal mares from one another from here to Santa Fe."

"Right, and there's the problem of finding hands to ride with two bunches," Baxter said.

"I may be able to help with that, at least for the daylight hours. Have you got an extra saddle?"

"Yes. What do you want with it?" Baxter's eyes narrowed.

"I want to borrow it for an hour or so."

"Does this have anything to do with getting me some help?"

"It does."

"You stay with the remuda, and if those stallions get into each other, rather than wait for one of them to be killed, shoot the one most hurt. We might just manage to get one of them to New Mexico."

With that, Baxter rode off, leaving Jonathan with the horses.

"Eli was right, Sam," he said, a smile brightening his face. "Morgan Baxter does think in a straight line. Let's go see if we can get that quarter horse off the white mare. The way he's nipping her, she won't have any hide left on her by midday."

Jonathan had dealt with stallions enough to know that if they are frightened, they can be dangerous. If not, and what you are doing interests them, they're likely to let you approach without fear of being bitten or kicked.

With that in mind, Jonathan began working Sam through the herd at a walk and doing his best to make his advance not look as if he was heading toward the chestnut. The stallion grew interested and stood with ears pricked, watching. The white mare took the opportunity offered and began moving away. Jonathan edged Sam between her and the stallion, and only then did he turn Sam directly toward the big chestnut. By that time, the mare had managed to work herself well into the herd.

A loud whistle turned Jonathan's attention away from the stallion. Morgan had returned and was waving at him, his horse bearing the requested extra saddle.

"Here," Morgan said, heaving the saddle onto Jonathan's lap as Jonathan and Sam drew level with him. "I see you got our quarter horse off the white mare. How did you do it?"

"Counted on his curiosity." Jonathan balanced the saddle as best he could. "I'm glad you came. I'd made up my mind to try to put my hand on him."

"You might have done it, unless he ran

out of curiosity," Morgan said without smiling.

"I'll put this on Chew and be back shortly, with or without her," Jonathan told him and rode off.

The Howard wagon was not an impressive construction. Whatever paint it once had was long gone. Its canvas cover, stretched over bent ash hoops, was stained and frayed at the edges, and flapped at the corners where the ropes had worn it through. Four sturdy oxen pulled it, moving in that swaying gait that once seen is never forgotten. There was something timeless and inevitable about yoked oxen, Jonathan thought, watching them.

Jane and a tall, lean woman with a narrow face were walking beside the wagon. "You come to complain about breakfast?" Jane said cheerfully when Jonathan, leading a saddled Chew, drew up beside her. "This here's my mother." She grasped the woman's arm. "Ma, this is Dr. Jonathan Wainwright. He rode with General Sheridan in the war."

"I'm pleased to meet you, Mrs. Howard," Jonathan said, taking off his hat.

The man walking at the head of the oxen must be Mr. Howard, but he showed no

65

interest in their visitor. That was not true of the five youngsters who came racing from whatever had been occupying them and skipped and jumped around Sam and Chew, talking and laughing. Jonathan guessed the youngest was about five, and the rest went up in height like steps. They were all tow-headed and almost identical in looks, but they did not look like Jane. The girls looked like their mother and the boys like the man prodding the oxen. Jane resembled neither, though she did share the children's blonde hair.

Mrs. Howard gave him a sharp look that displayed no pleasure in the introduction. "What was your rank, Mr. Wainwright?"

"I was a colonel, ma'am."

"I didn't meet many of your kind, Colonel," she said in a steely voice, "but I shore met enough of the scrapings to last me well into the future."

"Oh, Ma." Jane pulled the woman against her. "That's all over and done with."

Mrs. Howard threw off Jane's arm from around her shoulders. "Oh, no, it ain't," she said. "What do you want with Jane?"

"Mr. Parker has a job opening up that would pay her well. He needs someone to ride herd on the remuda a few hours a day. She would be well protected."

66

"You interested in that, Jane?" Her eyes drilled into Jonathan.

A smile lit Jane's face. "Oh, yes, Ma!"

"Speak with my husband, Jess, Colonel," Mrs. Howard said, with a nod toward the fellow trudging near the oxen, still not looking at her daughter. "I wouldn't get off the horse, were I you."

Jonathan didn't trust himself to speak. He touched his hat in thanks and urged Sam on, leading Chew along until he was abreast of Jess Howard. "Mr. Howard, may I speak with you?"

"What do you want, Wainwright?" Howard asked without looking up. He was tall, broad, and heavily muscled, wearing dark wool trousers and a collarless shirt He walked with his head thrust forward and his jaw set as if he were going into battle. Jonathan had seen a lot of men in a charge who carried themselves like that.

"Mr. Parker is shorthanded because the organizers of the train added extra livestock at the last minute," Jonathan said. "More horses came in last night. He's looking for someone to help Morgan, the wrangler, ride with the remuda a few hours a day. Jane's riding skills more than meet the requirements of the job. She will not be alone or exposed to any danger. It will pay well, though I don't yet know the exact amount."

"Who's going to be with her?"

"Morgan, Mr. Parker at times, and me when I can."

"What does her mother say?"

"She told me to talk to you."

"Ask Jane. If she wants to, she can try it," he said, finally looking at Jonathan, his square-jawed face knit into a scowl. He paused, then asked, "Did you shoot Mr. Callaway's hat off when he was talking to Parker?"

"I did." Jonathan's gaze drifted to the revolver Howard wore on his hip in a well-greased holster.

"That was a mistake, but you won't live to regret it."

Jonathan went still on Sam's back. "Are you threatening me, Mr. Howard?"

A wintry smile tugged at the man's lips. "Now, why would I bother to do that? Had I wanted to rid the world of another Yankee, you'd already be dead."

A dark impulse rose in Jonathan to shoot Howard right there, but he fought it down, telling himself the man's children were running around them, that he was Jane's father. Instead, his barely controlled anger came out in words. "Did you ride with Callaway, Mr. Howard, when he was burning people

68

out of their houses at night? Raping their women, shooting unsuspecting people in the back, and robbing settlers who had no way of defending themselves?"

Howard's face darkened, and he reached for his gun, but Jonathan's Colt was already pointed at his head.

"The war is over, Mr. Howard," he said, "but some people don't seem to know that. We've got another chance to make this country work. Why not be part of the effort?"

"In eighteen fifty," Howard said, his harsh voice cracking with fury, "our people moved into Missouri from Tennessee. Then in fifty-four they crossed into Kansas and staked out better land than they had in Missouri. We took our slaves with us. Everything went well until the Free Staters showed up and began agitating to make Kansas free. That led to a lot of killing on both sides. We took no part in that. In sixty-one there was a vote, and the Free Staters won. Our slaves left us. We were reduced to farming for ourselves. Surrounded by Free Staters, nobody would work for us."

Jonathan lowered the Colt, though he kept a sharp eye on Howard as he said, "And when the war came, the fighting along the border with Missouri increased. Men like

Callaway became renegades, preying on the Free Staters. Is that right?"

"It is. Mr. Callaway kept them off our backs 'til he was run off by your people. We hung on 'til now, but the Free Staters kept coming at us."

"Won't you run into people who oppose slavery in New Mexico?"

"We've heard it's hung on there. And, if not, we won't be known, and feelings might not be so rank."

"It's not my place to tell you anything, Mr. Howard," Jonathan said, sliding his Colt into its holster, "but I will take the liberty of saying you no longer need a killer like Rand Callaway to keep you safe. If he is foolish enough to attack us, for your children's sake, stay with the train." He didn't wait for Howard's answer but turned Sam and rode back to the women. "You're hired," Jonathan told Jane, passing her Chew's lead.

"What were you and Pa talking about?" Jane asked, once they were riding away from the Howard wagon. She sounded worried. While Jonathan talked with Howard, Jane had gone into the wagon and come out wearing deerskin leggings under her dress.

"Your family had a hard time in Kansas,"

he said by way of an answer.

"Yes." Jane turned her head away.

"You were a child through most of it. Are the people you call Ma and Pa your real parents?"

She looked back at him. "How did you know they're not?" she demanded.

"Your brothers and sisters are like peas in a pod. Aside from your hair, you look nothing like them."

"I think my people came from German stock," she said, her usual brightness fading from her face. "I was ten, or thereabouts, when the Howards took me in."

"Do you want to tell me about it? If you don't, that's fine."

She shrugged. "There's not much to tell. There was something they called the scowers that hit the town where we lived. It killed my mother and father, and most of the other people. I survived. I was living alone in the house when Mr. Callaway and his men found me. They went through the town, taking whatever they wanted, me included."

"Probably cholera," he said. "How did you find your way to the Howards?"

"I've heard that word, *cholera*," she answered. "Bad water, ain't it?"

"Yes." Jonathan said nothing else, not

71

wishing to add details.

"Pa had ridden with Callaway for a spell," Jane said, apparently not eager for more information about the sickness. "He'd complained about Ma not having any kids, and Callaway gave me to them. I've been with them ever since. Once I moved in, Ma started having babies like those peas you mentioned."

"Have the Howards treated you well?"

She shot him a hard glance, then said, "I won't complain. They've worked me hard, but Ma learned me to read and write."

He veered away from the subject. "I asked Mr. Howard to stay with the train if Callaway attacks us." He couldn't help wondering about her life with the Howards and her time with Callaway and his men. They were disturbing thoughts.

Jane gave a watery smile. "I figured you would get around to that with him. I don't expect you got an answer."

"No, because I didn't wait for one," Jonathan said, adding a smile of his own. "I don't think your pa is a man who takes well to pushing."

"I know he don't," she replied.

By then they had reached the remuda and Morgan. Jonathan performed the introductions. "Jane, this is the head wrangler,

72

Morgan Baxter. Morgan, this is Jane Howard. She can ride rings around me."

Morgan gaped at Jane, apparently struck
dumb. Then he stared at Jonathan as if appealing for help. Amused, Jonathan took
pity on him. "Jane," he said, "show Morgan
what you can do. See that sorrel with the
white blaze? Bring him over here."

She walked Chew into the herd. Because
she wasn't carrying a lariat, the horses
showed no alarm and parted for her as she
angled her way toward the sorrel. The
animal soon picked up on what she was doing and began maneuvering to escape.
Chew, however, understood what was happening. Being a well-trained cow horse, she
cut the sorrel off every time and soon had
Jane working it out of the herd. A few
minutes later, Jane walked the sorrel up to
Morgan and Jonathan.

"There's two stallions in this remuda,"
Morgan said, overcoming his shyness
enough to speak, but not enough to look at
her at the same time.

"I saw them soon as I got here," she said.
"You've got trouble."

"Uh huh." This time, he managed to
glance at her. "We're going to split this herd
even-steven with one stallion in each half.
That done, you take one of the new herds

south a mite."

She turned Chew into the herd. A few minutes later, Morgan said with wonder in his voice, "Lord above! Will you look at that girl work them horses."

Ten minutes after that, Jane's herd and the chestnut quarter horse were bunched and moving south at a smart trot.

"Am I working or still trying out?" Jane demanded when Morgan and Jonathan caught up with her.

"The job's yours." Morgan managed to look at her long enough to get the three words out. Then he turned to Jonathan. "I'll hold that other lot together and keep them coming this way."

"I'll be back in few minutes," Jonathan said and rode after Morgan, who had fled at a gallop. "You're not finished yet," he told the wrangler when he caught up with him. "That's my horse she's riding, and you're going to give her the one of her choice from these two bunches."

"Done," Morgan said without a second's hesitation.

"There's competition, you know." Jonathan was beginning to enjoy himself. "Eli's got an eye on her."

"I don't have *my* eye on her," Morgan protested. "I'm not the marrying kind."

"That's what Eli said, but I notice he's taken up washing and shaving and combing his hair every morning before he comes to breakfast, and he praised her biscuits so much she told him to put a sock in it."

"I'm not talking any more about it." Red faced and mad as a wet cat, Morgan rode off around the bunch, elbows out and shirt-tail flying.

Delighted with his achievement in stirring up Morgan, Jonathan went back to Jane and told her to start looking for the horse she wanted.

"I already know," she said. "It's that bay mare taking point on the other bunch, and there's something else needing attention. If I'm going to be keeping this bunch ahead of the others, I need a rifle and a scabbard. I ain't much good with a side gun, but with a rifle I'm moderately good at ending varmints' worries."

"Did you become your father's son after he lost the slaves?" Jonathan asked.

"Well, I done the work of one, that's right enough, and he taught me to use a gun so I could shoot any Free Staters that came looking for trouble." Her face and her voice both lost their cheer as she spoke. Jonathan saw he had touched a painful subject.

"I'll talk to Eli, and with luck you'll have

a rifle and scabbard by tomorrow. How's that?"

She brightened a little. "Good. I'll miss Chew. She's a good horse, quick on her feet and smart."

"Well, let's see how it goes," he said.

"Thanks, Jonathan. I know you didn't have to do any of this for me. I won't forget."

"Start filling up that hope chest," he said. "If I'm any judge, you'll soon have a line of men waiting on you."

"Jonathan!" she shouted, her face flaming, "you go along! It's my plan to be an old maid."

She reached out to poke him as she protested, but he caught her fist and said, "There was a cow ran up a tree," before releasing it and riding away with a wide grin on his face. For the past couple of hours, he had been enjoying himself, and he gave himself points for having wrestled down the black impulse that had told him to shoot Jess Howard.

CHAPTER 6

"Anyone here know how mounted Indians attack?" Jonathan asked ten days later.

Eli had called a halt earlier than usual, to have a meeting of the men who had agreed to do the fighting should the need arise. Jane, equipped now with a rifle, wanted to take part, but the men were so shocked, she had to leave. Thirty of the men were gathered around Jonathan and Eli, between the wagons and the herd of cattle.

"I've tangled with the Comanches a few times," one man said. Jonathan guessed he was in his fifties. He was dressed in a mixture of wool and deerskin clothes and wore his gray hair down to his shoulders. He sat cross legged, Indian style. A long Bowie knife hung from his belt in a fringed sheath, and a Sharps rifle lay across his lap.

"Let's hear what you have to tell us," Jonathan said.

"All right. They come at you strung out

and crisscrossing in front of you, shooting arrows and firing guns. The arrows are more of a danger. They can bring down a buffalo at fifty yards with one of them while riding at full gallop and sometimes hanging over the side of their horse."

Some of the listeners groaned in disbelief and made mocking comments, until Eli hushed them with an upraised hand. The Indian fighter ignored them.

"What's your name?" Jonathan asked.

"Jubal Smith," the man said. "I'm from northern Texas, and if you come from North Texas, you know a hell of a lot more about Comanches than you want to. Coming north with a herd of mules last year, we were attacked three times. None of us was killed, but we lost nearly half of the mules."

"What defense did you find most effective, Mr. Smith?"

"Bunch the wagons around what animals you've got and shoot from under the wagons, behind your saddles," Smith said. "If you stay in the open, they'll rain down those arrows 'til people look like pin cushions. You think I'm lying, but I ain't. They don't come in all the way in their charges. They'll come in shooting, swerve away still shooting, break up, and another bunch will come. Then the first bunch will come around again, riding hard, shooting arrows all the time."

"Thank you, Mr. Smith," Jonathan said. He looked around at the group, some of whom were still muttering. "While I was with General Sheridan, we heard a lot of stories about the Comanches and how they fought. Everything I heard supports what Mr. Smith's been telling us."

He paused to see if anyone else wanted to speak. Three of the oxen drivers, who had been travelling on the Santa Fe Trail since the outset of the war, confirmed Smith's account. "They don't like losing men, though," the oldest driver added. "If one or two Comanches go down, they'll gather them up and leave, deciding their medicine is bad."

Jonathan waited, making sure no one else wanted to speak. "As a cavalry man, I've often thought about their method of attack," he said finally. "We're dealing with a group of people who spend most of their lives on horseback and have developed ways of fighting while mounted that are murderously effective.

"I have a suggestion many of you will probably not like much, and it's this: Their strength is their weakness. At the first charge, we shoot their horses, and every man who makes it onto his feet after his mount goes down."

Murmurs of criticism rose from the group, along with louder comments about cowards from the younger men. Jubal Smith and the drivers, however, got to their feet and urged support. "You ain't seen what we have," the drivers said, almost in unison.

"For those of you who ain't seen one of their charges, listen up," Smith said. "Their ponies are fast and sure footed. The riders come at you yelling and blowing their whistles, and they ride with both hands free. They don't sit still a second, nor run their horses in a straight line. Instead, they're shooting arrows faster than you can fire, jack in a new shell, and fire again."

"I think the colonel is onto something," another driver said. "We none of us like the idea of shooting horses, but it's a damned sight better than being hung by the thumbs and skinned alive, which will happen if the Comanches get their hands on you."

"This here is their country," the second driver said. "It'd be smart to remember we live in their world as it is, not as we want it to be. The horses are a damned sight bigger target than those Injuns, flip-flopping all over the place. I doubt they'll charge more than once if they start losing their horses.

They're damned near helpless without them."

Smith sat down, in a silence thick enough to shovel. The driver's remark about being skinned alive had hushed the critics.

Eli cleared his throat. "As wagon master, I want you all to know I support Colonel Wainwright's plans, including shooting the Comanches' horses."

There was no more dissent, only a few grim nods. "Before we let you go, I have one further suggestion," Jonathan said. "If you've got any silk cloth, wear it like a loose vest. The Mongols, who conquered China, rode west in the twelve hundreds, all the way to Venice. Back then, they were probably the world's best bowmen. They learned that an arrowhead wouldn't penetrate silk but instead would push it into the wound, making the head much easier to pull out."

Nobody laughed.

"You figure they're ready?" Eli asked as he and Jonathan watched the men disperse.

"We won't know unless we're attacked," Jonathan said grimly.

Eli scratched beneath the brim of his hat. "What's your thinking about Callaway? I expected him to strike us by now."

"Assuming he still intended to stage an attack," Jonathan said, "he's probably hoping we'll let our guard down. My guess is, he's coming pretty soon."

Once the train was under way, and pretty well settled into its routine, Jonathan was up before dawn and had eaten breakfast by first light. Jane came every day to prepare it, dressed in deerskin leggings under a short skirt, a long-sleeved, blue cotton blouse, and a short denim jacket, with a waterproof cloak rolled and tied behind her saddle. She rode the bay mare she had named Katie to Eli's wagon.

"Lord above," Eli said in an awed voice, seeing her for the first time in her new outfit, "if you ain't the prettiest thing this side of Santa Fe, I'll eat a skunk raw."

"Is that supposed to be a compliment, Eli Parker?" she demanded, glaring down at him, a fist on one hip.

"Why, yes," he said, looking badly shaken.

Jonathan was adjusting the belly strap on his saddle as Sam munched on some oats and paused to watch the exchange.

"Well, the next time, leave out the skunk," she said in the same whipsaw voice, swinging off Katie and dropping to the ground in front of him. "What kind of thing is that to say to a woman? God Almighty, Eli, there are times I think you don't know a pie from a cow flap. Get out of my way. I've got another breakfast to make."

After Jane left, Eli looked up from the remnants of his breakfast, wearing a hang-dog expression. "It ain't easy to please a woman. I was afraid there for a minute she was going to bite one of my ears off. Did you hear any of that?"

"It's not as bad as you think, Eli," Jonathan said, struggling with his urge to grin. "If she hadn't liked the first half of your compliment, she wouldn't have gotten so angry over the part about the skunk. You went off message there a little."

"You having a laugh in your pocket at my expense?"

"Maybe a little, but I'm telling you the truth. I'd leave the animal comparisons out of future compliments. She's a fine woman, Eli. I'd hate to see you lose her to Morgan."

"Morgan wouldn't know what to do with a woman," Eli muttered, looking sour.

"You'd be surprised at how steep the learning curve is when there's a woman around to help out."

Eli's scowl deepened. "You going to mess with that belly strap all morning?"

"Just leaving," Jonathan said, climbing into his saddle.

■ ■ ■ ■

Since leaving Westport Landing the good weather had held, with a shower passing over them just often enough to lay the dust. Riding point had given Jonathan many hours to learn how to remain alert with a warm sun and a soft wind stirring the grass for company, and the occasional small band of antelope or deer, jack rabbits, and sometimes a skunk or badger hustling by. Overhead, the vultures, hawks, and eagles circled, surveillance and clean-up crews, riding the updrafts of air.

"I'd fall asleep if I was you," Jane told him one morning at breakfast by the fire, "with nothing to keep me thinking. That bunch of mine and especially that stallion give me work enough just holding them together. The quarter horse is some animal. I keep thinking that one day I might throw a rope on him and see how he'd take to a saddle."

"Don't you do more than think about it, Jane Howard," Eli said, scrambling to his feet. "That thing would kill you quick as look at you."

Jane colored a little. "Oh, don't fret yourself, Mr. Parker. I'm not as dumb as I look."

"You don't look dumb, and stop calling me Mr. Parker," he said, obviously flustered. "The name's Eli and you know it, and I don't want you getting yourself kilt, is all."

Having gotten a rise out him, Jane began to hum as she went back to turning the meat in the frying pan.

About halfway through the afternoon, Jonathan was amusing himself thinking about the merry dance Jane was taking Eli on. It occurred to him that his mind was becoming a little easier to live with, and he thought — though without much conviction — that perhaps Amos Pendexter had been right about leaving Boston.

He had told Sam what he thought and was about to give the horse odds that Jane had decided to corral Eli, and that their exchange at breakfast had been the opening moves in her campaign. He was just going to add that Jane would make Eli a fine wife when one of the principals in his reflections came up behind him, riding at a full gallop.

"I've come to fetch you, Jonathan," Jane shouted, turning Katie sharply enough to send dirt and dust flying. "Gideon Stockbridge was gored bad by a wild bull. Can't nobody get a rope on the animal. Two or three's tried. We got to hurry."

He was already turning Sam back toward

the train. "How bad is Mr. Stockbridge hurt?"

"Bad. Some of his insides is outside. Miss Stockbridge said would you please come? I've got one of the Bartlett youngsters riding with the horses, but I can't leave them long. That stallion would run the whole lot of them over the horizon, given half a chance."

She told him more as they rode. "Mr. Stockbridge saddled the little gray gelding that pulls their shay, took their buggy whip, and rode right at the bull. The bull knocked the gelding flat and gored Mr. Stockbridge before lighting out after Eli, who rode in and whacked the bull with an oak wheel spoke to get him off Mr. Stockbridge. That big horse of Eli's outran the bull, but the bull was so mad he tackled one of the red steers, and I reckon he's killed him."

Jonathan was only half listening to her. He was confronting what was being asked of him, and it was clear he'd have to do what he could for the old man, for Patience's sake if nothing else. The thought made him sweat, and he fought the anxiety down with a glance at Jane. "How are you around blood?" he asked her.

"I've seen my share of it, and back home I helped with half a dozen birthings," she said. "Come to think of it, I've stuck enough pigs to feed an army."

"You'll be bloody to your elbows," he told her. "Are you willing to do it?"

"If I pass out, you can douse me with water, and I'll get up and start again."

"All right, we'll get someone to relieve the boy."

The train had stopped, and a constantly changing group of people was gathered around Patience and four other women who had torn up precious sheets from their trunks and pushed them against the wounded man's body in an effort to stop the bleeding.

"You've probably saved his life," Jonathan said to Patience and the women with her, "but now I want just one of you to go on holding those cloths against his side. The rest of you get a fire going and get me two big kettles to boil a lot of water and find some yellow bar soap, two or three ground cloths, and the heaviest white thread you've got."

"I will hold the cloths," Patience said. She was white as the parts of the sheets that weren't red with Gideon's blood but could not be persuaded to let one of the stronger women take over the task.

"I've brought ether and morphine," Eli

said, hurrying up to them. "One of the bull's horns caught Stockbridge in the side of the head and knocked him cold. The critter's second swipe was what gutted him."

"Give them to Jane. She's going to help sew him up." Jonathan felt as if he might lose whatever he ate last. Added to that was a fear that he would not be able to do what he was being called on to do. He had not sliced human flesh with a scalpel in six years, and the thought of it made his head reel. But there was no backing out now.

"There are some things in the wagon I need," he told Jane. "I'll get them. You lay out one of the ground cloths, folded once, beside him. I'll be right back."

"You all right?" Jane asked, leaning close and speaking low.

"I'd better be," Jonathan said and strode away. When he came back, carrying a leather satchel, he was sweating again and still feeling ill, but Jane had arranged things as he had asked, and it calmed him slightly.

"The women have got the fires going in jig time, and the smaller of the two kettles is steaming," Jane said. "And you're sweating."

"Don't worry. You just keep a cloth by you to wipe my eyes if it gets any worse. Can you do that?"

"Sure can, Doc," she said, grinning.

"Now," Jonathan opened the leather sack. "These are the instruments I'll be using. Kneel down here beside me."

He knelt himself next to Stockbridge, whose breath came heavy as if he were snoring, and took the instruments out of the sack. He passed them to Jane one at a time, naming each one as he gave it to her. "Stethoscope, scalpel, scissors, saw, bone cutter, forceps, clamps, needles."

"These needles ain't no good," Jane blurted. "They're bent."

"They're supposed to be. You'll see. Tell me the name of each instrument."

Jane did.

"Good. Now drop them gently into the boiling water. Keep the forceps back and just put the ends in the water, and use them to lift the others things out. Have one of the women drop a large piece of cloth into the second pot and let it boil for a while. Where's the soap?" he asked, raising his voice.

One of the women pulled a bar from an apron pocket and passed it to Jane.

"Scrub your hands up to your elbows. Shake yourself dry," Jonathan told her. "I'll follow."

Two of the women rushed away and came

back with a pail and a large ladle and mixed boiling and cold water for them to wash in.

"Now we go to work," he said quietly to Jane when the instruments were laid out.

"What about Patience?" Jane asked.

"If she won't move of her own accord, we'll have two of the women lift her off him."

Patience did not move of her own accord. She struggled and yelled when the two largest women finally reached down and picked her up, wearing the expressions they must have worn dozens of times when dealing with stubborn children. Jonathan glanced around at the small crowd that had gathered, every person in it gone still. He knelt by Stockbridge again and beckoned Jane to join him.

"I'm short on prayers," she said, sounding uneasy as she sank down. " 'Now I lay me down to sleep' don't cut it."

"Brace yourself," Jonathan said. "It's going to look bad."

"Oh, Lord," Jane breathed as he lifted the pieces of sheet away.

"Take a couple of deep breaths." Jonathan's own insides felt like a block of ice. "We're fortunate he's still unconscious."

His hands were already exploring the gash left by the bull's horn. Blood began pud-

90

dling, its three sources clear from the torn veins and an artery.

"Clamps," he said.

One at a time Jane slapped them into his palm. Once he had the bleeding checked, he said, "Lean in with me, Jane, and very carefully we will ease the intestines back inside him. Move slowly, feel your way with your fingers, and if you encounter anything hard or sharp, pause and tell me."

"I hear you."

"On the count of three, move with me."

"A poem," she said and giggled.

He caught the note of hysteria. "Look at me," he said quietly.

Their eyes locked, and he said, "You can do this. Say it with me. 'I can do this.' "

"I can do this," she said, her voice steadying.

"Then let's do it."

With Jane increasingly adapting to his needs and his rhythm, they went ahead with the long job of putting in sutures, cutting away a shattered rib, and, finally, stitching Stockbridge together again. Jonathan put in the last stitch, then slowly passed Jane the needle.

"We've done all we can do," he said as they helped one another to their feet.

Throughout the two hours they had

worked over the wounded man, Patience, white as drifting snow, had stood as close to Jane and Jonathan as the other women would let her. She neither wept nor asked questions but stood still as a statue, her eyes fixed on her father and the pair working on him. Behind her and beside her, but standing further back, other people from the wagon train had waited in silence. Some stood with their heads bent, perhaps in prayer, while others appeared to be absorbed in Jonathan and Jane as they labored to save Stockbridge. Throughout their vigil, the only sounds were the wind in the grass and the dull bellowing of the bull. The animal had paced and pawed the earth, shaken his head, and roared his challenge as he chivied the cows at intervals.

"Patience." Jonathan turned to her when he had reached his feet. "We have done all we can for your father. He has lost a lot of blood. Caring for him now means getting him into a bed, keeping him warm, and keeping the wound clean, and we'll hope he regains consciousness. We'll have to wait to learn what kind of damage that animal's horn did to your father's head. Is there anything you want to ask me?"

She shook her head slightly. "Thank you, Jonathan," she said. "And thank you, Jane.

You were heroic. Both of you were. I don't know where you found the strength and the courage." Her pale cheeks flushed bright pink. "I behaved very badly. Were I not so grateful that Father is still alive, I would feel terrible."

"I thought you was about to faint dead away," Jane said cheerfully, "but now you've got some color back. Wanting to stay with your father when he's hurt bad as yours ain't nothing to be ashamed of."

Jonathan had stopped listening and was focused on the bellowing of the bull. "Excuse me." He turned away from Jane and Patience. Pushing through the people who had come forward to praise him, he went in long strides to where Sam was grazing, still saddled.

"Jonathan," Eli called. "Hold on!"

Jonathan made no response. Instead, he flung himself onto Sam. Urging the horse into a gallop, he rode toward the herd of cows and the bull. He heard Eli swear, then the thudding of hooves as the wagon master followed fast on his big gray, but paid Eli's pursuit no further heed.

He rode Sam straight into the herd. He knotted the reins and dropped them onto the horse's neck, reached down, pulled his rifle out of its scabbard, and jacked a shell into the chamber. The bull had seen him coming and was lowering its head, roaring in challenge as it slashed the grass with its horns and scraped clods of grass and dirt with its front hooves. The closer Sam and Jonathan came to the bull, the quicker the cattle between them scattered until only thirty feet of open ground separated them.

"Watch him, Sam," Jonathan said in a cold, hard voice, turning his mount sideways to the bull.

The horse needed no urging. His eyes were fixed on the beast, his ears cocked.

"Stand, Sam," Jonathan said, and the horse froze in place.

In that moment, the bull plunged forward. Standing in his stirrups, Jonathan shot the bull in its left shoulder. The animal slowed but kept coming. It had lowered its head, preparing to hook Sam, but Sam swung his hindquarters away from the charge, so when the bull's head came up, its target was gone. As the bull thundered past, Jonathan shot it between the ears. Momentum carried the great beast forward another stride before its legs buckled and it pitched forward, already dead, horns plowing into the ground in a cloud of dust.

Jonathan dropped back into his saddle. He cleared the empty cartridge, lowered the hammer, and slid the rifle back into its scabbard. For a few moments, he sat staring at the dead bull. He felt neither pleasure nor sorrow, but he did experience some gratification for having put an end to one stupid and murderous thing that, like war, destroyed everything in its path.

"Lord God!" Eli shouted, riding up to Jonathan and the dead bull. "It's a wonder you ain't dead. What were you thinking?"

"That it was time somebody solved the bull problem."

Eli leaned an arm on the pommel of his saddle. "You needed to kill something."

"Possibly."

As he said it, Jonathan realized it was true, though the knowledge unsettled him less than it should have. He wasn't yet ready to ponder why and said, "I also thought we might take some steaks off him."

Jane and Patience, along with the others, paused in their efforts to move Stockbridge. "What do you think, Patience?" Jane asked when the bull went down. "Is there a mite more to our gentleman friend than meets the eye?"

Patience had never witnessed this kind of violence. She had been terrified when she saw the bull charge Jonathan and shocked when he rose in his stirrups, fired his rifle, and killed the beast. More than shocked, in a way she had never before experienced. Mingled with the ordinary fear awakened by the charging animal and her concern for Jonathan's safety, the sight of him standing, the blast of the rifle, the upending of the huge bull, sent blood surging though her body and flooded her with unfamiliar emotions that reddened her face and left her gasping.

Having seen more than Patience of the barnyard side of life, Jane grinned at her response. "He's something, ain't he?"

Flustered, Patience cried out, "I must get Father into the wagon." She looked around wildly, then calmed a little as she saw the wagon approaching. Someone's husband was driving it up to where her father lay.

Jane and three other women eased Patience aside, then lifted Gideon Stockbridge into the wagon and onto his bed. As they climbed down and straightened their skirts, Jane laid a hand on Patience's shoulder. "We'll take turns looking in on you tonight. Try to get some rest if you can."

CHAPTER 7

Word of Jonathan's putting a bullet through Rand Callaway's hat on the first day of the journey had soon reached nearly everyone in the train over the age of seven and gave rise to considerable conversation. Of those who had been present, however, only Eli and Jonathan were still around to relate what happened. Since neither of them would talk about it, the shooting was soon reduced to nothing more than a story.

Jonathan's shooting the bull was something else again. A mere story seldom carries the weight of an event witnessed, and those who saw him ride straight at that bull and kill it as though it was something he might do any day he had a spare five minutes were eager to talk of the feat. It made a lasting impression on at least half of those in the train, and they chewed it over throughout the afternoon and into the evening.

Patience tried not to listen, focusing all her attention on her father even as she kept an ear out for Jane or one of the other women, coming to check on her and Gideon as promised. But it was Jonathan who was her first visitor. His sudden appearance at the wagon reddened her face as if she had been caught out in some misdeed, and she struggled mightily and with limited success to return to being the calm, confident, controlled person she was accustomed to being.

"Patience," he said, removing his hat. "I'd like to have a look at your father before dark. I hope I haven't startled you."

It was a warm evening, and Patience, like many others in the train, had rolled up the canvas sides of the wagon to let the breeze through. Jonathan stood by a rear wheel, looking in at her. She had been wiping her father's face with a damp cloth and shot to her feet at Jonathan's sudden arrival.

"Come in," she managed to say.

He climbed into the back of the wagon. A stethoscope hung around his neck, swaying slightly as he moved. "Has there been any change in your father?" he asked.

"Not that I can see," she said. "Perhaps his breathing is a little steadier."

"That's a good sign," Jonathan said. He

looked puzzled, and she wondered how much her nervousness showed. "I'd like to listen to his heart," he continued.

She nodded, and he put his stethoscope to use. When he was finished, he turned to look at her. "Your father's doing as well as can be expected. His heart is strong, and there's no sign of fever."

"Is he going to recover consciousness?" Patience asked.

"I don't know," Jonathan replied. "But you mustn't worry. Traumas like this can leave the patient unconscious for some time. If he's not awake by tomorrow night, we will make some efforts to wake him."

"I don't know how I will ever be able to repay you and Jane Howard," Patience said, her voice breaking.

Jonathan got to his feet. "You don't owe us anything."

He paused, and she had the sense he wanted to put comforting arms around her. Instead, he kept talking. "You have had a severe shock," he told her, "and you must be patient with yourself. If you feel frightened or overwhelmed, or if sleep doesn't come easily, I can give you something to help you cope. The good news is that time will rid you of these responses, should they grow troublesome. How are you feeling now?"

She stood very straight; hands folded at her waist. "I think I'm all right," she said.

He looked skeptical but didn't dispute her. "Good. I'll come back in the morning. I believe we're to have an early start. How are you managing with harnessing the mules?"

"Oh, Lord." She smiled, a little shakily. "I do that most days. Father's rheumatism makes it difficult for him to do that kind of lifting. I'm quite accustomed to it."

Jonathan thought it likely her father would never again lift much of anything, possibly even himself. He did not want to burden her more heavily than she was already, but he felt obliged to say, "Patience, your father's recovery may be very long and incomplete. The journey will only get more strenuous. It's not too late for you to turn back. I would be glad to go back with you to Westport Landing."

Her reply had steel in it that was new to him. "I have no intention of turning back, Jonathan. I know Father is teetering on the verge of death, but we all die. Were he able to speak, he would say, 'We have committed ourselves to relieving the suffering of those in pain and servitude. Push on.' That answer is also mine. Thank you for your concern."

"Very well." Jonathan felt he had been rebuked and found morally wanting. He strongly wanted to protest but could think of nothing likely to move her.

She managed a feeble smile. "I knew you would understand."

"Of course," he said, rallying. "Jane and the others will come by later. I'll come again in the morning. Is there anything I can do to help you now?"

"No, Jonathan," she said quietly, "but thank you for the offer."

"Goodnight then," he said. "I suppose you don't have a gun in the wagon?"

She said nothing, only stiffened her back a little.

"No, foolish of me to ask." He climbed out of the wagon and remounted Sam as quickly as he could, swearing silently at himself. One, for having asked the question and two, for feeling guilty about it.

Two days later one of the freight wagons broke a wheel. Eli sent word to Jane, Morgan, and Jonathan, out in front of the train with the remuda, to hold up. After the boy had relayed Eli's message, he asked Jonathan, "What's your take on Morgan's Injun woman?"

101

This was news to Jonathan. "What Indian woman?"

"Lord above, Doc. Ain't you heard? This Injun woman come out of the gloaming yesterday and told Morgan she's staying. It does look like she's sticking, so far. The whole train's talking about it. Some folks think it's disgraceful, other folks think it's the funniest thing that's happened since the fat man stepped on the banana skin, and some don't give a damn. Where do you fit in?"

Jonathan found the boy a pleasant addition to his day. "I'll have to give it some thought," he said, keeping his face straight. "Which group have you joined?"

"I ain't decided. Pa wouldn't give his opinion beyond saying he didn't want any goddamned Indians in the train, that they'd steal the last nickel out of a blind man's tin cup."

"That's a common opinion," Jonathan said, not wanting to criticize the father to the boy's face.

"Who's *common* when he's home?" the boy asked.

"In this case, it means an opinion of Indians that is widely held."

"Do you hold it?"

"Let's just say, your father's entitled to his

opinion."

"I like that word, *common,*" the boy said. "I'm short on words. I expect that's because I ain't had much schoolin'. We've been on the move a lot."

"What's your name?"

"Alvin Small. I was named after my father. My mother was holding out for Ebenezer. She had a brother died young and wanted his name for me, but she said she gave way for the sake of having peace in the house. The way I look at it is, if your last name's *Small,* you need a big name up front to make up for it. What's your opinion?"

"I think Alvin is a good name. Can you read?"

Alvin looked surprised. "I don't rightly know. The subject ain't come up."

Jonathan tucked away that information. "Let's go back and see how they're coming with that wheel."

The train had started again by the time Jonathan and Alvin reached Eli, riding a hundred yards or so in front of the Stockbridge wagon. Jonathan sent Alvin on his way and pulled up beside Eli. "What's this about Morgan and an Indian woman?"

"Beats me," Eli said, "but it's got to be the funniest thing we're going to encounter this whole journey. What I know about it

103

ain't much, but, from what Jane told me, she's an Osage who left her tribe because she didn't want to marry the man the chief picked for her." He stopped to take off his hat and scratch his head.

"Is that all?" Jonathan asked.

"Oh, no, we're just getting started. It seems she planned to find a sister who was married to a man living in another Osage band and had been travelling for a while."

"You've stopped again," Jonathan said.

"I hate to get to the end," Eli said, showing more energy than Jonathan had observed in him until now, "but here goes. The woman — her name is Yellow Leaf . . . I suppose that means she was born in September —"

"Eli."

"What? Oh. Well, her pony went lame, and Morgan came on her, walking west, trying to drag the animal after her. To add to her troubles, there was three half-starved wolves circling them, and her pack animal was trying to get loose from her so it could bolt."

"And Morgan shot one of the wolves, and the other two ran off," Jonathan said. "Then he cut the lame horse loose, put her gear on his horse, calmed down the pack animal, and they all walked off together."

"That ain't the end of it," Eli protested.

"First off, he give her one of the horses from the remuda. When dark came, she cooked him a supper, and, when he went to bed, she went with him. Scared him half to death. He jumped up and lit out running. But you'll recall a cold wind found us about moonrise, and Morgan was barefoot, in his long underwear and without his hat. He chilled down pretty fast and began thinking about rattlers and the night air on his bare head. Pretty soon he was back in bed with Yellow Leaf. I believe that, unless he beats her with a stick, she's there to stay."

"Interesting," Jonathan said. "Why didn't she take the horse and go on looking for her sister?"

"She's not much of a talker, and her English ain't anything to brag on, but he helped her with the lame horse and the wolves, fed her when she was hungry, and didn't have a woman of his own. So, because he met most of her expectations for a good husband, she decided to stay. That's what I figure, at least."

"I gather Morgan didn't have anything to say about that."

"She seems to think it was obvious he needed looking after."

Jonathan thought a little about it and found himself delighted with the story.

"Well," he said, "Morgan may find his life coming up in clover. Do you think her people will come looking for her?"

"Not likely."

"Have you seen her?"

"She's a good-looking woman, somewhat past her girlhood, I would judge. Why are you asking?"

"I'm wondering about disease," Jonathan said.

"Smallpox?" Eli asked, suddenly serious.

"And measles, whooping cough, cholera, diphtheria," Jonathan added. "From what I saw during the war, most of the Indians have something, thanks to us."

While they talked, the train had been moving past them. Jonathan soon set Sam into a lope to gain some distance on the train. When he reached the Stockbridge wagon, he pulled up beside Patience. "How is your father dealing with being awake again?" Gideon Stockbridge had regained consciousness sometime in the small hours of morning. He'd initially been confused, not understanding why he was strapped into his bed or remembering what had happened to him.

"He's asleep," Patience said with a happy smile.

"Good," Jonathan said. "How upset was

he to find he was wearing diapers?"

Patience blushed slightly but managed to keep facing him. "He raised the roof about a foot at first but seems to have become reconciled to his situation."

"Is he in any pain?"

"If he is, he's not letting on."

"I expect him to be sore, especially when he moves, but if he complains of sharp pains, send Alvin Small for me. And, speaking of Alvin, have you ever taught school?"

"Yes, on and off, usually to fill in when a teacher was ill. One left for personal reasons, and I finished the year in her place."

"Did you enjoy teaching?"

"I did, but Father kept involving me in other kinds of work that kept me away from the schoolroom."

"I've found out Alvin can't read or write, and my guess is that a lot of the other children in this train can't either. I must get out ahead of the train, but can we discuss this at another time?"

"Of course," she said and waved him along.

Jonathan rode away, pleased with himself. Since he'd mentioned Alvin and the other children's need of schooling, he was sure Patience would soon ask herself what should be done about it.

CHAPTER 8

Yellow Leaf was the first to see them. Two hours before first light, she had left her bed to answer a call of nature, and, because the night air was so full of the smells of earth and grass and tempting mysteries, drifting in the soft wind, she decided, against her better judgment, to walk around the quietly grazing horses.

She smelled them first, tobacco smoke. Edging into the herd, making sure to keep her distance from the stallion, she noted the horses had begun lifting their heads and drifting away from whatever was coming.

A few at a time, not hurrying, riders began taking shape in the darkness. The rumble of low voices told her they were not Indians. Keeping the horses between her and the men, moving with the horses, she put some distance between herself and the riders before breaking into a run. She found Morgan strapping on his gun.

"Where the hell have you been . . ." he began, but she interrupted.

"Many white men riding toward wagon train. I will tell them and come back. You get rifle, take bullets and food, ride horse very quietly toward sun. I will find you," she said. She grabbed one of Morgan's Spencers and a box of shells, and ran.

A few moments later, lying low over her horse's neck, she urged the animal into a trot, then a lope. The moment she was sure she had put enough distance between herself and the oncoming riders, she kicked her gelding into a full-out gallop.

Reaching the encampment, she raced around the circle of wagons, shouting, "They come!" at the top of her voice.

The commotion set the train's dogs barking. By the time Yellow Leaf reached Eli Parker's wagon, Eli was ringing the bell and Jonathan had pulled on his clothes and boots and strapped on his revolver and was pulling open the wagon's rear. No one needed to understand what the Osage woman was shouting to know trouble was coming.

In the preceding weeks, Jonathan had trained the men well. Eli's insistence that they circle their wagons every night, despite protests from vocal members of the train who were certain they wouldn't be attacked, had proved right.

Yellow Leaf pulled up, leaped from her horse, and ran to Jonathan. "Not Indians. Come from sun rising."

"How many?" he asked, unloading boxes of ammunition from the wagon bed.

"More." She held up both hands with her fingers spread.

"Where is Morgan?"

"Morgan with horses," she said. "Not good."

"No. Stay here."

"Not stay here," she said. "Can shoot. Will take care of him."

At that point, Jonathan noticed the Bowie knife in her belt and one of Morgan's Spencer rifles in the saddle scabbard. "We will come as soon as we can," he told her. "What will you do?"

"Hide him," she said. With that, she mounted in a single leap and was gone in a gallop.

Parker watched her race away. "I hope Morgan doesn't try to keep them horses from being run off."

"I hope he listens to her," Jonathan said. "Let's go." In the gray pre-dawn light, he saw the women and children running toward the center of the circle, carrying their bedding. "Damn!" Thinking of Patience, he started toward her wagon at a run, but Jane cut him off. She was running in the same direction, her skirts hiked up. "I'll fetch them," she shouted. "You get on with it."

"Watch yourself!" he called and ran for the spot where the men were gathering.

After a lot of grumbling, each wagon owner had agreed to fill bags with sand and dirt for the men to fire over. Now they were being unloaded with haste and no complaining. "Take the east side," he told the assembled men. "Get under the wagons. You know what to do. Remember: pick your target, squeeze off the shot. Now move. They're coming."

"Is it Callaway?" someone asked.

"Probably," Jonathan said. "Go, get one of those sandbags in front of you. Go! Don't start shooting 'til you hear the whistle."

The train had gone silent. Even the dogs had stopped barking. Eli and Jonathan passed out boxes of ammunition to boys who distributed them at a run along the line, while the eastern sky turned from gray to a pale cream. Then they heard the drumming of horses' hooves.

"Get set," Eli said and dropped under the last wagon covering the men at the south end of the line.

"Jonathan!" Jane appeared suddenly beside him, carrying a rifle. "I met Yellow Leaf, riding hell bent for election. She shouted, 'Renegades,' and I came. Where do you want me?"

He gaped. "You can't —"

"Yes, I can. I've shot more deer, rabbits, and bear than you have, and I've got a dog in this fight. Where's Eli?"

Jonathan pointed, and she darted off. He dodged under the wagon at the center of the line and pulled a whistle out of his pocket. He had bought it from Alvin Small for a quarter after lengthy bargaining. The men on both sides of him lay in position, rifle barrels over the sandbags.

"Hold your fire!" Jonathan shouted as the line of riders came into view, charging toward them at a gallop.

His order was echoed by others down the line. He gave it a few seconds, then shouted, "Pick a man."

That too went down the line. The riders were coming in fast, but still Jonathan waited. The horses' hooves pounding the ground were loud enough now to drown out his voice. When the raiders were within fifty yards, Jonathan raised the whistle to his lips and blew as loud as he could.

The defenders' rifles spoke almost in a single voice, and half the raiders flew backward off their horses. Jonathan jacked in a fresh shell and blew the whistle again. He and the others were firing now into a melee of riders who were fighting to pull their horses around and retreat. The screams of wounded men mingled with the squealing of terrified horses slamming into one another, their riders swearing, all of them engulfed in a cloud of dust.

"Hold your fire," Jonathan shouted.

A heartbeat later: "Attack! Attack!" someone from the raiders shouted, but no one appeared to be listening. A gust of wind whipped away the dust. Jonathan saw that only half a dozen men were still gathered around Callaway, who stood in his stirrups, revolver in hand, shouting and cursing.

"Do you want me to shoot him?" the man beside Jonathan asked.

"No," Jonathan said. "Let's wait a moment, see if they turn tail."

At that moment, Jane Howard stepped out from the wagons, her rifle halfway to her shoulder. "Callaway, you yellow bastard!"

The outlaw turned, saw her, and aimed his gun, but he was dead before his finger could press the trigger. Shot through the heart, he tumbled from the saddle. Feeling the reins drop, his horse bolted, dragging Callaway with it, one of the man's feet entangled in a stirrup. Jane slammed home the bolt of her rifle without lowering it. Instead, she held it on the remaining raiders and waited. At least twenty men from the train, including Eli and Jonathan, came scrambling over the bags, their own rifles pointed at the last of Callaway's men.

"Go!" Jonathan shouted. "Get out of here!"

The five raiders holstered their guns, pulled their horses around, and galloped away.

"Jane," Eli said. "Are you all right?" He had been standing behind her since she shot Callaway.

She dropped her rifle into the crook of her left arm. "I'm rid of a load I've carried a long time, Eli," she said.

The rest of the train's defenders crawled out from under the wagons in ones and twos, as if they couldn't quite believe the fighting was over. They stood in silence, staring out over the ground that had so lately been a churning mass of dust, men, and horses and the jarring slam of gunfire.

"We've got to look for injured men out there," Jonathan said, standing his rifle on its butt as the adrenalin began draining out

114

of him. He had just finished speaking when six women, led by Patience, came striding toward him. Two of the women carried a stretcher.

"We could use two men to get the wounded to the field hospital we've put together," Patience said, addressing Jonathan in a voice laden with what he heard as resignation, mixed with determination.

One of the three men close enough to hear her said roughly, "They would've likely raped you and murdered me, had they gotten hold of us. As far as I'm concerned, they can rot where they are."

Jonathan looked more closely at the man, one of the few drivers who wore his holster tied down. A gunman, Jonathan thought, bull necked and slope shouldered, a hard man in a fight. His eyes were too close to one another for Jonathan's liking, and darkness rose in him again. "Perhaps you would apologize to Miss Stockbridge for speaking to her as you did."

The fellow bristled. "I spent six months in Andersonville. If the war had gone on another month, I'd be dead. I had my fill of Southern hospitality. As for Callaway and his bunch, they weren't nothing but Confederate scum."

"I have not heard the apology," Jonathan

said. He kept his voice calm, but no one could mistake the threat in it. Beyond Jane, who still held her rifle, he saw Eli straighten his back.

Jane stepped between the driver and Jonathan. "Bill Johnson," she said, "you've got a mouth like a three-hole outhouse. God almighty, don't you know better than to talk like that to a lady?"

She snatched Johnson's hat off, which set the other men laughing. "Now tell her you're sorry, and get the hell back to your oxen." She shoved his hat into his stomach. "Well?"

His cheeks reddened, and he flicked a glance at Patience. "I'm sorry I spoke rough as I did, Miss Stockbridge, I forgot myself."

"It's quite all right, Mr. Johnson," Patience answered. "I'm sorry for your suffering. Not many lived to tell the tale of Andersonville."

"Now git," Jane said. Johnson turned tail and left, his companions slapping his back and laughing as they went.

Jane turned to Jonathan, speaking low enough that only he heard. "You can't kill the whole damned world." Then, more loudly, she said, "You and Eli ain't going to be carrying no stretchers. There's a whole train here needs to be put back together, and dead to bury, thank God none of them

116

ours. You've got work enough to do." She looked at Patience. "Miss Stockbridge, you and the others go out there and find out if any of them raiders is still alive. I'll get you some men to carry the stretchers."

Everyone scattered, leaving Eli and Jonathan alone.

"Am I right in thinking you'd have shot Bill Johnson if Jane hadn't stepped in?" Eli asked.

"Perhaps." Jonathan felt dissatisfied with the outcome of the face-off, and equally unhappy with himself. He'd thought he was doing better, conquering his darkness of soul, and now this.

Eli raised an eyebrow. "Was there something other than his mouth that got you going?"

Jonathan didn't wish to discuss it. "His eyes are too close together."

CHAPTER 9

Jonathan and Eli conscripted a burial crew, and by noon they had buried ten men. Not knowing their names, Eli had wooden crosses put up at the head of each grave, dug extra deep to keep the wolves from digging the men up. When that was done, he took off his hat and stood, holding in one hand the Bible he had brought from his wagon and his hat in the other. "These men died in violence, but that's over. The grass will soon cover them, and things will go on as God sees fit, or not."

He put his hat on and turned to Jonathan. "You want to say anything?"

"I think you've pretty well covered it," Jonathan replied. "Anyone else want to say something?"

The men shook their heads, put on their hats, and set off for the wagons, walking in silence save for the sound of the wind in the grass.

While the burials were going on, Morgan and Yellow Leaf had rounded up the dead men's horses, leaving Alvin Small and his older brother Lemuel, who had only one eye and had never been heard to speak, to keep the two remudas bunched — an easy task because the animals were in knee-high grass, and even the two stallions were satisfied to graze. Jane, having found two volunteers to carry the stretcher, set off with Patience and the other women to find the wounded, but they returned empty-handed.

"What was left of Rand Callaway's outfit must have gathered them up," Jane told Jonathan as she was cooking breakfast.

"I'm glad you and the other women didn't have to deal with them," Eli said.

"Amen to that," Jonathan added. "I'm glad Patience Stockbridge didn't have to see more blood or hear any more screaming."

Jane and Eli exchanged a quick smile, but neither said what they were thinking.

Two days later, the train having unhitched for the night, Jonathan and Patience walked away from the Stockbridge wagon so her father wouldn't overhear their conversation. "He's not recovering as rapidly as I would like," Jonathan said.

The last of the light was fading out of the sky, and the night wind had begun to murmur in the grass and shake the canvas on the wagons. The cooking fires had been lit, and the smells of coffee and meat frying drifted around them. The shouts and laughter of children and occasional lowing of the cattle broke the silence, only to be swiftly swallowed up by the encroaching darkness.

Patience shivered.

"Are you cold?" Jonathan asked. He started to take off his jacket, bought from a Kansa Indian woman who'd crossed his path the day before, riding alone and leading a pony carrying buffalo robes and deerskin jackets, dresses, and leggings. She spoke enough English to say she was going to a Kansa village where her husband's brother was being married, and people would want to drink whiskey and trade. She concluded their meeting by saying, "Have eyes in back of head, White Eyes. Kiowa raiding party passed me yesterday. I see them first. They not see me." That warning had stuck with Jonathan, and he'd wondered how serious the threat was as he watched the old woman ride away.

Patience said, "I'm not cold. It's just that sometimes at night, the prairie frightens me. I know it's foolish, but out here, human sounds like the children playing are swallowed in an instant, surrounded as we are by these vast distances."

"This open country does take some getting used to," Jonathan said, touched by the sadness in her voice. "But there is great beauty here, and, for the first time in a long time, I have found I take pleasure lying in my bed and gazing at the stars. During the day while you're driving, do you watch the antelope, deer, coyotes, and occasional badgers going about their business?"

"Oh, yes." Patience smiled briefly. "I think my favorites are the badgers. They seem purposeful and serious minded. I like watching them, but I'm not sure I know a deer from an antelope. I'm sorry. I've distracted you. Why is Father not progressing?"

"Age is probably one reason. Please don't think I'm dodging your question. As time passes, the human system seems to respond to challenges with less and less vigor. On the up side, your father has escaped infection, which is very important. The wound seems to be healing, but his heart is weaker than I like, and I don't feel he is as interested in his recovery as he should be. Perhaps you have something to say about that."

"I do," Patience said without hesitation. "Ten years ago, Mother died, and a light went out in Father's life that I have never been able to rekindle. He continues to be active, but to be perfectly honest, I don't think he is all that interested in living."

Jonathan caught himself just in time to avoid saying *I know the feeling.* Instead, he said, "Let's try brightening his life a little. Instead of staring at the canvas roof of your wagon all day, I think we can safely get him sitting up so he can look out at the world."

"Would that be safe?"

"I think so. Shall we try?"

"Well . . . yes. Let's see how he responds."

The following morning, with Jonathan for backup, Patience told her father their plan. Stockbridge looked at her for a while, then said in his usual somber voice, "Are you two trying to stir me up?"

"Now, Father," Patience said. "Jonathan says you're not progressing quite as rapidly as he would like, and that looking out on the world might increase your interest in your recovery."

To Jonathan's surprise, Stockbridge smiled. "Moved on to first names, I see."

"You're just trying to embarrass me, Father," Patience burst out, suddenly becoming very busy with Gideon's bedding.

"A change is just what the doctor ordered."

"I have to support your daughter in this, Mr. Stockbridge." Jonathan pretended not to notice how her face flushed at her father's remark.

"Very well." Stockbridge's voice sharpened a little. "Do what you have to. Truth to tell, I was growing tired of staring at this canvas roof."

Jonathan fetched Eli, and together they lifted Gideon's bed with him in it and moved him to the front of the wagon. Next, they raised Stockbridge into a sitting position so he could look out over the mules' backs at the prairie spread out before them.

"How's that, Father?" Patience asked when he had been propped up.

"It appears to be much as the Lord made it," he replied. "So, we must be content with it."

That answer didn't sound likely to make Patience feel much better, but she surprised Jonathan by saying cheerfully, "That is so, Father. We must praise His work."

"I wanted to say, 'I have seen room for improvement'," Eli said to Jonathan as they rode back to Eli's wagon.

"Yes," Jonathan said. "It seems to me that, starting with mankind, there is a wide range of available improvements for Him to choose from."

Later in the day, Jane trotted up on Katie to where Jonathan was riding point. "I heard you were visiting the Stockbridge wagon last night."

Jonathan nodded. "And this morning, Eli and I made another call."

Jane lost her bantering grin. "Is Patience's father going downhill?" She had turned up in a pair of deerskin leggings from someone's trunk, along with a man's collarless white dress shirt, caught around the waist by a red sash. Her skirt looked like the bottom half of a gingham dress, split front and back to let her straddle the mare's back. Her hat was a faded black felt with a wide brim and low crown, hanging down her back by a rawhide cord and mostly covered by the curling tumble of her hair.

"This is a change since breakfast," Jonathan said, so caught up in gazing at her that he'd forgotten the question. "You look just fine in your new outfit. I congratulate you. Has Eli seen you like this?" He wasn't flattering her, he told himself. Sitting erect in the saddle with the wind stirring her hair, her belted shirt emphasizing her figure, the fringed deerskin clinging to her long legs and her skirt afloat around her, Jane was a striking sight.

124

"No," she said, with an unmistakably pleased smile. "Pa told me I looked a mess."

"Go find Eli," Jonathan said, "but don't be surprised if he proposes to you on the spot."

"Then maybe I should stay clear of him," she said, pulling down her mare. Katie danced around and briefly came up off her front legs. "Are you taking an interest in Patience Stockbridge?"

"No," Jonathan said, perhaps a little too quickly. "And don't you start any rumor about that, either. I still have her father to look in on."

"That's a pretty good excuse. How about looking in on my father?"

Putting her heels into the mare, she raced away with a whoop of laughter.

"Well," Jonathan said to her dust, "if Eli won't propose to you, I just might." He rode off himself, suddenly grim, thinking he would do no such thing. Nor would he get close enough to Patience Stockbridge to do her any harm.

CHAPTER 10

"There's wagon tracks as far as I can see," Jonathan said, standing in his stirrups to look farther over the rough plains east and west.

"That's because a lot of trails are still feeding into this one," Eli said. He had ridden out to tell Jonathan the train would stop at noon, to rest the animals pulling the wagons and let them graze for an hour. It had rained heavily in the night, so parts of the track were knee deep in mud, and the creeks were cresting, making the oxen's work doubly hard in crossing them.

Jonathan sat back in his saddle. "Have the drivers complained?" he asked, surprised by Eli's decision.

"No, it's the draft animals. They need a rest or they will wear down. The trick is to work them hard but not so hard they begin to lose their weight."

"As a rule, how far do you plan to go

each day?"

"Fifteen miles on average," Eli responded, "and I have to rein in the drivers to hold to that rate of travel. Those men paid by the merchants try to get to the end of the trail as fast as possible. My task is to get the train and everyone in it to Santa Fe safely and in a reasonable time. So, I set the pace."

"All right." Jonathan held back a grin. "Now you can tell me why you really rode out here."

"Sharp, ain't you?" Eli said. "How many Indians have you seen in the past week?"

Jonathan had to pause and think. "There was that Kansa woman I bought the deerskin jacket from. As I recall, she said she was traveling to another village to trade. Three days ago, I saw a group of five men who stopped long enough to watch me for a couple of minutes, then rode on. They seemed to be in a hurry."

"They were armed?"

"They all had bows and quivers on their backs. Two had rifles."

Eli frowned. "That's just what Morgan and Yellow Leaf told me. Jane said she saw what she thought was a small war party. They were wearing paint. Were those men you saw painted?"

"No," Jonathan said.

"Kiowa, probably."

"A hunting party going after buffalo?"

"No. When they hunt buffalo, the whole village goes along. The women do the skinning and butchering." Eli fell silent for a moment, then said, "I don't like it. We should have seen more, some of them should have come pestering us for liquor or tobacco. The fact they haven't is bad news."

A few days after this conversation, Jonathan found an excuse to ride back to talk with Jane. She didn't tease him about Patience this time, or pretend he had come to court her. He saw at once something was troubling her. When he asked what it was, she said, "Pa."

"What's wrong with your father?"

She sat straight in her saddle, frowning, her body too full of energy for anything more than a slight sag of her shoulders. Jonathan had the fleeting wish he could paint her just as she was, with the wind in her hair and her green shirttails billowing. "I don't know, and that's where the trouble lies."

"Could he be ill?" he asked, regaining his focus.

"I don't think so, but he's meaner'n a bear with a sore tooth."

"Does he know you shot Callaway?"

"I don't think so, but, ever since that happened, he's been chewing on something he can't seem to swallow."

"Are we going to have trouble with him?"

"*We* being you and Eli?"

"Yes." He thought for a moment of telling her what had passed between her father and himself but quickly stifled the impulse. Knowing about it would only cause her pain.

She surprised him. "I overheard the two of you talking," she said, her eyes dodging away from his. "That day you gave me the horse herding job."

He felt cold, recalling how close he'd come to shooting Howard over nothing more than harsh words. "I'm sorry about that," he told her. "But I think he and I came to some sort of agreement. At least we put our guns away."

She turned to look at him again. "Jonathan," she said firmly, "the only reason you're not dead is you got the drop on him. There's something about Jess Howard you need to understand. Not only are you a Yankee, you faced him down. He hates the ground you walk on. If he gets the chance, he'll kill you and not be particular about how he does it."

He recognized in her voice the same steel she'd employed when she called out Rand Callaway before shooting him. Shocked by what she had said, and by her harshness, he tried to ease her away from the subject. "I'll make a point of staying away from him, then."

She frowned. "Now I think about it, that's probably why he's been in such a sour mood. He's been brooding over you mastering him and thinking about how to even the score."

Worse and worse, Jonathan thought.

"Jane, there's no way I'm going to let that happen, and I'm certainly not going to shoot him."

"Thank you for trying to make me feel better, Jonathan, but, unless I'm crow bait, the choice won't be yours. You should have shot him when you had the chance."

"How do you manage it?" Jonathan asked.

She gave him a hard look. "My father?"

"No, your anger."

"I guess the way you do," she replied, "by trying not to let it master me."

He hadn't expected that answer. "Then we have something in common, Jane."

"Yes, Jonathan, I noticed that."

They sat for a long moment, looking at one another in silence.

"You want to hear what Yellow Leaf told me yesterday?" Jane asked suddenly, breaking the spell.

"I'm ready." Jonathan felt oddly relieved to be set free but also that something vital had gone unsaid, without his knowing what it was.

"I met her near that creek you crossed getting here. She had gone down there for a bath. But it was Morgan she wanted to talk about." She stopped speaking and stayed quiet for so long, Jonathan became impatient.

"Jane, where did you go?" he asked.

She sighed. "Yellow Leaf said she'd gotten tired of Morgan not letting her throw her legs around him and decided to take matters into her own hands. Last night, instead of getting into her own bed, she pulled off her clothes and squeezed under his blanket. He fought to get out, but she got both arms around his middle and talked quietly to him, like you would with a spooked horse, until he quit struggling.

"Up until then, she'd been clutching him from behind, but, once he was lying still, she climbed on top of him. He was wide eyed with fright, she told me. That was when she realized this was his first go at what she had in mind.

"She thought about stopping but said to me, 'Is hard to turn around in teepee door.' So, she got astride him and showed him how it was done. That Morgan's got to be fifty if he's a day. I guess it's a kind of sad thing, but it had a happy ending."

"In the army," Jonathan said quietly, "I found a lot of men, probably half of them, had never made love to a woman, and a large number of them had their first experience with a bar girl."

Jane looked away. She said nothing for a long time. Then, "I was made a woman far too young."

He'd figured that from what he already knew of her history, but he hadn't wanted to think about it. "Callaway?" he asked.

She nodded, settling the question of why she had killed the man. He watched her as they rode, looking for some easing in her taut posture, but there was none. Slowly, his mind put Callaway's death together with her words about Jess Howard — *you should have shot him when you had the chance* — and made an appalling picture.

"Your father?"

She nodded a second time and lifted Katie's reins. As the mare threw up her head, Jane shot Jonathan a pain-filled glance and said in a voice grating with anger, "I

132

wish you had shot the bastard."

The mare sprang forward. Jonathan reined in Sam, who'd started after them, and sat watching Jane ride away with the effortless grace she displayed in everything physical she did. "All that grief, all those years," he said, feeling a sharp stab of sorrow for her.

Turning Sam, he made a vow, the darkness swirling inside him. *If Jess Howard ever again reaches for his gun facing me, it will be the last thing he does.*

After a while, growing calmer, he began to feel the full weight of what Jane had told him. He was faced with some difficult decisions. What, if anything, should he tell Eli? He'd heard similar stories from women in his practice, and he knew that younger women especially had to be approached with extreme gentleness and patience if they were ever to enjoy being made love to again. *Perhaps,* he thought, *I should talk to her about it.*

That thought didn't stick with him long, crowded out by another concern her revelation had raised. Why had she told him something this personal? Had she told Eli? Further reflection led him to think she likely hadn't. Because he was a doctor, then?

His mind hovered on the brink of the next step: if not because he was a doctor, why *had* she chosen to tell him? Instead of pursuing the matter further, he shut down his queries and kicked Sam into a gallop. "Let's go see if we can find any Indians."

Just when even Eli gave way and admitted they had been having beautiful weather, it decided to go in another direction. The change was sudden and dramatic. An hour after sunset at the end of a very hot, dusty day, during which the train had crossed a flooded creek that had mired four of the heaviest wagons. The water had come from somewhere to the west of them, and it had taken twelve teams of oxen and all the drivers, cursing more colorfully than Jonathan had heard since leaving the cavalry, three sweat- and blood-stained hours to get them out of the mud.

The storm began with a bolt of chain lightning, accompanied by a crash of thunder that sounded as if the sky had declared war on the earth, followed by a blast of hurricane force wind that quenched the fires in an instant and set the smaller wagons rolling. Only Eli's, the Stockbridges', and the Howards' wagons escaped being tumbled because the wind struck on their front ends instead of the sides.

Jonathan, Eli, and a dozen other men

saddled their horses as soon as they recovered enough from the shock of the blast to grasp the situation. "The stock," Eli said, meaning the animals in the herds in front of the train. "They'll have bolted." Leading their mounts, the men gathered outside the rectangle of wagons as soon as the center of the storm, racing with the wind, had passed over them. Stars were beginning to glimmer between the shredded clouds, and the moon came and went, adding its pale light.

Eli had to shout to make himself heard over the gusting wind and the rumbling of the departing storm. "Jonathan, take six men and get out to the remudas. Find Morgan or Yellow Leaf and turn those horses. The rest of you, follow me. Let's find the cattle."

Jonathan and his men were breaking away before Eli finished speaking. "Give them their heads," Jonathan told his companions. "They'll see the gopher holes before you will."

As he intended, the instructions brought a laugh. It was still too dark to see anything short of a lightning bug under their horses' bellies, but the laughter brought them together and lifted their spirits.

Before Jonathan spotted any horses, Yellow Leaf appeared out of the darkness, riding her paint bare-backed, coming toward them at full gallop. "Morgan need help," she shouted, spinning her mount in front of them without slowing the animal down much, her waist-long hair flying out like black wings. "Come! Horses run like hell."

"Lord God!" one of the men yelled as the group kicked their mounts into a gallop after her. "How does that woman stay on that horse?"

"I'm glad she ain't got the grip on me she's got on that pony," another man called loudly.

"I'd say Morgan fell into a pig pen and come out with a new suit," a third shouted, adding to the laughter.

The laughter faded quickly as they bent to the task of keeping up with Yellow Leaf, whose paint seemed to fly over the ground. Jonathan kept thinking he was back in the cavalry again, and the feeling was unexpectedly welcome. He did not have much time to enjoy it, because they swiftly drew close to the horse herd. Morgan was trying without any luck to turn the horses, led by the black thoroughbred, who apparently intended to take them all the way to Texas.

Wearing only his hat, long underwear, boots, and gun belt, Morgan saw them coming. He broke off and rode up to Jonathan.

"We may have to shoot that stallion," he shouted, over the drumming of the herd's hooves. "Get near him and he'll go for you. I made a couple of tries, then quit and tried turning this corner in. No luck. They can't be turned with him there."

"Where's the roan?"

"He's back of us somewhere. Yellow Leaf and Jane saw him cut out half a dozen mares and make off with them. Jane's probably following the roan."

"Jane!" Jonathan said, startled and angry all at once. "What's she doing out here?"

"The same thing we are. Ain't you hearing me?"

"Lord God!" Jonathan exploded. He started to say this was no place for a woman, but just in time thought of Yellow Leaf and kept the protest to himself.

"I haven't seen Him tonight," Morgan said, a joke lost on Jonathan, who was still steaming over Jane.

"Anyone got a rope?" he shouted, pulling away from Morgan and dropping back among the other riders.

Two of them, Jake and Rune Rawlings, swung up their lariats.

"We've got to try to take that stallion down without shooting him," Jonathan said. "How can we do it and not be run over by the herd?"

"If we can get ropes on him," Rune said, "he'll slow down to fight them. The rest of the bunch will spill around us. That's when the others can begin to turn them."

"You sure of this?" Jonathan asked.

"Hell no," Jake said, grinning, "but we can have some fun trying."

"Go," Jonathan said.

Much against his judgment, he kicked Sam into a gallop and followed the two men, riding at an angle in front of the thundering horses, moving all the time toward the black stallion leading them. The two ropers were nearly abreast of the stallion, and Jonathan, behind, drew his rifle as he went. The stallion had already sighted Jake and Rune closing in on him and swerved to challenge Jake, the nearest rider.

It was the moment Rune had been waiting for. Turning in his saddle, he dropped a loop over the animal's head and tightened it. The stallion turned on Rune with a scream of rage. Jake roped him the moment he swerved. With the ropes twisted around their pommels, both men pulled away from one another.

The stallion began to buck and gradually came to a stop, screaming and striking and fighting the ropes. As Rune had predicted, the herd split around the stallion and his tormentors. Jonathan was in front of the roped stallion now, his carbine in his right hand.

"Can you hold him?" he shouted, while the herd poured around them.

"Not for long," Jake answered. "One of us is likely to bust a belly strap."

Jonathan nodded. "Get ready to slacken your rope when he rears. I'll shout your name to warn you." He rode closer to Rune and called out, "Jake's going to slacken his rope when the horse is rearing. When it happens, pull him as hard as you can."

"Might work," Rune said.

They didn't have to wait long. The stallion, kicking and thrashing, threw his head and forequarters into a forward leap. Jonathan shouted, and Jake freed his rope. Rune, seeing his chance, threw his horse's weight against his own rope. The move broke the stallion's balance and brought him crashing to the earth.

As the herd surged around them, Jake anchored his rope again on the pommel and let his horse's motion tighten it. The stallion struggled to his feet, head down, defeated. Jonathan scabbarded his rifle.

"Bring him along," he yelled and swung Sam into the horses plunging past them, quickly moving toward the other riders. Their leader gone, the herd lost momentum and turned easily, soon slowing to a walk.

Jonathan went to find Morgan. "What do you want to do with them?"

"Move them back toward the wagons," the grizzled wrangler said. "If you get onto good grass, let them graze. They need to eat tonight. I'll go looking for Yellow Leaf and Jane."

"Shall I go with you?" Jonathan asked, hoping Morgan would say yes.

"Just let me find them and get some clothes," was his answer.

"All right," Jonathan said. "We'll keep them moving." He turned Sam and rode off, telling himself it was Eli's job anyway to look after Jane, trying hard not to worry and failing.

"Where's that stallion?" one of the men asked.

"I expect my boys have him licked by now," said an older, bearded man Jonathan recognized as Oral Rawlings.

"They have," Jonathan said, grinning, thinking the "boys" would never see thirty again.

CHAPTER 11

On the way back to the train, Jonathan found Jane and Yellow Leaf holding the roan stallion and his stolen mares in a tight group while they grazed.

"You had me worried," he said.

That brought a cynical snort from Yellow Leaf.

"This one like the rest," she said to Jane. "Worry only about belly and . . ."

Her final word was an Arapaho one that brought a roar of laughter from several of the men riding past. When Jane joined in, Jonathan felt his face light up like coals in a breeze. Luckily for him, it was still mostly dark.

"Where's Eli?" he said, hoping to stave off a verbal hazing.

"I ain't seen him this whole night," Jane said.

"Was herding cattle," Yellow Leaf said. "They not run far. Eli go back to help with broken wagons. Some people hurt. He with them."

"All right, what about Morgan?"

"He's getting some clothes on," Jane said, grinning. "He was riding around here in his long johns. Yellow Leaf sent him to get dressed. I about busted a gut listening to her. You got that black stallion tamed?"

"That might be an exaggeration," Jonathan said, glad to be on safe ground again. "The Rawlings brothers roped him and pulled him down, and he stopped fighting. The herd was turned, and they're grazing now, peaceful as sheep."

Talking with Jane had given him a chance to study her. Even in the half-light before dawn, Jonathan thought, the early morning breeze tumbling her hair around her face, her body from the saddle up silhouetted against the pale sky, he had never seen her looking so beautiful. For a moment, he allowed himself to feel seriously jealous of Eli.

"People need you to help," Yellow Leaf said sharply. "Not sitting on horse looking at Jane's things."

"Yellow Leaf!" Jane sprang up in her stirrups.

Jonathan sat staring at Jane, at a loss for words. Finally, he blurted out, "Well, I guess

I'd better go" and kicked Sam into a gallop. Yellow Leaf's laughter followed him.

By midday, with Patience working beside him, Jonathan had finished stitching the last cut and set the last bone. Things had gone so well because Patience had organized the other women, who washed wounds, bandaged those that had stitches, administered painkillers where needed, and helped Patience to stop the bleeding in the half dozen more seriously wounded.

"We've been working for nearly four hours," Jonathan said to her as they stood side by side, washing their hands in the basins one of the women had set out for them. "You must be very tired."

"It's a good weariness," Patience said, blushing slightly. "You have worked non-stop."

"We're lucky no one was killed in that storm," he responded, tossing her one of the dish cloths the women had gathered to serve as towels.

As they talked, he spied Jess Howard striding toward them. "You, Wainwright," Howard said, in a loud rasping voice. "Where's my daughter?"

Jonathan finished drying his hands, giving himself a few moments to decide how he was going to avoid a fight. Remembering what Jane had revealed about Howard made him want to do the man serious harm, but this was neither the time nor the place, and he didn't want to be the one to start trouble. "The last time I saw her was just before daylight, Mr. Howard," he said, in as near normal a voice as he could muster. "She was with Yellow Leaf. They were bringing in that roan stallion and the mares he tried to run off in the storm."

"She's been gone all night," Howard shouted.

Patience looked concerned by Howard's anger. "Mr. Howard, I understand you and your wife must have been worried, but as Jonathan just said, she's all right."

He glared at her. "When I want to hear from you, woman, I'll tell you."

Jonathan's voice hardened. "Mr. Howard, Miss Stockbridge is trying to ease your mind."

"I know what you and that Parker are up to with my Jane," Howard shouted, "and I'm not standing for it."

He reached for his gun, but, before it cleared its holster, Jonathan drew his Colt and slammed the barrel against the side of the man's head. With a groan, Howard went down. Jonathan made no effort to break his fall. He lay still on the ground. Patience stared at him, wide eyed.

"Is he dead?" she asked.

Three men repairing a wagon wheel nearby had stopped their work to watch the encounter. They dropped their tools and came running, the tallest of the three asking the same question Patience had. "Is he dead?"

"We seen him go for his gun," a second man blurted as they halted a few feet from where Jonathan stood.

Patience appeared rooted to her spot, her face white as snow and frozen in shock. She suddenly buckled, releasing her breath in a soft cry, and collapsed like a house of cards.

"That's two of them down, Colonel," the third man said. "People usually fall over around you like that?"

"Get me some of the women and be quick." Jonathan knelt beside Patience without touching her or looking at any of the three men.

They all dashed off toward a group of women nearby who were gathering dried clothes, spread over wagon wheels and the ends of wagon beds. A few moments later, half a dozen of the younger women hurried up to Jonathan, bearing a bucket of water, smelling salts, and a handful of cloths.

"You hurt, Doctor?" called a large, red-faced woman in the lead, her bonnet askew. "My name's Elsa."

Jonathan managed to tear his eyes away from Patience and shake his head.

"Then get out of the way," she said, still in a loud voice. "Jess dead?"

"No," the tallest man gasped, nearly out of breath from running.

"But he's going to have a sore head," the third one put in, equally winded.

"Agnes, Bessy," Elsa shouted, "get over here with me. Edith, Rosie, Dr. Wainwright, get busy on Jess Howard, even if he ought to be laid out. Too bad you didn't finish the job, Doc. Here, Agnes, give me them salts. Bessy, put a damp towel on her forehead, and watch she don't puke when she comes to."

"Hold a towel on Howard's head wound," Jonathan said, "while I get a look at his eyes."

"He ain't hit in the eyes." This came from Edith, a long-limbed, gaunt woman with a gold tooth.

"Looking in them will tell me if his brain is bleeding."

"Squint, Doc. If he's got a brain at all, it will be mighty small." This sally from Rosie, holding Howard's head, raised laughter from everyone but Jonathan, who was too absorbed in what he was doing to heed Rosie's remark. "You finding anything, Doc?" she asked a few moments later.

"No."

Jonathan got up, with a glance at Rosie's large brown eyes and pixie face. She couldn't be more than five feet tall, he thought, noting distractedly that she had everything necessary to break some hearts packed into that little body.

"I'm going to have to stitch that head wound, and I must fetch my bag," he said. "You three men, stay here. If Howard wakes and tries to get up, hold him down. I'll come back as soon as I can."

When he returned, Howard was still unconscious, and Jane had ridden up to the group. The men and women were ribbing one another and having what appeared to be a very good time, until Jonathan's arrival quieted them.

"I'm sorry about this, Jane," he said, "but it was either hit him or shoot him. I'm glad you're here. Help me with these stitches."

"Just so you know, Jane," Elsa bellowed from her spot next to Patience, "the doc didn't knock this one down. She fainted when the doc whacked your father." That produced a burst of laughter.

"How is he?" Jane asked, looking at Jonathan and not her father as she dropped to her knees beside him. Her shoulders drooped, and her face was pale, Jonathan noted and ascribed it to exhaustion. He felt sure she should help sew her father's wound up, if only to keep her occupied, despite all that lay between them.

"Too soon to tell," he said quickly. "I'm pretty sure his brain isn't bleeding. Before we start, you'd better wash your hands in that bucket."

"Here's soap," Rosie said, taking a yellow bar out of her apron pocket.

"How's Lorna?" Jane asked as she took the soap and plunged her hands into the water.

"There can't be much change, according to Ma," Rosie said. "She's pushing ninety and more than half blind. I think her falling into that wagon wheel about finished it."

"Shame," Jane said, drying her hands. "I like your grandma. You take after her."

Jonathan handed Jane a needle and thread. "If your mother wants, Rosie, I'd be glad to look at your grandmother. Something might be done to help her."

"Much obliged. I'll ask, Doc," Rosie answered quietly. "I hate the thought of losing her."

"I'm sure," Jonathan said. He took back the needle Jane had threaded. "Let's do this, Jane. Hold his head."

A few of the group watched with interest as Jonathan began working, but others turned away, shaking their heads. One by one those who had stayed drifted away, leaving Jane and Jonathan to their work, speaking quietly to one another. Patience was still unconscious, despite Bessy's demanding she wake up and Rosie's rubbing her hands.

"Now for the bandages," Jane said when Jonathan was finished.

He rinsed the needle and returned it to its box. "Well done, Jane," he told her.

"I've had a good teacher," she said, managing a smile. She braced her shoulders and sat back on her heels. "I probably know what happened here, but it would help to hear it from you."

He chose to make as brief an explanation as possible, to spare her as much pain as he could. "Your father was angry about your staying out all night," he said.

"I didn't smell whiskey on him."

"I doubt he had been drinking."

"Then he came planning to kill you," she said, anger and resignation in her voice.

Just then, Patience came to with a groan. She started to get up, but Rosie and Agnes caught her by the shoulders and laid her back down.

"Unless you want to fall flat again, young lady," Elsa said, "lie still awhile."

"It was seeing me hit your father with my gun that caused her to faint," Jonathan said. He and Jane stood with their heads close together, and he spoke almost in a whisper.

"Strange," Jane replied, lowering her voice more. "Patience can wade through blood but can't endure violence. I wish I had some of whatever she's got."

Jonathan was about to say, "I wouldn't change a hair on your head," when Jane asked, "Why didn't you shoot him? He's not going to stop coming after you."

"I do not want to shoot your father, Jane," he said, not allowing himself to ask why that was.

She looked down at her father's still form. "Then I may have to do it, because I'm not going to let him kill you," she said, suddenly sounding angry. "I'll see to getting him back to the wagon." Turning to Elsa and the other women nearby, she asked if they could sit with her father until she got back with some help.

"You go along," Elsa said. "He's not going anywhere. Rosie and I will wait."

"Thank you." Jane strode to her mare,

swung up, and rode away.

"Jonathan!" Patience sounded strained. Rosie and Elsa had allowed her to sit up, and she'd regained some color in her cheeks. "I feel such a fool. I have seen every kind of wound a soldier could have and helped to treat them. I look at a little blood on Mr. Howard's head, and I faint, causing all kinds of trouble for Elsa and Rosie. Jane must think me a nincompoop."

"No," he said, "she thinks you are to be envied."

"In what way?" Patience asked, while Rosie and Elsa helped her to her feet.

"For being the way you are. If you feel strong enough, please take my arm, and I'll walk you back to your wagon."

"What do you think, Elsa?" Rosie asked, watching them walk away, talking as they went.

"She's got some mighty stiff competition is what I think."

"I thought Jane and Eli were getting something together."

Elsa gave Rosie a shrewd look. "It's a way to stay close to the doc, wouldn't you say?"

CHAPTER 12

"We're behind time, and the hardest going is still ahead of us," Eli complained, swatting a huge green fly that was biting a piece out of his horse's neck. "We're only now coming up on Fort Dodge. We should have been here ten days ago."

The green flies had gotten so thick in the past week, they were making the animals miserable, and the mosquitoes at night bit any piece of human skin showing. Jonathan dreaded having to get out of his bed to relieve himself.

Eli pulled the faded blue bandanna from around his neck to wipe the sweat off his face. He had been riding hard, and Jonathan was nearly a mile out in front of the train, because three days earlier they had passed a small company of cavalry on reconnaissance and learned from their captain that the Kiowa had been raiding along the trail, which meant any day the Comanche might join them. Since then, Jonathan had been staying a full mile in front of the train in order to see trouble coming as soon as possible, and hoping it was far enough.

It hadn't helped that they were passing through dry, broken country with sparse grass that made it difficult to see very far ahead, especially when, he reminded himself, standing on the top of hills for a better view was a good way to shorten your life.

That the wagon master had come out on point at all told Jonathan that Eli was worried, and not just because the temperature had been climbing for several days, slowing the oxen. "The trail gets more difficult when we split off for the mountain branch," Eli said, clearly troubled by their loss of time.

"What's the mountain branch?" Jonathan asked.

"It's where the trail divides. One part is the Mountain Branch and the other is the Cimarron Cutoff, better known as the *Jornado de Muerti.*"

Jonathan blanched. "Does that mean what I think it does?"

"Yes. There's almost no water from Fort Dodge to the Wagon Mound, but it's shorter."

"So, we're taking the Mountain Branch for the water. Does reaching the mountains rid us of these flies?"

"Hopefully," Eli said. "Sometime in the next two days, we should reach Fort Dodge. Right after that, we bear west along the north bank of the Arkansas River."

"I don't think I've ever heard of Fort Dodge," Jonathan said.

"It opened in '65 and gained a bad reputation for dysentery, malaria, and pneumonia, from the unsanitary conditions the soldiers had to live in. They're most all Confederate soldiers who chose to fight Indians rather than rot in Yankee jails. Until recently, there wasn't a wooden building in the place, only dugouts with sod roofs for living quarters."

"Why are they here at all?" Jonathan asked.

"The Cheyenne and Kiowa call this area their hunting grounds, and they don't like what's happened to it. Americans and Mexicans have been travelling these routes since 1821, but not in the numbers that are passing through here now."

"How does that harm the hunting?"

"These Indians are horse people," Eli said, "living off the buffalo. They depend on the buffalo herds. We're interfering with the migration of the buffalo, as well as killing off the deer and nearly everything else wearing hair or feathers."

"The buffalo avoid us?"

"That's about the size of it. If the buffalo don't come, the people don't eat."

"I'm pretty sure I heard wolves last night."

"You did. Without the buffalo, they get hungry too." Eli sighed. "Tonight, I'm doubling the watch on the cattle and the remudas."

"I don't think you rode out here to tell me we're not making the time you hoped for," Jonathan said, looking up for a moment to follow the circling of a vulture. "I think that thing's following us."

"It always looks that way, especially if you're alone," Eli said. "There *is* something else worrying me. It's Jess Howard. He's talking about what he's going to do to you when his head heals. He's also drinking too much, and he's a mean drunk. I'm concerned about Jane, his wife, and those kids. I'm also concerned about you. He's a bushwhacker if I ever saw one."

"Thanks for your concern about me, Eli," Jonathan said, "but for several years I frequently had significant portions of the Confederate Army trying to kill me. I will keep an eye on Howard, but I think it's mostly the alcohol talking."

"Jane doesn't think so. She says the man's

a killer," Eli shot back.

"She might be right. He's several other unsavory things. As for worrying about his family, can you have one of the night watch go by their wagon every half hour?"

"I could, but the men would know right off it's the Howards I want watched. They'll ask why. I'd have to say, 'Howard's a mean drunk, and I'm worrying about his family,' which would lead to colorful comments about me and Jane that I might have to take exception to. I can't risk that. The people on this train are counting on me to get them to Santa Fe more or less in one piece and not getting kilt in a gunfight."

"You have a point," Jonathan said, grinning.

They rode along in silence for a few minutes.

"That vulture's still with us," Jonathan said, glancing up again. "Think we should be worrying?"

"That bird ain't your own personal vulture, and you ain't no Injun."

"I wonder what Yellow Leaf would say about us and the vulture?"

" 'Vulture minding own business,' " Eli said, in a fairly good imitation of Yellow Leaf's voice. " 'Try it.' "

"Okay," Jonathan said, then more seriously, "Jess Howard's been getting drunk for a long time without beating his wife and children. Has Jane ever told you different?"

"No," Eli admitted. "I'll give it more thought. I'd better get back."

He wheeled his horse and set off for the train at a gallop. Jonathan watched him go, wondering if Jane had told him what Howard had done to her. He thought not and still did not ask himself why she had told him.

Depending on whether Francisco Vasquez de Coronado's crossing of the Arkansas River in 1541, the Louisiana Purchase in 1803, or the 1821 opening of the Santa Fe Road by William Becknell is taken as the birth date of the Santa Fe Trail, first Indians, then Spaniards, then Mexicans, and, finally, Americans have been crossing and recrossing that part of the world for a very long time, and they have always had company.

"I've been seeing more rattlesnakes lately than I thought existed," Jonathan said to Patience as they stood outside the Stockbridge wagon, shortly after sunset. He had just finished examining her father, a ritual that brought him to her wagon three or four times a week. "You must be very careful where you put your feet when out of the wagon."

"Isn't it a little late to be warning me, Jonathan?" she asked in mock seriousness.

"I suppose you're right," he said, laughing. "I saw so many today while riding point, I guess they have filled my mind."

"Believe me," she said, "I am very careful. Is it true the Indians eat them?"

"I think it is. Cooked over an open fire or fried, they are said to taste like chicken."

"Not if they were cooked in Heaven, would I eat one of the wretched things," she said, her voice rising.

The sun slipped below the horizon, and over their heads there was a sudden booming sound that made Patience look up. "I've begun hearing that sound in the evenings. What's causing it?"

"It's a large bird called a nighthawk. When it dives and then turns back up suddenly, the wind blowing through its wing feathers makes the sound you hear. The males do it when they're courting, to impress females."

"Nature is most extraordinary," Patience said, laughing.

They were quiet for a few moments. Then, reluctantly, Jonathan said, "Patience, I feel compelled to say I'm not satisfied with your father's condition. His recovery is very slow, and I can't find any single reason why. His wounds are free of infection and are healing. But his heart is slightly weaker than it was, and his overall strength is fading."

She let out a soft sigh. "Thank you for being honest with me. Father pays little or no attention to what's going on around him or what he sees as we travel. It's as though he no longer has any interest in living."

"It's not uncommon when people are injured as seriously as your father was. But with him, I find it out of character. Does he talk with you as he always did?"

"No, he says talking tires him. Sometimes he'll drop off in the middle of a sentence, and he has lost all interest in our plans for Santa Fe."

"How old is he?"

"Seventy-three."

"I'm surprised. Did your parents marry late?"

"Father was twenty years older than my mother. She died when I was four. My memories of her are mostly of a woman in bed, in a room with the shades drawn. What's to be done about Father?"

The question came quickly, with all of Patience's concern in its delivery. It also came, Jonathan thought, with the warning that she did not wish to talk about her mother.

"At the moment," he said, "I don't have an answer. We can't improve on what he's eating. When I tell him it's time to get on his feet briefly each day, he only smiles and says, 'Let's wait a while, Jonathan.' "

They talked of other things for a few minutes, until Jonathan was ready to take his leave. "Remember, Patience, if your father's condition reveals itself as a failure to thrive, you are in no way responsible. A patient's failure to thrive comes when it comes and can almost never be reversed. For the time being, the best thing you can do for him is to take good care of yourself. Perhaps time will be on his side."

Sadness crossed her face, but without the fear he'd expected along with it. "Is that what is happening, Jonathan? Is he failing to thrive?"

"It's too early to say. I will tell you, one way or the other, when his true condition reveals itself."

"I will go on praying for his recovery." She laid a hand on his arm. "Sleep well, Jonathan," she said, with that calm acceptance he still marveled at. As he walked away, he asked himself why he was drawn to her. Was it the aura of peace he felt in her presence? Was it because she seemed to enjoy his company?

What did not concern him was that whatever warmth there was between them showed no signs of bursting into flames.

Despite Eli's warnings and those of many of the oxen drivers, Fort Dodge was a disappointment to many of the people in the train, especially the children. Misled by stories that circulated the length of the train, they expected Indians to be riding around the fort and the soldiers to be shooting at them. What they found instead was a sprawling and squalid set of low sod buildings, a few wooden shacks, and a handful of sullen soldiers marching back and forth on a burned-brown piece of prairie that served as a parade ground.

Once the wind shifted, the stench of latrines drifted over the travelers, causing the men to screw up their faces and swear. The women, pulling out handkerchiefs to cover their mouths and noses, grabbed up their skirts with a free hand and hastened their passing. The rocketing stink set the kids laughing hilariously, screaming and running in crazy circles, grasping themselves by the throat only to fall down in mock death, then leap up and race away, still yelling.

"It's the last fun they're likely to have," Jane said. Having run her horses ahead of the train, she'd left them in the care of the two long-legged Smithins boys, who had attached themselves to the remudas, and ridden ahead to visit with Jonathan.

"According to Eli," she continued, "we're entering some rough country, broken up by creeks with high banks just made for busting wagons."

"Are we going west or south?" Jonathan asked. "I should know the answer, but I don't."

"West," she said.

"Mountains." Jonathan nodded toward the broken line of blue mountains along the southwestern stretch of the horizon. He had been listening to Jane, but also studying her. Judging by her bright-red blouse and green split skirt, she seemed to have fallen under the influence of Yellow Leaf, who wore clothes of the most brilliant colors and equally gaudy cloths tied around her head.

"Jonathan," Jane said suddenly, "what are you staring at? Is there something wrong with me?"

"Oh, no," he protested. "You look fine." He wanted to say, "You look beautiful in those colors," but he thought that would be too personal, too admiring — something he was not supposed to be.

"You're a liar," she said, sounding hurt.

"You think I look like Yellow Leaf, don't you?"

Jonathan swore silently at his carelessness. This woman was sharper than a scalpel. He would have to be very careful how he climbed out of this hole.

"Actually, Jane," he said, "I was thinking red and green look good on you. It's a relief to see some color in this dreary landscape."

She gave him a skeptical eye. "Well, I ain't sure you're not lying, but being called a bright-colored piece of the landscape is better than nothing, and since I ain't nothing but a white Indian anyway, I guess I'd better settle for it."

"I assure you, Jane," he said, shocked by the pain in her words, "my compliment was spoken sincerely." He almost said it was heartfelt and swerved away from *that* just in time.

"Well, thank you, Jonathan," she said," but sometimes picking a way through your words is like being stuck in a thorn plum thicket."

With that, she whirled her mare around and rode off stiff backed, kicking up dust as she went. Jonathan sat for a while, watching her gradually disappear into the heat haze and even for a few more minutes after she was only a shimmer in the distance.

It had been a while since he'd examined his state of mind. His encounter with Jane, however, stirred something in him he had thought permanently tamed. He was keenly aware that in Patience's presence, the calmness of his mind was never disturbed, nor his desire roused. Recently, though, when he and Jane were together, he found she punched large holes in that calm and wakened the long dormant dragon of desire from what he had hoped was permanent sleep.

"I must not," he said grimly, pulling on Sam's reins. As they started off, he added, addressing the back of his mount's head, "And you and I know why, don't we, Sam?"

Chapter 13

As the train moved on beyond Fort Dodge, the days grew hotter, the biting flies an increased torment to the animals, and the oxen being bitten more often by rattlesnakes, usually on the legs, which could result in infection but was not fatal. However, a bite on an ox's or a horse's nose while they were grazing could swell their nostrils shut and asphyxiate them. The country became increasingly broken and drier than anything they had previously encountered. There was not, however, a lack of water, because the creeks, although shrunken and running between deep banks, were numerous enough for their needs. Unfortunately, the steep banks frequently halted the wagons.

"Jane told me you said we were in for trouble," Jonathan said, wiping his face with his bandanna and re-tying it around his neck. He and Eli were watching their wagon move off again after having foundered in a creek. It had taken three extra ox teams and all the men who could get their hands on the wheels to heave the wagon up the bank and onto solid ground. Earlier, two other wagons had each broken wheels, plunging down the bank when the wagon's brake let go.

Responding to Eli's commands, reluctantly, because it was extra work and took time, the drivers of the remaining wagons began adding ox teams to prevent a repeat of what had happened. It soon became their usual practice when confronting treacherous crossings.

"Another day's mileage shot to hell," Eli said sourly, then added, "She got it right. There's mountains and rock roads ahead and many miles of this rough going before the trail lifts and gives us some relief from the heat."

"Did that cavalry patrol that passed us this morning have any news?"

Eli lowered his voice. "I want what I'm going to say to stay between you and me for now. The captain told me the Comanches plan to start raiding wagon trains along this route. For a while they've let us alone. I guess the trains taking the other route have gotten too big and too well armed to be raided successfully. Daniel — Captain Mc-Bride — is a nephew a couple of times removed, I guess, on what's left of my mother's side of the family. He was posted here in April, been through a lot since. What he says, I believe. Tonight, I'll start having our animals brought inside the rectangle."

"What about the two stallions?" Jonathan asked, alarmed by the prospect of their harems being run together and the fireworks likely to follow.

"I'm leaving Jane and Morgan to wrestle with that problem," Eli said, sounding as if he'd dodged a bullet.

Jonathan decided not to question his decision. "Morgan and Yellow Leaf have all but adopted Jane. I think it's fair to say she's as good at handling horses now as Morgan is, if not better."

"Morgan won't admit it," Eli said, trying not to sound proud and failing, "but he's pretty much stopped telling her what to do, and even asks her now and then how she'd handle a situation. Two days ago, a wild mustang showed up and began pestering both remudas. It was only a question of time before he was going to challenge one of our stallions. He ran both of them, testing their strength, before backing away from a fight.

"Morgan told me he asked Jane what they

ought to do with him. 'Shoot him,' she said, and she did. I guess things are going bad with her father. Not just the drinking."

"What's gone wrong?" Jonathan asked. If there was serious trouble, Eli's not knowing the ugly truth of the relationship between Jane and Jess Howard meant he couldn't be much help to Jane.

"I'm not sure." Eli didn't sound very concerned. "The chick grown too big for the nest would be my guess."

Jonathan knew he was prying but risked the question anyway. "Is that what she told you?"

"No," Eli shot back, "it's my opinion. You think I'm wrong?"

He temporized. "I think Howard is a hard man and needs watching."

"Well," Eli said, his voice losing its edge, "we watched until Jane learned what was happening. Anyway, you would say that, given your run-ins with him."

"You're probably right." Jonathan felt relieved to have been given a way out of the discussion but figured Eli wouldn't be satisfied until he found out what Jane was referring to. He also thought she might have been seeking Eli's help without openly asking for it.

"Here's my plan for dealing with the

168

Comanche threat," Eli said, turning back to the subject that was clearly foremost in his mind. "I propose to take Rune and Jake Rawlings into my confidence. Put one of them out front with you and the other behind the train to cover our tail."

"We've had enough practice circling and laying out our guns for me to say we're ready to defend ourselves," Jonathan said. "I suppose you're adding Jake to my position to have another pair of eyes, but if you were to ask who I'd like with me, I'd say Yellow Leaf. She's got eyes like an eagle, and she knows what we're looking for, which is more than can be said for Jake and me."

"Morgan will fall down and chew grass, was I to ask her to do that," Eli said, bursting into laughter. "He clings to her like a beggar tick."

"Don't tell him," Jonathan said, forced to grin. "If she says yes, he'll fold."

"She does seem to have him by an ear," Eli admitted, wiping his eyes. "Jane says he'd crawl naked through a cactus patch for her."

The next day Jonathan was well out in front of the train. The weather had broken fair with just enough wind to keep the flies off. It was midmorning, and the ground mist had burned off, giving him a clear view of the blue mountains. He had been trying without much success to calculate how long it would take to reach them.

"Don't fall down," someone said scornfully, close behind him. "Already dead."

Jonathan was so startled he almost jumped out of the saddle.

"This one is watching for train," Yellow Leaf said, moving her brown and white pinto up beside Sam without looking at Jonathan.

He slid his Colt back into its holster and looked at Yellow Leaf. It was the first time he'd done more than glance at her. Her shining black hair, pulled back and caught in a bone ring, spilled down her back. She wore a red flannel shirt, its sleeves rolled up to her elbows, a braided rawhide belt fastened around her waist, deerskin leggings, and beaded moccasins.

She was, Jonathan thought, a very handsome woman. She also smelled good.

She was still talking, had been without interruption all the while Jonathan had studied her. "To keep scalp, must some time look around," she was saying as he began listening more closely. When she met his gaze, he was struck by how beautiful her eyes were.

"Onyx," he said.

A faint frown crossed her face. "Not know *onyx,*" she said.

"A black jewel stone. You have beautiful black eyes, like onyx."

The frown deepened. "I am just here, and already you are looking. First Jane's things, now me."

"Hold on," Jonathan protested. "I paid you a compliment. I didn't mean to upset you."

"What you pay me?" she demanded sharply.

Okay, get yourself out of this one, he thought. "A compliment," he said. "A *compliment* means I think something about you is very good, attractive, lovely." He was searching desperately for words she might know.

"You like women, Doc?" Her frown had given way to a smile, which brightened her face.

"Yes, I do," he said.

"Anything else you want to see?"

It suddenly dawned on Jonathan that he was having his leg pulled.

"No," he said seriously. "That's enough for today, and tomorrow will arrive with its own needs."

"You are also smartass," she said, trying

to smother a laugh.

"If I had a mirror, I would ask you to look in it. By the way, you smell very good. What is it?"

That bought him another smile. "Not know your word for it," she said. "Only know *flower*, tall and blue. Gather in fall, dry in sun, pound into small, and sprinkle on clothes when put away."

"Sage?" he asked, having heard Jane mention it.

"Is possible. My people use it for long time."

"Who are your people?"

"I am Osage," she said, her voice losing all traces of mirth.

Jonathan saw that his question had chilled the air between them. "Yours are a powerful people," he said, hoping to make up for it.

"Once," she answered, managing to glance at him.

"Eli says the Osage and Comanche are not friends."

"That is true. Together, we fought Kiowa and Pawnee and others."

She was quiet for a few moments, then said, as though she had settled something in her mind, "Too many enemies. In the time of my father, in the year of bad medicine, Kiowa warriors came into village and kill almost all the old people, children, women, cut off their heads. My father, my sister die there. Kiowa take away the *Taimay*. Osage not hold Medicine Dance for two years. From that time Osage are fewer and fewer."

It was clear to Jonathan that she assumed he would understand what these names referred to. While thinking hard about how to ask her what *Taimay* and Medicine Dance were, he looked around. Seeing nothing of any importance, he gave his attention back to Yellow Leaf.

"What you see?" she asked.

"Except for a creek ahead of us with willows and cottonwoods along its banks, just more prairie, dry and empty."

She climbed up onto her horse's back as if standing on a moving horse was what anyone might do.

"There, south," she said, throwing out an arm. "Six or seven antelope. West," she swung her arm in that direction, "band of mustangs. In front of us, buffalo, some young. Wolves follow. You need meat?"

"No pack horse," he said.

"Don't need. Shoot antelope. I skin it, wrap meat in hide. Throw over your horse or mine. Maybe shoot young buffalo. Good eating."

When she dropped back to sit on her

horse, Jonathan stood in his stirrups and scanned the landscape. Astonished, he said, "I can't see anything. Are you making a joke at my expense?"

"Your people have glass to look through. Things look closer. You have one?"

"Yes, but with you I guess I don't need it."

"You need it. Not seeing, not to laugh about. This one not always with you. Seeing might keep you alive."

She sounded as if she thought he wasn't going to last long. He turned to her and found her staring at him. With the sun on her face, accenting her high cheekbones, the broad curve of her forehead, the glow of her skin and the clarity and sadness in her gaze, Jonathan realized he was talking with a beautiful, mature woman who lived, like himself, with a knowledge of the darkness conferred by extended encounters with violent death.

"In the war I was a warrior," Jonathan said, feeling the shadows rising in his chest. "Many men died around me. My people won, but the suffering was great. Your people must not fight us, Yellow Leaf. We are too many. Do you believe me?"

"I do, Jonathan Wainwright, but my real answer is a story. Will you hear it?"

"Of course."

She nodded. "Long ago, in a place far to the north, before there were horses and we moved our villages with dogs, an old Arapaho warrior gave my people the *Taimay,* which is powerful medicine and was given to him by the Crow. It is only seen at time of what you call the Sun Dance and is for us a part of the ceremony, the *Kado.* The Medicine Dance is done once a year in honor of the sun."

"What is the *Taimay?*"

"I do not know how to tell you," Yellow Leaf said, frowning. "It is a figure made of deerskin head and body. No legs, but body is covered with short eagle feathers. It is kept on a pole during the dances. Then wrapped in antelope hide and placed in buffalo hide *parfleche* when dancing is over. The keeper of the *Taimay* decides when the *Kado* will be held."

She was quiet for a few moments, then said, "The *Kado* made the people strong in war, grass to grow, the buffalo to multiply, the women to have healthy children, and life to be good. But the dancing does not work now. The buffalo scatter and are few. Sickness has come among us, and what only makes your people sick kills us."

175

She paused again and straightened her back.

"That is the story, and I share my blanket with Morgan. You are a good man, a medicine man, Jonathan Wainwright, but you cannot help us. The happiness that was ours has passed from us. It is true also for the Comanche, but they will still fight you because they do not know what else to do."

"I am sorry, Yellow Leaf," Jonathan said. "Take my hand."

Looking puzzled, she did.

"I am here because I didn't know what else to do, but, as long as I draw breath, I will do all I can to make you and Morgan safe, and perhaps we will learn how to dance properly."

She squeezed his hand and smiled. "Perhaps in another time we might have danced to the whistle and drum, but let us now begin by killing young buffalo and make us welcome at the evening fires."

"Can you shoot with a rifle?"

"No, but I can skin a buffalo. Can you?"

"No, but I can shoot one."

"I want a rifle for Yellow Leaf," Jonathan told Eli the next morning.

"She know how to use one?" Eli asked, showing his reluctance.

"She will by this time tomorrow."

Finished cooking their breakfasts, Jane settled down between them. Jonathan had prodded Eli into inviting her to eat with them, and she'd accepted the offer as soon as it was made. "There's a lot of stress in that wagon," Jonathan had said when Eli expressed his surprise. "You might get another surprise if you asked her to marry you." No sooner had he spoken, than he felt as if he had stabbed himself in the stomach, a response he refused to dwell on. When Eli denied he had any chance of marrying Jane, Jonathan quickly changed the subject.

"How are you and Yellow Leaf getting along?" Jane asked, stirring her coffee.

Jonathan hesitated before answering, unsure how to respond. He felt certain it would be a mistake to share their conversation and final handshake with anyone.

"I find her an admirable woman," he said finally. "She is remarkably astute. She has a world of experience and has thought deeply about it. She carries a lot of sadness with her, but she can see animals and things far beyond my capacities. That young buffalo, for example . . ."

"Morgan better watch out," Jane said sharply, "or you'll have her under *your* blanket."

"She's a mighty fine woman," Eli said, plunging in with exactly the wrong comment, "but I can't see Jonathan hitching up with an Indian."

"Oh, I don't know, being *astute* ought to beat being an Indian."

"What does it mean, astute?" Eli asked.

"Damned if I know, but it must be something special if this one's called Yellow Leaf that." Jane banged her coffee mug onto the ground and rocketed to her feet, red-faced and ready for battle.

"It means she is intelligent and able to find the meaning of what she's observed," Jonathan said. "Don't forget, Jane, she's a lot older than you. Also, she's lost most of her people to sickness and war, starting with her father. Haven't you found her to be brave and kind?"

Jane turned away from them abruptly. "Oh, she's brave, all right," she said over her shoulder. "I wouldn't be surprised if, one of these days, she wrassled you onto the ground if nothing else worked, and it won't." By the time she finished saying all that, she was on her horse and on her way to the remuda.

"Good Lord and little fishes!" Eli said, wide eyed. "What in tarnation brought that on?"

"I've no idea." Jonathan watched her gallop away, her cloud of hair flying behind her. He was lying through his teeth, and his heart was thumping from the effect her outburst had on him. Admit it or not, he sometimes found her breathtaking. He was also thoroughly shaken by what she had said, and, while he was trying to deal with her revelation, he hoped for all he was worth that Eli didn't figure it out.

"I'll clean up here if you'll dig out that Spencer and a scabbard and a box of shells," he said. "We're behind time. Come to think about it, I haven't curried Sam." He was babbling and knew it and didn't care. Something in him made him want to smile, even laugh.

Eli looked lost in his own thoughts. "Do you figure Jane's worked up because she thinks you're making a move on Yellow Leaf? She's been telling me lately how happy Morgan is. You're not, are you?"

"Eli," Jonathan said, trying to sound offended, "have you lost your mind?"

"Well. Yes, you're right. It wouldn't make much sense," Eli admitted, adjusting his hat. "I don't really see you living in a teepee."

The thought seemed to bear in on him, and he laughed and slapped his leg. That gave Jonathan a chance to laugh, too, partially in relief that Eli had failed to understand the true cause of Jane's wrath, and partially because he felt so good about it.

CHAPTER 14

It didn't last. Jonathan had only to reflect on his proclivity for violence to lose all inclination to sing and dance over Jane's display of jealousy at his praise of Yellow Leaf.

By noon, he had taught Yellow Leaf the basics of loading, aiming, and firing the new Spencer rifle. Having worked with her hands from childhood, she had no trouble mastering the handling of the rifle, and it was a decided help that, although she was reluctant to display her feelings, she smiled every time she had the gun in her hands.

That afternoon, she in turn taught Jonathan how to bring antelope close enough to shoot. Having come upon a small herd, Yellow Leaf said, "Get off horse now. Bring rifle." Spencer in hand, she dropped to the ground. Jonathan followed, much less gracefully.

The grass was high where she had stopped

them, and they went through it, stepping carefully, until they reached a small stand of willows. There was a flash of steel, and a moment later she had cut a three-foot willow stick and trimmed off the small branches.

"Lie down," she said and instantly dropped full length on the ground.

"I don't much like —" Jonathan began, snakes on his mind.

"Lie down, not complain, not talk."

Muttering to himself, he did as he was told and rolled onto his back. Not having done this since childhood, he was astonished at the size of the daytime sky and the number of hawks and vultures riding the wind. He started to tell her what he was looking at, but she kicked him in the thigh.

"That hurt," he said and got kicked again.

He decided to be quiet and sulk. Yellow Leaf, meanwhile, had taken the red bandanna from around her neck and tied one corner to an end of the stick. Like Jonathan, she lay on her back while she worked. Now she grasped the other end of the stick, thrust it into the air, and began slowly waving the bandanna back and forth as it blew out in the wind like a little flag.

His curiosity overcame his fear of being kicked a third time. Jonathan inched closer to her and whispered in her ear, "What are you doing?"

Frowning, she whispered back, "Antelope will come. I will tell when to get up and shoot."

He lay for what he thought was several minutes, then turned his head and said, forgetting to lower his voice, "How much longer —"

He did not get to finish his question. A sharp elbow struck his upper arm and made him flinch. "How long is this going to go on?" he demanded, whispering this time.

"Until right time. I will tell you."

He lay quietly for a while longer, until the desire to laugh suddenly overcame him. As he sputtered and choked in his efforts to stop, her elbow hit him again.

"Hold rifle," she murmured. "Get up. Shoot. Now."

She dropped the flag, and they both scrambled to their feet. To Jonathan's surprise, five of the antelope were standing within an easy stone's throw. Jonathan chose the largest pronghorn in the group and shot it. Yellow Leaf brought down a smaller animal. The other three bounded away.

"How did you know when to stand up?" Jonathan asked when they began dressing the dead antelopes.

"Have clock in head," Yellow Leaf said, "and next time I not bring a child with me who cannot lie still and be quiet."

"I will have a black and blue leg where you kicked me," he said, "and the same on my left arm."

"Better than black and blue eye," she said, working swiftly over her doe.

Jonathan straightened up from his bent position, gutting the antelope. "You're having a lot of fun at my expense, aren't you?"

She paused long enough to look up and give him a false smile. "Someone is working instead of talking and is already skinning this antelope."

False or not, the smile brightened her face and made Jonathan grin. To his astonishment, he realized he was enjoying himself.

"Perhaps some person will help me skin this beast, or he will be doing it by starlight," he said.

"Perhaps someone will if someone else stops talking."

"You are a hard taskmaster." He went back to work.

"What is *taskmaster*?" she asked, stopping work herself to sit up and stare at him.

"Someone who makes others work very hard and kicks them and hits them with her elbow."

She burst into laughter, rocking back and forth with her eyes shut. Tears streamed down her face, startling Jonathan, who was not prepared for the outburst. He wasn't sure whether to laugh with her or be concerned at her response.

She stopped almost as suddenly as she had begun, picked up the knife she had dropped, wiped her face with her free hand, and then scuttled over to Jonathan on her knees. With a glance at the way he'd begun to skin the antelope, she said, "Legs first, then from neck. Finish with body lying on skin. Work with me. Do what I do."

She went back to her own antelope and worked in silence, with a speed he could not begin to imitate, but he mimicked her actions as best he could, and, in a surprisingly short time, the job was completed.

"Take meat. Leave bones. Watch."

Her knife began to flash again. In a very few minutes, the carcass was rolled off the skin and the meat lay piled on it. A few more slashes with her knife, and the meat was wrapped in the skin.

"Put on Sam," she told Jonathan, who had just rolled over his antelope carcass and pulled it away.

"Yellow Leaf," he said, sitting on his heels in front of her with the meat and skin between them, "you are amazing."

"That is like *taskmaster,*" she said, not smiling.

"No. It means I think you are very, very good. Wonderful."

She held his gaze for a long moment. "No one has ever said that about me, Jonathan Wainwright," she said quietly. "I will remember when pain comes."

"I hope you will remember and the pain never comes."

"I think it will. It always does, but I will have your words in my heart. Now help me with the other."

They finished quickly, but the sun was well down in the west when Jonathan put the meat, wrapped in the doe's skin, on Yellow Leaf's horse. As they parted for the day, Yellow Leaf said, "Perhaps tomorrow someone will bring glass."

"I will, and you will look through it also."

"Maybe I will see the next tomorrow," she answered.

"If you do, don't tell me what you see," he replied.

"Wise man," she said, turning her pinto toward Morgan's camp.

The train had been on the trail six weeks, and their progress was painfully slow, averaging little more than ten miles a day. Eli was nearly beside himself with frustration but doubled his efforts to increase their speed.

"Eli," Jonathan said, "this is not your fault. When a wagon breaks down, you can't tell the rest to go off and leave it. When there's a death — and we've had three: Mrs. Nichols from snake bite, Walter Fox from gangrene I couldn't halt, and the Needles boy falling under the wheels of one of the big wagons . . . That's three days mostly lost right there. Then there've been how many breakdowns, that each one cost at least half a day's delay?"

"Six by my count," Eli said gloomily.

He and Jonathan and Jane were sitting beside the last of the evening fire. After cooking it, she had stayed to eat supper with them, having admitted that she dreaded going back to the Howard wagon. "Pa's so nasty to me, Ma's been urging me to stay away as much as I can," she said.

She had apologized to Jonathan for her outburst over Yellow Leaf. When she finished, Jonathan had said, "Oh, were you angry, Jane?"

That earned him a punch in the shoulder. Eli laughed, but Jonathan thought it sounded forced.

187

"I think women have the idea I'm a punching bag," he said to Eli, trying to sound offended. "I'm still black and blue where Yellow Leaf kicked me for not lying still while she was drawing in the antelope. Now, this one" — pointing at Jane — "hits me for making a joke."

"That's because they can't get you into bed," Eli said loudly, followed by a more genuine laugh.

"Eli," Jane shouted, "you're asking for a bruise of your own!"

"I'll leave you two lovers to thrash this out." Jonathan grasped the opportunity to escape. "I'm going to bed."

Later, lying under his blanket, he relived Jane's explosion over his praising Yellow Leaf. It was clear to him she was angry because he had not responded to her overtures, subtle and not so subtle. He wondered briefly whether or not Eli was aware of what Jane's display meant, and he went to sleep hoping Jane would erase any doubts Eli might have about her affections.

Once again, he reminded himself that if he began a relationship with Jane there would be no extricating himself from it, and, aside from the damage he would do to Eli, at some point he feared the darkness would rise in him and destroy their relationship and her life. The conviction brought him the painful belief he could never marry, have children, enjoy the pleasures of a life shared. Instead, he would be forever alone. Finally, weariness silenced his thoughts, and he slept.

As the days passed, the trail gained elevation, and the country grew more broken and increasingly strewn with rocky outcrops. The grass was thinner and shorter, but stands of scrub spruce trees appeared, suggesting the region had more rain. In the distance, the pale-blue outline of mountains to the southwest looked no closer.

"Praise the Lord for this cooler night air," Patience said one evening after Jonathan had finished examining her father. A sickle moon with a faint circle of light its outline hung over their heads. The night wind, laden with the smell of earth and grass, blew gently around them, sighing as it went.

"I hope this slackening in the heat will give him better rest and an increase in strength," she said, into her companion's silence.

Jonathan stood for a few more moments, watching the wind stirring Patience's hair as she stared at the moon, while he decided whether or not to say her father was going to die. He could easily let her go on hoping, but his duty, he knew, was to tell her the examination had confirmed what he had suspected for several days. Gideon's body was gradually shutting down.

"Patience," he said finally, "I'm very sorry, but your father is not going to recover. His system is growing weaker with every passing day. Perhaps for too long, I have hung onto the hope I could reverse his decline, but I've failed."

He'd expected denial, even a few tears. Instead, she lowered her gaze to face him and placed a hand on his arm. "Perhaps I knew that, Jonathan," she said. "He told me last night that I must prepare to go on without him, and there was something in his voice that had not been there before. He knows he is going to die, and I must accept the inevitable."

"I am so sorry."

"I know you are. Father believed, and I with him, that what we encounter in the hereafter will be a continuation of God's love. We have experienced that love here and will experience it there. And, Jonathan, you did all there was to do. We are very grateful for your loving care."

He thanked her, feeling humbled. "I intended to comfort you, yet I'm the one who ended up being comforted. Did you figure I needed it more than you did?"

Her smile had some amusement as well as sympathy in it.

"You have been a great comfort to me, Jonathan, ever since Father's injury. I think it only right to extend the same to you for your long struggle to save him. Although you couldn't give him his life, you gave him care and company. We are only expected to do what we can, and that, I believe, begins with loving one another."

Jonathan returned to Eli's wagon a short time later, weary but strangely calmed by his talk with Patience. When he told Eli that Patience's father was dying, Eli said, "He was a good man, a mite stiff for my liking, but you couldn't be around him long before you saw in him a fellow who lived his beliefs. I think his daughter is much like him. Do you agree?"

"I do," Jonathan said.

"She'd make you a fine wife," Eli said quietly.

He didn't want to extend the discussion. "I'm not looking for one, Eli. Sleep well."

"Pa's gone," Jane said.

It was a gusty morning with a wild sky of scattered gray clouds racing east like a herd

191

of wild horses. The mountains looked higher, Jonathan had thought on rising. The air was drier and the nights increasingly colder.

"Where?" Eli asked, setting down his plate. He sounded concerned.

"I don't know, but there was a hard-looking man here yesterday just before dark. He and Pa had their heads together for a long while. Ma asked him who the man was and was told to mind her own business. This morning she told me Pa made her pack some clothes and jerky and a canteen of water. He didn't tell her where he was going."

"He took his guns?"

"Sidearms and rifle and extra ammunition, Ma said."

"Has he done this before?" Jonathan asked.

"Back when he was riding with Rand Callaway."

"Did you recognize the other man?"

"No, but he looked like the men Callaway used to have around him. I guess I'd better stay close to Ma and the kids until Pa comes back. Bad as he treats her, she gets skittish when he's not around."

"I can understand that." Eli picked up his plate. "I believe I would get skittish if I had all those kids to look after on my own."

Three days later, Jonathan and Yellow Leaf had just come up out of a creek's flood plain when she stood up on her pony, as she always did when they reached higher ground. Suddenly dropping back, she said, "Big war party, not hurry, but maybe come this way."

"Who are they?" Jonathan took out his telescope.

"Comanche," Yellow Leaf said.

Jonathan adjusted the spyglass. Surprise colored his voice. "I count twenty, possibly more, most carrying rifles. I don't think they've seen us. They are coming at a trot." He paused, then continued, "There are some white men with them."

"Renegades!" She turned her pony. "Very bad medicine. We go. Ride hard."

They had a good start, but Yellow Leaf's alarm was all Jonathan needed to keep pressing Sam until they reached the remudas. Jane's horses were in front. Jonathan pulled Sam up beside her. "Turn them back!"

"I take cattle!" Yellow Leaf called as she passed them.

"What is it?" Jane shouted as they began turning the lead horses and urging them into an easy gallop.

"Renegades!" Jonathan shouted back.

Jane nodded, short and sharp. "I'll run these into the other remuda. Worry about the stallions later."

The herd was pouring after the leaders, and, in a few minutes, they reached Morgan's horses. Jane had spurred ahead, yelling, "Renegades!" That single word told Morgan all he needed to hear to begin turning his bunch. Within seconds all the horses were running toward the train with Jane, Jonathan, and Morgan leading them.

The cattle, especially the milk cows, were slow to start, but Yellow Leaf had called out the same warning to the boys riding with them. The boys shouted and waved their hats at the lead bullocks and got them into a lumbering run toward the train. When the horses thundered past, raising a cloud of dust, the cattle seemed to get into the spirit of the thing and began running a little faster.

Eli and half a dozen other men had ridden out to meet the running animals. Behind them, at Eli's command, the wagons were already squaring.

"Get them inside," Eli shouted. The men with Jonathan and Jane slowed the horses to a trot and headed them inside the rectangle as it formed up on a stretch of prairie level enough to maneuver the wagons.

The horses ran inside the wagon ring, followed by the cattle, and gradually settled and began grazing. Jonathan rode along the train, gathering his armed men, aware that time to prepare themselves promised to be short . . . especially if anyone in the band of renegades had caught sight of him and Yellow Leaf as they raced away.

Eli had ordered Patience to put her wagon, the smallest in the train, inside the rectangle. Jonathan stopped beside the wagon and asked if she needed any help with her father.

"He's sleeping," she said. "I will gather the nursing team and set up the field hospital. I'll have one of the Smith girls stay with Father."

"Then I'll get on. Thank you for your work. Let's hope you don't have much to do."

To his relief, everyone remembered what had to be done. The moment the wagons were in place, the children were herded into the center with the animals around them. A dozen of the older women were left to tend them. The rest formed groups to break out pails and take the lids off the water barrels, preparing to douse any fires set by burning arrows, unload the ammunition wagon, and help Patience and her nurses lay out the field hospital.

Jane, Yellow Leaf, and half a dozen more women with rifles joined Jonathan, who had posted lookouts around the perimeter. Another twenty women, who would be the ammunition carriers, had also joined them. "Now we wait," he told the heavily armed group in front of him, "and remember, fight from under the wagons."

"They will ride around wagons," Yellow Leaf said. "Look for weak place. Ride away. Then come strong."

She had spoken without being asked, but her firm voice carried. No one questioned the accuracy of her prediction. Certainly, Jonathan didn't. In the time spent with her, he had developed a deep respect for the Osage woman.

"Do you know how to tell where they will attack?" he asked.

"Where they ride away. There they come back."

"What will stop them quickest?"

She showed some unease in replying. "There is no honor in it, but might shoot their horses. Might shoot the war chief. He will have most feathers. Do not be fooled when they run away. They will come back harder."

"Look here," said a tall, lanky man called

Edgard, wearing a wide-brimmed hat with the front of the brim pinned to the crown with porcupine quill. He stepped forward to point at Yellow Leaf. "That there's a squaw, and she can't be trusted to tell you whether or not the sun's up. And what's she doing with that rifle?"

Anger flared in Jonathan, but he wrestled it down.

"Keeping Morgan in antelope steaks," he said. As he'd meant, his audience burst into whoops of laughter at his response. "And I've got something more to say about Yellow Leaf," he added. "She saw the people coming at us before I could even see their dust. That gave us extra time. She says they're Comanches, and there's white men with them. This means they're renegades. So, thanks to her, we know what we're fighting. And if she has anything more to say, I want to hear it."

It was a long speech, but, when he stopped speaking, there were loud shouts of support and whistles. Edgard looked abashed and faded back.

"Yellow Leaf?" Jonathan said.

"Someone has this to say," she began. "Young warriors, to win honor, will jump horse into the circle, count coup, and then

197

kill any he can reach. Some must watch for that."

"What about the children?" one of the women asked.

"Not harm them. Take them. Tribes need children. Too many die," Yellow Leaf answered.

"Then we won't know at first where their attack will hit, until they pull back," Jonathan said.

"Jonathan," Jane said, "let Yellow Leaf and me and any of the other women get our horses and ride around, watching for any of them jumping into the circle. They do it, we shoot them. When they fall back, one or two of the renegades will see it and spread the alarm. Then we can pitch into the fighting."

He didn't like to think of her, or Yellow Leaf, in such danger, but the plan made sense. "All right, but when you give the alarm, shout out the compass point where they are. Now, the rest of you peel off and put two men under every other wagon. Make every shot count. I'll stay mounted and keep circling the ring until the women give the alarm. At that point, only one man from each pair runs to the attack area. Is that clear?"

Apparently, it was. The men broke off in pairs and were soon distributed among the wagons. Once mounted, Yellow Leaf and Jane rode back to Jonathan, who was just mounting Sam. "We'll come into the fight as soon as everyone knows where it's going to be," Jane said.

"All right. Keep your eyes open, and don't be reckless," he told her.

"Jonathan Wainwright," Yellow Leaf called out, thrusting her rifle over her head, "it is a good day to die."

"It is," he called out after her as she rode off, "but try not to!"

Yellow Leaf looked back, grinning. Jane just shook her head and rode after her.

A strange silence fell over the train. Under the late morning sun, none of the bullocks were bellowing. No children were shouting or crying. None of the drivers were cracking their whips and swearing, and none of the women were laughing and calling to one another. No smoke drifted over the wagons.

The only human sound was made by Henry Smithins, who was walking among the cattle singing *Nearer My God to Thee* in the clear, high tones of a boy whose voice has not changed. Jonathan sat listening, and soon Horace, deeper voiced, joined his brother, singing in harmony. A moment later, a woman's rich soprano joined the boys, and one by one around the circle of wagons, more men and women began singing.

The sound wrapped around Jonathan. Stripped in the war of any faith in God he'd ever had, he thought he'd never heard the hymn sung so beautifully. It stirred something in him deeper than belief and brought tears to his eyes, and wakened in him a kind of joy he'd thought was lost to him forever.

Shortly after the singing ceased and the silence of all but the wind rolled back, Yellow Leaf joined Jonathan, looking south between two wagons. They did not speak but went on staring, until Yellow Leaf broke the silence.

"They come," she said, dropping into a sitting position.

Jonathan opened his telescope and peered through it. "They certainly do." A sudden calm settled over him, as it had done during the war whenever the waiting was over.

"Are you afraid, Jonathan Wainwright?" she asked, her dark eyes searching his face.

"No," he said quietly. "I am not afraid of battle. I fear what comes after."

"What comes that you fear?"

He met her gaze and saw something in her eyes that cleared the way for him to answer. "I do not want to stop killing."

"Yes," she said. "Among my people, it is

so with many. Some stay on warpath until hair is white or spirit leaves them. Many die soon and are released. You have left your home."

There was no surprise, alarm, criticism, or fear in her. She spoke calmly, with understanding, without judgment. For the first time, Jonathan felt he had been understood. It came as an immense relief.

"Yes," he said. "The wish to kill is why I left."

She nodded and said again, "They come."

"And we go," he answered.

"Remember what I said before, and kill all you can," she called back as she turned her pony. "So will I."

And you left your *home,* he thought as he watched her sprint away.

CHAPTER 15

"I make it forty," Jonathan told Eli.

They were standing between two wagons, looking at the line of mounted Indians and half a dozen white men that fronted the south side of the train at a distance of about a hundred yards. In the center of the line sat their war chief, on a white horse. As Yellow Leaf had said, he wore the most feathers in his headpiece.

"Figuring out where to hit us," Eli replied.

Jonathan stepped back and led Sam along the line of wagons, calling out, "Hold your fire. Hold your fire. Wait for the attack, pass it along."

His order sped around the rectangle. Jane rode up to him, her rifle still in its scabbard, and leaned down to speak. "The ammunition is distributed," she said, "and women are posted to run it up where it's needed."

"Good work," he said. "I think we're ready

as we can be."

"Is it all right that I'm scared?"

"You'd be a fool not to be." He reached up and laid his hand on her knee.

She gripped his hand in hers. "Are you?"

"Of course I am. But this is the worst part, waiting. When it begins, you'll be too busy to think about it."

"Why does Yellow Leaf say, 'This is a good day to die'?"

"Perhaps to remind herself that death is ever present, perhaps to strengthen her courage."

Just then, the raiders broke into yells and kicked their horses into a gallop. Jane and Jonathan broke apart. Jonathan rode Sam to face the center of the approaching line. The war chief was riding straight at him. Jonathan guessed this charge was designed to test the train's firepower. He chose not to give that away.

"Hold your fire," he shouted, and the call went around the circle.

The hammering of the horses' hooves grew louder as the renegades approached. Knowing how unsettling a cavalry charge could be to those who'd never experienced one, Jonathan called out, "Steady!"

As soon as he shouted his order, the Indians in the charge broke into hoots and yells, screaming defiance and waving their bows, rifles, and hatchets over their heads. In the next moment, riders peeled off from both ends of the charging line and raced around the wagons, sending bullets and arrows into them.

"Hold!" Jonathan shouted. The attackers wheeled their horses and raced them back to their starting point. In a group, the raiders drew back, turned, and, in no discernible order, rode straight at the wagons, firing as they came, some shooting from under their horse's neck or turning and firing an arrow while looking back. Jonathan noted that the whites took no part in the showoff riding but gathered around the war chief, who sat watching.

Eli came to stand beside Jonathan, who kept his gaze on the war chief, holding back beyond handgun or carbine range. "Hand me your Sharps," Jonathan said.

Eli passed Jonathan the buffalo rifle.

"How much wind drift between us and the feathers?"

"Three inches at the most," Eli said. "It's a stretch, but it's worth a try."

Jonathan cocked the rifle, sighted high on the chief's chest, and squeezed the trigger. The rifle cracked, and the Indian's feet flew up over his head as his body was knocked backward off the horse. The white riders scattered. One, riding a big palomino, dodged among the braves still racing in and out, shouting at them.

Whatever he said pulled them back to where the chief had fallen. The man with the palomino swung off his horse, dropped to the ground, and bent over the chief. A few moments later, he stood up, shouted something, and pointed toward the train.

Jonathan, watching closely, gambled. "South!" he shouted. "Run!"

The men at the other points sprang up and charged, passing the pairs of women who were already transferring ammunition boxes to the south side of the circle. The men were crawling under the wagons facing the raiders when the renegades suddenly wheeled their horses and came straight at the train.

"Hold! Hold your fire!" Jonathan shouted, then threw himself under the nearest wagon.

From his new position, he had a clear view of the riders. He had been right, and he knew that if he could turn this attack, they could end the fight in minutes.

"Hold!" he shouted again, and the men waited. The attackers with rifles were already firing, but their shots were high and zipped through the coverings on the wagons.

All of the riders were yelling. Next came a shower of arrows, these also striking the canvas.

Jonathan kept shouting "Hold!" until the attackers were fifty yards away, then called, "Horses, fire!"

The men beneath the wagons fired almost as one. Half of the horses plunging toward them crashed to the ground, throwing their riders.

"Men, fire!" Jonathan called, as the remaining horses headed for the spaces between the wagons. All but a dozen of the riders on the ground and on the remaining horses went down under the defenders' concentrated fire. The raiders jumping their horses between the wagons were met by Jane and Yellow Leaf and the six remaining women on the ground with their rifles raised. The women fired, taking down eight of the men before they could turn their horses and flee. The few remaining attackers raced across the ring of wagons and jumped out at the north side, then broke and fled.

"Hold!" Jonathan said. Despite his order, when one of the Indians who had fallen sprang to his feet, he was shot dead.

"We have a dozen men with bullet wounds,

three with shoulder and chest wounds that will need your attention," Patience told Jonathan when he stopped by the jury-rigged hospital she and her women had put together. "And three of the women have arrows in them. There must be some of the renegades who are wounded as well."

"I expect you're right," he said, "but I doubt any of the Indians will let you touch them." All of the white men had been killed, apparently singled out by the defenders. When Jonathan examined their bodies, he found many had been shot more than once.

"What about Yellow Leaf?" Patience suggested.

One of the women found Yellow Leaf and brought her to the field hospital.

"Kill them," she said, after Jonathan explained the problem.

"We can't do that!" Patience protested. "They are humans and deserve help even if they are our enemies."

"It would be a great dishonor to help them," Yellow Rain said, apparently equally shocked at Patience's proposal. "If they go back to village, people will know you made him well . . . he cannot have honor. Children throw horse turds at him."

Jonathan contemplated the standoff and finally said, "Sometimes in the war, those wounded on the losing side who could not walk were shot in the head. Armies moved fast."

"Not time for stories." Yellow Leaf fixed him with her black gaze that always made him feel guilty, even if he wasn't.

Patience shot Jonathan a meaningful look. "Christians are brought up believing we must extend our hand to those in need of help."

"Another story." Yellow Leaf sounded disgusted. "That person on tree not here."

"He called on the Lord to forgive those who had crucified Him," Patience said, bristling. "He said, 'Father, forgive them. For they know not what they do.' "

Yellow Leaf made a scoffing sound. "Bad story. Crazy father let it happen."

Patience went white, and Jonathan thought she might light into Yellow Leaf. He spoke quickly to forestall her. "Patience, if any of them try to fight you off, leave them. We'll deal with the rest."

"Keep someone with gun always there," Yellow Leaf said, shaking her head. "If one wake, see knife can reach, will take and try to kill anyone there. Very dangerous thing you do."

She was right. An Indian with a head wound regained consciousness while two of the women were working over him. One had a pair of scissors in her apron pocket. The man sprang to his feet, grasped the scissors, grabbed her by the hair, and lifted the scissors to stab her but was knocked down by Yellow Leaf striking him over the head with the barrel of her rifle.

"Cannot tame a wolf," she said, staring down at the dead man.

Patience rushed over. "There was no need to hit him that hard," she protested.

Yellow Leaf wiped the barrel of her rifle with a square of bandage cloth. "You want have cup of tea with him?"

"I thank the Lord she was there," Patience told Jonathan later, "but she's a heathen and killed that man as calmly as I'd swat a fly."

"From what she's told me," he said, "I'd guess she's a more dedicated believer than you are."

"Jonathan! How can you say such a thing?"

"I asked her if her people believed in God. She said in her world, Father Sky and Mother Earth are very real, as is the Great Spirit that determines all things. Yellow Leaf is an Osage and has no commitment toward the Comanches — although she did say at one time her people were at peace with them. She has done nothing to regret. She is remarkably practical. She is also kind and gentle and very funny. She looks on the world with an eye entirely free of romantic misconceptions. She believes in an afterlife, and killing that Indian to stop him from killing Beatrice Langton was as rational as killing a snake that tries to bite you. She would tell you, if you asked her, she would tell you that the warrior died fighting and would go to the next life an honored man."

"Are you suggesting my Christian beliefs are 'romantic misconceptions'?" Patience demanded, clearly angry.

"No, but refusing to believe Yellow Leaf when she told you the wounded Indians did not want your help was. Beatrice Langton owes Yellow Leaf her life. I heard your women not only ignored Yellow Leaf as she stood by you, but some of them called her a *squaw.*"

"Some of those women have had relatives killed by Indians," Patience said. "They have reason for hating them."

"And what about Yellow Leaf? Her tribe has been decimated by smallpox, measles, diphtheria, gonorrhea, syphilis, whooping cough, all transmitted through us. We are driving them out of the lands they have lived on for generations. Where is her bitterness or hatred? She moved in with Morgan in part because she had no other place to go, and in part because she saw a man who needed her help. I think he's her project. He gives her something to do, a purpose for living. She is doing what Indian women have always done. They are the glue that holds the tribes together."

Patience gave a light laugh. "Jonathan Wainwright," she said. "I have never seen you so worked up. I swear, you have fallen in love with Yellow Leaf. She would make you a remarkably fine wife."

Jonathan wanted to be irritated, but he couldn't find the feeling and laughed with her. "You have changed the subject," he said.

"I'm sorry." She was still bubbling with amusement. "But that was the finest presentation of a subject that I can remember. You should have run for public office. That was excellent delivery."

"Now you're making fun of me."

"No, I'm not. You spoke the truth as you see it, and I admire you for it," she said, laying a hand on his arm. "It was a fine defense of a brave woman. I would be proud to be her friend, but a world separates us."

"Think how interesting it would be to explore those differences together," he said.

■ ■ ■ ■

While the burial crews were getting their instructions from Eli, Jonathan at Jane's request walked out to look at the dead white men scattered on the ground. Jonathan did not have to ask her why she was doing this. They had not gone far when Jane stopped by a man sprawled on his face in the tall grass, the back of his head blown off.

"I don't want to," Jane said, "but I'd best see his face."

Jonathan rolled the man onto his back. Jess Howard, lifeless, stared up at them. He had been shot in the right eye.

She let out a breath. "I thought so. Somebody had to do it. I'm glad it wasn't you."

For a full minute, she stood looking down at the dead man. Then she raised her head and looked dry-eyed at Jonathan. "Can we leave him be 'til I can fetch Ma? She needs to say goodbye and maybe say some words before he's buried."

"Go on," Jonathan said. "I'll stay with him until you and your mother come back."

He picked up the rifle lying beside Howard's body and passed it to her. "Perhaps you'll want to keep it for one of the boys."

"Maybe. Ma may think otherwise," she

said and left.

The Howard family gathered when the grave was ready. Jane's mother had brought her Bible, and when the men who dug the grave laid Howard in it and were pulled out, they took off their hats while Mrs. Howard read, " 'And I heard a voice from heaven saying, write this: Blessed are the dead who die in the Lord from now on. Blessed indeed, says the Spirit, that they may rest from their labors, for their deeds follow them!' "

She snapped the book shut and strode away, herding the children in front of her.

Jane looked wide eyed at Jonathan. "She read from Revelations. I don't know if she's wished him well or not."

"I'm not strong on Revelations, Jane." Jonathan watched Mrs. Howard depart, thinking of the final words she had read: *for their deeds follow them.* "You would have a better idea than I. Should you be with her?"

"I guess I'll be honest with you and say no. She knew what he was doing."

The following morning, the train was under way again, and Jonathan was out on point. Yellow Leaf rode nearby, silent and sour as a crab apple.

"Is there something you want to tell me?"

213

he asked.

"Too late," she said. "This one did not know how stupid you people are. No wonder trouble follow you like vultures follow dying buffalo."

"When you finish insulting me, tell me what's upset you."

She shot a fiery glance at him. "Last night, I make Morgan move horses and our sleeping place long way from where dead are lying. You did not go."

"Why should we have moved?" he asked, puzzled by her concern.

"A child know the spirits of the dead rise. You cannot bury their spirits. They are dangerous — bring illness, cause babies to come too soon and the worms to eat the corn. Why you not know this?"

Suddenly, he understood. *Of course. Pestilence may come from close association with the dead. Superstition, serving a good cause.*

"It was good to do what you did," he said. "Perhaps we have left soon enough."

She rode in silence for a few moments, then said, "All died while fighting. Perhaps this time their spirits, rising with honor, did no harm. Long, long ago the People learned of the danger. You must not forget."

"Let's hope there will be no more dying for a while."

When she replied, her voice had softened somewhat. "Sometimes, Jonathan Wainwright, I think you still a child."

CHAPTER 16

The wounds, physical and emotional, were healing quickly, and there was at least one good result from the renegades' attack. It quelled the petty bickering that had plagued the train ever since setting out for Santa Fe. Eli began to lose the frown lines between his eyes, and Patience's father — who had watched the battle from beneath a huge freight wagon with men firing from both sides of him — asked, once under way, to be propped up so he could see the land through which they were passing. Some things he began to see, besides the blue sky, were a prairie still dotted with colorful flowers, flocks of quail bursting out of the grass, herds of antelope, and, as the days passed, increasing numbers of buffalo.

"Follow fires," Yellow Leaf said.

She and Jonathan were on point, and he had called her attention to the buffalo. Because she was not quick to explain herself, it took Jonathan a little while to understand why she had said it. They had ridden into an area where the grass was green and less than a foot high for as far as he could see.

"This must have been burned," he said, but his eureka moment did not impress Yellow Leaf.

"What you do with eyes and nose?" she demanded, turning sharply on her pony to glare at him.

This morning she was wearing a rolled red bandanna tied around her head. The weather had turned colder, so she'd put on a beaded buckskin jacket and doeskin leggings. He had praised her appearance, and her response was a sharp "Look like old crow." But she was smiling.

"I guess I hadn't noticed," he said, somewhat surprised. "Now you mention it, there is a slight burned smell in the air."

"Buffalo kick up old burned things. Jonathan Wainwright, someone must use eyes and nose to know what is here. You go places like child or old man asleep on horse. World has bad things. Wind carry messages. Open eyes. Open ears."

She was quiet for a moment, apparently studying the scattered groups of buffalo. Finally, she said, "There will be many more

in one more sun. Form large herd. Dangerous then."

"Why?" he asked.

"Frighten, then run together. Not stop for
long time."

"Stampede?"

"Not know that word."

"All running fast together. Not turning
aside for things."

"Yes, sometimes whole villages broken
down by those running."

"Have you ever seen this happen?"

She grunted assent. "One time. Lodges
broken. People dead. Not get on horse soon
enough and ride fast." Then she added,
"Plenty is seeing once."

"I can imagine," he said, looking at her
and thinking about her life, compared with
his own.

The train, moving across the prairie, did
not drift along like the clouds, sedate and
silent. The wagons creaked and groaned.
The huge wheels, greased or not, squealed
and grated. Canvas flapped and banged on
the iron frames. The oxen roared at unpre-
dictable intervals, and their drivers swore,
shouted, and cracked their whips. The
children, at least those old enough to run
along with the wagons, were constantly

shouting and yelling. The women, most of whom walked beside the wagons, often called to one another or walked in groups, laughing and talking at the top of their voices to be heard. Sometimes, things went wrong.

The day after Yellow Leaf and Jonathan talked about the buffalo, Jake Rawlings came after him, riding his dun horse hard. "Jonathan! You best come with me. A boy's cut hisself real bad! He'll bleed out if something's not done."

Jonathan passed Jake his rifle. "You stay here with Yellow Leaf," he said and spurred Sam back toward the train.

Eli rode out from it to meet him. "It's Timmy Messering," he said. "The fool kid was chasing his sister with their father's Bowie knife and fell on it, and laid open his leg. His mother took one look, and it scared her so bad she fainted. Woke up, scrambled to her feet, saw it again, and fell flat.

"Two of the women in the train had to give her smelling salts to get her on her feet again and into her wagon. By chance and good luck, one of the women who's been in Patience Stockbridge's nursing bunch was nearby, and she tore off her petticoat and wrapped it around the boy's leg. That's slowed the bleeding but ain't stopped it."

"I'll need my bag and some ether and a bottle of whiskey." Jonathan turned Sam toward Eli's wagon.

"You planning to get the boy drunk?"

"No. We can't boil water, so I'll have to sterilize the wound and the needles as best I can."

Patience had heard of the accident, turned her mules, and come back to the Messerings' wagon. Jonathan found her there along with several of the women who'd trained under her, all gathered to offer help. Adele Messering, on her feet again, was with her son.

"How are you feeling, young fellow?" Jonathan asked as he unwrapped the blood-soaked cloth from Timmy's leg.

White as snow, clearly trying to be brave, the boy said, "I've felt better. Pa, I'm mighty sorry about the knife."

"We'll talk on that later," Karl Messering said. "Right now, you do what the doctor tells you, you hear?" Messering was a big man with coal-black hair and beard to match, but what showed of his face was nearly as pale as his wife's. She sat pressed against him, trying not to cry.

"Yes, Pa."

Patience and two of her nurses were kneeling on both sides of the boy, having laid out the needles and cloths beside Jonathan. Patience held a brown glass bottle where Timmy couldn't see it, a folded cloth pressed to its top.

"Timothy," Jonathan said quietly, "this is quite a cut you gave yourself, but I'm going to sew it up and make you good as new. We're going to put you to sleep for a bit while we patch you up. How does that sound?"

As he spoke, the two nurses put their hands on the boy. "Now," Jonathan said, and Patience pressed the cloth over the boy's nose and mouth. The odor of ether filled the wagon.

For a few seconds, the boy's entire body fought to free itself from the stifling ether. Adele gave a cry of alarm as Timmy's body fell back, completely limp.

"Splash the wound with whiskey," Jonathan told Patience.

From then until Jonathan had put in the last of the twenty stitches needed to close the wound, there was no sound in the wagon save the wind.

"Bandages," he said, and the work was done. A sigh of relief rose from everyone around the boy as Jonathan pinned the last bandage in place.

He looked up at the Messerings. "Tim will

be sore for a while, and he is not to run or jump down from the wagon or jump anywhere else. I'll come around to look at the wound from time to time. And for God's sake, Mr. Messering, keep that knife where your son can't pick it up on impulse."

Karl Messering was not accustomed to being spoken to that way, and his face flushed, but he nodded. Adele, released from the worst of her fear, turned on him and shouted, "You and that goddamned knife!"

"I never heard Adele Messering so much as raise her voice," Patience told Jonathan, sounding slightly shaken, when they had climbed down from the wagon.

"It was a near thing," Jonathan said. "Another half inch and the boy would have severed his femoral artery. Had he done that, we would have been too late to save him. I thought it best not to tell his mother."

"You have a sardonic sense of humor, Jonathan Wainwright," Patience said.

"I'm surprised to learn I have any sense of humor," he replied, and they went on walking in silence.

It happened with little warning. Jane was the first to notice something, although Yellow Leaf probably noticed it at almost the same time. The fact they were nearly a mile apart meant it was not known until much later. The train had been passing through a stretch of mostly high, rolling country, heavily spotted with scattered stands of scrub spruce and piñon pine, a feature that would take on great significance.

Morgan had sent Jane ahead of the remudas, to scout the grazing. For several days, there had been brief bursts of wind and rain, falling mostly during the early morning hours, and it was Yellow Leaf who called Jonathan's attention to the pale-green shoots thrusting up through the taller and drier grass.

"Remember about buffalo following rain for new grass," she said. They had seen an increasing number of buffalo lately, scattered over the land in small groups.

"We have more than enough meat," he said, his mind occupied with the problem of Timmy Messering's leg, which was not healing as well as he thought it should.

"Not dream, pay attention," she said, sounding irritable.

"What's wrong? You've been grumpy all morning."

"Something," she said, without taking her eyes off the sky to the southwest.

Their horses also seemed grumpy, sidling

and tossing their heads, refusing to settle when standing. "What's got into these two?" Jonathan asked, irked with Sam's uneasiness.

"Maybe what make me *grumpy,*" Yellow Leaf said.

The morning had been mostly sunny, with huge banks of cumulus clouds racing over their heads. By noon the wind had shifted to the southwest, blowing fitfully and occasionally with a blustery strength. The sky over the mountains darkened as thunderheads formed, black as night. They advanced like giant ships, driving the white cumulus clouds before them like fleeing sheep.

"Did you bring your oilskin?" he asked her.

"Not worry about rain," she said. "Something else."

Lightning burst out of the dark clouds in sudden flashes that struck the earth with jagged spears. The huge storm was too far away for them to hear the thunder, but at the rate the storm was swallowing the blue sky, they would hear it soon.

Before Jonathan could ask Yellow Leaf what the "something else" was, Jane came riding toward them at full gallop. She pulled up and shouted, "A mile or so ahead of you

— I was on the ground, looking at the new grass, and I swear I felt it tremble."

At that, Yellow Leaf dropped to the ground and pressed her ear to the earth. A few seconds later, she rose to her feet and leaped onto her pony. "They come!"

"What's coming?" Jane and Jonathan demanded.

"Buffalo, many, many! Earth shake! We must ride! Build fire!"

Their mounts needed no encouragement and ran like racehorses for the whole mile back to the train. Once at its head, and having found Eli, Jonathan told him what was coming. Yellow Leaf added, "Stop train. Build big fire in front, put on burning water, and throw match when hear their feet."

"Scrub spruce and coal oil," Eli said. "Jonathan, round up some men, bring axes, and start cutting."

"What about Morgan?" Jane asked.

Yellow Leaf said, "Morgan know what to do. He will hear and run everything to side."

"The boys!" Jane's voice rose. "They're with my remuda!"

"You will think of small ones here," Yellow Leaf told her, mounting her pony. "I will care for them." She called the last words over her shoulder and took off.

Eli turned to Jane. "Yellow Leaf's right.

I'll give you the hand bell. Ride down the train, spread the word, and see to it everybody gets into their wagons."

Jane set off with the bell and began ringing the stop signal, pausing at intervals to say there was a buffalo stampede. Within a minute or two, the dreaded word *stampede* had been shouted from wagon to wagon the length of the train, bringing it to a halt and those walking, running for the wagons. After setting their brakes, the drivers all clambered onto the backs of their lead oxen, so the huge beasts would know they were with them and stay calmer.

Jane kept on riding until she had gone the length of the train and made certain all the children were in their wagons. At the head of the train, Jonathan and a dozen men were chopping down the spruce brush while another dozen dragged the cut brush into a pile thirty yards in front.

Eli had found a three-gallon can of coal oil and set it beside the growing pile of brush. That done, he rode out another thirty yards, got off his horse, knelt down, placed his hands on the ground, and waited. Several minutes passed before he jumped up and raced back to the brush pile.

"Get to the wagons!"

The men scattered, leaving Eli and Jonathan with the brush pile and the oil can.

"Pour it on," Eli said.

Jonathan carried the can around the pile, splashing oil over the brush as he went.

"Here goes." Eli pulled out matches and made to strike one.

"Stop, Eli!" Jonathan shouted. "We're too close. This thing is going to explode. Back off. We'll pour some oil on a branch, light it, and throw it onto the pile."

They did exactly that, and the pile lit all at once with a roar that sent a ring of fire and smoke shooting out all around it.

"Lord a' mercy!" Eli said, nearly falling down in his effort to dodge away from the flames.

Jonathan grasped his arm and steered him back as they sprinted for the train. "Get to your wagon," he said. "Tie your horse to the nearest wheel in case you need him. I'm going to the Stockbridge wagon and if there's time, hobble their mules." He could feel the ground shaking under their feet and hear a faint rumble, low and persistent.

"They're coming," Eli said. "Let's pray that fire splits the herd."

Jonathan glanced at the fire as he mounted Sam. The flames were shooting fifteen feet high, the entire pile ablaze. He reached Patience's wagon as the sound of the running buffalo echoed like distant thunder. The lamps hanging from the canvas roof swung and jingled like bells.

Jonathan swiftly set the wagon's brake and hobbled the mules, then took the reins from Patience's hands. There was no point speaking; the thunder of thousands of hooves drowned all other sounds. He settled himself on the seat beside her just as the first of the herd shot past them. The fire had done its work. The herd had split without slowing and was pouring around the train on both sides at an astounding speed. Jonathan and Patience were instantly immersed in the heavy, pungent smell of the hundreds of animals racing past them.

Behind them, Gideon Stockbridge had propped himself on his elbows and was watching the stampede with an expression of wonder on his ravaged face. Patience stood on the wagon seat, her hands clasped in front of her, gazing wide eyed and enraptured at what she was witnessing.

The mules, their ears pricked, watched first on one side and then the other without stirring, apparently mesmerized. Awed by the spectacle, Jonathan tried to follow just one of the racing animals, but he found it impossible. He did see a large bull stumble and go down, and the animals behind him leap over him as if they were in a steeple-chase. The downed bull lay unmoving. At least a hundred animals went over him, some of their hooves striking him in their passing.

The stampede ended as suddenly as it began. The silence rushing in, as the thunder of the buffalo swiftly faded, was uncanny, nearly as unsettling as the terrible hammering of the buffaloes' hooves.

Still standing on the wagon seat, Patience looked back over the canvas roof in the direction the buffalo had gone. "Father, I expect to live the rest of my life without ever again witnessing the equal of what has just swept around and past us."

Jonathan had gotten down and taken the hobbles off the mules' feet. He climbed back onto the wagon, eager to hear what Gideon would say in response to Patience's surprisingly emotional statement. There was no answer. Looking past Patience, Jonathan saw her father's immobile face and sightless eyes and knew in an instant what had happened.

He took her by the waist and sat her down, keeping her back turned to the inside of the wagon.

"Jonathan," she cried, "what are you doing?"

"Patience," he said quietly, "please forgive my taking this liberty, but you need to sit."

She folded her hands in her lap, her face gone pale. "Is it Father?" she asked.

"Yes. He's gone. I'm very sorry."

A little shiver went through her. "He didn't answer me," she said. "I should have guessed."

"With your permission, I will close his eyes," he said quietly.

"Please do." She swallowed hard. "I hope he saw the buffalo running."

"I think he went right after the herd passed us." He had no idea if that was true but thought it would ease the shock if he told her so.

"Unless you want me to stay with you," he said, "I think I should lay him down and move his bed back into the wagon."

Tears welled up but didn't spill over. "Yes, please do that. It must be done."

He stepped past her and gently closed Gideon's eyes, then straightened him on his bed, crossed his hands on his chest, and pulled the bed as close to the tailgate as possible, in preparation for the inevitable moment when he must be lifted out for burial.

CHAPTER 17

Nearly every person in the train who had any contact with Gideon Stockbridge gathered on the small hill, chosen by Patience, beyond the last tracks on the eastern edge of the trail. Even half of the drivers came, the others guarding the oxen. Eli and half a dozen mounted and armed men also stayed with the train.

Gideon had been sewn into a canvas sack and carried by four men on a pair of planks, laid on two wooden cross pieces, taken from the repair wagon. The day had broken fair with a light west wind, and Jonathan, Jubal Smith, and Duncan and Burchard Harley had gone out at first light and dug the grave. Eli and Patience had agreed the burial would take place at the time the train usually got under way, and, when the burial was over, the train would leave.

Jonathan and the burial team lowered Gideon into the grave with two ropes. Then the Horner brothers freed the ropes and moved away. Patience, carrying her Bible, stepped to the head of the grave.

"Nothing I can say can add to the life of my beloved father, Gideon Stockbridge, who died as he lived, quietly and without complaint. So, I will content myself with readings my father cherished and were the beacons that lit his way. The first is from Isaiah, Chapter Six, Verse Eight. 'Also, I heard the voice of the Lord, saying, whom shall I send, and who will go for us? Then said I, here *am* I; send me.' The second is John, Chapter Fifteen, Verse Twelve. 'This is my commandment. That ye love one another as I have loved you.' "

She paused for a moment, looking down into the grave. "I have lived all my conscious life knowing that the Lord giveth, but only now do I know what it means when He taketh away."

She turned abruptly from the grave and hurried off toward the train.

Jubal Smith pulled his hat back on and reached for a shovel. "I guess it's up to us."

The other three men broke loose from the silence that still enveloped the gathered people, who remained either staring at the grave or watching Patience walk toward her wagon. Jubal's words appeared to set them free, and one by one or in small groups they slowly made their way down the hill and back to the train. From time to time, one of the people turned and took a few steps backward to stare at the small, wooden cross already sinking into the grass.

When the train had lurched noisily into motion without a wheel breaking or an ox getting a leg over the chain, Jonathan rode up to Patience's wagon and dismounted to walk alongside her. He had rehearsed what he would say but was still unsure of himself, despite his determination to offer her his help.

"Patience," he began, "I found your words very moving."

"Thank you, Jonathan." She sat very straight on the driver's seat, pale and looking as if she might collapse at any minute. "Even knowing it had to be done, leaving Father alone in this wasteland is the hardest thing I have ever had to do."

"Will you let me get Burchard Harley to drive for you while you lie down and rest?"

"No," she said firmly. "I have had a lot of time to prepare for this moment and what is to follow. I have prayed and listened and with God's guidance found my way forward. I know what I am to do."

She turned to Jonathan and managed a

smile. "Please don't worry about me. I am shaken, but that will pass. I will go forward and do the work that Father and I would have done together had God not called him. I thank you for your concern, but now I think I must spend some time with my own mind."

"With your permission," he said, feeling a bit guilty for having imposed himself on her, "I'll stop by from time to time and help you as best I can, even if it's nothing more than talking for a few minutes."

"I will look forward to that," she said. Her tone was polite enough, but it was clear to Jonathan she wanted him to leave.

"I misjudged her," he told Eli later in the day. "She's a lot stronger than I thought. In fact, she all but told me to go away. I still don't know how I feel about that. Or even if I should have left her alone at such a time, whether she wanted me to stay or not."

"I suspect you did the right thing, going and coming," Eli said. "From what I've seen of Quakers, it's my conclusion they don't ever feel alone, not the way the rest of us do."

"She said she'd been praying and listening and has seen what she's going to do."

"And didn't make any fuss about it."

"No, nor express any doubt."

■ ■ ■ ■

After an early start and a few hours of journeying, the train slowly began to climb. The changing landscape was reflected in the stands of low spruce, juniper, piñon pine, and sagebrush. Ever since their run-in with the renegades, Eli had kept the train going forward with a minimum of two wagons abreast. That morning, the wagon master had organized them to advance three wagons abreast, because they were travelling over slightly rolling land, and the trail accommodated the arrangement. He did not tell the travelers they were going deeper into Kiowa and Comanche country.

"I think we've got mostly clear going for the rest of the day," he had told Jonathan over breakfast.

"Those mountains are beginning to look a mite closer," Jane put in, sitting cross-legged on the ground with her tin dish in her lap.

She seldom missed eating breakfast with them. The three were not aware of it, but there was a lively debate among the rest of the people in the train, excluding Patience Stockbridge and Jane's family, over which of the two men she was going to marry. Those leaning toward Jonathan were fewer in number because those favoring him were nearly matched by those, mostly women, who were sure he was going to marry Patience.

"They got a name?" she asked, getting to her feet.

"The Spanish Peaks," Eli said.

"We've been watching them for weeks," Jonathan added, "and they seemed to be retreating as we advanced."

"We've still got a piece to go before we reach them," Eli said, standing, and added, "Today, Jonathan, you and Yellow Leaf get an extra-long lead on us. And make good use of that glass of yours. Morgan said he saw half a dozen braves travelling east. He said they weren't wearing paint, but they did take a long look at him and the horses before going on."

"Try to keep your eyes off Yellow Leaf long enough to see what else is 'round you," Jane said in a voice that made Eli laugh.

Her jokes about him and Yellow Leaf made Jonathan uncomfortable. He couldn't laugh at her jibes, and always denied he spent any time at all looking at Yellow Leaf. That response, of course, only made Eli laugh louder and Jane look away.

Six hours later, Jonathan and Yellow Leaf were two miles ahead of the train and seated on a low ridge in knee-high grass, eating and giving their horses a chance to graze. Yellow Leaf had provided their lunch of flat bread and pemmican. The first time she gave him a stick of the latter, he had viewed it with considerable doubt, but after a bite or two he was soon singing its praises, so much so that Jane had told him to shut up about it or she would pound *him* into pemmican.

The mid-day sun was warm and made sitting in the grass very pleasant. During the morning, they had seen nothing to alarm them, and at the moment, a little west of them, a pair of coyotes passed close enough to reveal the markings on their tawny coats. In front of them a badger was scrabbling along, ignoring both the people and the coyotes. To the east, a small herd of antelope were dividing their time between watching Jonathan and Yellow Leaf lunching, and grazing while swishing their tails. Almost as close, a bull buffalo and three females were absorbed in feeding while their calves bobbed and bounced around them.

"Those mountains are looking bigger," Jonathan said. He had found that Yellow Leaf could go without talking for long periods of time, so if he wanted a conversation, he had to start it.

"Bigger ones beyond it," she said.

"They have a name?"

"Sangre de Cristo," she replied, wiping her hands on the grass, having finished eating.

"Blood of Christ," he said. "I have heard of them."

"Leaving or returning sun makes red color on tops of mountains. I have seen it in other places where the sun goes before night comes."

They were in Colorado, having crossed into the territory the day before. Mentioning that fact had prompted her to tell him white people and Mexicans were crazy, giving names like Kansas or Colorado to pieces of land.

"What's wrong with doing that?" he asked, curious to hear her answer.

"Is child play. Not real. This not Colorado. That river is not Arkansas. It is *river.*"

"But if you give it a name, we will know which river you are talking about," he said, enjoying himself.

She gave him a pitying look and laid a hand on his arm, the first time she had touched him. "If you live here, you know which river it is. Perhaps horses are tamed in a special place in it. Perhaps one place is where you can cross in spring. But it is just a river. Is not *Arkansas.* Rivers know they are rivers. Not need name."

Jonathan saw he had taken this as far as he should. "White people have a story about names. Want to hear it?"

"Yes, this person likes stories," she said. Her smile lit up her face and for a moment wiped away the deep sadness that all too often lined it.

"In the beginning, there were only animals," he said, "and God looked at the world and said, 'I will make a man,' and He made one and called him Adam. Then He saw that Adam would be lonely and made a woman, calling her Eve. Then He thought it would be a good idea to give Adam something to do.

" 'Adam,' he said, 'you see all these things around you and all the animals and birds?'

"Adam said he did.

" 'Then you give them all names.' God went back to Heaven, and we have been giving things names ever since."

"This is true?" Yellow Leaf asked.

"I don't know, but it is true we give things names."

"Yes. I am glad to hear that story. Jonathan Wainwright looked happy telling it. What has made it hard for you to be happy?"

"That, Yellow Leaf, is a long story."

She studied him for a long moment. "One

day, perhaps, I will hear it."

It was not that day, nor the day after. Now, Jonathan lifted his spyglass to his eye and scanned the land to the southwest of them. He thought he saw dust in one place but was unsure and passed the telescope to Yellow Leaf. "Point that over those coyotes and tell me what you see."

She did so. "Something moving this way," she said. "Dust too thin for wagons."

"Or a herd of mustangs running from wolves?"

"Too small. We should ride that way and see."

"You think it's Indians, don't you?"

She gave him one of her dagger glances. "Better to go look than ask smartass questions."

They mounted up and rode off together, with Jonathan explaining to her why it was not a smartass question and she keeping her face turned away from him, apparently struggling not to laugh.

Twenty minutes later, he said, "Stop" and passed her the telescope. "Do you see what I see?"

She raised it to her eye. "Eight of them, all Comanche. Five with guns. Bad medicine."

"Could they be hunting?"

She shook her head as she passed the telescope back to him. "No horses to carry meat. Wear paint. War party."

"Very small," he said.

Another shake of her head. "Somewhere back of them. More."

She was sitting very straight on her horse, fist on one hip, staring at Jonathan. With the gusting wind lifting the heavy black braids off her breasts, and the intense colors of her long-sleeved red blouse and black split skirt and closely fitted doeskin leggings, Jonathan thought she was the epitome of a strong and beautiful woman. Briefly, the image of Jane rose in his mind, and he thought, *Snow White and Rose Red.*

Her black eyes bored into him. "You want sit here and lose your hair?"

"What say we go back to the train and tell them the good news?" Jonathan tucked the telescope away and turned Sam.

"Not gallop," she told him sternly, moving her paint ahead of him. "Not make dust."

Despite the fact they had a Comanche war party on their heels, Jonathan felt almost light-hearted. He did not ask himself what part his "Snow White and Rose Red" or, perhaps, Yellow Leaf's company played in his high spirits, but, without any reflection at all he suddenly said with a grin, "Mother says, 'Not make dust.' "

"Idiot." She kicked her pony into a trot, calling back over her shoulder, "Someone should not leave lodge without grown up to look after him."

Her riposte delighted him. Slackening his reins, he sent Sam flying past her and shouted, "Dust be damned!" Yellow Leaf came hammering after him, swearing a blue streak. Luckily for him, Jonathan had no idea what she was saying.

Upon reaching the train, Jonathan told Eli what they'd seen. "The Comanches were coming up the trail and couldn't miss the train," he said.

Eli nodded. "Get some of our riflemen out there to protect the herds."

"Yellow Leaf has Rune and Jake Rawlings helping Morgan, and Burchard and Duncan are on their way to help Jane. I've got eight more men coming."

"We'll assume an attack before the day's out. I'll square the train," Eli said as Jonathan's men rode up, heavily armed.

As Eli predicted, it didn't take long before the war party arrived. The Comanches began riding in wide circles around the remuda, shouting and waving guns and bows over their heads at Burchard and Duncan and Jane, obviously preparing to peel off from their circle and attack.

"The rest of them must be after Morgan and Yellow Leaf," Jonathan said, pulling up to weigh the odds. "Let's rid ourselves of these four and go on to Morgan. Just don't shoot one another."

That brought laughter from the men as they spread out and rode toward the Indians. One of the Comanches, a big man with a livid scar on his face, ran straight at them, yelling as he came, guiding his pony with his legs as he raised his rifle to his shoulder. Jonathan and his men reined in. The Indian fired twice and was turning his pony, too late. He had come within range of Jonathan and the riders. Their barrage of fire threw the warrior off his pony. When the other three Indians pulled up to watch their companion's display, Jane and Duncan and Burchard took advantage of the pause, rode up on them, and opened fire, killing another outright. Duncan, who said later he wasn't a very good shot, downed one of the horses from under a third Comanche, forcing the two survivors to race away.

"You better go on and help Yellow Leaf and Morgan," Jane told Jonathan, somewhat breathless. "I don't think Morgan's much of a hand with a rifle. That Rune and Jake Rawlings ain't much better. By the way," she added, her eyes flashing and her face flaming, "you don't need to get yourself shot, either. I saw your bunch watching that crazy Indian shooting at you."

"I'm glad someone's watching me," he said.

Her face got redder. "Go on. Get out of here. Go save your Osage maiden."

She paled abruptly and swung her mare away from him as if fleeing her own words. Jonathan watched her go, certain that what he had intended as a joke had become something else, but this was no time to think about that something.

He heard the shooting just as they reached the cattle. The animals were grazing quietly, unmoved by the sound of gunfire or the riders racing past them. Bursting over a low hill, they found four more of the Comanches and Morgan, Yellow Leaf, and the Rawlings brothers exchanging fire across the bunched horses, who were surging back and forth between the shooters.

Jonathan pulled to a stop on the hillock. "Four with me. The rest take the other side. And for God's sake, don't forget to stop firing if some of ours get between us."

Off they went, but, long before they could begin firing at the four warriors, the Comanches had raced away to the west, not even shouting threats as they fled.

"Someone decided not to kill any Comanches today," Jonathan said, finding himself beside Yellow Leaf as the three groups of riders came together.

"Very young," she said. "Someone could have been their mother."

"I'll take four men and head the cattle toward the train," Morgan shouted, riding past them.

"We bring in horses," Yellow Leaf called after him.

"If you had been their mother," Jonathan asked, "would they be out here with a raiding party?"

She gave him a slit-eyed glance that he had learned presaged trouble. "Where is the Comanche woman who could have stopped it?"

"Not yet born?" he asked.

She ignored his response, and he regretted the question, guessing too late that his first one had wakened some deeply buried concern.

"My people will now fade away," she said after a moment, meeting his gaze. "The warriors will fall into the earth. The buffalo will go, and the lodges will be without children. Our way is ending."

Jonathan tried hard to find a way to say it

would not happen, but he knew it would. Even the Comanches, fierce as they were, would be corralled, broken.

"Yellow Leaf," he said quietly, "I am sorry. It is true there are many, many more of us coming. We will fill this land with farms and roads and towns. But I hope you and Morgan can live together and be happy. Perhaps many of your people will learn to live as we live and still preserve your traditions."

She did not speak at once when he finished. When she finally did, Jonathan was shaken by the sadness in her voice.

"Jonathan Wainwright, I have heard you. Morgan and I may make a life together. A few Indian people may come to live as you do. Or not. But our way of life is our tradition. I think many more will die. The drumming and the dancing will end. The buffalo will die. The singing will stop, and our day will sink like the sun into darkness. These are the things I have seen."

"You have seen terrible things, Yellow Leaf. I am sorry."

"Perhaps I should have shot those boys and sent them to what follows, where there will be no pain. But I could not."

He wanted to take her pain away and had only inadequate words with which to do it. "I think you should have done just what your heart told you to do. It was the right thing."

"Jonathan! Come along!" one of his men shouted.

The interruption came as a relief, and not only to Jonathan. "How long will it take you to get the horses back to the train?" he asked her.

"The big hand on your watch will go half around. Longer for the cattle," she said.

"After starting the horses, send one of the men to tell Morgan if he has not reached us in half an hour, he must leave them and come to the train. If you are not at the train by then, you and the men must come in. Do you understand, Yellow Leaf?"

"I understand. I will run horses in. May need help stopping them," she said as Sam and her pony began to pull apart.

"We will have riders waiting. Be careful. If you see more Comanches, or their dust, leave the horses."

She grinned suddenly. "Village worrier," she called, putting her heels into her paint's side and leaping away.

"Remember, leave the horses!" he shouted after her.

CHAPTER 18

Jane and Yellow Leaf reached the train together, both remudas thundering in and circling the squared wagons twice before finally being slowed to a walk. Half an hour later, Morgan arrived, he and his men having managed to prod the cattle into a trot, the cows bellowing to be milked.

The horses were corralled inside the square, but the cattle, which could not be run off so easily, were left outside to graze. Half a dozen women, with five armed mounted men watching over them, ran out with pails to milk the cows, pushing their way through the beef cattle as casually as if they were walking in their gardens.

"If they're coming, they're running late," Eli said to Jonathan. The two men were sitting on their horses outside the square, staring south, the prairie glowing like gold in the last rays of the sun.

Yellow Leaf and Jane joined the two men

in time to hear what Eli had said. "Yellow Leaf says they ain't coming," Jane put in.

"How do you know that?" Eli demanded, turning to face her.

"Come just before sun rises," Yellow Leaf said, being more than usually laconic.

Jane showed some impatience. "She might say why, was you to ask her."

"Yellow Leaf," Jonathan said, "could you tell us what makes you think that?"

"Eat now. Have rest. Listen to chiefs. Good medicine to go into battle with sun at their backs."

"Then they will attack from over there." Eli pointed to the darkened east. "Probably out of them hillocks."

"We're going to lose some cattle," Morgan said.

"Would they take the time to herd them unless we were wiped out?" Eli asked.

"Put arrers into them," Morgan replied. It took Jonathan a second to realize he meant *arrows.* He wondered briefly what a conversation between Morgan and Yellow Leaf sounded like. He would have liked to let his imagination work on that question a little longer, but Jane disrupted his thinking.

"Why would they want to kill those bullocks and cows?" Jane demanded, looking as if she was already angry just from hearing

249

of such a thing.

"Bullocks pull wagons. Cows feed you," Yellow Leaf said.

"Out of meanness," Morgan added. "Skin you alive if they catch you."

"Is that true?" Jane asked Yellow Leaf, who only shrugged in response.

"I have told everyone to save one bullet for themselves," Eli said, quickly adding, "but it's not going to come to such a pass. We're ready for them."

That broke up the conference, and Eli had spoken the truth. Having fought off the renegades, they all had some knowledge of what to expect. The ammunition was distributed. Patience had organized her field hospital and its crew. Jane's ammunition crew had completed their work two hours earlier. Jonathan's riflemen were ready to take their positions, and they had more carefully constructed their barricades to fight behind.

Once the women were in from milking the cows and the cooking fires were lighted, Jonathan told his men to eat in shifts, to guarantee a third of them were always on watch. Then the question of the night watch was settled. After talking with Yellow Leaf and Morgan, Jubal Smith, the Texan who had fought the Comanches in the Panhandle, and Eli, having listened to Yellow Leaf, decided not to post any men outside the square.

"They creep in the grass with a knife and make no sound," she had warned. "They will kill men outside in the dark. Keep men inside and have horses tied close, to smell them if they come."

"Her paint shies whenever I come near her," Jonathan had said. Ordinarily such a remark opened the way for someone to suggest he be freer with the soap and water, but it was not a time for joking. No one laughed, and there wasn't much of the usual talk around the cooking fires. Even the children, sensing the tension in their parents, ate in silence and went to bed without complaining.

Once the half-moon's light had replaced the sunset's afterglow, Jonathan rode slowly inside the square of wagons, checking on all the men on watch, then returned to speak with Patience.

"I find waiting like this very hard," she told him. She was sitting on a low stool, staring into the last coals of her fire, with a dark shawl pulled around her shoulders. "I don't know how people sleep, but Jane's mother and the children have been asleep this last hour."

"I'm surprised people sleep at all," he said. "I watch the sky a lot most nights."

He'd tried to make light of it, but Patience was too sharp to think he was joking.

"Do you relive the war?" she asked.

"Now and then, but often sleep just eludes me."

He had no intention of telling her the truth about the horrors that danced in his head when he closed his eyes. Men with half their skulls blown away, fields of grass and earth soaked with dead soldiers' blood. He could hardly bring himself to admit that, of late, these nightmare visions had begun to decline in number and intensity — "for fear," as Eli would say, "they had only let up for a better hold."

Quoting Eli to himself, and other things like listening to Yellow Leaf talk about the world around them and how to see it, were indulgences he had never allowed himself until now, and it surprised him how much pleasure he found in them. He acknowledged the change in himself, but he could not believe these simple things capable of altering who he'd become since the war, or the threat he still was to the world.

"Jonathan?"

"I'm sorry, Patience. What did you say?"

"You were saying sleep often eludes you."

"Ah, I'm sorry. Some people have more active imaginations than others. Do you feel prepared for tomorrow?"

"As much as possible. As long as the walls hold, I think we'll be all right. If not . . ."

"They will hold. Try to sleep. Tomorrow will come without your waiting up for it."

"Will you keep watch all night?"

"No, I'll turn in soon."

He did not get off Sam's back until past midnight. To be sure, he had three men on the last watch tasked to call him an hour before sunrise. He was up two hours before first light. For him, to rise well before a battle was routine, as was encouraging the men by being present and reviewing with the officers their plans and, if possible, to eat and make certain the men were fed.

It was a cold morning. As Jane made breakfast over their small fire, she and Jonathan and Eli huddled around it. At similar small fires dotting the inside of the square, other women warmed and served the gruel that had been cooked along with dinner the night before. They ate mostly in silence, Jane for once as quiet as the others.

When they had finished eating, Jonathan kicked the fire apart and stamped the coals into the damp ground. "We should take heart from knowing we are as prepared as it is possible to be."

"My people are ready," Jane said, setting the pan and tin dishes aside. "I'd best get to them."

"Let's try to come through this." Eli adjusted his hat.

"All right." Jane glanced at Eli and then Jonathan. "You two take care, and, Jonathan, don't you do nothing brave and foolish. You tell him, Eli."

"Don't do nothing brave and foolish, Jonathan," Eli said with a crooked grin, "but the main thing is, coming here to begin with was his greatest mistake, and it's too late to do anything about that." With that, he got on his horse and rode off.

Jonathan mounted Sam, and noted the thin line of light above the eastern horizon with a tightening in his stomach. "You're working with Yellow Leaf, right?"

She frowned at him. "You know I am."

"Watch her. I'm not sure she will shoot any Indian threatening her. She wouldn't fire on the young men who were crowding her and Morgan."

"I was counting on her to have my back," Jane said, sounding alarmed.

"Don't count on it, and don't put yourself in a place you can't get out of without her. If she starts shooting, make sure she's hitting something helpful before you count her in."

"All right." She stiffened her spine, bracing herself. "I want you on your feet when this is over, you hear?"

"I hear you, Jane, and if any of them get inside the square, shoot from a standing position if you can. You'll double your effectiveness."

Jonathan rode Sam around the square, calling out to all the men as he went, and finally took up his position with Eli where he could look out between a pair of the big wagons on the east side of the square. Located on both sides of him within easy shouting distance were men to whom he could give commands, and receive information to and from the four sides of the square by compass location, letting him shift men from one position to another without having to send a messenger.

"The sun will break the horizon any minute now," Eli said.

No sooner had he spoken than a shower of flaming arrows arced into the sky and came down, some still burning as they landed among the horses.

"Morgan and the Harley brothers are with them," Jonathan said calmly. "Clever — might have started a stampede in here."

"Cruel bastards," Eli said.

The sun came up, and a moment later a howl like all the banshees in creation crying out at once splintered the air.

"Hold!" Jonathan shouted.

There was nothing for the moment but the yelling to fire at, but within two minutes silhouettes of the attackers rose over the hillocks and came pouring down toward the train.

"Hold!" Jonathan called a second time. It was still too dim to see the yelling men racing towards them. Then, as though bursting out of the earth within fifty yards of them, the attackers were visible.

"Fire!" Jonathan shouted. "West to east."

The steady, withering gunfire pouring out from the wagons broke the advancing lines. The attackers' shouting stopped. In its place came a second rain of arrows, aimed at and under the wagons. Half the fighters from the west section threw themselves beneath the east's wagons and opened fire, driving the men in front of them back.

"What are those devils up to now?" Eli asked, clambering to his feet and pulling back beside Jonathan.

"Hold," Jonathan shouted.

A stunned silence fell over the square. The sun, gaining some altitude, also gained an angle favoring the men under the wagons. Jonathan did not get to answer Eli because, at that moment, thirty or forty riders came over the hillocks. They split and began to race around the train, pouring arrows into the wagons and into the open center.

"Shields!" Jonathan shouted. As the command was passed along, those in the center of the squared wagons grasped their homemade shields and squatted with them over their heads.

"Clear," Jonathan called as new riders, many armed with rifles and muskets, replaced the bowmen, who darted toward the wagons and then suddenly spurted away.

"They're beginning to hit north and south," the two watchers closest to Jonathan shouted.

"Are north and south holding?" Jonathan called back.

"South has men on it. Firing is coming from a hilltop."

"Eli, get down there," Jonathan said. "See what you can do. I'll get you some support." As Eli dashed off, Jonathan shouted over his shoulder, "Men with Sharps, come here."

Jubal Smith and two ox drivers, who had been buffalo hunters, came on the run.

"Get to the south line," Jonathan said.

"They've got snipers on a hill. Eli's headed there. See what you can do, stay low, and shift positions often. Go!"

"Doc," Duncan Harley called, coming at a run from the north end of the east line, "we think they're bunching for an attack over there. They've all pulled together, and most of them's got guns."

"Get back there and say help is coming."

Duncan turned and ran off. Jonathan said, "Call in Jane."

She was there on her mare in a minute, and Yellow Leaf was with her.

"Go around and, without shouting, take five men from each of the south, west, and north sides and get them to the north end of the east line. Something's building there, but you two stay away from it. Up on those horses, you wouldn't last five minutes."

"Have been told of this, maybe," Yellow Leaf said. "They will ride down on this place and come inside. At same time, others will attack other sides."

"Thanks, Yellow Leaf. Go! Go!" As they left, he shouted out fresh orders: "Ammunition to all sides. Stay sharp."

The sun was climbing. The wind had picked up and was flapping the canvas covers on the wagons. Jonathan stood in his stirrups, looking around the square. The ammunition carriers were moving as fast as the weight of the shells allowed. Patience and her women were working on three men with arrow wounds, while armed defenders were running toward the northeast corner, responding to Yellow Leaf and Jane's call.

A high, piercing yell from behind the hillocks split the air.

"They are coming, all sides!" Jonathan shouted, just as twenty mounted warriors burst over the hillocks and drove down on the northeast corner of the square.

"Horses first!" Jonathan stood in the saddle to get a better view of the attack. "Fire!"

Rifles spat. All the attackers' horses in the first rank pitched forward, hurling their riders to the ground and breaking the momentum of the riders following. The strengthened line of defenders kept firing steadily, reducing the riders to six and decimating those who had leaped from their horses to continue their charge on foot.

Two riders survived the hail of bullets and jumped their horses into the square, shooting a woman carrying ammunition and the man with her. As they turned their attention to Patience and her helpers, Jane and Yellow Leaf shot both warriors from different sides of the square. The attackers' riderless horses panicked and bolted, their hackamores flying. One knocked a man down who had run out to grab it, and the other plunged through a corner of Patience's hospital, flattening a woman. Yellow Leaf pulled her pony to a stop, leaped onto its back, and shot both horses through the neck. They crashed to the ground, stone dead.

Jonathan dropped back into his saddle and rode to the corner. Behind him, a constant crackle of gunfire sounded from the remaining three sides. Satisfied the northeast corner was holding, Jonathan rode around the square to see if any of the sides needed more help. He had hardly started when the shooting suddenly fell off. The surviving Indians, taking with them the wounded who could pull themselves onto a rider's horse, galloped back over the hillocks, yipping and shouting as they retreated.

Slowly, the men of the train backed out from under the wagons and got to their feet. Only Patience's women went on with what they were doing. Swift conference with the men and with Patience told Jonathan what their casualties were.

"We've lost five men and two women," he told Eli when the wagon master walked up to the field hospital.

"Three are seriously wounded and may not live," Patience put in. "Ten are less seriously wounded, and one of the men knocked down by those Indian ponies Yellow Leaf shot has a broken arm. Jane and I set it."

"And we haven't counted the Indians wounded or dead," Jane said.

"Perhaps you will decide to kill those not dead," Yellow Leaf said. "If not, leave them. In morning will be gone. Dead will be there."

"Will we be leaving today, Eli?" Jane asked.

He glanced at his shadow. "It's about midday," he said. "We have some dead of our own to bury, and we can't leave them dead Indians for the critters to feed on."

Yellow Leaf said, "Perhaps someone will tell their spirits it is time to go. Then bury what is left behind."

There was a quick outbreak of muttering, and a woman shouted, "Shut that heathen's mouth."

Patience turned to face the woman. Gently, but loud enough for all to hear, she said, "Let us grieve our losses and say our prayers together. This is not a time for anger. This woman you call a heathen shot those Indian ponies running wild inside the square and kept injuries to a single broken arm. She is

261

asking to be allowed to perform a religious ceremony honored among her people. We should remember that 'God works in mysterious ways his wonders to perform.' "

She turned to Eli. "I ask the wagon master to thank Yellow Leaf for her service to us today, and to ask her to go among the dead Comanches and release them for their journey to the next world."

"I second that request," Jonathan said. "Yellow Leaf has been our eyes for many weeks now, and working with her has been an education."

The listeners stirred, but, before anyone spoke, Eli came to stand beside Patience. "Yellow Leaf deserves all our thanks. I hope she knows she has it. Yellow Leaf," he added, turning to her, "will you go among the dead Comanches and say what needs to be said so that we may bury them?"

She bowed her head slightly. "I am not a one who has been touched by the Great Spirit, but I will do what needs doing."

"Thank you," Eli said. "Do it now."

Jonathan had been running his eyes over the gathered people, and he saw two men he thought would do what needed to be done. "Burchard Harley, Bill Johnson, would you come up here, please? And Yellow Leaf."

The two men, still wearing holstered pistols and carrying their rifles, came up to Jonathan as the rest of the small crowd scattered back to their wagons, arguing as they went. Yellow Leaf stepped closer to Jonathan.

"You'll all remember after the first raid," Jonathan said to them, "the trouble we had trying to treat the Indians who were wounded? We may have the same trouble here, especially from those able to lift a gun."

"Can Yellow Leaf walk among them safely?" Jane asked, sounding doubtful.

Jonathan glanced at Yellow Leaf. "Can you?"

She shrugged.

"But you want to release the dead to begin their journey."

"Yes," she replied firmly.

They all looked at one another for a few moments. Then Jonathan said, "Eli, I suggest we take down the canvas on the wagon closest to where the fallen are lying and stand up there with our rifles. If one of the injured men tries to harm Yellow Leaf, we will shoot him."

"Y.L.," Jane said loudly, starting to laugh, "just don't step between that wagon and the wounded Injun coming at you."

Yellow Leaf did not laugh. Neither did anyone else except for the Watsons' retarded son. Finding only Toby laughing with her, Jane went white. She dug her heels into her mare's side and rode away. Watching her go, Jonathan wondered what demons had prodded her into saying so thoughtless a thing.

"Not be angry with her, Jonathan Wainwright," Yellow Leaf said quietly. Then, more loudly, "I will carry my Spencer and decide who will die."

"You shouldn't be doing this at all, Yellow Leaf," Morgan burst out. "That bunch would put a knife in you quick as blink."

"What would Morgan do with a gun pointed at him?" she asked calmly.

Morgan turned to the people gathered behind him and threw up his hands. Then he swung back to her. "I might as well talk to a log."

"You want to take log under your blanket?" she asked with a straight face.

The audience exploded with laughter. Even Patience couldn't hold it in.

"You're outclassed here, Morgan," Jonathan said, dropping a hand on the man's shoulder, which was enough to make Morgan laugh along with the rest. Then Jonathan turned back to Yellow Leaf. "Eli and I will be your backup."

Yellow Leaf went among the fallen warriors, pausing beside every dead man to bend over him and speak. Those still alive that she passed showed no hostility. Some were singing their death song, the sound reaching the train only faintly. If any spoke to Yellow Leaf, only she heard them.

Just before dark, six men with Burchard Harley at their head came to Eli and suggested setting up an ambush and killing all the Indians, wounded and not.

"Give us a chance to rid the earth of that scum," Burchard said. "If we don't, they'll just go off and kill somebody else."

Jonathan managed to keep the anger he was feeling out of his voice. "Burchard, you were in the war. Remember how, after battles, both sides were allowed to reach their wounded in safety? I think it's best we do the same here."

"But them was white men we was fighting," Burchard replied, "not these animals."

Eli intervened. "The way I see it, we whupped them good. I don't see us having any more trouble from them. I'm for leaving them be."

The men pulled back and argued a few minutes. Then Burchard broke away and came up to Eli and Jonathan. "Most want

265

to let it lie, and I will go along with them, but I hate to give up the chance to kill more of them murderous bastards."

"Good choice, Burchard," Eli said, shaking the man's hand. "Now you men get yourself a good night's sleep. You've earned it."

They buried the dead the following morning. As Yellow Leaf had predicted, during the night many of those still alive were taken away on travois, tied to the ponies. Several dogs barked when the riders came to retrieve them but were quickly silenced, and many of the men in the wagons sat up with their rifles across their laps until the removal was finished.

Shortly after sunrise, the train got under way again. Except for those who left loved ones in graves that would never be revisited, most of the people were eager to put distance between themselves and the scene of the battle.

"I find this departure has reopened the wound in my heart caused by my father's death," Patience told Jonathan when she led off the train. In the rosy light of the huge, red morning sun, Jonathan saw how drawn her face was. He had intended to reach her in time to harness her mules but got caught up in helping to hoist a wagon wheel out of a badger set that had collapsed under the wheel's weight while they were forming yesterday's square.

"I am very sorry you have had to go through this twice," Jonathan said. "I would like to keep you company for the morning, but Eli is still nervous about our safety and is sending me on ahead, to see if there are any more war parties in our path."

"Well, I guess I'd rather have you and Yellow Leaf out there than have you waste your time sitting with me. I wouldn't make very good company. It's not Father's death that is foremost in my thoughts. It's the loneliness of his grave and the knowledge I will likely never see it again."

It dawned on Jonathan that his being with her was only preventing her from working through her grief. Promising to call on her that evening, he put Sam into a gallop to gain distance from the train.

"She says the hardest part is having to leave her father and know she won't see his grave again," he told Yellow Leaf as they were making their way into foothills, leading toward the mountains heaving up before them.

"My people moved often, following the buffalo, moving north in the spring with them and back again in the fall. Perhaps that we do not speak of the dead or go near the platforms in the trees where dead lie, wrapped in hides, makes that part easier for us."

"You have lost your family," Jonathan said.

"They still with me in memory," she said and paused. "Have you lost your family?"

He hesitated for a moment. Then, with a sudden sense of loss, he said, "Yes."

CHAPTER 19

Save for those who had lost a loved one in the Comanche raid, the approach to the mountains was dramatic enough to replace in the rest of the travelers' minds memories of the fighting with the challenges of the new trail. For one thing, the relatively smooth going on the high prairie track between creeks and occasional hills was replaced by a trail studded with rocks and outcrops of granite. To compensate, the days were cooler and the insects fewer that had tormented people and beasts, especially the bullocks, victimized by huge horseflies that drew blood when they bit.

"Adam musta had goddamned poor eyesight," said Jacob Drew, a Vermont Yankee driver, "to have mixed a ox up with a horse when he named this cussed pest a horsefly."

Lanky, square-jawed and gray-haired, Drew had not spoken a dozen words to anyone but his oxen since the train formed, and his sudden burst of eloquence had gone the length of the train like a gust of wind, creating hilarity as it went. The idea of Adam having poor eyesight made the adults laugh until tears rolled down their faces. The children just looked at one another and shook their heads.

The changes in the trail and the sharpening of the air brought about changes in the mood of the travelers. People talked more with one another, and there was increased snap in their walk.

"Ma was singing this morning," Jane said as she was making breakfast. The day was crisp, with a heavy dew and a fat, yellow sun rising from behind the horizon. "I ain't heard her sing since before Pa died. She even gave me a hug as I was leaving. I hope she ain't coming down with something."

"Maybe she's just feeling happy," Eli said, always inclined toward hopefulness where Jane and her family were concerned.

"What's she got to be happy about?" Jane said sharply. "She's got five kids, one in the hopper, and no husband." Gripping the frying pan in one hand and the red-handled, three-tined fork in the other, Jane looked at Eli as though deciding whether to stab him or bang him with the skillet.

"Let me have some of that fry bread

before you do anything rash," Jonathan said, forgetting who he was talking to.

"Perhaps you don't care about my mother, but I do." Jane brought her glare to bear on Jonathan. "I've a good mind to turn this bread over your head."

Eli, as was his wont, was using the last piece of venison on his plate to wipe up the remaining grease and not giving his full attention to Jane's demeanor. "Jane, you nearing your uncomfortable time?" he asked without looking up.

Jonathan froze. He had leaned forward to pick up his coffee cup from the rock they were using for a breakfast table. Only Eli missed the significance of the ringing silence.

Very carefully, Jane set the fork and the frying pan on the rock, untied her apron, and let it fall to the ground at her feet. Then she turned and walked to where her mare was grazing with Sam and gathered the reins. Once in the saddle, she walked the mare up to the rock and stared down at the two men.

"Eli Parker," she said quietly, "if you ever again make any reference to my *'uncomfortable time'* . . ." She shouted the rest at the top of her voice. "I'll wring your scrawny, goddamned neck!" She jumped her mare over the rock, sending plates and cups flying and landing Eli and Jonathan on their tails.

As he got to his feet and dusted off the seat of his pants, Eli grumbled, "I was looking forward to that flatbread." Jonathan decided not to bring up the subject of Jane and her uncomfortable time, for fear he might wring Eli's neck himself.

Later that day, riding with Yellow Leaf, Jonathan found Jane's outburst was still with him, not dislodged by their approach to the mountains. Increasing numbers of mule deer and buffalo dotted the landscape, in small herds that were scattered within sight in all directions. Since midmorning, dusky grouse had been exploding from the stands of low spruce and piñon pine as he and Yellow Leaf passed, and the day was brightened by the chickadees and gray jays, nutcrackers, and pine grosbeaks flitting among the scrub brush, chirping, singing, or, in the case of the jays, squawking at intervals, pretending a calamity was occurring.

"Need pepper gun to have grouse for supper," Yellow Leaf said, following a long silence. "When young, we caught them in grass nets. Takes long time. We gather nuts and seeds and spread them under net. Then wait for them to come to eat. Then drop net on them. Good eating."

"I have a shotgun," Jonathan said. "Tomorrow, I'll bring it along."

"You quiet today," she said. "Not used to you not talking. You trying to become Indian?"

"You good at keeping secrets?"

"What trouble you?"

"Jane. I'm worried about her."

"You also worry about Patience Stockbridge."

"If you don't want to talk about Jane, just say so."

"Someone is quick to anger and kill somebody. Maybe me."

Jonathan felt the heat rising in his face. "This morning," he said, "as we were eating breakfast, Jane got angry with Eli and me. She jumped her horse over us, knocking breakfast seven ways to Sunday. One of the mare's hooves missed Eli's head by a hand's breadth."

"Is your fault?" Yellow Leaf asked.

Jonathan told her what had been said and what had happened before Jane jumped her horse over them and sent the pan and the fry bread flying.

"What Eli say?"

"That he had been looking forward to eating the fry bread."

"Lucky to escape with scalps still on heads."

Jonathan laughed, but it was uneasy laughter. Yellow Leaf did not join him. Instead, she sat on her pony with a leg crossed in front of her, an elbow resting on her thigh, studying him.

"What?" he asked.

"You think she marry Eli Parker?"

"I hope so. He's a good man."

"Good for what?"

Jonathan found he didn't like how talking about Jane marrying Eli made him feel.

"You marry Patience Stockbridge?"

"No."

"Why not?"

"She wouldn't have me, and I'm not in love with her."

"You love Jane?"

"Where did you get such a crazy idea?" he demanded, his face burning.

She finally laughed. "Maybe dusty grouse tell me."

At that moment, a young mule deer raced around a hillock into their path, followed by three gray timber wolves. Before Jonathan could respond, Yellow Leaf had pulled her rifle out of its scabbard and shot the deer and two of the wolves in quick succession.

The third wolf skidded into a sudden turn, sending up a shower of gravel, and belted back around the hillock.

"Dinner and wolf skins," Yellow Leaf said, when the third wolf was out of sight, jacking a fresh shell into the gun's chamber with no trace of excitement. "Better to shoot them in winter, fur thicker. You want fur collar for winter coat? Not frost. Warm."

"Yes. Thank you. How in God's earth did you react to the deer and the wolves so quickly?"

Yellow Leaf laughed, not something she often did, and slid her rifle back into its case. "Need two things to live," she said, "food, clothes. Once you learn that, not need to think. You stop to think. Perhaps someone not do that."

"Are we going to dress out these animals?" Jonathan asked, feeling she had let him down easy but let him down all the same.

By the time Jonathan bled the deer and gutted it, Yellow Leaf had the wolf carcasses out of their skins. From time to time, he paused in his labors to watch her, sitting on her heels, the eight-inch blade of her bone-handled knife flashing in the sun as she worked with what to him was astonishing speed and certainty, as though her knife moved of its own volition.

"Someone should be working and not looking," she told him, shaking him out of his reverie.

"You're right, but it's a pleasure watching you skin that wolf."

"You are strange person." She sat back on her heels for a moment to look at him. "Sometimes you are child with mother."

"My mother never skinned a wolf," he replied.

"Not make me feel too much needed," she said, going back to work. "Someone might roll up her buffalo robe and come to live with you."

"I sleep outside."

"Parlez-vous Français?" she asked, looking surprised.

"Like a Spanish cow," he said.

"Not know Spanish cow. You will tell me of your mother's tribe."

She stopped what she was doing. Jonathan stopped with her, knowing she would not move until he complied.

"In the white world, people who have about the same amount of money live within walking distance of one another and have parents who also lived in the same part of the city. Also, they all speak the same way. Beginning as children, they seldom speak to anyone not in the tribe."

"This I have not heard," Yellow Leaf said, sounding astonished. She paused then said, "Then you are of this tribe?"

"I am."

"Is why when you talk, you do not sound like anyone except Jacob Drew and not quite like him?"

"You have a good ear. We both come from the part of the country called New England."

"I am liking how you sound. Easy to understand. Some talk as though have thumb in their mouth. All your tribe sound like you?"

"Yes."

"I will try talk like you. Maybe become one of your tribe someday."

Jonathan, thinking she was joking, started to laugh, caught himself in time, and said, "My people would be honored."

Their tasks finished, they loaded the deer meat and wolf skins on their horses and mounted up again. Their conversation soon turned to the country through which they were riding and the multitude of opportunities it provided to bushwhack those coming along the trail. Fortunately, this day had proved very peaceful, and, when the sun was about a yard from the mountains, they turned their horses. They were trotting back toward the train when they met Jane riding hard along their trail.

"There's trouble!" she shouted, pulling her mare to a stop so hard that she nearly set her on her tail. "There's bad trouble," she repeated, a little more softly.

"Someone should tell us what it is." Yellow Leaf said it sharply enough to make Jonathan wince, in preparation for Jane's hair-trigger temper kicking in.

To his surprise, Jane seemed not to notice. "If something ain't done, there's going to be a shooting. The Harley brothers are sayin' Rune and Jake Rawlings stole a rifle from their wagon. The train's stopped, and the Rawlingses have given them an hour to back down from what they've said, or they'll come at 'em with their guns. Jonathan, Eli wants you in there *now.*"

"All right, but you've got to stay with Yellow Leaf," he said.

"Go!" Jane jumped down to tighten the mare's belly strap. "Those four are fighting mad. And don't you do some damned fool thing and get yourself shot."

"This is time to think," Yellow Leaf said quietly, holding his gaze.

Jane scowled at her. "What's that got to do with anything?"

"I shot deer without thinking, also wolves.

278

Someone will think before he shoots."

"I'll think hard," Jonathan told her, turning away and lifting Sam into a gallop.

Jonathan found Eli backed against his wagon with thirty or more men and women all talking at once, many shaking their fists at him. The other wagons were halted every which way, with women rushing around, rounding up their children and herding them into the wagons only to have many immediately pour out the back ends, yelling and leaping with excitement.

He eased Sam through the mob until he reached Eli and sat for a while, looking at the crowd until the racket they had been making gradually faded away. "Why's everyone all riled up, Eli?" he asked, leaning an elbow on his pommel.

Eli aimed for calm in his reply but didn't quite make it. "It would appear four idiots plan to shoot one another," he said.

Seeing Burchard Harley in the crowd, Jonathan called out, "Burchard, what are you troubling Eli about?"

Before Burchard could answer, a tall, hard-faced woman named Dina Watkins said loudly, "Dr. Wainwright, the answer to your question is that four idiot *men* are planning to shoot one another where stray bullets are likely to do more damage to us than the Indians did. I've got ten children, but I don't have any extras. Instead of standing around here jawing, some of you men should go to them and shake them 'til their teeth rattle, and they agree to put an end to this foolishness."

That brought whoops, cheers, and laughter from two-thirds of those listening. Jonathan laughed as well, and even Eli, harassed as he was, managed to grin.

"Mrs. Watkins," Jonathan said, "what if I go and talk with them first and see what comes out of that?"

She looked skeptical. "It's my experience that talking is all right, but a rap on the side of the head gets quicker results."

That produced another round of laughter, but the anger had drained out of the group, and another woman said, "You go talk to them, Doctor. It's likely they'll see their mistake."

Half a dozen more said, "Talk to them, Doc."

Jubal Smith added in his drawl, "And if'n they don't see the light, remind them dying is permanent, and two or three of us have rifles and are fairly good shots."

Jonathan thought for a moment. "Jubal, bring out our men. Tell them to come armed. Bill Johnson, go with him. Do this fast. I'll slow the four idiots down as much as I can." He turned to Eli. "Where are they?"

Eli took out his pocket watch. "They're in their wagons. They'll be coming out in about fifteen minutes."

Jonathan turned to the crowd again. "Go to your wagons. Keep the children with you. I think we can do this without anybody getting hurt."

The crowd broke up. The train's militia came streaming toward Eli's wagon, and, when they had gathered, Jonathan said, "We're going to stop this fight by scaring the bejesus out of them."

"What started it?" one of the men asked.

"A woman, of course," someone said, creating a ripple of laughter.

"Actually," Eli put in, "it was four men and a woman. Duncan Harley and Jake Rawlings were courting Ginger Stearns. For some time, Miss Stearns managed to keep each man thinking he was the only one in the running."

"How come the brothers mixed in?" Bill Johnson asked.

By this time the men had crowded around, giving Eli their full attention. A few were taking sides as to who was in the wrong,

Ginger or the two men. Arguing broke out. "Hold on," Jonathan said in his colonel voice, bringing the bickering to a halt. "Eli, can you get through what remains to be said quickly?"

"There ain't much more to tell," Eli said. "Miss Stearns blundered, and the two of them turned up at the same time, expecting to take her for a walk. They accused each other of butting in. Jake pushed Duncan, and Duncan punched Jake, knocking him down. Jake, being considerably smaller than Duncan, ran for his brother Rune. Duncan figured what was coming and fetched Burchard, who said he'd give the opposition an hour to either apologize or come wearing guns."

"Here's what we're going to do," Jonathan said. "One, we're going to form a half circle around that foursome, and I'm going to tell them we'll riddle with bullet holes the first one of them that reaches for his gun. Two, I'll tell them none of them moves until they shake hands and swear to settle things peacefully."

"Them two youngsters running the Stearns girl ain't much more than kids," one of the men said. "I don't fancy shooting either of 'em."

"Neither does the colonel," Eli said.

"Nobody's going to shoot anybody. My guess is that, by now, all four of them are scared half to death."

"Let's do it," Jonathan said.

The four young men soon climbed out of their wagons, followed by their families. Both fathers were carrying rifles. They came together at the designated meeting spot and stood looking at the half circle of armed men watching them. Jonathan, still mounted, rode Sam forward and told the four men and their supporters, loud enough to be sure everyone could hear him, what was going to happen.

The silence following his warning had grown uncomfortably long when it was broken by Ginger Stearns, who came marching toward them through the tall grass, holding up her skirt, her dark-red hair flowing down the back of her gingham dress and blowing around her shoulders in the fitful wind that had picked up. Jonathan had expected to see a girl, but Ginger Stearns was twenty if she was a day and a full-bodied woman. Later, he recalled thinking it odd she wasn't married.

When she reached the four young men, she stopped and briefly looked down for rattlers. Then she looked up and said in a clear, high voice, "Duncan, Jake, this here's my fault. I never intended things to go as they did. And I ain't going to allow you two to get hurt because of me. I asked Ma what should I do, and she said, 'You got yourself into this mess. Get yourself out.' That's what I'm doing right now. From here on in, I ain't walking out with either one of you. I'm sorry for the trouble I've caused, but that's how it was, and this here's how it's going to be."

For the first time she looked at Jonathan and the armed men behind him. "I've said my piece," she told them. "You can get on with what I interrupted."

With that, she turned away, hiked up her skirt again, and set off for her wagon, her head up and her back straight.

"Gentlemen," Jonathan said to the Rawlings and Harley brothers, torn between amusement and admiration, "we have been told what to do. I suggest we do it. You would be wise to shake hands now and let this train ready itself for dinner."

There was some shuffling and rubbing their hands on their pants among the would-be combatants, but, a moment later, the two sets of brothers shook hands. With their families gathered around them, they set off together, talking and laughing as if nothing had happened.

Jonathan watched them go, then turned to his men. "Miss Ginger Stearns appears to have stolen our thunder. Dismissed."

CHAPTER 20

"In a week or so, barring an accident," Eli said, "we ought to reach Raton Pass."

"Should we worry about that?" Jane asked, having made her peace with Eli.

It was a clear, chilly evening, and the three of them were eating dinner. Jonathan thought their truce would be short lived but had made up his mind to stay out of their affairs as much as he could. He saw no need to revisit the mare-jumping incident, but the calm did not lessen his uneasiness over Eli and Jane's relationship.

"I could say no and not be a liar," Eli replied, "but I wouldn't be altogether honest either." He went back to eating as if he had answered her.

"Eli," she said, impatiently, setting her tin plate aside on the square of canvas they had begun using for a table, "stop eating and answer my question properly."

Eli sighed heavily but set aside his plate.

Jonathan watched this exchange with increased irritation. *Is Eli being deliberately stupid?* he wondered. *Why doesn't he at least make an effort to engage with her?*

"Well," Eli began by taking off his hat to scratch his head. "It's the major pass on this trail for crossing the Sangre de Cristo Mountains, and the going's almighty rough. The trail's been improved some in the past couple of years, but there's no way to improve granite outcrops and ledges. I expect we'll have to take some of the wagons apart to get them over the worst places."

"Which ones?" Jane asked.

"Hard to tell." Eli put his hat back on and reached for his dish.

"Eli Parker!" Jane said loudly. "Getting information out of you is like trying to wring blood out of a stone."

"Well, I'm right in the middle of eating my supper," he protested. "I can't talk with my mouth full."

"No, I suppose you can't," Jane said.

Her voice twisted Jonathan's insides. That Eli couldn't hear the pain in it made him grit his teeth to stop himself from telling the man to open his damned ears.

"Jane," he said, "wagon trains have been passing this way for years. Try not to worry about it. One way or another, we'll get you

287

and your family through the pass."

"I suppose so." Jane avoided looking at him.

"And there's bound to be some spectacular scenery," he added.

She looked up at him and smiled. "It's all right," she said, somewhat sadly, Jonathan thought. "Ma quotes the Bible to me now and then. Once she said, 'You can't make a silk purse out of a sow's ear.' "

"Speaking of sows," Eli said, "I was at a shindig in town the last time I was in Santa Fe, and they had some roast pigs that was, I think, the best eating I ever had."

"I better ride around and make sure everyone is accounted for and all right." Jonathan got to his feet, thinking he'd like to wring Eli's neck. Instead, he said, "Excellent dinner, Jane. I congratulate you."

She started to speak, but Eli spoke first. "Before you bed down, Jonathan, find out where Morgan and Yellow Leaf are. I ain't seen either of them since yesterday."

"Are you trying to get rid of me?" Jonathan asked, hoping to make Jane laugh. "Yellow Leaf is likely to shoot me if I ride up on them in the dark."

"I'll give you odds she'll know it's you before she can see you," Jane put in.

"How's she going to do that?"

"I'm not telling," Jane said, "but I'll bet you a quarter."

"You're on," Jonathan said, pleased to hear the liveliness in her voice.

His first stop was Patience's wagon. Her mules were staked out close by, feeding quietly. They raised their heads to blow softly at his approach and then went back to grazing. There was a lamp burning in the wagon, and, to his surprise, the shadows of two people were dimly outlined on the canvas covering. Seeing she had company, he started to ride past but changed his mind. He wanted her assessment of the two men and one woman still not recovered from injuries acquired in the Indian raid. Also, he wanted to know if the person visiting Patience needed his attention.

He rode around to the front of the wagon but avoided looking in. "Patience, it's Jonathan. May I speak with you?"

"Jonathan!" she cried. "You startled us. Won't you step in?"

A moment later, two heads appeared in the opening, nearly side by side. The lamplight falling on them revealed one head with dark hair and one auburn.

"Hello, Doctor," Ginger Stearns said with a broad smile. "Do you and Patience need some privacy?"

"No, Ginger," Patience said quickly, beaming at the young woman. "I expect Jonathan has a question for me concerning our patients. Is that so, Jonathan?"

"That's right. I haven't seen them for two days." He glanced at Ginger. "Miss Stearns, my quickest way of learning how they are progressing is to ask Patience."

"Please call me Ginger," the young woman said. "Can you believe this, Doctor? I'm learning how to write more than my name. And I'm getting help with my grammar, which ain't nothing to write home about."

"You are fortunate in having Patience as your teacher. I won't keep her long. Patience, how are they?"

"There's no cause for concern," she answered, still smiling. "The two drivers will be on their feet tomorrow, and Annabelle Thompson is walking again."

"Then I will leave you to your work." Jonathan lifted his hat. "Good night."

The two heads vanished inside the wagon, and Jonathan rode away with their chatter and laughter in his ears. He could not recall seeing Patience in such high spirits, even when her father was alive. And seeing Ginger again confirmed his recollection that she was a beautiful young woman.

He found Yellow Leaf and Morgan easily

enough. Morgan was playing his banjo, and Jonathan caught the sound of it and rode straight to their camp. Yellow Leaf was sitting cross-legged beside a small fire with her back to Jonathan, roasting meat on a spit.

"Jonathan," she called without turning her head, "come and help us eat these grouse."

"And how did you know it was me?" Jonathan demanded, getting down from Sam.

"You never see that no two people walk the same?" she asked. "Horse also."

"Hello, Morgan. I owe Jane a quarter. She bet Yellow Leaf would know it was me before she saw me."

"Ain't she something? She knows when I'm taking a nap instead of watching the horses, or she did before you run her off to ride point with you."

He spoke in a friendly way, but Yellow Leaf glanced up at Jonathan, caught his eye and shook her head very slightly. The message was clear.

"I don't think a herd of wild horses could run her off from you," he said. "By the way, Eli sent me out here to find you. He said he hadn't seen the pair of you for two days. Everything all right?"

"Fair to middling," Morgan said. He had

been sharpening his Bowie knife when Jonathan arrived and now resumed his task. Its blade flashed softly in the firelight as it slid back and forth over the whetstone.

"These birds ready," Yellow Leaf said. "Morgan, eat now. Sharpen later. Jonathan Wainwright, sit here."

She had pulled four tin plates from the hide sack beside her. Jonathan sat across the fire from her, watching with admiration as she drew her knife from her belt and sliced the two large birds into four halves more quickly than he could have taken the birds off the spit.

"Yellow Leaf," he said, "you move as if that knife is part of you."

"Is," she said. "Morgan, eat." As she spoke, she put cooked wild onions and garlic on their dishes. They ate in silence, which Jonathan gathered was habitual with them. When they had emptied their plates and Jonathan had praised the cook — and meant every word — he turned to Morgan and asked, "How should I take that 'fair to middling' comment?"

"Grazing's getting harder to come by," the wrangler said. He picked up his knife and whetstone and began sharpening the knife again.

For the most part, people didn't bother

trying to talk with Morgan, agreeing in general with Eli, who had said early on, "I'd get more satisfaction out of talking to my horse." Jonathan nodded at Morgan's brief explanation and waited a short while in case the man said more, then gave up and took his leave of them.

"He says enough," Yellow Leaf had told Jonathan, when he asked if Morgan talked with her. She had paused after making that answer and added, sounding puzzled, "I think I talk more with you than all my life before."

"What do you think about that?" Jonathan had asked, amused by her comment.

She hitched around on her mare to stare at him, frowning slightly. "Don't know," she said, as though seeing him for the first time. "When we talk, I feel you in my head. Very strange. Until now, I have always been one person. Now two people and am troubled, but then I listen some more and feel better. I am glad you are with me."

Jonathan waited a moment or two before answering. She usually wore her hair in two long braids, but today she had brushed it out and let it fall over the shoulders and down the back of her red blouse. The sun glistened on the shining black waves and matched perfectly the light in her large, dark eyes. For a moment he experienced a sharp stab of despair and a crushing awareness of being forever cut off from having such a beautiful, strong, and intelligent woman for a wife. With great effort, he beat down the thought and freed himself from it.

"There is a word in English for what you describe," he said, trying to sound cheerful. "*Intimacy.* It means a closeness between two people. It can be of several kinds. There is the kind you and Morgan have, and there is the kind you and I have, which is friendship."

"We say, 'You are in my heart,' if we love someone," she said quietly, "but I think this is different. This is sharing inner place. Not know this before."

"I think there is room in our hearts for many people. Do you think that?"

"Am I in your heart, Jonathan Wainwright?"

"Am I in yours?"

"I think Jane is in your heart, but you won't say so."

He shied away from that, as well as from what she had asked him. "Why won't you tell me if I am in your heart?"

"Maybe," she said, "for same reason you not tell me if I am in yours."

"You are my friend, Yellow Leaf," he said.

"And you are mine, Jonathan Wainwright. Someone hopes," she said more softly but as sincerely, "later he will tell her why he will not let himself take any woman into his heart."

"Perhaps," he said, "I will learn how to do that."

Which was the closest he had ever come since skirting around it with Dr. Pendexter to admitting he had shut down his hopes to love someone and be loved.

Eli had called a meeting for an hour earlier than their usual stopping time and had not told Jonathan what his concerns were. When the sun had another two hours before setting, the train drew into its square, and the people drew together at Eli's wagon. It had been a blustery, chilly, uneasy day with the sun dodging in and out of herds of gray clouds, racing from the west, that had galloped over them all the day long.

The ominous quality of the weather added to the unusual silence of the men and scattering of women gathered in front of Eli's wagon. Jonathan was not standing with Eli on the wagon bed as he usually did at these events. He had not been asked, an omission that puzzled him, though at that moment he attached no significance to it.

"Up until now," Eli began, "we have travelled two, three, and four wagons abreast. That's all over with. We're going in a single line from now on until we're clear of Raton Pass."

He paused, apparently to let the news sink in, but, as the pause lengthened, it came to Jonathan that something was troubling Eli.

"Eli!" Dina Watkins shouted. "Get on with it."

"Yes, well," Eli said. He cleared his throat. "Stretched out the way we'll be, we'll be more exposed to raiders attacking individual wagons, especially those that fall back from the train. I'll leave it to Jonathan to work out a way to have some of his men ride shotgun on us."

Jonathan was surprised to be hearing about his part in things for the first time. Normally, Eli would have sounded him out before making public mention of it. More evidence that Eli was distracted by something.

"Now, about the animals," Eli went on. "We're going to take the cattle through the pass first and hold them on the first good piece of grazing land they find. We'll hold the horses here until the wagons are through, because we can guard them more safely here than on the other side of the pass. Any questions?"

"How long will it take us to get through the pass?" one of the drivers asked. "We're already getting short on grazing. We're seein' more rocks than grass."

There was a murmur of agreement from the rest of the drivers present.

"I'm concerned about water," a woman said, "for us and our critters."

"All right," Eli said, showing more energy. "With any luck, we should get all the wagons through in two days — that's if we don't have breakdowns or have to dismantle more than one or two wagons. As for the water, there's a few springs, but that's about it. Make sure you fill your barrels before starting into the pass."

"We losing the river?"

"Probably tomorrow," Eli replied. "At Bent's Fort, the Arkansas River turns south. There's a crossing, and that's the last we'll see of it. We have about five days to the pass from the fort. There are creeks to cross. The water flow has been good so far. The creeks should take us to the pass. Let's get started."

While Jonathan waited for Eli to climb down from the wagon, Jane came toward him, accompanied by a tall, lean man wearing a Texas hat, a gray shirt, an unbuttoned leather vest, and denim trousers, the legs tucked into tooled leather boots. A revolver hung low on one hip.

"Jonathan!" Jane called, "Don't go! There's someone I want you to meet." She wore a tight black skirt with a crimson blouse tucked into it. When she reached him, he saw she was slightly flushed from walking and obvious excitement.

"This here is Daniel Longstreet Raintree," she said, a little too loudly, "but don't call him Dan. He goes mostly by D. L. Raintree, and he comes from Texas."

"Pleased to meet you." Jonathan held out his hand.

Raintree nodded. "I ain't much for hand-shakes."

Jonathan took a second look at the man's revolver, noting the ivory grip and silver trimmings. Almost faster than his eyes could follow, Raintree whipped the gun out of its holster, tossed it up, caught it by the barrel, and passed it to Jonathan. "That's real ivory and real silver," he said with a mocking grin.

"Impressive," Jonathan said, keeping his voice neutral. He carefully returned the gun to Raintree. "Are you travelling south or north?"

The smirk didn't leave Raintree's face. "I reckon I'll string along with Jane's family for a while. Perch Taylor and me run together for a while in Kansas."

Jane tightened her hold on the man's arm. "He and Ma are kin of some kind."

"You planning to help Jane with her remuda?" Jonathan asked.

"Maybe. Sorry to be stealing your cook." His tone made it clear he had no such regret.

Jonathan let the remark pass. He had no wish to make any show of emotion in this man's presence. "Eli and I will miss you, Jane."

"I've got Realia Green to fill in for me while Daniel's here," she said, giving her companion's arm a squeeze.

"Very good of you." Jonathan avoided the sneering grin still on Raintree's face, though he felt quite certain now of what was troubling Eli. "I must leave you. This is a peaceful train, Mr. Raintree. I hope it's to your liking."

"If it ain't I'll change it," he said.

"Jane." Jonathan tipped his hat and turned to Sam.

As Jane and Daniel wandered off, Jane still clinging to him, Eli joined Jonathan. "What do you think?" he asked.

"He's a killer, and his draw is faster than greased lightning. I'd be no match for him."

"Is he going to be trouble?"

"Not sure," Jonathan said. "My guess is he's on the run, from the law or bounty hunters. But I'm serious now, Eli. Don't let him rile you. Unless he's just laying low here, I think he might try to do that."

"Jane seems to have taken a quick liking to him," Eli said, stone faced.

"She's no idea what she's got hold of." Jonathan sighed. "I'd better get some men together." He didn't want to get into a conversation about Jane, not only because it was obvious she was telling Eli he was out of the running, but because he did not want to explore how jammed up he had felt, seeing Jane hanging off that young gunman's arm.

CHAPTER 21

That night, Jonathan and his patrol drove off three Mexicans and a Chinaman wielding machetes, having caught them trying to break into one of the goods wagons.

"Shoot high," Jonathan said, as they bore down on the thieves. The four outlaws scrambled onto their mules and fled with bullets zipping over their heads. "Too bad," Jubal Smith said as they pulled up. "I'd have liked to have that pigtail to hang in my wagon."

"What in the world is a Chinaman doing down here?" someone said when the laughter faded.

"I don't know," another man said. "But I been to the northwest, and they're like ants. You see one and the rest are coming."

"They came into California with the Gold Rush," Jonathan said. "I suppose, like our own people, only a few of them made enough money to live on, and the rest had to find work."

"The year the war ended," another man put in, "the Central Pacific railroad began advertising for them."

The riders made another sweep of the train and, encountering no intruders, turned over the work to the midnight riders.

Their progress toward the Raton Pass was slowed by heavy rain and wind that made the trail a mud pie, wearing on the animals as well as turning the advance into a slow slog. For Jonathan and Eli, Jane's absence reduced their breakfasts and dinners to a tragic mockery of the meals she'd cooked. On the fourth morning, however, their depression lifted, when Jonathan returned from watering Sam and found Jane working over a newly lit fire.

His rejoicing was short lived. Getting closer, he realized her hair had not seen a brush that morning. Her clothes looked thrown on, and a bruise ran around her lower right arm. She had tried to cover it with a bandanna, but the cloth had slid down as she worked, exposing the injury.

He tamped down his anger, determined to wait and see whether or not she would explain why she was there and what had caused the bruising. He had already guessed its source. "You're a welcome addition to our fireside," he said.

He had forgotten Eli, only now stumbling down from the wagon, still unaware of Jane's presence. Jane paid no attention to either man, but the moment Eli opened his eyes and saw her, he said in a loud voice, "Jane, I thought you was staying back to make breakfast for your cousin, and why do you look like you've been drug through a thorn plum?"

Jane straightened and glared at him. "I've fed him, and I've been up for a couple of hours working. If you don't like how I look, turn away. How long have you been sleeping in that underwear? I can smell you from here, and it ain't a bed of roses."

"We're very glad to see you Jane," Jonathan put in hurriedly. "It's a pleasant surprise. Isn't that so, Eli?" He raised his voice at the end of the sentence, hoping to make an impression on Eli as to what should be said.

"Yes," Eli replied, "but Jane, you been sick? What brings you back?"

"You go wash, change that underwear, and maybe I'll tell you."

Muttering, Eli went around the wagon to the water barrel. Once he was out of sight, she turned to glower at Jonathan. "I know what you're thinking."

Careful, he thought. "I can see the finger marks in the bruise on your arm, if that's what you're referring to."

"Make yourself useful as well as ornamental," she snapped. "Do something with this damned fire while I slice the deer meat Yellow Leaf sent over."

Caution was the better part of valor. Jonathan set about reviving the fire with some dry spruce limbs he had stored in Eli's wagon, out of the rain, the day before. While he did that, Jane unwrapped a large chunk of venison, slapped it into the frying pan, and set about cutting the meat into slices.

For a few minutes they worked in silence, until Jane straightened up. "He ain't got no money. I came back to earn some and loan it to him. I got savings, but I ain't said anything about that."

"Was it your idea?"

"No," she said after a pause. "It wasn't."

"Did that bruise come out of the discussion?"

"It might have."

Eli came around the back of the wagon. "There. I don't want to hear no more about how I smell. What did you do to your arm?"

"I fell down, and my horse stepped on it," Jane said, tossing a large piece of the fat Yellow Leaf had wrapped with the meat into the frying pan. The fat began to sizzle and hiss as soon as it touched the hot iron. Jane began forking the meat into the fat, giving herself cover to stop talking.

"In fact," Jonathan told Yellow Leaf as they rode point later that day, "it was the last thing she said before leaving. I don't know whether she's coming to cook our suppers or not."

"Bad medicine." Yellow Leaf's gaze continued to sweep the dark, broken land surrounding them. "Someone not like this place." They were riding in deep shadow through a narrow gorge, its shattered granite walls dotted with small, twisted dark-green spruces looking old as time itself, clinging to life in the crevasses.

"This place or D. L. Raintree?"

"Maybe both," she replied, settling on her mare's back and shooting Jonathan one of her slashing looks from half-lidded eyes that spoke paragraphs. This one, Jonathan decided, was part amusement and part a jab at his being so thick headed.

"What has she said to you about him?" he asked.

"Nothing. What needed? You saw her arm?"

"Yes."

"Jane's mother afraid of him. He hit small

ones if disturbed by them. I told her to stick a knife in him while he sleeping."

Jonathan did not doubt for an instant it was what she would do.

"Sometimes, hunting a smart animal," she continued, "there must be first time to watch it, see where it goes, where is the sun, where is the wind. Then be there, wait, kill it."

Jonathan understood precisely what she meant. "He is very dangerous, very fast with his gun."

"You have rifle. Shoot him in back."

How to explain to her why he couldn't do that? He decided to try. "If I shot D. L. Raintree in the back, I would lose my honor. I would be called a coward. Do you know that word?"

"Yes. Do you wait for rattlesnake to strike before you kill it?"

"People aren't rattlesnakes."

"This one is."

The problem of honor in cultural differences was put aside as three mule deer burst over the top of a rocky outcrop to their right. The two does and a yearling skidded briefly and then leaped down the rock face, scattering the shale as they ran. A moment later, a large mountain lion came racing after them, its feet seeming to scarcely touch the rocks and gravel as it pursued the deer.

"The yearling's mine," Jonathan shouted as he and Yellow Leaf reached for their rifles.

"Cat," she said.

The yearling went down in a graceful somersault, shale rattling after it. The cat twisted in the air, intending to race away the instant its feet touched the rocks, but it died in mid-fall and crashed down on the dead deer.

"You shot that cat in the head," Jonathan said in astonishment when they reached the fallen animals.

"Not want hole in skin," she said, dropping down from her mare, knife already in hand.

They had some difficulty getting the lion skin onto their pack horse, but Yellow Leaf wrapped her bandanna over the horse's eyes and quieted the animal long enough to let Jonathan strap the dressed deer and the cat skin onto its back. Once they were on their way again, Yellow Leaf pulled her paint closer to Sam. "Jonathan Wainwright's honor will not get him shot. Does he hear?"

She had carefully avoided looking at him while she spoke, but turned to him for an answer.

"I hear Yellow Leaf," he said, smiling despite himself. "I think she speaks wisely."

"You have saying I have heard," she told him, still sounding very serious. " 'Many ways to skin cat.' I do it one way because shortest. Maybe could do it another."

"I'm sure you could," he said, this time without smiling. "I will think hard about ways not to get shot."

Eli listened without comment as Jonathan described Raintree's treatment of the Howards. "You'd better put together a few of the men from your group who know how to handle guns," he said, then added, "Count me in as one of the men going to face him down."

"Much as you want to, Eli," Jonathan told him, "you can't. The train can't risk losing its wagon master, and there's some risk involved in this, no matter what plan we settle on."

Eli snorted in disgust. "I suppose you're right, but it galls me not to be in on it."

By evening, Jonathan had spoken to five of his best riflemen. He asked that they meet after dark at Eli's wagon but not to tell anyone, their wives included, where they were going.

"I'm glad you called on me," Orrington Rowe said when Jonathan finished telling them why he'd arranged the meeting. "Word of what that skunk is doing to Jane and her family has been in the wind for a day or two."

Orrington was the oldest man in the group, large and steady. He'd been a mountain man for twenty years before returning East to fight with the Union Army. Jonathan was glad to have gained his support, because he knew the other four would be quick to follow Rowe's lead.

"Our problem is, no one of us could come out of a gunfight with Raintree alive," Jonathan said. "Yellow Leaf suggests shooting him with a rifle when he's not looking. It seemed an obvious solution to her. My comments about honor left her laughing."

"Anyone got any better ideas?" Merced Kinsell asked in a Vermont twang, grinning broadly at the example of what had become known throughout the train as the Yellow Leaf solution.

"I suppose we could all shoot him at once," said Fence, a tough, lean driver whose shoulder-length hair was prematurely gray. A Rhode Islander, Fence claimed he didn't know how he came by his name. He had enlisted under the name of Smith and served as a sniper in the war.

"I believe we'd be charged with murder, were we to do that," Kinsell put in.

"We're back to you, Colonel," Rowe said.

Jonathan thought a moment. "Here's another suggestion. I go to him unarmed and tell him to pack up his gear, ride out, and not come back. My guess is he'll laugh at me, insult me, something like that. I'll call him out and tell him to meet me tomorrow morning as soon as there's light enough to shoot by. Right after I leave, you call on him unarmed and tell him if he wounds or kills me, the five of you will shoot him."

There was a long silence after Jonathan stopped talking with none of the men looking at anyone else, except for Rowe, who watched Jonathan closely. Jonathan was about to suggest starting over when Rowe said, "It might work, Colonel. I'd say it's worth a try."

"We ought to remember that snake has a wagon full of women and kids to mess with," Kinsell said.

That broke the jam, and all the others started talking at once "Hold up!" Jonathan said, pushing out his hands. "One at a time."

In the end they agreed it was unlikely Raintree could use Jane's family to any advantage, and if he left in the night with Jane, they would ride them down and shoot him.

"Remember," Jonathan said as the riflemen departed, "go in right after I leave."

He found Raintree a little way off from the Howards' wagon, a bit of luck for which he blessed whatever deity might be watching over him. At least he wouldn't have to contend with Jane overhearing and taking some rash action. Raintree took his challenge pretty much as Jonathan expected, a sneering laugh and a few choice insults accompanying his flat refusal to clear off — the mildest of which was, "I don't take orders from no stinkin' Yankee."

"Tomorrow morning, then," Jonathan said, fighting down an intense desire to leap at Raintree and throttle him bare handed. The darkness inside him was harder to master than it had been with Callaway or Jess Howard, and he reflected later that it was just as well he hadn't brought his Colt. He'd have shot the bastard clear through the heart, or tried to, and likely broken his promise to Yellow Leaf not to get himself shot first.

When Jonathan returned to Eli's wagon, to tell the wagon master what he'd done and what came after, he found Morgan and Yellow Leaf sitting around the last of the dinner fire, small yellow flames licking up amid the coals. "We were just talking about

Jane Howard's problem with that Raintree fella," Eli said. "Come and sit down."

Greetings over, Jonathan said to Morgan and Yellow Leaf, "You two may as well hear this. Just don't repeat it to anyone." He laid out the plan and then said, "I'll go out tomorrow morning, but I don't expect to see Raintree. I'm hoping he will have left."

"With Jane?" Yellow Leaf asked in a flat voice.

"If he takes Jane, we will bring her back, I promise," he told her.

"If you do," Morgan said, "shoot the bastard, or he'll circle back and bushwhack you." A long speech for him, Jonathan thought.

Yellow Leaf had asked nothing more, but she never took her eyes off Jonathan. "You don't think much of this plan, do you?" he asked her.

She shook her head but said nothing.

Jonathan did not sleep that night. The oxen were restless. For the past several nights, a small pack of wolves had circled first one team and then another in the dark, never getting up the courage to tackle one of the huge beasts. Jubal said the wolves were testing the animals, looking for a weak one. This night, they had chosen to pick on the teams picketed nearest Jonathan's bed, causing Sam and the pack horse and Eli's mount to stamp and snort and the oxen to bellow and rip up turf with their horns and hooves at intervals all through the night.

He rose gratefully with the first line of gray in the east, washed up, watered Sam and the pack horse, finished dressing, strapped on his gun, and set out for the Howard family's wagon. He and Raintree had agreed to meet on the east side of it. The light grew steadily and the morning wind picked up as the sky brightened. The dew had fallen, but his boots were already wet from watering the horses.

He stopped and looked around, from habit of estimating advantages and disadvantages of battlefields. To his left was the line of wagons, the Howards' being the third and, he judged, about thirty yards from him. Beyond them, the oxen were staked out, although most were lying down. To his right, a long, low rocky hill broke the landscape, with clumps of spruce between the rocks and a jagged ledge zigzagging along its middle like a low wall. Turning back, he saw his men spread out a few yards behind him in a fan, rifles resting in the crooks of their arms.

A sharp cry made him look forward again, in time to see Jane picking herself off the ground behind her wagon. Raintree leaped down behind her, grasped her wrist and yanked her to her feet, twisted her arm behind her back, and walked her out toward the hill. When he saw Jonathan, he stopped and pulled Jane in front of him. "Thought you were smart, didn't you, Yankee," he said in a grating voice, speaking over her head.

For a moment, Jonathan thought the man might be drunk but quickly decided he was just gloating.

Raintree snickered. "You're not half as smart as I am. And, when I'm ready, I'm going to shoot you, and there won't be a goddamned thing you and that dog shit behind you can do about it. Didn't think I'd —"

A rifle cracked, and the top half of his head disintegrated. Jane flinched away from what was left of Raintree, rubbing her wrist. Jonathan spun around to see which of the men had shot him, but they were all looking toward the hill. Jonathan ran to Jane, started to speak to her, but saw that for the moment she would not hear him. Instead, he caught her in his arms and realized for the first time that her hair was splattered with Raintree's blood and brains.

He held her until her mother reached them. Crying, "Thank God! Thank God!"

she took Jane from Jonathan and walked the stunned young woman to their wagon.

The men behind Jonathan had run in and stood staring down at Raintree's remains, glancing every now and then at the hill from whence the bullet that killed him had come. "Lord above, will you lookee there," Fence said, staring at the hill as the day brightened around them.

Jonathan and the rest of his men looked up. With the newly risen sun as a backdrop, a rider was coming around the hill and moving toward them at a leisurely pace. "He's carrying a rifle across his saddle," Jacob Drew said.

"Not wearing a hat," Kinsell added. "Might be an Injun."

"You're in for a surprise," Jonathan said, having recognized the rider.

A moment or two later it became clear to all of them that the rider was Yellow Leaf on her pony, dressed in fringed leggings and a belted doeskin jacket, her rifle across her thighs and two slashes of black paint across her cheeks. Her hair, caught in a rawhide band around her head, fell around her shoulders and down her back. The men watched her come in silence. She rode slowly up next to Jonathan, then halted briefly and looked down at the corpse, then at Jonathan.

"Damn fool man," she said and rode on toward Jane's wagon.

"Was that Raintree she was talking about?" Orrington Rowe asked.

"No," Jonathan said, "it was me."

CHAPTER 22

At the crack of Yellow Leaf's rifle, the wagons all along the line began to empty, and, by the time of her arrival, a large crowd had gathered around the Howard wagon. None of those present knew what Yellow Leaf had done, but dressed as she was and wearing war paint with the rifle across her lap, the crowd split without any complaint to let her through.

Sliding from her mare at the Howards' wagon, still holding her rifle, she twisted the hackamore once around a wheel and patted the paint's shoulder. "Not touch," she told the gathered people. "Will bite, kick bad."

That caused some grumbling, but nobody tested the warning, perhaps persuaded by the way the paint trampled, tossed her head, and rolled her eyes when anyone came near her once Yellow Leaf had climbed into the wagon. A few minutes later, Jonathan arrived, having fetched Patience to check on Jane and work out as to how Raintree would be buried.

Some of the men said he didn't deserve to have anything said over him, but, from up on the wagon bed, Patience responded, "There is no doubt he was a wicked man who perhaps deserved to die, but we have been taught to forgive even those who have broken all the 'shall nots.' That being so, let us commend his soul to God and feel thankful we have ended our responsibilities concerning D. L. Raintree."

Yellow Leaf stuck her head out the back of the wagon. "Better not to speak of the dead after telling them they can go. That way, be sure he not come back."

Several of the people crowded around began muttering about "heathen talk," but Patience spoke up in Yellow Leaf's defense. "What Yellow Leaf said has its echo in Christ's Sermon on the Mount. Not mentioning the names of the dead acknowledges the powerful connection between them and those they leave behind. The dead have gone to the next place, and bringing them back by talking about them increases our grief. Christ tells us, 'Take therefore no thought for the morrow: for the morrow shall take thought for the things of itself. Sufficient unto the day *is* the evil thereof.' Let us not add today's sorrows to those of tomorrow, because tomorrow will have sorrows enough of its own."

The grumbling ceased, but Jonathan saw that the hostility toward Yellow Leaf had not lessened. He climbed up beside Patience.

"I think I should get Yellow Leaf away from here," he said quietly. "I'm impressed by what you said, but too many out here are not. Tell her to go out the front. I'll meet her there. How's Jane?"

"She'll be all right," Patience said. "Having that man's head explode in her face terrified her, but she's a strong young woman, and I hope to God she's learned a lesson. Putting your hand in the fire is a damned inefficient way to get attention."

She got down off the wagon, and Jonathan was surprised to find Ginger Stearns waiting for her, looking very much at ease. He decided to think about that later and also about her parting remarks. Patience Stockbridge seemed to be showing a new, tougher side to her character.

Later, as he rode with Yellow Leaf back to Morgan's camp, he said, "You probably saved my life, and I want to thank you for it."

"I am finding white people just as different, one from other one, as Indians," she said, "and stubborn. I disappointed with you, Jonathan Wainwright."

Jonathan was surprised to find her statement stung. He opened his mouth to protest, then closed it and thought a moment. "Do you know why I did what I did?"

"You think I don't know?"

"You said you are disappointed with me. I think you should let me explain myself."

"I listen."

"It's the only plan we came up with that had any chance of working without someone getting shot."

Yellow Leaf broke into a wide smile that he had never before seen on her face. For once, she looked genuinely happy. "Sometimes, Jonathan Wainwright, you sound like child I never had. You did not think a bad man like that do what he did?"

"I didn't think he would, no."

"He had no honor?"

"None."

"Then, is a good thing I shot him?" she said.

"Yes, for Jane's sake and mine. He would have shot me, but I am sorry you had to do it." A shiver went through him as he recalled his own desire to do exactly what she had, the risk of his own death be damned. "I've shot people. I don't want to have to do it again."

"Not even bad men like Raintree?"

"Not even them. I'd rather no one has to shoot anyone, ever."

For the past few hours, with the sun still east of midday, the train had been ascending the trail leading up to Raton Pass. Jonathan and Eli had worked steadily since first light in an attempt to keep the wagons close to one another, but then misfortune struck. In the first narrow pass of the trail, Elijah Hutchins — a gray-haired, heavily muscled, and slow-speaking man — drove the rear right wheel of his huge wagon into a ledge, smashing the spokes with a cracking sound like gunfire and collapsing the rear right side of the wagon.

"No use crying over spilt milk," Eli said, though Jonathan could see he was fuming mad, while Elijah waved his straw hat and turned the air blue over his mistake.

"I took my eyes off that lead team one goddamned second, and Possum, the greedy bastard, heaved to the right to grab a bite of grass and took Charley with him. Of course, the rest followed, turning the front wheels in just enough to take this rear wheel into the rock before I could stop them."

"Jonathan!" Eli shouted, "Fetch me half a dozen men, and we'll need three of our biggest jacks and a twelve-foot oak four-by-four."

Jonathan lifted his hand to indicate he had heard and turned Sam. The first mounted person he met was Alvin Small, bursting with excitement. "Colonel," the boy began, "I ain't never seen nothing like these mountains before. A couple of them look like they'd hook any cloud hurrying by."

"They do, Alvin. There's a wagon broken down further along. Could you ride to the head of the train and tell them what's happened, and to hold up until someone brings word to start again? And ride back as soon as you're finished. Now repeat what I just said."

The boy did and went off with his message, grinning ear to ear.

"We'll use that four-by-four as a pry," Eli said as soon as he had the men gathered, "and lift the back corner of the wagon high enough to plant the jacks under the bed."

"What if she won't lift?" one of the men asked, eyeing the length of their pry doubtfully.

The other men groaned.

"We unload the wagon until she does," Eli said.

But it didn't come to that. With the pry in place, everyone piled onto the four-by-four and, using the ledge as a fulcrum, lifted the wagon a few inches at a time until all three of the jacks were in place and ready to take the weight.

"Someone lend a hand here," Elijah called from inside the wagon when the broken wheel had been removed.

After a lot of grunting, groaning, and swearing, six men wrestled an iron-shod replacement wheel, tall as the men handling it, out of the wagon and onto the ground, to loud cheering and shouts of encouragement from the small crowd that had gathered as the work went forward. But, before the huge wheel could be mounted, more men wielding sledgehammers had to break away the offending chunk of ledge and make space for the wheel to be rolled into place and lifted onto the axle.

"The goddamned pass," Eli croaked to Jonathan as people began hurrying back to their wagons and Elijah sent his oxen's shoulders into their yokes by shouting their names, all the while pistol-cracking his whip above their backs.

Eli turned to walk to his gray, but he had

taken only three steps when he flinched, grasped his left arm, groaned, and would have gone down if Jonathan had not been close enough to catch him when his knees buckled. Some of the stragglers who had stopped to talk saw Eli go down and came running as Jonathan eased him to the ground and put his hat under his head. He checked Eli's pulse and chafed one of his hands, telling him to just lie quiet. "What's your last name, Eli?" he asked. "Do you know where you are?"

"Parker," Eli said, but it was little more than a whisper.

"Good. Are you in pain?"

"Chest tight . . . hard to . . . catch my breath," Eli gasped.

"Lie still. It will pass. Don't try to get up."

"Is the train moving?"

"Yes. No. Lie still. We'll see about your getting up later. Is the pain lessening?"

"I . . . think so." His breath was coming easier now; Jonathan could hear the difference. "I feel . . . mostly tired all at once."

"All right, Eli, that's all right. Try to stay awake." The huddle of people around him and Eli, leaning in to offer advice or ask if the wagon master was going to live, momentarily cost Jonathan control of his temper. "Stand back!" he snapped. "Back away!

Now!" The crack of command, his colonel voice, startled everybody around him, including himself.

He drew a deep, calming breath. "We're going to put him on the gray," he said, the volume turned down, and gestured to three of the men nearby. "You three plus me, two of us on each side to steady him. Then we'll walk him to his wagon."

Alvin had returned and was among the onlookers. Seeing him, Jonathan called, "Mount up and lead this gray to Eli's wagon. When that's done, ride back to the head of the line and start them off. How much lead do they have?"

"I ain't much of a judge," the boy replied, "but I'd guess an hour."

"On second thought," Jonathan said, checking himself, "ride alongside Elijah, and, when you catch sight of the train, ride up and tell them to start. Remind them to stay in single file."

"I'll do it," the boy said. "Then I'll come back to hear how the wagon master is. Don't let him die on us. I don't think Pa could stand it. As it is, he's whittled himself down to a splinter worrying."

As the three men and Jonathan were getting Eli back to his wagon and into bed, Jane arrived on her mare. "Alvin told me

Eli is sick. Is he?" she said when Jonathan stepped down from the wagon.

She did not, he thought, look especially worried, but ever since Raintree's death it was difficult to judge what she was feeling. Sometimes, she gossiped as she'd always done while making their meals. At other times she remained silent, as if her thoughts were somewhere else.

"Yes, but how ill I'm not sure."

She frowned down at him. "That don't tell me much."

Jonathan took a moment to study her more carefully. She looked much as she had at breakfast. Her hair was still uncombed, and her clothes still looked as if she had slept in them.

Laying his hand on the mare's shoulder, he said, "He's sleeping quietly, which probably means he's out of pain. He may have overdone himself working on the wagon wheel. If so, he should be fully recovered in a couple of hours."

"And if not?"

Jonathan pondered the question and decided nothing would be gained by lying to her. "If not, he's probably experienced *angina pectoris.*"

"A what?"

"It's a Latin phrase. It means 'strangling

in the chest.' His heart would be afflicted."

She blanched. "Then he's going to die?"

He moved his hand and briefly pressed her knee. "I won't mislead you, Jane. If it is *angina pectoris,* he is seriously ill, but he may live for years with the condition and die of something else."

"But that's not likely."

"No."

"Will he need any looking after?"

"Give me a few hours, and I'll give you an answer."

She bit her lip. "I've got to get back to the two kids watching the horses." She lifted the reins, kicked her mare, and jumped the animal out from under Jonathan's hand. He watched her ride away with a tightening in his own chest, but it wasn't *angina pectoris.* It was something much more common and, while not fatal, often very painful, but he would be damned if he would give in to it.

The narrowness of Raton Pass made maneuvering the team oxen difficult, with six and eight animals scrabbling for footing in the rock and gravel as they heaved their weight into the yokes. Their drivers sometimes walked on their backs, shouting encouragement as well as directions in the effort to keep them moving and find a path for each wagon's wheels that would not tip it over. There was a continuous slamming and groaning sound as the wheels rolled over the exposed granite, loose rocks, and gravel of the trail.

Eli's wagon had been put between two of the biggest wagons. He was awake when the time came to go through the roughest part of the pass, though Jonathan would not allow him to get up. He had Eli lifted out and carried on a stretcher over the worst of the pass and put back to bed once the wagon reached him. Jonathan asked him a few simple questions, which he answered easily, but noted that Eli showed little interest in what was happening around him and slept again as soon as Jonathan stopped pestering him.

"What do you think, Colonel?" Jubal Smith asked when they were out of the wagon.

"Too soon to say, Jubal, but the attack has taken its toll."

"His color's bad, and his gaze don't stay fixed anywhere. I've seen that too many times, and it ain't good."

"No, it's not, but let's not bury him yet."

Jubal chuckled. "You're right, Colonel. No need to hurry. We won't run out of burial space any time soon."

Jonathan watched Jubal lift himself onto his black horse and thought, *there are men, and I'm one, Jubal's another, who have seen too much dying.*

There were sore backs from the heavy lifting, and the drivers were hoarse from shouting, but only Eli was bedridden. A bright spot was the continuing fair weather throughout the travelers' ordeal, which took place in a setting of astonishing beauty. At nearly eight thousand feet of altitude, the air in the pass was clear as crystal. The climb, the sinking of the sun, the clouds drifting over the peaks and valleys made a magnificent sight. And the moon, turning the rocks and ledges a quiet silver and deepening the shadows, made the mountain tops look close enough to reach out and touch.

Morgan, Jane, and Yellow Leaf were the first over the pass. With a lot of conscripted help, they'd herded the horses and cattle safely through and down the New Mexico side to grazing and water. They held the animals where they were for the next twenty-four hours and then cornered Jonathan, who had made the trip on Sam. Both he and Sam showed the wear. They were ready to sleep standing up — easier for Sam than Jonathan.

"We can't hold these horses here more than another day," Jane said.

Morgan limited himself to a nod and three words. "Not enough grazing."

Jonathan was pleased to find that the challenge of getting the herd to safe ground had apparently helped heal Jane's emotional wounds. Although her hair still looked a mess, and she had not slept any more than the others, she had regained her edge and her confidence. What she thought about the shooting of Raintree, Jonathan had decided, was a subject she would have to broach first.

"Cattle drift," Yellow Leaf told him.

"You've got four more hours of light. Walk them toward Fort Union for a couple of hours," Jonathan said. "If you run into grazing, hold them. I'll send some men to help you guard them, and I'll have the wagons already through the pass follow you as close as they can, to give you all the cover we can."

He knew, as she did, the risk she and the others with the remudas, including the Smithins boys, faced alone with the animals. In addition to raiders, the wolves up here in the mountains would be a greater menace than ever. He also knew it would take part of another day to get the last of the wagons through the pass. Dividing the train weakened their defenses, but he found splitting it temporarily was his best option. Some of the travelers would object strenuously, but he was determined to give as much protection as possible to the animals and those guarding them.

He rode along the line of wagons that had made it through the pass until he found Jacob Drew's. "Jacob," he said, "can your wife drive the oxen while you round up Jubal Smith and a couple more to catch up with Jane and Morgan, and ride guard on them until sundown? I'll get someone to take your places before dark."

"Annabelle," Drew called. "Can you keep these oxen moving for a couple of hours?"

Annabelle Drew, a freckle-faced woman with a fine smile and a sharp wit, stuck her head out from under the canvas. "Does a bear shit in the woods?"

Then she saw Jonathan, and her face flamed crimson. "My apologies, Doc. Yes, I'll drive 'em," she said, dropping to the ground, light as a butterfly. "Jacob, don't you come back drunk or I'll skin you."

"You ever married, Colonel?" Drew asked him as they rode away.

"Never that fortunate," Jonathan said.

"Best thing that ever happened to me," Drew said with a faraway look on his face,

331

"was my stepping up to Annabelle at a corn husking and asking her if all that curly brown hair was a wig. She shoved me back about three paces and threatened to black both my eyes. I asked if I could make up for insult by marrying her. Lord, I was lucky."

Jonathan laughed, but he wasn't amused. He felt suddenly old and solitary beside this happy man.

"When you've gathered the others," he said, "go right through the pass and find Jane, Yellow Leaf, and Morgan and the Harley boys. Take plenty of ammunition, and keep your eyes open."

"Will do. How's the wagon master? I heard he was poorly."

"I really don't know, Jacob. I wish I did."

"If he don't make it, you're going to have your hands full."

With that cheerful assessment, Drew went off to collect the others. Trying to clear his mind of rain clouds, Jonathan threw himself back into the task of getting wagons through the pass. At dusk, he called a halt and sent a relief group to take over guarding the animals. Before the final wagon, a huge goods wagon manned by two drivers with eight oxen drawing the behemoth, left to join the rest moving down into New Mexico, Jane's mother and three other women arrived laden with food, clothes, and blankets.

"Can we send these cooked grouse, antelope steaks, and bread with this wagon, to Jane and the others?" Mrs. Howard asked.

"And there's blankets and things," another woman added, which was timely because, although the days were hot, in the mountains the nights were cold.

"They will take them and make the deliveries," Jonathan said. He called half a dozen men down and told them their lives depended on getting the food and gear to Jane and the rest of those guarding the animals.

That done, he turned back to Mrs. Howard and asked how Jane was taking Raintree's death.

"We're not supposed to gloat over the dead," she replied, her jaw tightening, "but that Raintree was bad trouble. I regard his death as the Lord's work. He must have been plain sick and tired of His creation. I know I was."

Listening, Jonathan suddenly realized that this woman had not cut her teeth in Missouri but somewhere on the coast of Maine. Once heard, the local accent was never forgotten. He suddenly felt a kinship to her and found himself smiling.

She paused for a moment as if searching for words, or so it seemed to Jonathan. But when she spoke again, her words crackled and flew like sparks. "This here business with Jane is beyond my curing, Doctor. Why she let that trash near her is more than I know. When I tried to talk with her about it, she near snapped my head off. If you cornered me, I'd have to say she didn't give a pig's squeal what happened to him. But that's not the end of it. Something's eating into her, Doctor."

She paused and let her searching gray eyes rest on his, and he felt them bore into him. "She's an unmasted ship on a lee shore, Dr. Wainwright, and, unless the wind shifts, you will be the ledge she'll founder on."

With that she and her companions picked up their skirts and stalked off.

Not on this light snow, Jonathan thought, feeling slightly sorry for himself and unaware he had completely misread Mrs. Howard's message.

CHAPTER 23

Early on the second morning after clearing Raton Pass, a dozen Comanches, Mexicans, and what turned out to be escaped Genizaros struck the train's remudas. The horses and cattle were being moved nearer one another and closer to the train, a caution insisted on by Eli, still in bed but rebelling at his captivity. The raiders, apparently, had assumed the two women and Morgan would turn tail and run at first sight of the yelling band.

"Go at them," Jane shouted to Yellow Leaf, who had already drawn her rifle and swung her horse toward the charge.

Morgan rode in from the side and began shooting. His aim was poor, but just the sight of him riding hard toward them, firing, meant the raiders faced a counterattack coming from three directions. And the women were deadly. Three of the raiders in the front rank had lost their saddles, and four more behind them abruptly remembered they had come to this outing to steal horses, not to get shot, and reined their horses in so hard they nearly sat down. Two more men close to them screamed and fell across their horses' necks.

Neither the women nor Morgan thought they could hold off the raiders, but they had broken the charge. Before the milling horse thieves could reorganize, the three defenders rode pell mell towards the wagon train. They soon met Jonathan and most of his still-mounted men, who'd raced toward the front of the train as soon as they heard the shooting.

"There's six or eight of them left," Jane told Jonathan. "They're probably stampeding the remudas."

"Good work." He turned to Yellow Leaf. "Your pinto got a nick on her rump."

"Same bullet burned hole in my legging," she complained. "I will come with you and kill somebody. These new leggings, finished last night."

"You three go look for the cattle," Jonathan told her, trying to look severe but falling short, "and don't get into any more shootouts."

Feeling the old rising of his spirits before

a battle, he sensed the same in her and said so.

"Two the same," she said, meeting his gaze. "I will stop this one bleeding, then round up cattle and try not to shoot somebody. You come back. Don't be damn fool."

With that advice given, she rode off. He sat for a moment, watching her until she joined Morgan and Jane. She was, he thought, one of the most interesting persons he had ever known.

"Colonel!"

The shout broke his reverie, and he turned in the saddle to see Jubal Smith at the head of his men, waving a rifle over his head. "We're ready!"

With hard riding through broken scrub land, they caught up with the rustlers in less than an hour. Coming around a sharp bend in the canyon the rustlers had chosen for their escape, Jonathan pulled Sam up. In front of them was a cloud of dust.

"I suggest we divide and ride down both sides of whatever's in that dust," he said, as his men milled around him. "Anyone got a better idea?"

"I think the colonel's nailed it," Jubal Smith said. "We ride down each side, hell for leather, shooting everything with two legs until we get to the front and turn the horses."

"Agreed?" Jonathan asked.

"I've got two legs, riding four," Merced Kinsell put in dryly. "I'd as lief not be shot."

"I believe there's some among them not more than kids," Jonathan said when the laughter stopped. "If any of the bunch runs, let him go."

"Good idea," Smith said. "It will cut down on burials."

"Let's do it." Jonathan gave Sam his head.

Having run the two remudas together, the thieves, their numbers seriously reduced, were having difficulties driving the horses because the stallions, reunited, were more interested in fighting with one another and holding onto their mares than running. Also, having been exposed several times to men rushing around, firing guns, the horses weren't bothered enough to run at more than a half-hearted gallop. Added to that, they didn't like the smell of these new people, so the oldest of the mares kept trying to turn the others around and go back to the place where people smelled better.

"How are we going to do this without shooting a horse or three?" Merced Kinsell asked Jonathan, pulling up beside him. "I ain't done this before, so far as I can recall."

"You and Orrington put yourselves near Jubal. Do what he does," Jonathan said with a grin.

"Pa said I was damned fool to set off as I did," Merced said as he pulled away. "I believe he could've been right."

"We'll take this side," Jonathan shouted to Jacob Drew, who stood in his stirrups and waved the five or six riders closest to him toward Jonathan. The rest followed Jubal.

The broken sides of the canyon were strewn with large gray rocks and shattered ledges, dotted with sagebrush and occasional clumps of stunted spruce. The stolen horses were spread out across the narrowing valley and resisting the loud, frantic efforts of the thieves to bunch them and increase their speed.

Jonathan had seen the narrowing and realized they would be among the rustlers when they rode into the dust cloud. In preparation he drew his handgun and waved it over his head, hoping to give his men the message. Then into the dust they rode. He found it hard to estimate distance, but, using the horses running beside him to judge by, he guessed he could see about thirty feet. Almost at once there was an outbreak of shooting from across the herd. A moment later, right in front of him, a man on a horse suddenly took shape.

"He's mine, Colonel," Jacob Drew shouted, racing past him, Colt in hand.

The rustler turned in his saddle, a startled look on his dark face, just in time for Jacob to strike the side of his head with the barrel of the revolver. The blow knocked the man right out of his saddle and sent the knife in his hand flying. Sam leaped over the fallen man. Swearing under his breath, Jonathan urged Sam forward.

Then Jacob reappeared out of the dust, racing toward Jonathan, closely followed by two Indians in deerskin leggings and moccasins and not much else. The one in the lead, his hair flying, held a hatchet and was drawing his arm back to send it into Jacob's back. Jonathan shot him. The second Indian, gripping a knife, rode straight at Jonathan. Counting on Sam's size to spook the pony, Jonathan rode right at the oncoming rider. With a wild yell, the Indian slashed at Jonathan, but, at the last moment, the pony sprang away from Sam toward the thundering horses flashing past.

"Look at that idjit!" Jacob shouted, having turned his horse and pulled up beside Sam. The Indian's cayuse had suddenly cast its lot with the herd and plunged into the streaming horses. The Indian had sprung up to stand on his pony's back, to save his legs in the crowded race.

"What turned you around?" Jonathan asked, staring after the Indian as the raider disappeared into the dust.

"They was two of them," Jacob said. "I reckon I folded. When it come down to it, I didn't want to shoot them. I suppose I was yallar."

He sounded crestfallen.

"No, but it was the wrong time for philosophical reflection," Jonathan said. "If I hadn't been there, you would be wearing a hatchet between your shoulder blades. Now, let's get on."

With few exceptions, the rustlers, seeing the riders, headed in ones and twos for the mountains. The three who tried to fight, died. The herd was quickly slowed and turned and was soon headed back the way it had come.

"Jubal," Jonathan said to the Texan, "will you take these horses to the last creek we crossed, find some decent grazing, and hold them on it until the train catches up with you? How many men will you want?"

"Glad to. Let me pick five," Jubal said.

"Do it. We should be with you before dark. I'll go back and hurry the train along. I also want to be in calling distance of Eli."

"How bad is he, Colonel?"

"I'd say he's got a fighting chance. The best news is, he hasn't had another attack. He wouldn't have survived that."

"He called me Clemmy," Jane said, her face drawn and her voice strained. "He ain't done that before."

"Her name was Clementine," Jonathan said.

They were riding well away from Eli's wagon, to be sure he would not hear them. Jonathan had examined Eli after coming back from recovering the horses, but he had not seen him since then, the demands of the train and keeping it moving having eaten his day. It was now mid-afternoon, and Jane had left the cattle with Morgan and Yellow Leaf, for a brief look at Eli. When she came away, she found Jonathan and Sam waiting for her.

"Did he recognize you at all while you were with him?" Jonathan asked, concerned.

"I don't think so. I asked him how he was feeling, and he said, 'It is up in the apple tree.' "

"When they were young, he and Clementine used to leave notes for one another in an apple tree."

Jane gave a short laugh that conveyed little

humor. "It's hard to imagine Eli as a child," she said.

Jonathan had not talked with Jane for any length of time since the shooting of Raintree. He saw that she was thinner and looked very tired. She no longer ate with him and was there at the fire and gone with few words shared.

"Jane," he said, "forgive my asking, but are you sleeping at all?"

"Why *are* you asking?" she demanded.

He decided *in for a nickel, in for a dime.* "Because you've lost weight, and you look exhausted, and if I can help, I want to."

"Do you care?" she asked in a dull voice.

"Of course I care. I care a great deal."

That last bit popped out before he had time to censor it. Her question had rattled him. He found he did not want her doubting that he cared about her.

"Like Clementine and Eli?" she asked sarcastically.

Now he was in much deeper than a dime would buy. "Why won't you answer my question?"

Her shoulders sagged, and she looked away. "It's been harder with Pa gone," she said wearily, "and Ma seems to have lost interest. The kids pretty much depend on me."

"Could you hire one of the train's grown girls to come in during the day?"

"I've got to save what I can for Ma and the kids. When we get to Santa Fe, I'll lose my two jobs, and their care will fall on me."

"I must look at Eli," he said abruptly, not knowing how else to end the conversation. "Give me time to think about what you've told me."

His examination of Eli was soon completed, and he did not like what he found. The man had weakened significantly in the past twenty-four hours. He could no longer stand alone, and his mind was, as Jane had said, wandering back through his childhood. Jonathan reviewed his options and found none likely to be of any more use than what he had been doing. Most frustrating was that he had no clear medical understanding of what had happened to Eli.

Having taken his pulse and found some satisfaction that, for now at least, Eli was comfortable, Jonathan left to find Dina Watkins.

"Well, Jonathan, how can I help? And don't be long winded. I've got a passel of young'uns and these four mules to keep going in one direction."

"I'll be quick, Mrs. Watkins," he said, keeping Sam close to where she sat on the wagon seat. "I need a reliable girl to ride with the Howards a few hours a day and do what Jane would be doing. The girl will be paid whatever you think right."

"I heard Mercy Howard ain't well. That right?"

"Jane said she's 'lost interest.' I'm not sure what that means." Jonathan knew well enough, but he also knew Dina would enjoy telling him.

"Happens to some women at the change of life," Mrs. Watkins said. "I was glad to see an end to being pregnant. She lost her husband and saw her daughter nearly ruin her life. It takes it out of you. My Erma is fifteen and been taking care of kids since she was ten. She's strong and good tempered. Pay her three dollars a week with Sundays off, and she'll tend to the kids and do as much of the cleaning and cooking as they need."

Jonathan leaned over and put out his hand. "Done, and thank you, Mrs. Watkins. You have eased my mind."

She shook his hand and released it, and he was glad to get it back. She had a grip that came with handling reins day in and day out. "Before you go, Doctor," she said. "Why don't you marry Jane Howard and put both of you out of your misery?"

Had it been a man who asked him that, there might have been blood in the water. But since it wasn't, Jonathan could not seriously consider violence as a response. "I think she's looking elsewhere, Mrs. Watkins," he said and put his heels to Sam's belly.

"There was a cow ran up a tree," she called after him, burning his ears.

For the remainder of the day, at irregular intervals, Mrs. Watkins's question popped into his mind, roiling his thoughts, and the image of the cow climbing the tree continued to make his ears burn. Worse still, telling himself his state of mind disqualified him as husband material seemed to have lost its power to squelch his inclination to rethink that decision.

Reviewing his behavior over the past weeks, he found no indications of bloodthirstiness on his part. Shooting that rustler was an act of defense, and one that had given him no pleasure. Lying under his blanket that night, watching the stars and listening to coyotes yipping from a mesa to the west of their campsite, the image of Jane sitting on her mare, fist on her hip, looking at him with those blue eyes filled with pain, twisted his heart.

A different Jane met him the following

morning.

"What's Erma Watkins doing at Ma's wagon?" she demanded, brandishing the skillet at him.

"The company hired her, agreed on wages and hours," Jonathan began. "You can't be in two places at once. Your mother has more on her hands than she can manage. You're needed on the remudas. That's why Miss Watkins is in your wagon this morning."

"Who's paying her?" Jane asked, lowering the skillet a little.

"The company," he said.

"You ready for breakfast?"

"After I've seen to Eli."

"He's not going to make it, is he?"

Jonathan looked at her and made a decision. "The odds are heavily against it, but I have seen patients come back from this, to live an ordinary life."

"Thanks for telling me the truth," she said, her scowl fading. "You're 'the company,' ain't you?"

"Does it matter?"

"I don't understand you, Jonathan. Move along, breakfast is coming."

Jonathan lingered to look at her a moment longer. Her hair was washed and brushed. Her red blouse and yellow skirt were clean and ironed. She moved with purpose and energy. Her entire body seemed to him an expression of her beauty and vitality.

If only, Jonathan, he thought. *If only.*

Jane had said she didn't understand him. Jonathan might have made the same observation about himself.

Coming back from examining Eli, he said to her, "He's asleep. Let's eat, and when we've finished, you can try to get him to eat something. Don't be surprised if you can't."

"I might try some of that cream Alvin Small brought over," she said. "That might tempt him."

"Good idea."

They ate in companionable silence for a while, the sun slowly rising through the ground mist, the quiet broken toward the end by Jane asking Jonathan if he had any idea what Morgan and Yellow Leaf were going to do once they reached Santa Fe. "I've heard it said that, being an Indian, she might have a hard time there. I've also heard some of the rich Mexican families still have Indian slaves, called Genizaros, living with them."

He nodded. "I've heard there are a lot of Pueblo people living in the area, but the Genizaros are mostly Navajo — why, I can't say."

She frowned. "Ain't Santa Fe a part of

the United States?"

"Yes, it is."

"Is somebody going to do something about it? The slavery, I mean."

"Patience plans to, but I don't hold out much hope for her success. The Mexicans and the Genizaros have been living together for a couple of hundred years."

"She won't be working alone from what I hear," Jane said, her face turning red.

"Oh?" Jonathan pretended not to have noticed the blush.

"Ginger Stearns has moved in with Patience," Jane said, getting redder. "Ginger's mother about busted a gut when Ginger told her what she was doing."

Jonathan continued playing the innocent. "Why do you think she's done that? Is she working for Patience?"

"Jonathan Wainwright!" Jane burst out. "You been having me on! Ain't you?"

"I think you look very pretty when you're blushing," Jonathan said, unable to suppress a grin.

Jane grinned back. "I blushed a lot as a girl. Not much anymore, but I am kind of knocked sideways by Patience and Ginger."

"The world can be an interesting place," Jonathan said. "Are you convinced they're a couple?"

"I came on them kissing one night a while back. They didn't see me, so I backed off and left them to it." She gave him a curious look. "Did you see much of that kind of thing when you was doctoring?"

"I worked mostly among the well-to-do, which made it possible for them to hide a good deal. But, yes, there were a few women living together. More were married and lived something like a double life. And there were a few who could find a satisfactory relationship with both men and women."

"Lord above! I didn't know that. Yellow Leaf wasn't at all shocked when I told her what I'd seen. She shrugged and said it was all flesh. I'm still not sure I know what she meant, but I didn't dare ask. She says things that curls your hair."

"I think she sees the world for what it is, and if it is, then it must be all right. She's a pragmatist."

"What's that when it's home?"

"She doesn't think first, or even second, whether something's right or wrong. She asks if it does what it's intended to do. Neither does she carry a sack full of Christian guilt."

"What?"

"She doesn't divide the world into the sinners and the redeemed, or worry if she's redeemed."

"She's superstitious," Jane said. "I've seen her turn away from what she was going to do because a black crow flew across her path."

"What happens if you break a mirror?"

"Seven years bad luck. All right. Jonathan, are you in love with Yellow Leaf?"

Jane had suddenly gone serious. Jonathan didn't respond immediately. He didn't want to hurt her feelings, and he certainly did not want to lie.

"I admire her, Jane," he said finally. "She is in many ways a remarkable person. I also recognize that she carries a burden of pain over the fate of her people. The fact she's not bitter is remarkable. Despite all that, she has brightened Morgan's life and made a new man of him."

"I'm still waiting for an answer," Jane said stiffly.

Jonathan knew she had a short tolerance for listening to him praise Yellow Leaf, but if she wanted an honest answer, he couldn't avoid it. He waited another moment, watching the approach of Elsa Smithins, who'd been helping nurse Eli. Elsa reached the wagon and climbed aboard, without speaking to Jonathan. *No reprieve there,* he thought.

"No, Jane, I don't love her. Were she and I living together — and we're not — I think I would come to love her, but that's altogether different from being in love with her."

"Would you come to love me if we were living together?" she asked.

Elsa poked her head out from under the canvas. "Doctor, you'd best come in here."

The urgency in her voice was unmistakable. Jonathan ran to the wagon, sharply aware of Jane following.

"I found him this way when I came in," Elsa said, as Jonathan dropped down beside Eli and pressed a finger against his neck.

Eli had fallen onto his right side, and Jonathan rolled him roughly onto his back. Raising his fist, he struck Eli a smashing, hammer blow on the left side of his chest, waited, searched for a pulse. Finding none, he struck again, with no better success.

His shoulders sagged as he reached out and closed Eli's eyes. "He's gone," he said and got to his feet.

Elsa stared down at the wagon master's body. "So, whether we live or die, we belong to the Lord." She clasped her hands and pressed them against her breasts. "The Lord giveth and the Lord taketh away."

"So we are taught, Mrs. Smithins." His

throat tight with a sense of failure, Jonathan turned to Jane. "If there is no objection, we will bury him in the morning."

"I'm sorry I'm not crying, Jonathan," Jane said. "He was a good man, but I didn't love him. I should have no say in when to bury him."

"If you wish, Doctor," Mrs. Smithins said, "two or three of us women will lay him out. It only seems right to do it."

"Yes, that would be a good thing."

"And he shouldn't be left alone," she added, "but you must rest. Come morning you will be the wagon master and all that entails. I will see to the vigils."

The weight of it settled on him as he and Jane stepped down from the wagon, and, while Elsa needed no help, they both reached up their hands to see her safely to the ground.

"Why do you suppose we did that?" Jane asked, after Elsa walked off.

"There is a formality that comes with a peaceful death," Jonathan said. "People are anxious to see things are done right. Like when Gideon Stockbridge died."

"I remember," Jane said, then burst out, "God, Jonathan, I feel awful. It's come on all at once. Oh lord, I'm going to bawl."

She raised her arms, tears streaming down

her face. Jonathan stepped forward and embraced her. She locked her arms around his neck and buried her face in his shoulder, sobbing violently, her body shaking with whatever was sweeping through her. She had fallen against him like a stricken child and clung to him until the spasms of weeping stopped wracking her. When they ended, she caught her breath and gradually loosened her grip on him and finally stepped back from his embrace.

As for Jonathan, holding her close had not only deepened his sympathy for her but wakened a fearful joy at having her in his arms. Among his churning emotions, the one that hurt most was the sense of utter rightness at the warmth of her body pressed to his. And when she stepped away from him, he felt she had taken a part of him with her.

CHAPTER 24

Eli Parker was buried at sunrise the following morning. Jonathan had declined to lead the burial ceremony, and it fell to Jacob Drew, who had a copy of the Book of Common Prayer from which he read portions of the burial ceremony. He began with, "I am the Resurrection and the Life . . ." and ended with, "O God, whose mercies cannot be numbered: Accept our prayers on behalf of thy servant Eli, and grant *him* an entrance into the land of light and joy . . . Amen."

For a moment, as the sun cleared the eastern horizon, the rising breeze paused and a profound silence settled over the small group gathered around the grave. When the wind picked up again, Jubal Smith settled his hat back on his head and said in his loud Texas voice, "I say we take it that old Eli jumped the fence."

A ripple of laughter and "Amens" ran through the crowd as it began to dissolve, and Yellow Leaf and Morgan stopped by Jonathan.

"Best one so far," Yellow Leaf said, "but I miss singing."

"Me too," Morgan said, then frowned at having said so much.

"Patience usually starts us off," Jonathan said, looking around. "Come to think of it, I haven't seen her. Was she here?"

Dina Watkins, passing Jonathan and overhearing his question, paused with a frown of disapproval. "She and that young hussy Ginger Stearns are staying out of sight. Well they should, or they'd have gotten an earful from me." She went on walking with her chin thrust forward, scowling under her bonnet.

"Christian charity," Yellow Leaf said, straight faced, "not everywhere?"

"You can say that to me," Jonathan told her, "but you must not say it to anyone else. In fact, don't talk about it at all. I don't know how many people in this train know about Patience and Ginger, but Dina Watkins won't be the only one who thinks they are breaking God's law. Somebody could be hurt."

Yellow Leaf gave Jonathan that flat look that presaged trouble.

"And you needn't look at me like that,

either," he said.

"I take you under my blanket one day," she said and walked off.

"Morgan," Jonathan said, "she doesn't mean that."

"She does mostly," he said, not seeming troubled as he started after her. "She's like the wind. Blows where it will."

An hour later, Jonathan became the wagon master by acclamation. He wasn't sure whether the whoops and hollers after the vote were cheers or jeers. Having crossed the Raton Pass without mishaps, they began passing near and through dusty and impoverished Mexican villages baking in the sun, apparently lifeless save for barking dogs and naked children, that sprang to life with the arrival of the train. Men and women appeared from the squat adobe dwellings to run beside the train, hawking corn tortillas, grilled onions, tomatoes, green peppers, and squawking chickens swung by their legs.

Their first sight for some time of an American presence, except for the scattered groups of Union cavalry in the largely empty country through which they had passed, came at Fort Union, a sprawling encampment of the Union Army and the largest military post in the Southwest.

Jonathan was surprised his people did not show more interest in the fort. But, as Oral Rawlings remarked, "their sights are set on Santa Fe."

He thought that made sense. Glancing up at the nearly white sky, he saw the silent and memorializing turkey vultures, patiently circling.

Once through the Raton Pass, Jonathan had taken advice from the drivers and then Jane, Morgan, and Yellow Leaf, all of whom agreed the animals needed water and grazing. That settled, Jonathan pushed the train forward to the joining of the Cimarron and Mountain routes. The spirits of the travelers rose as they told one another they had only the Sangre de Cristo mountains, rising in the distance, challenging their passage to Santa Fe.

However, that was not all they were telling one another, without telling Jonathan. When fresh trouble erupted, on an evening otherwise much like any other, the event caught him uninformed and unprepared.

The train had formed its square in the middle of a small valley, with hills to the east and foothills to higher country on the west. The grazing was good, and a clear, low-banked creek provided adequate water for the people and the stock. The weather was fair with a fine red afterglow on the eastern clouds following the setting of the sun. A cool breeze was blowing. Fires had been lit, spreading the smell of meat frying. Jane and Jonathan had finished eating and were sitting and talking over cups of coffee.

"How is Erma Watkins getting along?" Jonathan asked, aware that raising the subject might result in fireworks.

Jane surprised him. "That girl is going to make some man a fine wife," she said without a trace of sarcasm. "I didn't know how much I needed her. The kids love her. So does Ma, but she won't admit it. When I'm outside the wagon, I hear them jawing away like a pair of magpies."

"I'm glad to hear it," Jonathan said. "I was worried it wasn't going to work out."

Jane glanced down at her coffee. "I'm sorry I was such a horse's behind about it. You were right. I wasn't going to hold up."

Watching her across the remains of the fire, Jonathan thought she looked like a new person. Color had come back to her cheeks. Her hair was clean and brushed. Her eyes had regained their life and her body its spring. Tonight, in her gingham dress, she looked beautiful. The awareness filled Jonathan with pleasure, struck through with flashes of pain. He could not bring himself to admit he loved her and wanted her. Dina Watkins's question burned though his mind: *why don't you marry Jane Howard and put both of you out of your misery?*

"Jonathan! Where are you?" Jane asked with a laugh. "Have you heard a word I said?"

Jonathan started to speak but was cut off by a piercing scream.

He and Jane jumped to their feet and began to run. They had scarcely started when they heard people shouting and another loud scream. "It's near Patience's wagon," Jane said, racing beside Jonathan, her skirt pulled up to her knees.

Other people were jumping down from their wagons and running toward the small group of women, who were shouting and apparently beating someone they had knocked down. With a chill, Jonathan saw Patience trying to reach the fallen person but constantly being struck and thrust back.

"They've got Ginger!" Jane shouted.

They reached the melee seconds later. Jonathan grasped two of the shouting, kicking women by their arms and threw them back, clearing a path for him and Jane.

"Get off her!" He flung two more of the angry women to one side and shoved others off their feet until he had reached Ginger and planted himself over her, with Jane also straddling the fallen girl, her back pressed against Jonathan's.

"She's getting what she deserves!" one of the attackers shouted, struggling to her feet.

"That's right," Dina Watkins barked. "She's a foul sinner, and so is Patience Stockbridge!"

Bertram Small, a heavy, bull-necked, bald man with a turned eye, elbowed his way up to Jonathan. "You touch another of these women, who are doing God's work, and you'll answer to me, Wainwright."

Turning slightly to his right and planting his right heel solidly on the ground, Jonathan swung back and struck Small a powerful blow on the chin. Small rocked back on his heels, hung for an instant, then went down like a tree falling and did not stir.

"Get back from her," Jonathan said, in a voice they had not heard before. Then: "Patience."

"I'm here," she said. She was kneeling beside Ginger now, holding her head. Her dress was torn, and her nose had clearly been bleeding.

"We're going to take Ginger to your wagon." Jonathan raised his voice. "Who's with me?"

Jubal Smith, Duncan and Burchard Harley, Jacob Drew, Merced Kinsell, and Orrington Rowe pushed forward, stepping over the prone Bertram Small.

"There's more of us, Colonel," Jubal said, "should you need us."

"You'll do," Jonathan said. "Before we move her, I've got to see how badly Miss Stearns is hurt."

"I can't move my left arm, and my shoulder hurts real bad," Ginger said weakly, her words slurred.

Jonathan addressed the crowd. "I want you to return to your wagons. There's nothing more for you to do here."

"I want these two sinners driven out of this train," Dina Watkins shrieked, pushing forward, her chin thrust out and her bonnet askew.

Jane advanced on the older woman. "Shut your mouth, Dina Watkins. If anyone should be kicked out, it's you, along with the other cowards who ganged up on Patience and Ginger, two women who never did any of you any harm. Shame on the whole damned bunch of you. Now git out of here."

Jane was a strong woman, and, when she was angry, she looked formidable. Dina Watkins shrank back, turned, and hurried away, her supporters trailing after her.

Jane turned back to Patience. "I'd like to

take a horse whip to the lot of them."

Jonathan beckoned to her. "Jane, I need you here a minute." He stood up from examining Ginger and murmured into Jane's ear. "I think her left shoulder's out of its socket. I can put it back, but I need you to help me."

"All right, but how can you do it?"

"You take her in your arms and brace your feet. I'll pull her left arm out and let the shoulder pop back into its socket. I need you to hold her tight. It will have to be done fast, and it's going to hurt her, but the pain will be brief."

Jane frowned at him.

"It's the only way to do it," he said.

Turning back to Patience and Ginger, Jonathan moved Patience, and Jane took her place. She lifted the young woman's head and shoulders into her arms and tightened her grip while Jonathan reached down and grasped Ginger's wrist. He straightened abruptly and gave the arm a sharp pull. There was a popping sound mingled with Ginger's scream, but it was all over in a moment.

"Sorry," Jonathan said, sitting on his heels to speak to her. "Your shoulder will be sore for a while, but you'll have the use of it. Now, Jane and I are going to carry you to the wagon."

The last of the sunset glow was nearly gone, and Patience had gone ahead of them to light a lamp. Carrying their burden carefully, they reached the wagon without incident and boosted Ginger into it.

"Did I lose any teeth?" Ginger asked with obvious difficulty when Jonathan laid her on her bed.

"No," Jonathan said, carefully opening her mouth, "but you've got a swollen lip." He let go his gentle hold on her jaw. "Did someone punch you?"

"Yes, but I was being struck from all around, even when I was on the ground. My side hurts most now."

"Probably cracked a rib." Jonathan ran his hands over her arms and legs, pressing now and then when she flinched, bringing a cry of pain. "A lot of bruises but no broken bones. Let's see the side that hurts."

As he'd thought, a rib was cracked but fortunately not broken. The examination over, he stood up. "Someone kicked you. Did you see who it was?"

"No, but I felt it," Ginger managed to say, with emphasis on *felt*.

Patience was hovering over Ginger while Jonathan worked and Jane looked on. "She's covered with bruises," Jonathan told Patience. "Bathe her carefully. Keep her in bed for a day or two. Then get her onto her feet even if she protests. Make her move that left arm, lifting it a little more each day until she has full use of it. She can't harm it, but it will be sore."

He and Jane left shortly afterward. Jane, leading her horse, was quiet for a few minutes as they walked toward Jonathan's wagon. Then she said, "Do you think they . . ."

Her hesitancy amused Jonathan, but he said seriously, "Yes, I'm sure they do. I'd guess they're in love."

"I wonder how . . ." Jane began.

Jonathan interrupted. "I think I'll leave that to your imagination."

That night, thirteen wagons slipped away from the train and were out of sight by morning.

"Good riddance to bad rubbish," Jane said over breakfast.

"We'll have to find someone to replace Erma Watkins," Jonathan said.

"She didn't leave," Jane said brightly, vigorously stirring the venison strips in the frying pan. "She's staying with Ma and me from now on."

Erma's leaving home and the attack on Ginger and Patience kept them talking all through breakfast, and it was with reluctance they finally left for their day's work.

CHAPTER 25

The train never did catch up with Dina Watkins and her followers, and, according to Jane, Erma had not mentioned her mother or the rest of her family. Neither, apparently, did she suffer in silence at their loss. Before they reached the Sangre de Cristo mountains, she had changed her name to Isabell, begun spending some of her free evenings with the older of the Smithins brothers, and learned to dance the Boston Fancy at the evening fiddlings, a freedom her mother would never have allowed her.

Once out of the town of Raton, Jonathan was relieved to find safe but hilly traveling through high, dry country. A day later, they paused midday at the Clifton House, a trading post and stage station. The travelers stocked up on salt, sugar, bacon, boots, clothes, and whiskey. Those wanting flour were told they'd have to wait to buy that until they crossed the Cimarron River and stopped at the Aztec Mill in the town of Cimarron.

Questioning Jubal Smith about the mill, Jonathan learned it had been built in the town to provide flour for Santa Fe wagon trains and the nearby Apache Indian reservation. They crossed the Cimarron River with no problems and paused to check on all the wagons, then gathered at the Aztec Mill, bought the needed flour, and were soon on their way again.

After crossing the Cimarron, the travelers began to imagine Santa Fe as something other than a distant arrival point. The campfire conversations turned more and more frequently to what life there would be like. One evening, Yellow Leaf and Morgan came to see Jonathan shortly after Jane had left.

"Perhaps we will sit by the fire and eat something sweet," Yellow Leaf said after she and Morgan had hobbled their horses and left them to graze. At the Clifton House trading post, she had eaten her first sugar cookie, after which she bought all Morgan would pay for and guarded them as rare treasures. Her having brought them told Jonathan that she and Morgan had something serious to discuss.

"I believe there's coffee in the pot," he

said, "to go with something sweet."

As his guests were settling themselves, Jonathan swung the pot over the fire, got out the tin cups, and joined them. "It's good to have you here," he said. "We have not talked for a while."

Yellow Leaf obviously approved of the formality, because she nodded and said, "There is always a place for Jonathan Wainwright at our fire."

Since Jonathan had taken Eli's place, she had been riding point alone, with occasional help from Jane, who let the Smithins boys take over her remuda when the weather was good and the trail open, without creeks or heavy scrub growth to negotiate. Jonathan had hired them to work with Morgan and Jane, chiefly as extra eyes, having become more alert to rustlers following the raid on their animals.

"How are the boys coming along?" Jonathan asked Morgan, aware the man would not speak unless encouraged.

"Good riders," Morgan said, staring into his empty cup.

Yellow Leaf waited, to be sure Morgan was not going to say more before speaking. "Alfred Smithins is quick to learn," she said. "Holden Smithins very slow. Quiet and willing, but all parts not working. But he sings if horses troubled. They listen and grow quiet. Very strange."

"Very," Jonathan replied, reaching for the coffee pot and filling their cups.

Yellow Leaf passed out the sugar cookies and took a tiny bite from hers. "Perhaps it is time to say some things."

Jonathan glanced at Morgan, but he was sitting cross-legged, holding his cup with his hat on one knee and staring into the fire. He'd tucked his cookie into his shirt pocket. No help there.

"Is it true we are going to some place that we don't know?" Yellow Leaf asked.

"Yes, it's true," Jonathan said, with no idea where this conversation was going.

Yellow Leaf took another bite from her cookie and followed it with a sip of coffee, then sat for a while, apparently enjoying the taste of the cookie melting in the coffee. Jonathan took a bite out of his own cookie and also tasted some coffee. Not bad.

"Someone may not know what to do there," she said at last, putting the rest of her cookie back in the sack it had come from.

Just then, an owl hooted in the scrub growth on the hill beside them. Jonathan started to put down his cookie and coffee, but Yellow Leaf stopped him.

"Is night bird," she said. "What will Jonathan Wainwright do?"

"He might buy a ranch," he said, surprising himself. It was the first time he had shared that thought with anyone, and he was glad he had, particularly with these two. He also liked the solid sound of it.

"Is first time I have heard someone sound as if he might be somewhere tomorrow. It is good."

Was it good? Jonathan wondered. Sitting beside this fire with two people from whom in most ways he was separated by worlds of experience, he nonetheless felt completely at ease. The feeling that he was an outcast, a danger to all around him, a man who killed without hesitation and without remorse, had been lifted off him, and, although he was sure it would not last, for this hour he was a man who could say, and mean it, "I may buy a ranch."

"I hope you do," Morgan said, looking up from the fire to address Jonathan. "You have earned some peace."

Jonathan found it startling and moving to hear Morgan say so much and with so much feeling.

"Someone may take a woman onto that ranch," Yellow Leaf added. "It would be good."

That possibility, Jonathan could not allow himself to consider. It took him further than he could go with any conviction. "What do you two want to do?" he asked quickly. "Yellow Leaf, have you asked yourself what you would like to do in Santa Fe?"

Morgan simply shook his head and returned to studying the fire, which lit their faces softly. The owl had fallen silent, but, somewhere in the hills, coyotes had begun serenading the newly risen moon, and up above, the night hawks were diving, the wind in their feathers making a soft booming sound. Yellow Leaf, who had been watching Jonathan closely, said, "I will tell you a story Grandmother told me when someone came into the village and tried to steal a horse. Others killed him, and I cried."

She reached out and laid a hand on his arm. "This is what she said, holding someone in her arms: 'Long, long ago, when Great Spirit made things, he made people last when he was tired, and made a mistake. Some did bad things . . . killed more than the people needed to eat and stole horses. Great Spirit thought so long about it, when he stopped thinking, there were too many people and too many bad people for him to take the time to kill them himself. So he made some people to do that work for him.' "

The three of them sat quietly listening to the low crackle of the fire and the other night sounds.

"You're saying the Great Spirit made me to take care of his mistakes," Jonathan said, unsure how to feel about what Yellow Leaf had told them.

After they had sat in silence a while longer, Yellow Leaf said, "Grandmother also said, 'If you find wampum belt, pick it up.' "

"Don't think too hard on it," Morgan said and downed the last of his coffee. "Half the time I don't know what she's talking about."

Jonathan was still focused on Yellow Leaf. "This wouldn't be connected to your saying I should take Jane Howard under my blanket, would it?"

"Some questions need slept on for answers to come," Yellow Leaf replied. "What is there for Morgan and someone else to do in Santa Fe? Have never lived in place made of houses."

The three discussed the problem until the fire had burned down to coals and the evening star had set, without finding any answers that satisfied both Yellow Leaf and Morgan. After they left, Jonathan lay a long time, watching the stars and thinking about

Yellow Leaf's grandmother stories before sleep caught him.

Soon after leaving Cimarron, they passed the town of Rayado, where the Mountain Route met the Cimarron Cutoff, but they were the only southbound train in the town that day, although for several days they had encountered a scattering of traders, a dozen or fifteen in a group moving north, made up of loaded wagons, accompanied by heavily armed mounted men and one riding shotgun.

In spite of the increasing heat, the weather was good with only occasional thunderstorms, and the train moved south steadily some fifteen miles a day. The country through which they were passing was dry and the grazing poor, so Jonathan pushed the herders to keep the animals moving. The morning they came on a small river, called Ocate Creek, lifted everyone's spirits, and Jane, Yellow Leaf, Morgan, and their young herders had a struggle holding the remudas and the cattle together. Once the animals smelled the water, they began pressing forward, every animal setting its own speed. They plunged into the water in their eagerness to drink, casting caution to the winds.

"Even the stallions drink side by side,"

Yellow Leaf told Jonathan, laughing more happily than he had ever seen her.

He had ridden ahead of the train, worried about the horses and the cattle, and found her sitting on her pinto with one leg crossed in front of her, watching the animals milling around her. The animals having drunk their fill, Jane, Morgan, and the boys, a hundred yards down the river, were starting the work of separating their remudas from the cattle and herding them out on the south side of the river.

"How are Patience and Ginger doing?" Yellow Leaf asked, growing serious. "Not see them for a while."

"Their bruises are starting to fade, and Ginger's shoulder is working," he said. "I think it was a warning to both of them to be careful how they conduct themselves around people they don't know well."

"Someone has seen that sometimes, married women liked another woman more than husband and trouble followed, but mostly not. More often, woman who lost husband took another one like her into teepee. People nodded and said it was good. Not good to be alone."

"Are you worried now about Santa Fe?" he asked, aware that he had not been of much help to her that evening at his fire.

"Have heard Indians not liked much there," she answered, looking away from him. "Some be made to work but Mexicans not pay them."

"Have you talked to Patience about this? She and her father were going to work to end that practice in Santa Fe, and she knows something about it. Eli did also but would say little of it."

"Those who work have name, Genizaro, someone has heard."

"You have Morgan," Jonathan said. "Also, people make up stories."

"I see why you are doctor," Yellow Leaf said, turning her horse away and giving him one of her slashing glances that made him feel twenty-five. "Like to make people feel better."

Jonathan watched her ride away, thinking again how beautiful she was. On a sunny morning a few days later, Jonathan led the train down from the high, dry country into a wonderfully green valley with grass and trees and land being farmed. In the center of the valley lay the largest town they had seen for many weeks, and the trail led them into its plaza.

Jubal Smith was riding with Jonathan when they entered the valley, and they reined in together, to take in the welcome wonder.

"Las Vegas, it's called," Jubal said. "From what I've heard, it began in 1835 as a Santa Fe Trail town. Eleven years later, so the story goes, General Stephen Kearney, standing on the roof of one of them adobe buildings in the plaza, claimed the New Mexico Territory for the United States. It's been a growing trading town ever since."

Most of the train had cleared the crescent, and a lone woman's voice rose strong and clear from somewhere in the train: " 'Come ye thankful people come,/Raise the song of harvest home;/All is safely gathered in,/Ere the winter storms begin . . .' "

"Come Ye Faithful People, Come," Jubal said, smiling. "My mother loved that hymn. We always sang it at harvest time."

The lone voice had been joined by others, and, coming down the winding trail into the valley, everyone but the oxen seemed to be singing. The singers had reached the second stanza, and Jonathan joined in with, " 'All the world is God's own field,/Fruit unto his praise to yield.'

"It's this green valley that's done it," he said, his memory kicking in.

Not to be outdone, Jubal broke out in his rusty baritone, " 'First the blade, and then the ear,/Then the full corn shall appear.' "

Getting into the spirit of the thing, rackety tenor and rusty baritone finished the stanza with " 'Lord of harvest, grant that we/ Wholesome grain and pure shall be.' " The two men rode on, very pleased with themselves, their backs a little straighter, accompanied by the choiring voices behind them.

In Las Vegas they lost half a dozen of their traders and their drivers, who one by one found Jonathan to shake his hand and ask if he was thinking of organizing a train back to Missouri.

"I am not," he told them. "I'm thinking of taking up ranching."

"Colonel, first a trail boss and then a rancher," one of the older, bearded men said, grinning as he gripped Jonathan's hand. "You are a glutton for punishment."

Jonathan laughed with the man, but it was a little startling to think that he might be. *A penitent?* he wondered but quickly shook off that idea. The train had passed through the town's dusty plaza before stopping, but, interesting as Las Vegas was, the remaining members of the train were eager to press on. "Then it's wagons ho," Jonathan told the group who had gathered around him, urging him to leave the town, pretty as the valley was. "If we can get the animals off the grass." And indeed the horses and the cattle were grazing, switching their tails, looking the happiest they had been for many weeks.

"We've got a choice here," Jubal told Jonathan. "There's two passes a couple of miles ahead of us, Kearny Gap and the *Puertocito Pedregosa,* or rocky little door. Three days beyond the passes is Santa Fe, if the rope holds."

"Which do we choose?" Jonathan asked.

"I'd go with the Puertocito," Jubal said without hesitation. "It's a mite rough but nothing like the Raton."

"Then that's the one we'll take," Jonathan said. "Let's spread the word we're moving."

CHAPTER 26

"Are you really considering becoming a rancher, Jonathan?" Patience asked.

He had tied Sam to her wagon and joined her on the wagon's seat, vacated by Ginger as soon as he rode up beside their mules and lifted his hat in greeting.

"I didn't intend to chase Ginger away," he said, troubled by her jumping to the ground and running ahead of the mules to begin walking.

"She sometimes forgets she doesn't have to leave me whenever an adult engages me in conversation," Patience said with a smile. "What about my question?"

He studied her for a moment, concluding he had never seen her looking better. The observation pleased him. Her inquiry surprised him a bit, and he said, "Do you think I shouldn't?"

"I'm not sure." Patience tilted her head a little as she turned to look up at him.

"Neither am I. How are things going with you and Ginger?"

"That's a bold question, Colonel Wainwright," she said, her face brightening.

"Not nearly as bold as what you two have done, Miss Stockbridge," he said.

"No, I suppose not. Move along, mules," she responded in a louder voice, giving the reins a shake. The animals pricked their ears and lengthened their strides for a few moments, then settled back into their all-day pace.

"I'm so happy, Jonathan, I feel positively sinful," she said quietly, keeping her eyes on the mules. "I suppose I shouldn't say such a thing, but I know I can trust you to understand."

"Yes, you can, and thank you for your trust. I'm very happy for you. How fortunate you and Ginger found one another."

"I know I'm shameless. I'm almost old enough to be her mother."

Jonathan found himself smiling.

"Nonsense," he said, "even if you were old enough, I wouldn't tell."

Patience elbowed his ribs, and he gave an exaggerated groan. At that she gave him another elbow poke for good measure, and Jonathan thought when her father was alive, she would never have dreamt of doing such a thing.

"How is Ginger?" he asked, more seriously. "Has she recovered?" From more than her injured shoulder, he meant.

Patience's gaze drifted to the young woman striding along ahead of the mules. "She still cries out in her sleep once in a while. But it's becoming less frequent."

"I'm glad to hear it."

He paused and then said, uncertain of his ground but feeling compelled, "Once you reach Santa Fe, you might do well to say Ginger is your niece. I know it's not my business, but these people are likely to be more difficult than much of our group has been."

"More rigorously religious, you mean?"

"Jubal Smith reminded me the Catholic Church has pretty much run the lives of the people in Santa Fe for the past three hundred years. American Protestants have been proselytizing down here for some time, but they haven't made much headway."

"And the Pueblo peoples?" she asked.

"I haven't learned much about them, but it seems they cling to their own beliefs."

"Well," Patience said, straightening her back, "we'll just have to see, won't we?"

It really wasn't a question.

"I've walked myself out," Ginger said, returning to the wagon. "Is there room for another one on that seat?"

"Come aboard." Jonathan reached down a hand to her.

She took it and with his help swung up beside him. "It's yours," he said. "I've been enjoying myself too long. You are looking fully recovered, Ginger. I'm glad of it."

"Much obliged, Doc," she said, flashing him a grin. "Thanks to you, we're not six feet under."

On Sam again, Jonathan had time to reflect a little on the life these two so very different women had set out on. He thought it encouraging that they had been drawn more tightly together by the beating, but their road ahead was going to be a rough one.

"Why you look so grim?" Yellow Leaf asked, overtaking him without his having noticed her coming.

"You keep doing that, and someone's going to shoot you," he said, trying to frown but not quite making it.

They had mastered the Puertocito Pass with no difficulty and crossed the Tecolote Creek, running well inside its banks, without miring any of the wagons or having too much trouble with the cattle deciding it was a good place to spend the rest of the day. The country they were heading into was rolling and broken but still green with grass, scattered with piñon pines and junipers.

"That there's Starvation Peak," Jubal Smith said as he came up. He'd taken to riding with Jonathan a part of each day. He was pointing ahead of them at a huge mesa with long, sloping sides and a flat top, thrusting into the air amid much lower ridges and hills.

"From here it looks about a mile-high blown volcano," Jonathan said.

"It's just a particularly big mesa, but it's often called Starvation Peak. Story is that sometime in the past, a tribe of hostile Indians drove thirty-some people up onto the mesa, where they either starved or died from lack of water. Oddly, at the foot of the thing there's a watering place called Bernal Springs. Close by, there's a stage station. Might be a good place to camp if the time falls right and it ain't too crowded."

Jonathan glanced at the mesa, then at the sun. "It will be a little early, but we might stop, if the people will let me. They've been hurrying me along for a while now."

"I'll carry the suggestion back along the line and let you know," Jubal said. Then he added, "Santa Fe ain't really much more than a big Mexican town with a lot of northern traders mixed in. That and the pueblos. The people in them are not what you'd call sociable."

"Is it a wealthy town?"

Jubal shrugged. "There's a few Americans and some Mexicans who are sitting on some money. A lot of it's in gold jewelry, taken in to cover loans to Mexicans who were never able to repay. There's some hard feeling over it, but the wealthy families pretty well run the place. People who complain too loudly tend to disappear."

"Are these the same families who are said to have Indian slaves?"

"The Genizaros," Jubal said. "They're a kind of tribe made up of Indians captured young or bought from the Comanches, who took 'em from the Navajo, Pawnee, Apache, and other tribes in their constant wars with just about everybody. Today, most of the Genizaros are Navajos. I've heard some gossip saying the daughter of the Quaker preacher who died plans to try to free them."

"That's what she says," Jonathan agreed.

"Big mistake. Santa Fe may be part of the United States, but it's really a Spanish/Mexican town, running on their rules. They don't operate much like us."

"I'd heard there's been a government here for more than three hundred years."

"Well, that's true," Jubal said, "and the original building is still standing, but the law they handed out don't look much like ours."

Jonathan frowned. "Are our people likely to run into trouble in Santa Fe?"

"People can always do that," Jubal replied, then grinned. "You Yankees might grow a bit impatient with the speed at which things don't get done."

"We Yankees come in for a lot of knocks, is what I think."

"No offense intended, Colonel," Jubal said, losing his grin.

"None taken, Jubal. None taken, but I have the feeling I haven't heard the whole story."

There was some grumbling about stopping at the giant mesa, but the novelty of Bernal Springs and the presence of the stage station worked to outweigh the minority's urge to press on, and the train spent the night there with the added interest of two other trains joining them before dark. The musicians found one another, and, shortly after nightfall, with lanterns lit, they gathered and swung into a jig that brought the travelers running.

The man among them who had drawn the caller's straw jumped to his feet and shouted out a Virginia reel, "The Irish Washwoman." Grabbing up his fiddle, he glanced at his fellow fiddlers and the two accordion players, and off they went on the count of three. For the next hour, the grass in the almost flat ground that was their dance floor took a severe beating as the contra dances kept the lines moving.

Jonathan was watching the dancers and feeling a bit left out when Jane found him and slipped her hand through his, eyes sparkling with excitement. "Come along, Jonathan! I need a partner!"

Allowing himself to be led forward, he began to say he had never in his life taken part in one of these country dances or even been where they were performed, but cut himself short. The last thing he wanted to do was remind Jane of the difference in class between them. *In for a penny, in for a pound,* he thought as the two of them broke into a run. By the time they were well into the crowd, the caller had announced the next dance.

"The Boston Fancy!" Jane shouted. "Get over there where that line is forming, and, when I start toward you, you start toward me, and when you ain't with me, do what the person next to you does."

And that's what he did. There must have been fifty people in the two lines. The fiddles sprang to life, the caller called out the changes, and Jonathan followed as best he could as the speed of the movements increased. He found himself on Jane's side of the lines, and she grasped his left hand in hers, placed his right hand in the center of her back, put her own hand on his back, and began to twirl to the music.

"Lean back!" she shouted over the joyous noise when he stumbled forward.

He did, and in a moment caught on and began to twirl, balancing his weight with hers. It was so extraordinary an experience, he broke into a broad grin. He found she was quite capable of matching him, and around they went in the dim flickering of the lanterns and the starlight and light from the sliver of moon rising, while the fiddles and the accordions filled the night, with the dancers sashaying up and down the center, crossing over and twirling again.

"Next, we'll do the Lady of the Lake," Jane said as the Boston Fancy ended, and they stood catching their breath between sets.

"I don't know that I'll have the wind,"

Jonathan said. "I haven't moved like that since I was a child."

"Did you like it?" Jane asked, still holding his hand.

"I'm surprised to say, I did. I never would have believed I would."

He was genuinely astonished at his response. Just as they had stopped walking and turned back toward the milling crowd on the trampled-grass dance floor, the orchestra struck up "Good Night, Ladies."

"Come on." Jane pulled him back toward the crowd. "We can waltz to that if the caller can hold down the fiddlers."

Jonathan felt a most extraordinary sensation of having abandoned reality. He had danced the waltz many times in Boston homes but always dressed in tie and tails and wearing white gloves, dancing in a gas-lit room on a parquet floor with a woman in a ball gown and held at arm's length. He could hear an owl hooting somewhere.

"Where did you learn to waltz?" he demanded, walking with her onto the dance floor.

"At barn dances!" She swung around into his arms, and away they went, catching their boots every now and then on a hard bunch of buffalo grass.

"You dance divinely, Miss Howard," he

said, recovering from a stumble.

"And so do you, Colonel Wainwright, when you're not stepping on my feet."

They laughed along with the other dancers, struggling to waltz, but they all grew quieter as the music drew toward its end. Jonathan and Jane held each other closer, moving under the stars together as if they intended to go on waltzing forever.

Chapter 27

"That there's Borieta Pass," Jubal told Jonathan, "and on the western end of her is Apache Canyon where the Union forces licked the Confederates in the first skirmish of the war in these parts."

"They regrouped, didn't they?" Jonathan asked, staring up at the twisting trail that rose through brush-covered, rocky slopes and gullies, dotted with scattered piñon pine and junipers. They had been gradually climbing all through the morning, and the air was sharp with pine and juniper scents.

"They did," Jubal said, pushing his hat back on his head and then pulling it back in place. Jonathan had noticed this often-repeated move on Jubal's part whenever he talked about something that caused him uneasiness. "We've got another pass to manage after this one, and a battle was fought here that ended Confederate hopes of hooking onto the California gold fields."

"In '62 wasn't it?" Jonathan asked. "Were you mixed up in that fight?" He kept his question deliberately casual, giving Jubal plenty of room to get away with a simple yes or no. Jubal had never mentioned which side he supported in the war, and Jonathan didn't care to press him.

"No, I fought under General John C. Pemberton."

"Were you at Vicksburg?"

"I was."

"Facing Grant and his seventy thousand men with unlimited support behind them."

"I believe that about says it, and thank the Lord, if He had any part in that war, that it's over."

"Amen," Jonathan said, making no reference to Pemberton's loss of Vicksburg and his finally surrendering of a starving army and the city's civilians to Ulysses S. Grant.

"We're almost at the end of this journey," Jubal said.

"We are," Jonathan responded, happy to put an end to a conversation on a very dangerous subject. The war might be over, but the violent struggle between the adversaries, and the hatred that had burned so high, was still fresh in the minds of men on both sides of the conflict.

"Have you made any plans?" Jonathan

asked as he and Jubal began riding again with the train snaking along behind them. The cattle and the two remudas were well ahead, climbing slowly toward the Borieta Pass under a cloudless sky, with the temperature in the middle seventies.

"Not yet, but every time I've been here, I think of staying. The sun shines most of the time in this country, and it's high enough to keep the temperature livable, especially at night, when you'll want to have a jacket handy. What about you?"

"Like you, I'm partial to this high country. I'm thinking of taking up ranching."

"You could do a lot worse. So far, I've always taken another train back to Missouri, working for one or another of the traders. I'll probably hang around here for a while and see how things go. What are Morgan and the Indian woman going to do?"

"Odd you should ask. I was just thinking of them."

"It ain't none of my business, Colonel, but she ain't likely to get a very favorable reception in Santa Fe."

"I've been told that, but I still don't understand where the trouble lies. Is it because she is an Indian?"

"It's a mite more complicated. You recall what I told you the other day, about the

Genizaros? I know some of their history. They've been part of Santa Fe ever since the Spanish came. Most of them were taken into the homes of the wealthy Spanish and made to work off the cost of their purchase. That usually took twenty to thirty years. The males, on reaching manhood, were sometimes conscripted into the army, and it's said they made good fighters."

"Sounds like the Janissaries, who made up the Turkish army in the days of the Ottoman Empire," Jonathan replied. "They spent their lives as slaves, serving as soldiers."

"In the case of the Genizaros, once they were let go, no one would hire them, and they began settling together, seldom returning to their tribes."

"How does this affect Yellow Leaf?"

Jubal made a sour face. "Colonel, she ain't no spring chicken, but she's a damned fine-looking woman, obviously in good health and not attached to any of the pueblos and not a Comanche. She could disappear, and no one would come looking for her."

"Why the devil not? Who would take her?"

"For a long time in Santa Fe, wealthy Mexicans, Spanish, and a mixed bunch from all over have had their own way by supporting the alcaldes."

"That would be the governors?"

"That's right, which is to say, what law there is. Them and the Church, which looked the other way as long as the money came in. Odd thing is, for some of the time, a Genizaro could complain to the alcalde about how he or she was being treated, and the alcalde would step in and clean up things a little. The populations of several small towns around here are made up almost entirely of Genizaros who have gained their freedom."

"I thought the nation put an end to slavery," Jonathan said. What Jubal had told him raised his ire and upset him in several other ways he didn't bother to explore.

"Santa Fe's a long way from Washington," Jubal said with another sour grin, "and old habits die hard."

"Let's get over this pass and see where our cattle and horses are," Jonathan said, still angry. "Old habits may be running them off."

Having sent Jubal ahead to locate pasturing for the animals, and satisfied with his report, Jonathan slowed the train despite protests and sent Jane, Morgan, and Yellow Leaf, with a dozen armed men from his company, to guard the herders and their charges until the train reached them.

Jane sought him out before leaving her re-muda and asked him to look in on her mother when he could. "She's none too good, Jonathan, as you probably know. If she goes off her feet, Erma's going to have a load on her back, what with the kids and Ma both needing care. I don't see how she can do it and drive the horses."

"It will be all right, Jane," he told her. "I'll take care of it. One of the boys will be glad to earn some money driving for your mother, and I will go by often enough to be sure everything is being done right."

He wasn't happy with Jane's appearance. Her clothes were every which way and none too clean. Her hair was a muddle, and her mare looked as if she hadn't been brushed that morning, something he couldn't recall happening in all the time they had been on the trail. "Are you ill, Jane?" he asked.

She scowled. "What's your complaint? Ain't I working hard enough?"

"Whoa!" Jonathan raised both hands as if to ward off a physical attack.

"I'll just get to work, Doctor. Now I won't be cooking your breakfast any more, it seems that's all I'm good for."

With that remark and a slashing look that, had it been a knife, would have taken his head off, she whirled her mare and thundered off at a gallop, leaving a cloud of dust behind her.

Jonathan would have liked to think a little about that outburst and figure out what to do about it, and possibly feel sorry for himself a little. He didn't get the chance. Bill Johnson and Burchard Harley, drivers still with the train, found him. Their cargoes were going all the way to Santa Fe, whereas many of the other drivers and their wagons had been dropping off in twos and threes to deliver loads to the owners waiting for them in the towns and stations between here and the Raton Pass.

Bill Johnson was a slow speaking man and so lanky that no shirt Jonathan ever saw him wearing had sleeves long enough to cover his wrists. Today was no exception. Jonathan had plenty of height, but standing beside Johnson made him feel like a kid brother. Usually, the sensation made him want to grin, but not today.

"Reckon we'll close in on Santa Fe today, Colonel?" Johnson asked.

"Does it depend on what you two are going to tell me?"

"We've got four steers down," Burchard said. "We figure they got into the Jimson weed."

"Three of mine," Johnson said. "One of Burchard's."

Jonathan took a deep breath. "That makes twenty-three oxen we've lost to bad water, poison weeds, broken legs in gopher holes, and failure to thrive. Can they walk?"

"With some prodding," Burchard said, showing little conviction.

Jonathan turned to Johnson. "Bill, how many does that leave you with?"

"Six."

"Burchard?"

"Five."

"I suggest you chain the two wagons together, and, Burchard, you put three of your oxen into the spaces left by Bill's loss. Then add four more, to make a twelve-ox team. Trail the one left over. Share the bull whacking."

Burchard looked at Johnson. "It should get us into Santa Fe."

"Good as done," the big man said.

They went off discussing how to manage the chaining, and Jonathan mounted Sam and rode to Patience's wagon. There, he found the two women were harnessing and hitching up the mules.

"Hello, Jonathan," Ginger said, smiling brightly. She was working without her bonnet, and her auburn hair drifted over her shoulders in the morning breeze. She finished hitching the off-mule's traces to the evener and stood up, resting a hand on the animal's rump, then stepped out to wipe her hands unselfconsciously on her hips.

"What brings you out here? I hope we're not held up," she said, still smiling.

"No, I'm just stopping to see if you are ready," Jonathan said, thinking how good the young woman looked, how happy.

"Good morning, Jonathan," Patience called, straightening up to look at him over the mules' backs. "Just give me a minute."

She disappeared and then reappeared after coming around the front of the mules' heads, stopping briefly to rub their noses. Jonathan watched the freedom of her walk and the absence of stress in her expression. She smiled as easily as Ginger.

Jonathan set his hat on the pommel of his saddle and leaned forward, bringing himself nearer the two women.

"We're in good order," Patience said, coming to stand beside Ginger, who caught her hand without apparently pausing to think about what she was doing. Jonathan noticed and approved.

"What are your plans once we get to Santa Fe?" he asked, breaking a promise he had made to himself not to ask the question.

His concern for them, however, proved the stronger decider.

"Find a place to live!" they said in unison and laughed together.

"Ask a silly question and get a silly answer," Jonathan said.

"We can't answer more fully," Patience said, much more soberly, "until we have learned what needs doing and how we can make a difference."

A spurt of anger, unexpected, began to elbow out concern. "You mean, don't you, that you intend to find out whether or not there are any Genizaros being kept as unpaid servants?"

"That's the idea," Ginger replied, a bit brassily.

He turned to hear Patience's response before saying more.

She spoke with somber conviction. "Jonathan, we came here to spread the Quaker message that God intended us to love one another, and that enslaving another human being breaks God's intention for us to live together in love and harmony. It is our responsibility to expose slavery and anything by any name that holds people in bondage."

He adjusted his hat and revised the first thing he found himself wanting to say, which might have led to his being stoned.

"An admirable objective, no doubt," he said instead. "As I remember, we fought a war over the issue. The thing is, although there were a couple of skirmishes between Union and Confederate forces here, the issues that separated North and South in the war had little or no significance among the population of Santa Fe."

"What are you getting at?" Ginger asked.

He thought about Jubal's local history lesson. "They're Americans here in name only. They've been under first Spanish and then Mexican rule since the sixteenth century. The people in power here have been doing things the way they wanted for a long, long time. They are not accustomed to being told they need to make changes. Their solution to opposition has been to eradicate it."

Ginger's face flushed, a sign of a storm rising. Patience tightened her grip on Ginger's hand to stop the younger woman from speaking. "We appreciate your concern, Jonathan, and we don't doubt what you have told us is true, but we have no intention of barging into the citizens' houses demanding they change their ways, nor will we march in the main street, carrying a banner with *FREE YOUR GENIZAROS* stitched on it. We intend to move very slowly and carefully, studying the existing situation thoroughly. Only when we see a way to approach things gently and rationally will we act."

"Honey attracts more bees than vinegar," Ginger added.

Jonathan saw he was going to lose the argument. "Very well," he said, readjusting his hat, "though if we're passing out homilies, here's one: 'Fools rush in where angels fear to tread.' "

Patience merely smiled. "Are you still thinking of buying a ranch?"

"I know you're not fools," Jonathan said, "but I do think you're naïve, a state of affairs that can put you in harm's way just as quickly."

"We will be careful," Patience replied. "Now, about that ranch."

"Perhaps. You sure you wouldn't do better opening a school? The two of you —"

"Jonathan," Patience said, frowning.

"All right, I'll stop. Goodbye."

He rode away convinced that no good would come of their plans, and just as convinced there was nothing he could do about it except try to keep track of what they were up to.

CHAPTER 28

The sun was just poking its head above the mountains as the train creaked and bumped its way into the Santa Fe Plaza to the shouts and cracking whips of the bull whackers, amid a pale cloud of dust. Its arrival was observed calmly by a line of Indian women already sitting cross-legged on the floor of an open-fronted shed attached to the low, gray, single-level adobe government offices for the town and surrounding pueblos and villages, their corn, peanuts, and chilies piled in front of them.

Yellow Leaf caught up with Jonathan just as he was bringing the much-shortened train to a halt.

"Animals are with water and grass," she said, throwing a leg over her mare's withers. "Cannot stay there more than two suns."

"Thin grazing?" he asked, looking into her sparkling black eyes and thinking that in her weathered leggings, fringed jacket, and red bandanna rolled and tied around her head, her black hair floating around her shoulders, she looked as beautiful as if she wore a silk gown.

"Yes. What you want me to do?"

"Get Jane and bring her in with you. Tell Morgan to keep the Smithins boys with him and that I'll send the Harley brothers as soon as I can. Also say I'll be out as soon as I finish my business with Preston Miles at the freight company."

"Where we find you?"

"Stay with Eli's wagon. I'll find you."

"Never learn," she said, shaking her head. She touched her heels to her pony and rode away.

"Never use the name of the dead," he finished for her, but she didn't hear him.

For the next hour, Jonathan was very busy, his first task being to find the Santa Fe Freight Company office and its owner, Preston Miles.

The office had its own squat, stucco building, shaded by aspens and located on a stretch with a land office on one side, a livestock dealer across the way, and a livery stable at the end of the street. Miles was a tall man with a bald crown and long black sideburns stretching down his square jaw. He wore pressed trousers, tooled boots with a rider's high heels, and a leather vest with a gold watch chain across it.

"You must be Wainwright" were his first words, talking around the cheroot stuck in his mouth. "What the hell happened to old Eli? Your note the stage driver gave me said only that you'd buried him and taken his place."

Jonathan didn't like the man's looks or the sneer in his drawl. Since Miles gave no indication that he wanted to shake hands, Jonathan remained standing just inside the door, the leather satchel holding all the train's paperwork hanging from his left shoulder, leaving his right hand free.

"Heart failure. I gave him what care I could, but it wasn't enough."

"You a doctor?" Miles asked, showing some surprise.

"I was, before the war. Then I became a colonel in the Union Army and rode with General Philip Sheridan from the Shenandoah Campaign to Appomattox."

"Another Yankee," Miles said, bringing laughter from the three men working at desks behind him.

"Were you in the war, Mr. Miles?"

"I was," Miles replied, losing his sneer.

"It's best we put it behind us, wouldn't you say?"

Miles apparently mistook Jonathan's olive branch for cowardice. "I shot every Yankee I came across during the war, and I only regret I can't keep up the good work."

There was more laughter, until Jonathan said, loudly enough for the whole room to hear, "You might be able to shoot the one in front of you if you wish to arm yourself and try."

The room went silent.

"Ah! Gentlemen!" Miles turned slowly toward the desks. "Have you heard the man? He has challenged me."

Yet more laughter. Miles spun back suddenly with a derringer in his hand. Jonathan shot him in the right shoulder. Miles screamed, staggered, and sank to his knees as his derringer skidded across the wood floor. He fainted and crashed down, blood soaking his shirt and leather vest and beginning to puddle under him.

"Perhaps one of you gentlemen would fetch a doctor," Jonathan said, watching the three desk sitters closely as he holstered his gun. He supposed he ought to feel regret — *the first thing I do here is shoot a man* — but instead he felt oddly calm. "I will do what I can to stop the bleeding, but he'll need more help than that."

One of the men dashed out of the office.

Jonathan addressed the younger of the two remaining. "Run to the bar on the corner and bring back a pitcher of whiskey. Tell the bartender Mr. Miles needs it in a hurry." Pointing at the third man, a red-haired fellow, he said, "Come over here and help me get his vest and shirt off."

"Why are you doing this?" the man asked, a stunned look on his face as he came around his desk.

"I had in mind keeping him from bleeding out," Jonathan snapped. "Are you going to help or not?"

The red-haired man broke out of his shock enough to kneel down beside Jonathan, and he held up Miles's shoulders while Jonathan pulled off the vest and tore open the shirt. Jonathan peeled the fabric away from the wound, balled up the rest, and pressed it against the bloody bullet hole.

"Ease him down," he said.

The first man came running back into the office, gasping for breath. "Doc . . . ain't . . . in . . . town."

Damn. "The wagons are in the plaza," Jonathan said. "Get up there as fast as you can. You'll find two women in the first wagon or near it. Tell them to get here with my black bag, ether and chloroform, and cloth for bandages. Can you remember that?"

"I think so."

"Repeat what I said."

The man was in no shape to remember anything.

"Paper and a pencil," Jonathan said.

The man scrambled to his feet and brought them.

"Write it down: 'Black bag, ether, chloroform, bandages. Come as fast as you can.' Go!"

In the next few minutes, Jonathan managed to get the red-haired man to hold the blood-soaked shirt against Miles's wound while he went to the front windows of the office and pulled down one of the tan-colored drapes, which weren't as dust laden as they might have been. He set to work tearing them into squares. He hadn't worked long when his assistant said in a weak voice, "This here shirt cain't hold no more blood, and it's running over my . . ."

He fainted before finishing his sentence and pitched headfirst over Miles, who had begun to stir and groan. Swearing quietly, Jonathan grasped a handful of the torn drapes and strode back to Miles and the unconscious redhead. Grasping the man by the collar, he dragged him off Miles and clamped one of the folded cloth squares against Miles's shoulder, thinking that if the bullet hadn't killed him, whatever was in the drape might.

Ginger burst into the room, carrying Jonathan's bag. "Thank heaven! The idiot you sent left us thinking it was you who'd been shot!"

She probably would have said more, her green eyes big as marbles, but Patience caught up with her, laden with the things Jonathan had sent for. "Give him the bag," Patience said, giving her a push. "Is the bullet in him?"

Patience knelt beside Jonathan, piling the things in her arms in an arc around them for easy reach.

Miles suddenly opened his eyes. He started to sit up but slumped back, yelling in pain.

"Ether," Jonathan said.

The youngest of Miles's men ran into the office holding a bottle of whiskey in each fist. "Who's drinking this?" he asked, thrusting the bottles at Jonathan.

"Nobody. It's going into our friend's wound." He grasped one of the bottles, uncorked it, and splashed whiskey over the injury. The wound bubbled. Miles's eyes shot open, and he tried to sit up, yelling.

"Get down here," Jonathan said to the man still holding the second bottle of whiskey. "You're going to sit on his chest. I'll hold his arms while the women administer the ether. Move!"

And that was how they knocked Miles out, giving Jonathan time to halt the bleeding and extract the bullet. With Ginger and Patience's help, he closed the wound and wrapped the man's shoulder in bandages. The three of them had washed their hands in the whiskey before starting, and the room reeked of it. They used the second bottle to wash the blood off their hands and wrists. The floor looked as if a pig had been slaughtered there.

While he, Patience, and Ginger were cleaning up, Jonathan asked, "Is there an undertaker in town, and a hospital?"

The red-haired man said there was.

"Get the undertaker over here and hope he's not burying someone. Tell him we need his hearse to move Miles to the hospital."

"Who's going to pay him?" the redhead asked. "He's tighter than the paper on the wall."

"Tell him the Santa Fe Freight Company will foot the bill." He turned to the older of the men still standing. "I have papers from the train along with records of the wagons that stopped before getting here and what they were carrying."

"I can handle that," the fellow said, extending his hand. "The name's Burke, Samuel Burke. Preston Miles got what was coming to him, and we'll testify to it, but you may have made a mistake in saving his life. He runs with a bunch of hard cases here in Santa Fe, led by Lawrence Murphy and Emil Fritz. Murphy owns L. G. Murphy and Company. He and Fritz call it a land business, but their bunch, made up of lawyers and businessmen, are crooked as a corkscrew. They specialize in selling land they don't own to farmers and ranchers, and later on forcing them off it and claiming all the stock, buildings, and improvements. Miles and Murphy and them are likely to come after you — that is, if you're planning to stay."

Jonathan found the man's seriousness both welcome and amusing.

"I spent several years being chased by the Confederate Army," he said, shaking Burke's hand. "I'm accustomed to it."

When Jonathan had seen the still-sedated Miles off to the hospital and finished his work with Burke, he was pleasantly surprised when Burke said he would see that

Eli's wages would be paid for the time he had led the train. "And if you decide you want to take up being a wagon master, we have a place for you."

"I doubt your boss will be pleased with that hire," Jonathan said.

"Miles is, or was, a manager of the company. I'm the owner. From now on, we will not be seeing much of Mr. Miles around here."

"Thank you for the offer, but I have ranching in mind. Is there anyone selling land in Santa Fe I *can* trust?"

Burke gave a broad smile. "Yes, Horace Grover and I have some land looking for a buyer. In fact, we have a ranch the owner recently put in our hands to sell for him. It's fair sized, thirty-nine thousand acres, fifty percent farmland."

"What crops are usually grown?"

Burke though a minute, stroking his mustache to help the process along. "The Indians have been raising beans, squash, and corn for as long as they've been here, I guess," he said. "On the more arable land, there's sorghum, upland cotton, chili peppers, onions, pecans, and, of course, hay."

"And cattle?" Jonathan added.

"And cattle. There's even some dairy cows kept for their milk, but it's hot here summers, and there's no use having much extra milk on hand."

"Well, Mr. Burke, after I get some other business taken care of, perhaps we'll have more conversations about this ranch and even have a look at it," Jonathan said. "But how do you account for no lawman turning up here after the shooting — or will I be seeing him later?"

"Call me Sam. We don't have a sheriff or marshal. What we've got is the governor's office, and there's a company of Union soldiers posted close by, but that's mostly for Indian trouble. Your trouble is more likely to come from the Ring crowd — Murphy and those fellas I told you about — than anywhere else. Watch your back."

"I'll do that," Jonathan said.

Before leaving Burke, Jonathan got the name and location of the rancher who handled Burke's livestock. By dark, and with the help of Jubal, Morgan, Yellow Leaf, Jane, and her young men, Jonathan had the re- mudas and the cattle in the rancher's pastures. In the meantime, the wagons, halted in the plaza, were dispersed to their various owners. Burke had sent one of his men to collect Eli's wagon, having told Jonathan to come along whenever he was ready and take whatever he wanted from it.

Patience and Ginger made arrangements with the boardinghouse and livery stable they had chosen to accommodate them, their wagon, and their mules.

Morgan and Yellow Leaf had gone off somewhere, and Jonathan settled his nagging anxiety about the Osage woman with the thought that Morgan would keep her safe from any trouble. He wondered where Jane was, then told himself not to be ridiculous. *She'll be with her family. She doesn't need me.*

He'd loaded his worldly belongings into leather packs, now on Sam and Chew. Jubal had done the same with his horses.

"I could use a bath and a steak and a glass of whiskey," Jubal told Jonathan as they swung the pasture gate shut. "What about you?"

"Sounds about right," Jonathan answered, "but I want a room first."

"The Red Steer Saloon has rooms. I believe I'll throw down there," Jubal said. "It might be a mite noisy, but I can eat, drink, and sleep right in the same place."

"You plan to be here long?" Jonathan asked.

"Probably until my money runs out. Then I'll cast around for a train going north." Jubal swung into his saddle.

"Good luck, Jubal." Jonathan reached up to shake the man's hand. "Thanks for the help these last weeks."

"My pleasure. I hope you find that ranch you been thinking about."

Jonathan watched the man ride off and then walked his horses out of the plaza.

"For a clean bed and good food," Burke had told him, "go out of the plaza past the adobe church. If you have to ask where it is, ask for *La Parroquia,* and you will soon find it. There's been a Catholic church there for a hundred years or more, and the word is there's going to be a big new one built . . . St. Francis Cathedral. No more adobe church."

"Is there opposition?" Jonathan asked, somewhat surprised.

"Some. People here don't much like change, especially in the pueblos, but building a cathedral will put a lot of people to work."

Jonathan found the church with no difficulty and his inn on a rise of land soon after. The inn had a dining room with half a dozen tables, and a small livery stable attached. The inn was run by the Aguadosses, Bruno and Eliana and their five children aged six to sixteen, three girls and two boys. The family made up the staff, save for the man in the stables. Once Sam and Chew were rubbed down, fed, and watered, Jonathan accompanied his luggage, carried by the two boys, to his rooms. He had fallen a bit behind them and started to run up the stairs to catch up, only to find after the third leap that he was out of breath and had to stop for a few seconds before walking the rest of the way.

"We live up high," the younger of the two boys, tall and gangling, said with a grin. "Air is thin. If you stay, by and by you will be better. Where do you want your things to go?"

"Leave them on this bed," Jonathan said, struggling not to pant.

He had rented two adjoining rooms with clean, cream-colored walls and sizeable windows looking out over the town and the Santa Fe Mountains, a part of the Sangre de Cristo range. Because he expected to be living there several weeks, he had the bed removed from one of the rooms and a writing desk, a table, two straight-backed chairs, and a reading chair and lamp stand installed beside the wood-burning fireplace, a job that brought out the whole family, even the six-year-old girl, who carried in the pillows for the bed and the cushions for the reading chair.

Once everything was arranged and his bed made up to Mrs. Aguadoss's satisfaction, she turned to him and said, "You are happy?"

Jonathan had seen at once that she was the organizing element in the family. She was tall for a Mexican woman and had a beautiful complexion and a well-kept figure that, despite the streaks of white in her long black hair, made her look more like her oldest daughter than a woman in her forties.

"I am, thanks to you and your fine family," Jonathan said.

"Muchas graçias, Señor," she said, coloring slightly. "We will eat at the sixth hour."

She snapped her thumb and finger and pointed at the door, and her husband and children filed out. She followed them but paused in the doorway to say, "At first, here, one tires soon. Perhaps you will rest."

"Yes, I think I will," Jonathan said, amused by her words. He suspected she had given him an order rather than asked a question.

There were further surprises in store for him. When he came downstairs to dinner, the eight-year-old son met him at the foot of the stairs and thrust out a hand. "I am Fedro."

"Hello, Fedro," Jonathan said. "I'm glad to meet you. I'm Jonathan."

"*Madre* says I am to call you Mr. Wainwright," the boy said seriously.

"That will be fine." Jonathan gave the boy's hand a good shake.

"She also says I am not to . . ." He paused, frowning, and finished more slowly. "Indulge in frivolous talk." He beamed at having gotten through it.

"Well done," Jonathan said, smiling. "If we can't indulge in frivolous conversation, what shall we do?"

"I'm to take you in to dinner and show you to your place."

"Lead on."

CHAPTER 29

There were two men and a middle-aged woman, the latter wearing *pince nez* glasses low on her nose, already seated when Jonathan entered the room. Mrs. Aguadoss took over the introductions, beginning with the woman — Miss Abigail Whitcomb, headmistress of Hollingworth Academy, a school for girls. Though Jonathan put on his best manners, Miss Whitcomb seemed unimpressed by either his Boston origins or his recent stint as a wagon master, remarking unfavorably on "a man of your social standing leading a wagon train on the Santa Fe Trail."

The two men were the Wiseman brothers from Philadelphia. They were in their fifties, enough alike to be twins — the same double chins, round bellies, heavy black eyebrows, and bald heads. They frequently completed one another's sentences, though they were not especially talkative. They had opened a clothing store in Albuquerque and were now opening a second in Santa Fe. When dinner was served, they stopped talking altogether and ate without looking up from their plates.

It did not cross Jonathan's mind until he sat down that it was the first time in many, many weeks that he was sitting at a table to eat, instead of sitting cross-legged beside a fire, an ant hill, or a large rock. He had a moment of unease, worrying that he might have forgotten how this ritual unfolded and what was expected of him.

The grace, said by Mr. Aguadoss in Spanish and ending with the family crossing themselves, gave Jonathan time to study the way the forks and knives and spoons were laid out, and, since there was only one of each, his appetite returned. He regained confidence and began to enjoy the experience.

The bed, when he reached it a couple of hours later, presented a more formidable challenge, made worse by his initial eager anticipation. He clambered into the bed, pulled the covers up and, because he had been awake since before dawn, hoped to sleep until morning. It didn't work out that way, at least for the first half hour. His bed was fitted with a cornhusk mattress, which, while a bit noisy, was soft and comfortable. The sheet and blanket were welcome because the temperature had gone down with the sun, and Mrs. Aguadoss had opened one of the windows, bringing a distinct chill into the room.

Jonathan had dug out his nightshirt earlier and had looked forward to wearing it at his first opportunity. The moment had come, and he slid it over his head and eased himself into bed with great expectations. He did not expect visions of sugarplums to dance in his head, but he was looking forward to a good night's sleep.

To his surprise, once in bed with the covers up under his ears, he began to feel uncomfortable. He sat up and punched his pillow, shook the sheet and blanket, and settled back, only to find that his nightshirt had worked its way up to his waist, compelling him to get out of bed and push it down before clambering back in for a third start.

Things did not improve. Despite the comfort surrounding him, he found he was uncomfortable. With the lamp out, the room gave him a choky feeling, added to the sensation that the sheet and blanket were stifling his movements. He rolled over and tested another position, to no avail.

For the past several weeks he had slept on the hard earth with his head on Sam's saddle. After another half hour of struggle,

Jonathan threw off his covers, pulled his nightshirt off over his head and tossed it onto the bed, and put on his underwear. Next, he stripped the blanket off the bed, unfolded the spare blanket and spread it on the floor under the window, laid down his boots for a pillow, and stretched out. As he pulled the blanket over him, he looked up and through the window saw a patch of sky, sprinkled with stars. Within minutes he was asleep.

Pounding footsteps in the hall woke him. He sat up, yawning in the morning light, pulling the blanket around his shoulders as Mrs. Aguadoss burst into the room. His face flushed as he realized his bare legs were sticking out, and he wondered at the relief that flooded her face.

"You couldn't sleep in the bed, I see," she said, ignoring his attempts to cover his legs as she picked up a mug of tea someone had left and brought it to him. "And you wanted to see the sky," she added, passing him the mug, which was still steaming. She reached over him and closed the window.

"I hope I haven't caused you any trouble," Jonathan said, now wearing his blanket like a toga.

"No, but my daughter Rosa will be disappointed. It was she who brought your tea.

She told me you had been murdered in your bed and dragged to the window. There was no blood, she said, so you must have been choked to death."

The corners of her mouth twitched, and her eyes were dancing. She and Jonathan burst out laughing together.

For the next week, Jonathan familiarized himself with the town and the surrounding areas half an hour's ride from the plaza. He also spent several hours with Samuel Burke, looking at the ranch he had mentioned, its deeds, buildings, and its land and water. There were two wells close to the sprawling adobe house and wood-framed barns and a small creek in the highest part of the ranch, emanating from a spring that, Burke assured him, ran the year around at the same rate. The spring came out of a fissure in a ledge, thrusting up in a dense stand of pine and spruce that, left uncut, suggested permanence.

"I don't know why it hasn't been done before," Burke said as he and Jonathan stood in a grassy opening below the spring. "A water tank could be located right here and enough of the water diverted to keep the tank permanently filled. The excess water could be shipped back to the creek through there." He pointed to their left where a grassy dip in the ground led to the bubbling water.

"What about winter?" Jonathan asked.

"It gets a mite chilly," Burke admitted. "But the spring runs under the ice. We don't get a lot of snow here. Up there, it's different."

Jonathan followed Burke's gaze to the top of the mountain above them, and to the northeast at the peaks several miles away. "Does this mountain have a name?" he asked.

"Not that I know of," Burke said. "We've got too many of them, and this one's not tall enough."

"What is the altitude in Santa Fe?"

"Around seven thousand feet, making for hot summers and cold winters but not much rain or snow. As you can see around us, however, there's a lot of green growth and good grazing."

Looking back and down to the farm buildings below them, half a mile away, Jonathan saw mostly grass, dotted with piñon pine, a scattering of juniper, and occasional granite outcroppings. All in all, he thought, a fine pasturage that reminded him of Maine and New Hampshire, where, as a boy, he had spent several summers.

"Indian women from the pueblo will come through in the early fall," Burke said, breaking into Jonathan's brief reverie. "If you let them, they'll gather piñon nuts." Burke paused, then added, "They been doing that since time began, I guess."

"There's a lot of history here," Jonathan agreed.

"True, and much of it bloody. Still is, unfortunately."

Nevertheless, as Jonathan stood looking over the ranch spread out below him and imagined the Indian women walking among the piñon pines — all bearing a close resemblance to Yellow Leaf — something moved inside him. He felt himself living here with no self-dread, simply him and horses and cattle on the land around him, and Sam and Chew in the home corral.

Watching him, Burke said, "Dr. Wainwright, has the elevation sickness caught up with you?"

"No, Mr. Burke. I have not felt this well in a very long time, and you have a buyer."

Burke nodded but looked grave. "I would not sleep through the night if I did not tell you that Preston Miles is out of the hospital and has rallied the Santa Fe Ring. They are coming after you."

He'd expected that. "How many are we

talking about?"

"Six or eight, at least. It's how they operate. They'll send hardened men from their ranches. Men who were raiders along the Santa Fe Trail until the Ring hired them as enforcers. Nobody, not even the governor, has been able to control them."

"Have you any idea when?"

"If they follow their usual practice, they'll wait until you've stocked the place. Then they'll come, kill you and all the hands, and claim the ranch under some invention of money being owed."

He should have been afraid, or angry. Instead, resolve settled inside him. "How soon can you have the deed ready for me?" Jonathan asked.

"If you plan to make the purchase, against my advice, I can bring them to you this afternoon. The deed will take twenty-four hours."

"How long do the Planfords need to vacate?"

"They're already gone. The place is empty. How do you plan to pay?"

"The money is in the First National Bank. You will have it when you hand me the deed."

"Excellent," Burke said, with a warm smile. "You may as well have these." He reached into a pocket and passed Jonathan a heavy set of keys.

Jonathan took them and shook Burke's hand. "Draw up the papers. When they're ready, leave word with Mrs. Aguadoss."

"You're a brave man, Doctor," Burke said, retrieving his hand. "I'm not sure you're a wise one."

That night, Jonathan told Mrs. Aguadoss that he would be leaving at the end of the week if his plans worked out as expected, but he would like to hold onto the rooms for an additional week regardless. He had made a note of the inn Jubal had chosen, and, the following morning, he found Jubal in the inn's dining room, which was part of the bar, adding whiskey to the smells of breakfasts being fried. Once seated with a mug of coffee, Jonathan told the Texan he had bought a ranch and needed a foreman.

"Are you interested?" he asked.

Jubal studied the remains of his steak and eggs, then looked up. "I'm your man."

"Something comes with the job you might want to think about."

"That is?"

"The chance of being shot." Jonathan gave Jubal a quick description of what Burke had told him about Preston Miles and the Santa Fe Ring.

"How many men do you figure you're going to need to run that spread you're buying?" Jubal asked.

"Well, there's about forty-five thousand acres of upland grazing to stock, and I'm thinking of beginning with fifty acres of lower arable land, in upland cotton, chili peppers, and corn and another fifty or thereabouts in sorghum. So, I'll need some fencing. Then, if things go well, I want to run beef cattle and breed horses. I'm wondering how many of our *posse comitatus* are still in town or nearby. Add in Yellow Leaf and Morgan, and Jane Howard." The final name gave him pause even as he said it, but Jane had handled herself in plenty of danger on the trail . . . and he found he missed her, and Yellow Leaf, more than he cared to admit.

"Sounds like you'll need about ten or a dozen men," Jubal said. "You know, there's still a fair number of men from the train drifting around town. I've seen a few in the bar. If you want, I'll round up as many as I can. What have you got in mind for Jane Howard, Yellow Leaf, and Morgan? By the way, he's as good a man with horses as you're likely to find, and those two women are better than three average men because they work like men and can both cook."

He paused to laugh, then said, "As I recall, for a while there was a lot of talk on the train about you and Patience Stockbridge, until the Stearns girl moved in with her. Then they began pairing you up with Jane and Yellow Leaf, one or both."

"Jane was planning to marry Eli, and Yellow Leaf has Morgan to look after." Jonathan was anxious to drop that topic. "But this place will need someone who knows horses, and someone to take the ranch house in hand as well as the bunkhouse and the men's meals. And then there's going to be gardens and sheep, milk cows, pigs, and chickens to look after."

"Well," Jubal said, grinning, "looks like we'll have Jane, Yellow Leaf, and Morgan back with us after all."

"Maybe," Jonathan said, trying not to grin himself. "I was told the Ring usually waits until the property is developed before striking, but I don't think Miles will wait. I'd give us two weeks at the most to get those people back together and start planning how we're going to deal with the Ring when their guns come."

"I'll start now."

"Shall we discuss wages, Jubal?"

"I'm glad to be working with you, Colonel. We can settle the wages later. Right now, we've got our work cut out for us, and I'm glad of it. Shall I meet you at your boarding-house?"

"First thing in the morning. I'm lucky to have you with me, Jubal," Jonathan replied, shaking his new foreman's hand. "If you can find Bill Johnson and hire him, keep him with you. Wear your guns and watch your backs."

His years in the Union cavalry had conditioned Jonathan not to dwell on those he had killed or wounded, but in the case of Preston Miles he was surprised to find himself thinking at odd moments about the shooting. He felt no remorse for what he had done but was pleasantly surprised to feel relieved he had not killed Miles, a response completely new to him.

He experienced another change almost instantly after buying the ranch. It was a burst of something akin to joy, added to by his decision to offer work to Jane and Yellow Leaf, Morgan, Bill Johnson, the Harley brothers, Jacob Drew, and the rest of the men from the wagon train that Jubal was setting out to find and, hopefully, hire.

Alone this time, Jonathan returned to the ranch in the late afternoon and rode Sam up the rising land behind the house, with the early purple shadows on the small valleys and ravines, drawn out of the rugged landscape by the sinking sun. While Sam grazed, he leaned an arm on the pommel and let the sound of the wind, the shapes and smells of the earth, the glimmer of the mountains soak into him.

His mind, drifting over this new place, plucked a memory from his childhood: *I will lift up mine eyes unto the hills, from whence cometh my help . . .*

He focused for a moment on the highest of the peaks, reflecting a pale, pinkish glow in the late afternoon sunshine. "How wonderful it would be," he murmured as he tightened the reins and turned Sam toward the ranch house.

There was no bitterness in his thought, only a kind of peace, as if he half believed he had finally found the right hills.

Chapter 30

Yellow Leaf found him without Jubal's help. He came out of the boardinghouse the third morning just as the sun was burning the last of the gray mist off the mountains. She was sitting on her pinto as he had so often seen her sit, her left leg over the pony's withers, an elbow resting on her knee, watching him walk toward her as if he were a complete stranger.

"Morgan in bar," she said. "No money to get him out."

"Why can't he get out?" Jonathan asked, knowing any greeting would be ignored.

"Maybe too drunk. No money. I went, but man in bar tell me 'not let no fucking squaw in.' "

"I'll get Sam," Jonathan said.

On the way to the bar, Jonathan managed to drag out of Yellow Leaf that Morgan had not been able to find any work. Also, that if he took a drink, it led to a second, and so on.

"Never see him drink before," she said. "Lost all money gambling."

In the distant past, the bar's name had been painted on a plank that now hung, one end lower than the other, over the doorway. Enough letters were still legible enough to make out the weather-worn words Riverside Tavern. The building was a two-story shanty on the dusty edge of town with no river in sight, and the only rooms to let were those where the whores conducted their business. Jonathan pushed through its bat-wing doors and saw a large man with a patch over one eye, wearing a white apron and polishing glasses behind the bar, facing four bleary-eyed men with beer mugs in front of them who were clearly beginning their day.

"You got something on your mind?" The barman fixed his eye on Jonathan, who lingered at the door, studying the room.

"Are you holding a man who can't pay his bar bill?"

"What if I am?" The bartender put down the glass he was polishing, and his other hand dropped out of sight.

"Bring your hand back up empty," Jonathan said, "and I'll pay the fellow's bar bill and take him away with no trouble. That

433

hand comes up with anything in it, I'll shoot you and find the man myself."

The hand came up empty.

"Now you and I will find him with you walking in front of me," Jonathan said.

Morgan was passed out on the floor of a locked storeroom, an empty whiskey bottle on its side near his head. "Pick him up," Jonathan said.

"I'll need fifty dollars for whiskey and the room," the man growled, turning his one-eyed scowl on Jonathan.

Having noted the man's long, heavily-muscled arms, Jonathan stayed well back from him. "Twenty-five dollars," Jonathan said, "and you will carry him out of the saloon."

"Like hell," the man said.

"It's that or I shoot you in the leg and you get no money."

The men at the bar watched in silence as the little procession passed them on its way to the door, with Morgan over the bartender's shoulder and Jonathan following.

"Lay him over the pinto's withers," Jonathan said once they got outside.

Yellow Leaf was standing at her pony's head and grasped the bridge of its nose to steady the animal while Morgan's limp body was being flopped over it.

Jonathan mounted Sam. Yellow Leaf was already back on the paint. "Your twenty-five dollars is on the floor, just inside the doors," Jonathan said.

Without further conversation, she and Jonathan rode away at a quick trot, Morgan hanging over the pinto's sides, limp as a rope. Assuming Yellow Leaf had no place to take him, Jonathan took advantage of the moment to ask her if she and Morgan would be willing to work for him.

"Do what?" she asked, her eyes widening slightly. For her, that counted as a display of vast surprise at the question.

"Help me run my ranch."

"You want hire one drunk and one fucking squaw?"

Jonathan saw he had walked onto thin ice and scrambled for a second try. "Morgan is the best horse man I'm likely to find," he said. "He may be drunk, but he'll sober up. He didn't drink the whole time he was on the train."

Yellow Leaf was silent for a few minutes, and Jonathan gave her time to work through whatever she was thinking.

"If he work," she said finally, "he not drink."

"I think you're right," Jonathan said. "Will he work for me?"

"Working horses?"

"Of course. Now, will Yellow Leaf do me the honor of working for me?"

She frowned, looking confused. "What is *honor*? I never do that."

"It means, I would be very glad and thank you if you would help me run the farm. You are a very brave and smart woman. I would be honored to have you work with me."

She gave him that penetrating gaze of hers that seemed to go right through him and stirred the hair on the back of his neck. "Jonathan Wainwright, I would go to edge of world with you. Yes, I will work for you and, if you want, with you."

"That's settled, and I am very pleased," he said quietly. "Now, let's get Morgan to the hospital. He is going to be very sick when he wakes up. Then I will take you to the ranch."

At the hospital, Yellow Leaf refused to enter the building. "These ones not want someone in there . . . or anywhere else. Bad place," she told Jonathan as he shouldered Morgan. "Sit out here. You see Jane Howard yet?"

"No," Jonathan said. "Do you know where she and her family are?"

"Maybe not tell. Keep you for myself."

Jonathan smiled as he carried Morgan into

the building, thinking how good it was to have Yellow Leaf near him again.

Within a week Jubal had rounded up all the men he had chosen, and no one had turned him down. He also found Jane, working behind the bar in the Rio Grande Hotel's dining room, but she had turned his offer of work down so hard, he had spun on his heel and walked out, deciding Jonathan didn't need to hear that story.

The story leaked out, however, and Yellow Leaf heard it from Morgan, now dry and repentant, who had heard it in the hospital from one of their ox team drivers, wounded in a knife fight during a card game. Having thought about it a while, Yellow Leaf waited until she had an opportunity to talk to Jonathan the first time she caught him alone.

It was not easy, for the first week was busy. As Jubal led the men onto the ranch or they found their own way there and work began on raising the bunkhouse, most of the cooking for everyone was done outdoors over open fires, under the direction of Yellow Leaf. Every morning at daylight, Bill Johnson and Burchard Harley rode out with a pack horse to hunt for mule deer, the day's meat, and, early in the week Jacob Drew and Merced Kinsell, driving Eli Parker's wagon, had bargained with the nearby pueblos and returned, the wagon heaped with corn, onions, potatoes, squash, and long bunches of green and red chilies. The remainder of the week, the wagon traveled frequently from stores in town to sawmills north of them and back to the ranch, transporting lumber and all the things needed for the building going forward.

Within ten days, the constant sawing and hammering tapered off, and Jubal declared the bunkhouse and four-hole outhouse finished . . . the latter firmly settled in a scattered stand of piñon pine and juniper. All that was needed were beds and stoves for the living quarters and tables, benches, and the biggest cookstove Jonathan could buy for what Jacob Drew called the grub house, a name that stuck.

The next day, Yellow Leaf caught Jonathan returning from the christening of the back house — the ceremony achieved by sprinkling whiskey over the seats, then passing the bottle around and giving everyone a swallow. The bottle was buried outside the swinging door.

"We will talk," she said, leading him to the cooking fires sunk in the ground, where she was roasting the hindquarters of a mule deer on two large iron spits. The air was filled with the mouth-watering odor of venison roasting over red-hot coals.

"Turn this spit," she told him. "I will do the other. Then we talk."

"Anyone who can smell this without wanting to eat is tired of living," Jonathan said. He managed to turn the spit without getting burned by the crackling fire or the hissing and popping juice dripping into the glowing coals.

Yellow Leaf turned to face him but avoided his gaze. "I have not told truth about Jane Howard."

He felt his heart turn over. "Yellow Leaf," he said, "has something happened to her?"

"Maybe." She straightened her back and looked him in the eye. "She work in bar at Rio Grande Hotel. She bark at Jubal Smith when he offer her job. He think, better not say anything more about her."

Jonathan's first response was white-hot anger, but he squelched that, realizing Jane must have said something about him that Jubal did not want to repeat. Erasing the anger left him with a sudden and profoundly painful sense of loss. "Is she safe there?"

"Not know. Jubal say not bad as saloon."

"This is my fault," he said, adding guilt to

439

loss. "I left her to look after herself and her family."

Yellow Leaf studied his face. "Go talk. Someone can't go. Fucking squaw."

Jonathan closed the space between them and put his arms around her. "Yellow Leaf, you are a woman of honor, an intelligent and a remarkably courageous one. I am proud to call you my friend."

For a brief moment she rested her forehead against his shoulder, then stepped out of his embrace. "I will not say it anymore," she told him. "I think you and I not white man and Indian woman. I don't know how it happen, but we are one man and one woman."

"Yes, I think you are right, as you almost always are." He paused for a moment. "I am reluctant to go to see Jane. I think it's pretty clear she doesn't want to see me."

"Turn that spit," she told him, "and listen. If you do not talk to her, you will hurt both of you."

He turned the spit, planning to tell her he had made up his mind that Jane was better off without him but was called off to deal with a problem the team had in laying out the new barn and corral. He was briefly glad of the excuse, but it didn't last, and not even the work eased the upwelling of a dull,

440

persisting sadness that soon began to settle over him, causing him to think Yellow Leaf's warning may have been on target.

The following day, clouds came up with the sun and burst over the mountains, giving them a rare shower. The work went forward, but it was a cold rain that vanished into the dry earth, kicking up tiny puffs of dust as it fell. Dark herds of scudding, wind-driven clouds blocked the sun periodically, spat out their cold drops, and, in general, soured everyone's satisfaction with life.

In the late afternoon, the rain ceased, and the sun managed to peek over the last of a tumble of purple clouds before vanishing from sight and ushering in bad news. Jonathan, Duncan Harley, his brother Burchard, and Jacob Drew had just driven the fourth and final stake, finishing the task of squaring the foundation for the barn, when Jubal arrived at a gallop.

"I signed on Orrington Rowe and Isaac True," he told Jonathan hurriedly, dropping down from his saddle. "They're the last of the posse that ain't headed north again on the trail. That's the good news. I picked up some bad news looking for Rowe and True, though. There's been a meeting of the Ring. Miles is coming after you, and he won't be coming alone."

"Round up the men and take them to the bunkhouse," Jonathan told him. "Jacob, get Yellow Leaf and bring her to the bunkhouse as well."

The bunkhouse smelled of newly cut pine lumber, and the men's boots rang loudly on the freshly laid floor, their raised voices seeming to bounce off the bare walls. Jonathan waited to speak until everyone had assembled. "Here's what we know: Miles is coming, but we don't know when," he told them. "From right now, I want all of you to strap on your sidearms and carry your rifle with you all the time you're out of your bedroll, and have both with you when you bed down.

"Here's the hard part. I think we'll need at least four men keeping three-hour night watches, with four watches from six to six. For the day watches, we'll need two mounted and one watching the ranch road in four-hour shifts. Jubal will tell you the positions and help you decide how to divide up the watches. Any questions?"

"There ain't but twelve of us, Colonel," Jacob Drew said. "Day and night work will wear us down pretty fast."

"Where everyone sleeping?" Yellow Leaf asked.

"In here, where it's dry," one of the men

said dismissively, bringing some laughs from the group.

"Send two on foot in the dark. Pour kerosene around here," she said, making a sweeping gesture with her hand. "Drop match. Flames go up. Others, waiting, ride in. Here, everyone runs out, get shot."

"We're going to have people watching," Jubal said.

"She's got a point," Jacob Drew said. "They're going to know we have people watching."

Arguing broke out, and in an instant everyone was talking, and no one was listening. Then Jubal gave a piercing whistle, and the room fell silent.

"Those of you on night patrol will be mounted," Jonathan said. "Jubal will fill in the details. You will check on the bunkhouse and the ranch house at staggered intervals. Will that meet our need?"

"I will watch road each night from midnight to first light," Yellow Leaf said. "Then another will come. I will make fires and cook."

"You will be exhausted," Jonathan said, instantly concerned.

"Maybe you will come and help me rest." That brought a roar of laughter, whistles, and boots pounding the floor, making

Jonathan's face burn and setting him laughing at the same time.

Her remark made Yellow Leaf an instant success with the men. "Tomorrow, Leafy," one of them shouted, "we start building you a cookhouse."

A cheer went up, and her christening stuck.

Although Jonathan knew she would not allow herself to laugh, he saw she was beaming with pleasure and felt happy that, at least for the moment, she was letting herself experience the warmth of the men's affection.

Chapter 31

Four nights later, an hour before dawn, Jonathan was sitting on a folded horse blanket he had placed on a rock under a stand of junipers. The moon threw a cold, pale light over the low hills and shallow gullies behind him, and the ranch road below him was a pale twisting line running south between low hills. He was too chilled to fall asleep, even though, in the past couple of hours, all he had seen was a pair of coyotes trot up the road toward the ranch buildings, and a badger shuffle across the road and chase off a red fox that was nosing the remains of a jack rabbit the coyotes had ignored.

"You asleep, Jonathan Wainwright?" Yellow Leaf asked him.

He jumped to his feet and had his Colt nearly out of its holster before he turned enough to see her standing behind him, rifle in the crook of her arm. Her pony was looking at him over her shoulder.

"Lord!" he said, shoving his gun back into its holster. "I wish you wouldn't do that!"

"Two steers feeding on other side of road. You see them?"

"No, where are they?"

"Good thing I come," she said. "They coming this way, find you off Sam, will try put horns through you. Maybe you sleeping."

"I was not, and I don't see any steers," he protested.

"We get on horses," she said calmly, mounting her pony. "They in road behind you. Bad medicine."

"I'll be . . . Whoa!"

Jonathan ran for Sam and was barely in the saddle when the two longhorns reached his seat, having come up the slope at a trot. Seeing both people mounted, they stopped, snorted and blew a little, and pawed the ground. Then, losing interest, they lunged away, vanishing around the hill with scarcely a sound.

"Maybe you ask Bill Johnson shoot one of them," Yellow Leaf said. "Have change from deer. You like steak?"

"I do."

"Good."

If she was going to say anything else, it

was lost. She straightened herself on her horse's back. "Something coming," she said, just above a whisper. "Not move."

The two horses had raised their heads, ears pricked. Jonathan could hear nothing, nor see anything more than rocks, grass, dirt road, and shadows.

"Two come," Yellow Leaf said. "Look at road. Not move. We will follow. The others come soon."

Finally, Jonathan could hear the faint thud of hooves. A moment later, two riders on ponies emerged from the darkness, walking briskly and nearly in silence. There was something tied around their ponies' feet. The riders were stripped to the waist. Both carried rifles and wore feathers in their long hair, and straps across their horses' withers supported what looked to Jonathan like bundles of something.

Leaning toward him, Yellow Leaf whispered, "Hooves wrapped, not make sound. Cans. Oil. Not move yet."

The two silent riders faded into the darkness. Yellow Leaf sat still, apparently waiting. Jonathan wanted to follow the two, but she dropped a hand on his arm.

"Soon," she said.

It occurred to Jonathan that she was quieting him as though he were a child.

He wasn't sure whether to be amused or irritated.

"Go now," she said finally and turned away from the road. "We ride fast." She touched her heels to her pony's flanks. Her pinto flew away, followed closely by Sam. Yellow Leaf led them in a westerly curve that allowed them to pass the two Indians without being seen and reach the ranch road again well ahead of the two raiders.

"The bunkhouse," Jonathan said as they pulled up near the ranch house.

"Hide horses," she said.

"The watch."

"Walk horses to bunkhouse?" she asked.

"Let's do it."

When they were fifty feet from the building, a voice told them to stand where they were. Two men, one on each side of the bunkhouse, stepped out of the shadows. One was Merced Kinsell, the other Orrington Rowe.

"It's Jonathan and Leafy," Jonathan said, just loud enough to be heard, hoping the name *Leafy* would identify them. "We're going to have two visitors, carrying lamp oil, and we don't want any noise in dealing with them."

"All right, Colonel, we'll get the drop on them and whack them on the head," Kinsell said, coming closer, followed by Rowe.

Yellow Leaf broke in. "Let them get off horses and put down guns to get kerosene."

"Sounds good," Orrington said. "Then we jump them."

"They're bound to have knives," Jonathan said. "We'll club them down with our rifles."

"If one runs, someone will stop him," Yellow Leaf said.

"She will stop him," Jonathan said, to clarify for the other two men.

"How?" Merced demanded.

"With horse," she replied.

"Colonel?" Orrington sounded worried.

"If she says her horse will knock him down, she'll knock him down," Jonathan said.

They laid their plans quickly and retreated into the shadows of the piñons scattered over the area. Yellow Leaf led her pinto to some grass and vanished behind the animal.

Jonathan had found while he was in the cavalry that he was not at his best having to wait somewhere for the enemy to show up while being chewed by mosquitoes or suddenly having the urge to scratch his back. Usually, his horse handled itself with more stoicism than he did. Standing behind his piñon pine and not moving around, clearing his throat or taking off his boot, which suddenly had a pebble in it that was jabbing his foot, he found himself blaming Yellow Leaf for not letting him shoot the two Indians when he had the chance.

Two shadows detached themselves from the deeper shadows and turned into two horses moving almost silently toward the bunkhouse. Twenty feet away from the building, the two riders let themselves down from their horses, put down their rifles, and lifted the straps holding the cans over their horses' withers. Jonathan forgot the pebble and burst out from his tree with Merced and Orrington.

"Leafy!" Orrington shouted as the Indian farthest from the men sprinted for the road.

Jonathan reached the closer Indian and saw the flash of the man's knife blade as he crouched to spring. Not pausing, Jonathan closed with him, swung up the butt of his rifle, and knocked the man to the ground. At that moment, Yellow Leaf flew past him on her pony. A moment later she overtook the fleeing man and kicked him in the back of his neck, knocking him head over heels.

In a few minutes, they had the two Indians tied and gagged and planted safely in the bunkhouse. As soon as that was done, Jonathan called on the rest of his men, wakened by Orrington while waiting for the

Indians. Dressed and armed, they poured out of the bunkhouse.

"Time for the bonfire?" Merced asked Jonathan.

"Soak it with the kerosene," Jonathan replied, then added, "Be sure to step back before you light it."

Between the ranch house and the bunkhouse, there was a pile of ends and leftover split and broken boards from their building, as well as the piñon and junipers that had been torn up on the building sites. Merced and Orrington went off, carrying the cans by their bails. In the east, the faintest brush stroke of gray showed over the mountains.

"It is a good day to die, Jonathan Wainwright," Yellow Leaf said.

He turned to find her standing beside him, her rifle in crook of her right arm. Her paint was eyeing him over her head.

"Look," he told her, "there are enough of us to handle this. You could ride up to the spring and wait it out. I don't want you getting hurt."

She gave him one of her penetrating stares. "You are clear as spring water, Jonathan Wainwright. We all die sometime. But it is good to hear that a person wants someone to live. You are the one who should go to spring. But you won't, even if some

451

people need you."

"I'll stay with them," Jonathan said, watching her closely and with admiration.

She smiled slightly. "I will cook you breakfast when shooting stops."

A little later, right after someone shot Jonathan's hat off, he thought of their conversation and was startled to recall neither of them had mentioned Morgan. At that moment, Morgan and half a dozen of Jonathan's men were lying behind a granite ledge, firing as fast as they could jack shells into their rifles and take aim. In fact, the skirmish was seriously one sided and lasted about four minutes. Preston Miles and his men had ridden straight past the house and toward the bonfire, and into a hail of bullets sent their way from shooters they could not see. For several seconds they faced the guns, firing back at gun smoke in the half-light. Then the few left on their horses turned to escape, but someone, shooting from a stand of junipers to their right, killed two of them. The remaining five pulled in their horses and threw up their hands. The firing ceased.

"Dismount! Drop your guns! Step away from the horses!" Jonathan shouted.

The men dropped their gun belts, laid down their rifles, and lined up in front of their horses. Yellow Leaf clambered to her feet and walked down the slope toward them. Gradually, all of Jonathan's men came into view, following him, walking slowly toward their captives. The new day was with them, and aside from the crackling of the fire that was still burning, a deep silence had settled over the scene.

With the help of three volunteers, and taking advantage of the remains of the bonfire, Yellow Leaf fried venison and eggs, stuck large pots of beans into the glowing coals, and kept frying until the three helpers had served everyone breakfast. The prisoners, including the two Indians, who'd settled cross-legged on the ground, ate everything the three servers brought them, appearing in the best of spirits. Initially, still fired up from the shooting, Jonathan's men leaned toward shooting the seven survivors, but, having eaten, they swung over to Jonathan's plan of taking the raiders back to town and handing them over to Governor Nicasio Oroño.

It created a significant stir in Santa Fe when the line of horses rode into town, seven carrying dead men slung across their saddles, another five bearing men riding upright with their hands tied to their pommels, flanked and followed by Jonathan's fully armed men, Yellow Leaf riding beside the first dead man and Jonathan leading the procession.

By the time they reached the plaza, their procession had accumulated nearly fifty people of all ages, including men, women, stray children and three dogs. Jonathan halted them in front of the building housing the governor's office. Someone must have seen what was coming and run ahead to warn Governor Oroño, because he stepped out of his office onto the wooden walkway and stood with his hands in his pockets, studying the company.

Oroño was a heavyset man, in a dark suit and vest with a gold watch chain across his substantial stomach. He took one hand out of a pocket and stroked his full, dark beard. "With whom do I have the honor of speaking?" he asked in a heavily accented voice.

Jonathan dismounted. "Jonathan Wainwright. I bought the Planford ranch."

"The man who shot Mr. Preston Miles in the shoulder, no?"

"Yes. He's lying across the saddle of that bay horse behind me."

"I gather he and these other men did not meet a natural death."

"No. Governor, my men and I shot them, and we have brought you five prisoners who

454

survived Mr. Miles's attempt to kill us. I believe the Ring had a hand in this business. Would you know anything about that?"

"No, Mr. Wainwright, I have no knowledge of whatever any of these men or those who hired them planned and attempted to carry out." He sighed. "The doings of the group called the Ring have far more to answer for than trying to kill you. Unfortunately, I have had little success in halting their depredations. I expect you will want me to take these five men and put them in jail, but it is my sad task to tell you they will be tried and found innocent."

"Thank you for telling me the truth, Governor. Your job is not an enviable one."

Oroño nodded slightly. "Fortunately, my duties extend far beyond this wretched town, Mr. Wainwright. My principal task is to create a functioning state from the violence scarring this part of the southwest. That, and the threat of Indian attacks."

"Well, Godspeed, Governor. I suppose someone will want to bury the remains of the dead men. It's my understanding that this Ring has attorneys, political people, businessmen, and land speculators in it. My message to them is: leave my ranch and everything and everyone on it alone. If they don't, they will come home across their saddles."

Oroño drew nearer to where Jonathan stood. Lowering his voice, he said, "Is that Indian woman working for you?"

"Her husband is, and, yes, until I can hire a cook, she's keeping us fed. I intend to have her managing a part of my ranch as soon as possible."

"My advice to you is to keep her out of the town. I suppose you know about our Genizaros."

"Yes. I was hoping she could keep the ranch stocked with whatever we need from the stores in town."

The governor shook his head. "Is bad idea. Other than the Pueblo people, and we have a lot of them, Indians from the wild tribes are kept as servants of one kind and another. Many of our male Genizaros serve in the militias, whose task it is to hold off the Comanches and other raiding tribes that attack us from time to time."

"How does that affect Yellow Leaf?"

"She appears to be a strong woman in the prime of life. Is she?"

"Yes." Jonathan figured where this was going and his anger rose. He controlled it, with some difficulty.

"She would bring a high price on the market. Keep her out of Santa Fe. There

456

are people here who have been capturing and selling Indians for a very long time. She would be whisked away before she knew what was happening. Also, Mr. Wainwright, by winning this encounter with the Ring you have made dangerous enemies. Watch your back."

"President Lincoln ended slavery in this country," Jonathan said, trying not to snap out the words.

"Ah, yes." The governor smiled. "So he did. Good day to you, sir."

When Governor Oroño had gone back inside, Jonathan regained his saddle, turned Sam, and told Jubal to cut their prisoners loose.

"Ain't somebody going to jail them?" Jubal demanded, visibly upset.

"The governor said they would only be found innocent in a trial. The Ring apparently has a choke hold on the court."

"Well, I swear!" Jubal said in disgust. "We'll only have to shoot them next time they come for us. It would make more sense to do it now."

"We've accumulated quite a crowd here." Jonathan turned in his saddle to take in the gathering, which was increasing in number as word flew out through the town. "If we don't want to shoot our way out, I suggest we tie the dead men's horses to the hitching rail in front of this building and free the prisoners."

Jonathan's men were calling out similar warnings, and Yellow Leaf rode up to him, having been sworn at by some of the people in the throng. Jubal freed the prisoners, prompting a cheer to go up from the rowdies and bar flies, and grim muttering among the rest.

"Not safe here," Yellow Leaf said to Jonathan, resting the butt of her rifle on her thigh.

"Stay close," Jonathan said. He moved Sam to put her between himself and Jubal, then called, "Move out."

His men closed ranks behind them, and they pushed their way through the crowd. Once clear of it, Jonathan picked up their pace, and they were soon out of town.

Once clear of Santa Fe, Jubal said, "I should have thought the people would be glad we shot up Ring's gunmen."

"We shoot their people," Yellow Leaf said.

"You better stay away from town," Jonathan told her. "Governor Oroño told me you would not be safe there alone."

"You just afraid I find a better job," she said, bringing a snort of laughter from Jubal.

"Don't upset her," Jubal said. "She's all

the cook we've got."

"Ever heard of Genizaros?" Jonathan asked her, then belatedly recalled that she had.

"Slaves," she replied. "Many bought from Comanches."

"How much would you have brought, Yellow Leaf?" Jubal asked.

"Not funny," Jonathan said. "According to the governor, trade in people is still a thriving business."

"Do you believe him?" Jubal asked, sober now.

"Yes, and what I heard made makes me uneasy thinking of Patience and Ginger poking their noses into that rats' nest."

"They live with others in house in town," Yellow Leaf said.

Jonathan glanced at her. "Do you know where?"

"Dove Street at north end of town. Someone met Ginger and talked."

"What did she tell you?" Jonathan felt impatient.

"Just told you."

"Getting information out of her is like squeezing blood out of a rock," Jubal said.

"No blood in rock," Yellow Leaf said flatly.

The two men exchanged glances. "What else did she tell you?" Jonathan asked.

"Can't find more people like Patience Stockbridge. Need to find work soon."

"They short on money?" Jubal asked.

"Don't know about short money. They don't have much more, tall or short."

"No wonder Morgan spends so much time with the horses," Jubal remarked.

"Only someone Great Spirit touch think blood in stone." She dug her heels into her paint and galloped ahead.

"She ought to be a leader of her people," Jonathan said, watching her ride away. "Instead, she's cooking for us and taking care of Morgan. There's room for improvement."

CHAPTER 32

The milk cows came, and a crew had to rush to construct in the barn a place to tie them up and install a set of stanchions to hold them in place, and mangers to hold their hay while they were being milked.

"Not know how to milk cow, just eat them," Yellow Leaf told Jonathan, expressing alarm when he led her into the barn and said he wanted her to take care of the six Guernsey cows standing on the milking platform. "Cows eat, shit, take care of themselves," she added, folding her arms across her chest and staring at him, stone faced.

"You ain't thought this through, Doc," Isaac True said when he and the other three men had stopped gathering their tools to laugh at Yellow Leaf's comments. "How's she going to grain and milk these cows twice a day and feed us breakfast and supper?"

The question stymied Jonathan, who only

at that moment realized he had no idea when cows should be fed and when milked, or how to go about either task.

"Alright," he said bravely. "Any of you know how to milk a cow?"

"We better find out soon, because if those cows ain't milked, they'll dry up," Karl Messering said. He was a big dark-haired, serious-minded man with a heavy black beard that gave him an Old Testament look. He was also the only married man among the hired hands. His family was living in a *casita* in town, and his wife was taking in washing.

"Like tumbleweed?" Yellow Leaf asked, looking astonished.

"Stop giving milk," Messering told her.

"Karl, can you milk a cow?" Jonathan asked.

"I ain't for a while, but I can. So can my boy and my wife."

"Your wife's name is Adele, isn't it, and Timothy's your boy's name?" Jonathan asked. "I remember stitching him up after he cut himself on your Bowie knife."

"We all thought Adele might be going to cut Karl's throat with that knife when you finished," Isaac put in.

That set the men laughing, and even Karl was grinning broadly.

"Do you think Adele would consider coming to work here? Wait, is Timothy in school?"

"From what I can tell, there ain't a school outside of the church school in town, and we ain't Catholics," the big man replied. "Well, we was brought up on farms. I could talk with Adele. She don't speak Spanish, and not many around us speak English. Outside of housework, she don't have much to do."

"Thank you, Karl."

Jubal joined them, and Jonathan told him about their need for someone to milk the cows. "There's a couple of the youngest hands can fill in until you find someone to take over," Jubal said, then turned to Yellow Leaf. "Leafy, you want to learn how to milk a cow?"

"Too old to learn new things, when new things mean more work" was the answer he got. That pleased the men, and they sent up a ragged cheer.

"Never mind," Jubal said. "I'll get young Jefferson in here. He went off to war, he told me, to get out of barn chores. So, hurry up and find someone else. I don't want to lose him. He's the best horse doctor we've got — excluding you, Colonel."

That brought a chuckle from all of them.

"All right, let's get back to what we were doing," Jonathan told the group. "Jubal, get these cows fed, watered, and milked. Yellow Leaf, wait a bit, I want to talk to you."

Jubal went off in search of Jefferson, and the other men finished gathering their tools and left. When they had gone, the barn fell back into its dusty slumber, disturbed only by the soft sounds of the cows, chewing their cuds and switching their tails at the occasional fly.

"You mad I don't milk cows?" Yellow Leaf demanded, apparently determined to defend her boundaries.

"Not at all," he said and meant it. "I don't want you milking the cows."

"You think Adele Messering do a better job?" she asked, bristling.

"You've got more corners than a five-sided box."

"Box has four sides."

"Some caskets have six corners. Some hat boxes don't have any."

"What is *casket*?"

"It's the box white people bury their dead in. Can we stop doing whatever it is we're doing?"

The corners of Yellow Leaf's mouth twitched, but she was not giving ground.

"No," he said, not waiting for an answer,

"I don't think Adele Messering would do a better job, once you learned how to milk a cow. I don't want you milking the cows. I want to put you in charge of the barn and everything that goes on in it and around it."

Yellow Leaf lost her braced stance, and her eyes widened. "What goes on?" she asked, obviously both alarmed and puzzled.

Jonathan paused, thinking about how to answer her question, and suddenly realized what he wanted for this ranch.

"Yellow Leaf," he said, feeling a surge of purpose, "we're living near a town that's going to grow, Ring or no Ring. The population is going to increase whether the railroad comes here or not. I want this ranch to support all the people who work on it. To that end, I am planning to raise crops that will be sold to Santa Fe and the other towns within easy reach. In addition to cattle for the northern cities and horses, I want this ranch to feature dairy cows, milk, butter, hens, eggs, pigs, sheep, and mules for the northern market. These Guernseys are just a beginning.

"We'll have chickens and roosters so we can have eggs to eat and sell to the stores in town. We'll have pigs, to fatten and eat and sell. We'll have cows for milk, and young cows to raise to make more milk and butter, which we will also sell in town as we become more settled. I wanted Jane to take charge of the ranch house and oversee the cookhouse and the furnishing and care of the bunkhouse, but she does not want to be around me."

"If I do what you ask, you will need a cooking person," she said quietly, looking a little uneasy. "Someone not knows if she can do things you said."

"With one hand tied behind your back," he said.

That made her laugh, breaking the tension. "Not like having hand tied at back," she said firmly.

"Then we won't," he said, "and you're right. This place is going to need at least one full-time cook. Are you willing to go on cooking for now?"

"Yes, but I think you wrong about Jane Howard."

Jonathan didn't care to discuss that. He shut down their conversation, saying, "We've both got work to do."

The next day, Yellow Leaf cooked breakfast and lunch but was nowhere to be found at supper time. The fires were not even set. Word spread among the hands, and they all gathered outside the bunkhouse to shoot questions at Jubal, who had no answers.

"Where's the colonel?" Burchard Harley asked.

"Gone to talk with Morgan. Morgan won't leave the horses for another hour."

A few minutes later, Jonathan rode in. "Morgan says this morning, she said something about talking to Jane. Did she talk to any of you?"

The question met with silence.

"All right, start the fires, and settle among yourselves who's going to do the cooking tonight. Jubal, a word."

Jonathan got down from Sam and took Jubal a short distance away from the others. "You found Jane, didn't you? Where is she? I know she doesn't want to see me, but I need to speak to her."

"About Yellow Leaf?"

"Yes. I've got a bad feeling about this."

"Well, it shure ain't like her to have left without telling us."

"That's it. There is no way she would have done such a thing. Where is Jane?"

"Well, you might think twice about going to see her. She said some pretty rough things to me when I finally tracked her down." Jubal looked uncomfortable telling Jonathan this, and Jonathan was quick to respond.

"I appreciate your concern, Jubal," he said. "I might have done the same thing had it been you. But the situation has changed. I'm thinking, if Yellow Leaf went into town alone, someone may have grabbed her. If that's happened, word of it will get around, and a bar would be a likely place to hear about it. Whatever Jane thinks of me, she was a close friend of Yellow Leaf. I want to ask her to listen for news, and if she hears anything, to get word back to me."

"Ain't you getting ahead of yourself, Colonel?" Jubal said. "We don't know Yellow Leaf's missing. She might just have lost track of time."

"Did you ever know her to lose track of time? When we were riding point together, she could tell me what time it was within three minutes of what my watch said any time I asked her."

"I guess I don't want anything to have happened to her."

"Neither do I, but if she's been grabbed, I think they'll have to break one of her legs to keep her."

"Or chain her up."

"God, I'd hate to have that happen."

"So would I. Jane's working at the bar in the Rio Grande Hotel. It's a fancy name, but it looked like a pretty tough place to me. She wasn't exactly welcoming. That's why I didn't tell you."

"Water under the bridge. I'll risk being thrown out."

The Rio Grande Hotel was in a sprawling adobe building with mostly single-story adobe houses and shops lining the nearby streets, which were still choked with wagons pulled by draft horses and mules. Their drivers turned the air blue whenever they were forced to stop and wait for people to cross in front of them, or found their way jammed by other wagons and struggled to undo a tangle. Jonathan found the hotel easily enough, with half a dozen sleepy horses tied to the hitching rail.

Before adding Sam to the line, he took in his surroundings and decided that if he left his rifle in its saddle scabbard, he would come out of the hotel to find it gone. With some reluctance, he took the rifle into the hotel with him. He needn't have concerned himself because no one he encountered, including the desk clerk who pointed Jonathan toward the bar, took any notice of it.

The daylight was nearly gone in the bar when Jonathan reached it, and an aged man in a blue-striped apron and less-than-white jacket was on a tall stepladder, lighting lamps suspended from the wooden ceiling.

Jonathan quickly took in the empty tables and chairs scattered around the room. More light glowed from hanging lamps at the bar itself, increased by the broad mirror on the wall behind. Half a dozen men were leaning on the bar, each with one foot braced on its brass rail, two talking quietly and the rest studying their whiskey.

"No guns in the bar," a woman said in a harsh voice Jonathan would have recognized anywhere. A voice totally without the brightness it had once carried.

"Hello, Jane." Jonathan stepped out of the shadows and walked to the unoccupied end of the bar. "May I speak with you? It concerns Yellow Leaf."

Jane had been polishing glasses. She came toward him, the polishing cloth thrown over a shoulder. Seeing her was more disturbing than Jonathan expected. Her hair was piled on top of her head. She had lost weight, and, in the tight-fitting top to her dress with its flounced skirt, she looked brassy, aggressive, and hardened.

"Was she in here, to talk with you?" he asked, his mouth strangely dry.

"Is that all you have to say to me?" she snapped.

He stiffened. "I have been led to believe that you do not wish to talk with me. Had I not reason to believe Yellow Leaf is in serious trouble, I would not have forced myself on you. Have you seen her today?"

"Yes, I saw her. Did you send her to talk to me?"

"No, I did not. I'm sorry if she left you with that impression."

Jonathan was finding the conversation extremely painful. Despite her obvious hostility, her new role, and change of appearance, he wanted, above all else at that moment, to restore himself in Jane's good graces. He felt badly rattled by her rejection.

Her face softened slightly. "What's happened to Yellow Leaf?" she said.

"Early this afternoon, she rode into town. Morgan said she came to see you. She has not come back to the ranch, and I have reason to believe she may have been abducted."

"Haven't you told her to be careful in town?" she demanded.

"Of course I have. I also told her not to come in here alone, but you know her. She does not take directions seriously if following them prevents her from doing something she wants to do."

"Yes, you might as well try to harness the wind." Jane relaxed enough to smile. "She

471

tried to get me to come work for you. I told her I'd wait for you to ask me yourself before saying anything."

Her face had hardened again. His heart sinking as he met her gaze, Jonathan thought he knew how she would answer that question. "Did she say where she was going when she left you?"

"No."

"Will you listen for comments by any of the men coming in here that hint at a woman having recently been abducted, especially an Indian woman?"

Her shoulders slumped a little, and her voice was softer when she replied. "I'll do that, and I'll ask Oscar — he's in charge of the bar — to do the same."

"Thank you, Jane."

He paused, wanting to ask how she and her family were getting along, but told himself he had no right to inquire. As for asking her to come work for him, he was pretty sure her answer would be *no*.

He couldn't face it. "I hope I'll find her at the ranch when I return, but I doubt I will. Can you let me know as soon as you have any leads?"

"Of course. I'll get word to you as soon as I hear anything."

He thought she spoke to him much more

warmly in saying goodbye, then shut down the notion as being an expression of hope and not reality.

His ride back to the ranch was one of the longest he had ever taken, despite pushing Sam hard all the way. When he reached it, he found what he had dreaded was true. Yellow Leaf was not there. The men were clearing away the remnants of their supper and were, Jonathan saw, in a frame of mind as glum as his cavalry unit when one of their comrades had died in combat.

"Jubal," he said, "we'll keep a fire tonight where she can see it coming up the road. You take the first watch. I'll relieve you at midnight."

"Colonel," Jacob Drew said, "if you build a fire, don't sit by it. We can't afford to lose either one of you. In fact, a couple of us older men will keep watch tonight. You and Jubal have had a long day, and I doubt you've eaten. There's some steak and Yellow Leaf's bread and drippings set aside for you."

"Drew's right, Colonel," Jubal told him. "He and whoever sits up with him can sleep in tomorrow. Neither of us can."

Reluctantly, Jonathan gave way and turned the night watch over to Jacob Drew, who went off at once to recruit two more men to share it.

Jonathan ate and made his bed, but he lay awake a long time. Concern for Yellow Leaf occupied his thoughts, but, as the first hour passed, he began to think also about Jane. He ran their conversation over and over in his mind, focusing increasingly on her saying she was waiting for him to ask her to come to work at the ranch. His cowardice in not making the request right then shamed him deeply. Did he still think he was unfit to marry? He found he could no longer bring himself to say he wasn't. Turning that fact over in his mind, exhaustion finally shut him down, and he slept.

CHAPTER 33

Yellow Leaf did not return the next day or the one after, but, at midmorning on the third day, Jubal found him. "Colonel, a boy just rode into the ranch yard. Want me to talk to him?"

Jonathan had spent the previous day inspecting the barn and found light coming through the roof in several places. He and some of the men were splitting shingles out of pine blocks, sawn into shingle lengths from the trees they had felled earlier in the day and twitched down to the barn. The rest of the men were on the roof, tearing up the rotted shingles and laying fresh ones.

"I'll go," Jonathan said and left at a jog, hoping there was news from Jane.

"You Colonel?" asked the skinny, dark-haired Pueblo boy, astride an aged mule, when Jonathan reached him.

"Yes. Who sent you?"

"Miss Howard. This for you." He pulled a

folded piece of paper out of his boot and passed it to Jonathan, who opened it and read, *Come in armed. Bring men.*

He glanced at the boy. "What's your name?"

"Cuerno," the boy said.

"Are you hungry?"

The boy nodded.

"You see that building?" He pointed. When the boy nodded, he said. "That's the cook shack. You go in there, and you eat anything you want to eat. There's milk in a pitcher. It's fresh. You drink it. You'll ride back to town with us in a while. Will that be all right?"

Grinning, the boy nodded. "Eat first?"

"Yes," Jonathan said, "you eat all you want."

A quarter of an hour later, Jonathan and his men were armed and mounted. "We're going into town a few at a time," Jubal told them while Jonathan fetched the boy. "We'll gather at the Rio Grande Hotel and go in together. Keep the talk down, and, Jacob, you keep that boy with you until the colonel tells you to let him go."

"We don't know yet where she is, right?" Jacob asked.

"That's right, and if that boy were to tell certain people what we're doing, we'd lose our advantage. So, don't let him out of your sight."

"Will do."

Jonathan and the boy joined them. "This youngster's name is Cuerno. Cuerno, this is Mr. Drew. He will look after you. Stay close to him. We're going to move fast." Jonathan wasn't sure how much Cuerno had understood of what he had said, but the boy nodded.

"Come over here, son." Drew reached out and shook the boy's hand. "You have a strong name. It means *horn* in English. Shall I call you Horn? I had sons of my own. You do any deer hunting?"

Jonathan did not wait to hear Cuerno's answer but rode to the head of the men. He raised his hand and signaled forward, moving Sam into a trot.

"I don't think the boy's mule is able to keep this pace," Jubal said a few minutes later, pulling up beside Jonathan.

"Put him up behind Jacob. That big black of Drew's won't even notice the added weight. I doubt the kid weighs eighty pounds. He's mostly skin and bones."

"All right," Jubal replied. "Damned shame to neglect a kid that way. I'll lead the mule." He turned away to deal with the boy, and Jonathan put his mind on what was ahead of them.

At the hotel, Jane was waiting for them in the empty bar. "They've got her in a hacienda about three miles south of town," she told Jonathan, as the last of the men entered. She looked much like her old self, all the hardness gone. She had abandoned her barmaid outfit for a blue and orange blouse and long skirt, and her hair was brushed down over her shoulders. Jonathan wanted to drift indefinitely on the blue oceans of her eyes but wrenched himself away.

"What can you tell us about the place?" he asked.

"It used to be a ranch," she said with a slight frown, as if her mind was elsewhere.

"What is it now?"

"A hangout for some really bad people, gunmen for the most part. They're smugglers, and reports have it they trade in people a lot of the time. We don't see much of them in here, thank the Lord, but last night two of them came in, stood at the bar with a bottle between them, and talked together for half an hour. Both Americans, I think. They spoke English with a Southern accent." She paused. "Really hard looking — like those men with Rand Callaway, if you remember."

"Not likely to forget," Jonathan said.

"They paid me no mind, and I busied myself near them and was able to put together enough to learn they were with the hacienda outfit. When one of them said, 'For an Injun, she fought like a cougar,' I began to pay closer attention."

"I'm glad you did. Is the place walled?"

"No, but it's big and sprawling. I can't tell you much more. I didn't feel safe asking questions. It don't pay to be too nosy about that hacienda. The other day, a stranger drifted in and began asking people about it. When he left, three men followed him. The next morning, he was found beside the river with his throat cut. The walls have ears in this place, and the streets have eyes. I don't doubt that someone has carried word out there that you and your men are in town."

"Then the quicker we act, the better," Jonathan said, pushing back from the bar.

"You be careful, Jonathan."

"I will." He stood for a moment looking at her. "Perhaps we will talk when this is over."

"Let's," she answered.

Jonathan walked away, feeling as if his feet were lifting off the floor, and called his men together. In the next five minutes he told them what they were going to do, finishing with, "And let's hope Yellow Leaf is still there and has not been shipped off some-where."

"We'll get her, Colonel," Jubal said.

"What about Horn?" Drew asked. "I don't think the boy's got any place to go."

"Jane," Jonathan called, "where does that boy you sent out with your message live?"

"I don't know," she replied. "He was standing outside, and I gave him a dollar to ride out to your ranch. I had some doubts about that mule of his making it."

"Can you keep an eye on him 'til we come back and get somebody to feed and water his mule?"

"I can do that. I'll get one of our people to put the mule in our stables."

Drew led the boy to the bar. "You're go-ing to stay with Miss Howard and not be a nuisance."

"Are you coming back?" the boy asked, looking as if he might cry.

"You bet we're coming back for you, Horn," one of the men shouted and was echoed by the others. Jonathan, surprised and pleased, realized that the ranch had acquired a new resident.

The hacienda was located in a shallow val-ley, behind a small creek lined with old, gnarled cottonwood trees whose leaves rattled softly in the hot wind. Jonathan had taken advantage of the cover the trees provided and brought his men under them, to study the buildings.

"One-story adobe," Jubal said. "That simplifies matters a little. Mighty quiet place."

And it was. In fact, the scene was one of peace and sleepy morning sunlight. The building had once been painted a pale cream, but, where the paint had worn away, the walls were gray. There was a large door in the center of the main building, with small windows on either side.

"That door puts us at a disadvantage," Jubal said, "and the windows ain't big enough to shoot out and jump through."

"You take the first six men behind us and ride hard to the back of the building. Shoot your way into the house if you have to. I'll wait for your first shot and take the rest of us in that front door. Start with your rifles, and, once inside, stack them and use your sidearms. Some of the defenders will probably fall back into the two wings of the hacienda. Clear the rooms one at a time, with one of you watching your backs."

"What if they hold their prisoners in front of them?"

"Don't let them out of the room. When

the shooting stops, we'll negotiate. Go."

Jubal and his men broke out from under the cottonwood trees and belted into the yard and around the house. A moment later, several shots were fired at once.

"Let's do it," Jonathan said, and away he and his men went. At the front of the hacienda, they dismounted and blasted the door open with their rifles, then raced through it into the house. The men spread out in an arc in the empty parlor with its immense stone fireplace and made for the doors leading off it.

Expecting heavy resistance, Jonathan had sprinted into the house with his Colt drawn. It soon became clear, however, that there was no resistance. The firing from the rear of the house had ended almost as soon as it had begun.

"Start checking rooms," he ordered, "and don't just walk into any of them. Kick the door open, wait, look around the doorframe and wait again. Go in with your gun in front of you. Take your time."

The hacienda, he found as they slowly advanced toward the back of the building, must have been built in haphazard sections over the years, with no effort to create a system of hallways that ran in straight lines. Finally, as they found room after dank, airless room with only broken furniture, unmade beds, and the dank odors of mildew and unwashed bodies in them, Jonathan called a halt.

"Does anyone have any idea where we are?" he asked. "I expect any time now to encounter the Minotaur."

Merced Kinsell raised an eyebrow. "Who's that when he's home?"

"He lived on the island of Crete in a labyrinth under a king's castle a couple of thousand years ago. He ate people. A man named Theseus killed him."

"I heard about that," Merced said. "Was that story in a book?"

"Yes. Were you ever in school?"

"I may have been. I can't say for sure."

The discussion of Greek mythology came to an abrupt end when the blast of a rifle echoed through the hall where they stood, and a bullet slammed into the door frame a few inches from Jonathan's head. Everyone scrambled to get out of the hall. Jonathan and Jubal dodged back into the nearest room, one on each side of the door.

"All right, Jubal," Jonathan said, just above a whisper, "on the count of three. Go out in a roll. I'll go first. One, two —"

And out he went, falling and rolling. He stopped on his stomach, his gun in both hands. A moment later, Jubal followed. The barrage of firing came from two men down the hall, blasting away. Jonathan spread his legs to steady himself, chose the man on his right, and shot him. Jubal took out the second man.

Jubal got to his feet after Jonathan did, groaning a little but keeping his gun on the fallen shooters. "I ain't as limber as I once was," he complained, making a face as he rubbed his hip.

"It doesn't say much for our physical condition," Jonathan said as the other men came out of the rooms they had dived into. The hall was filled with gun smoke and the smell of burned powder.

"Colonel, that you?" Isaac True shouted.

"Come along. The way's clear," Jubal answered.

"We've got Leafy and two others. She ain't in the best shape," Isaac said as he and three others came down the hall. "Jacob's with her."

"Let's get her out of here. Any of you men hurt?" Jonathan asked.

"Nope. We've got three of her jailers tied up."

"What will we do with them?" Jubal asked.

"String 'em up in one of them cotton-woods," Burchard Harley suggested.

"Cut them loose," Jonathan said grimly. "The town government won't take a side in this confrontation, and they're all the local law there is here."

Jubal looked disgusted but nodded reluctantly. "I guess. I don't see my way clear to shooting them."

The rest agreed, and Jonathan said, "Let's get Yellow Leaf and get out of here. A couple of you men fetch her pinto from the stable and watch yourselves. The pinto can't always control her dislike for whites. Can she ride, Isaac?" he asked.

"Maybe. We'll fetch the horse if she'll let us. She may need to see Leafy to cooperate."

Two of the men left for the barn. The rest followed Jubal and Jonathan into the room where Yellow Leaf was being held. Seeing her almost changed Jonathan's mind about cutting her captors loose. She was sitting on the floor, her back against the wall. Her right eye was swollen shut, the flesh below it midnight blue, streaked with orange. Her lips were swollen and crusted with blood. Her leggings and doeskin jacket hung off her in tatters, blood stained and torn.

"They've been at her," one of the men muttered.

"Bastards," another said.

Jonathan dropped onto his knees beside

her and took her hands gently in his own. "It's Jonathan. You're safe now."

"About time," she said in a defiant croak, fixing him with her good eye.

Jubal, standing behind Jonathan, said, "Did one of them who did this to you have a white eye?"

She glanced up at him and nodded.

Jubal turned to the man beside him. The man pointed at two more of Jonathan's men, and the three slipped out of the room. While this was going on, Jonathan drew his knife and carefully cut away the leather collar padlocked around Yellow Leaf's neck and chained to a ring in the wall above her head.

"Can you stand?" he asked.

Instead of answering, she gripped his arms and slowly pulled herself to her feet, her face twisting slightly as she rose. "Sore," she said.

Jonathan did not have to ask where. The bruises on the insides of her thighs told it all.

"Do you think you can ride your paint?" he asked. "We'll carry you if you can't."

"Maybe can ride," she croaked. Jonathan noticed more bruising on her neck.

The silence of the hacienda was splintered by three gunshots.

"That's taken care of, Leafy," Jubal said.

"They won't be hurting nobody no more."

"Good," Jonathan said for both of them and, more quietly to Yellow Leaf, "Let's get you home."

Chapter 34

Once Yellow Leaf was in the ranch house and in bed, the full seriousness of her condition became clear, along with the realization on Jonathan's part that none of the men, including himself, had any idea how to ease Yellow Leaf on her road to recovery. Much of the care she needed involved treating the injuries to the lower parts of her body.

"I will do this," she had insisted after Jonathan had examined her and explained the extent of her injuries.

Having him doing the examination had been excruciatingly painful to her physically, but more so emotionally. When he said he would have to remove the bandages daily for a while and wash and apply ointment to the wounds, Yellow Leaf said she would kill either him or herself before letting that happen.

Jonathan emerged from the bedroom

shaken and told Jubal, who had been waiting out in the hall for him to finish, "Tomorrow, you are in charge of the place. I'm going to town and ask Jane if she can help me find someone to come out here and nurse Yellow Leaf."

"Colonel," Jubal said, following him into the living room with its big rough-stone fireplace.

Jonathan more or less collapsed on the horse-hide sofa. Jubal perched on its edge and continued speaking, clearly nervous but plunging ahead anyway. "If that ain't the worst idea you've had since I first come to know you, it's a close second. You and I both know you could probably get Patience and Ginger out here. The last I knew, they were both treading water. Now then, you ain't going to like what I'm going to say, but the worst thing you could do is go to Jane Howard and ask her if she knows anyone who might come out to the ranch and lend a hand with Yellow Leaf. You've got to go in there and tell her you need *her* help and would she come out here with her family and work for you."

"She's got a full-time job," Jonathan began.

Jubal gripped his shoulder. "You go ahead and ask her to come out here and work for you. You know we need her here, and so do you."

"I don't think I *need* her," Jonathan protested.

Jubal shook his head. "This may cost me my job, Colonel, but it needs saying. You go talk with all three of those women and get them out here as fast as you can. We need a cook. Yellow Leaf needs a nurse, and you need a housekeeper and a bookkeeper. If we don't get a cook, the hands will start leaving. With no one to care for her, Yellow Leaf will probably die of sepsis. Your ranch house will become a rats' nest, and your finances will grow more tangled than a briar patch. And the boy Horn needs looking after that you and I can't give him.

"One more thing: this ranch needs your full attention. It's a big spread you've got here. If you want to do those things you've talked about doing, it'll take all the work and thinking you and I can bring to it."

Jonathan took off his hat and studied its headband for a while. His first impulse was to fire Jubal. Getting over that, he confronted the question of asking Jane to come out here with him. He saw the sense of it, and maybe Jubal was right about the ranch. Having found good reasons for doing what Jubal suggested, he felt very much better.

"Jubal," he said, "your job's secure. Ask the men to please hang on. A cook is coming."

"God in heaven, Jonathan Wainwright," Jane said. "I had damn near give up on you."

She had been cleaning the bar when he recited Jubal's list of needs at the ranch and then asked her if she would consider coming to work for him.

"There's all kinds of room in the place," he said, almost certain she would turn him down flat. "You and your family can live there if you want to."

She untied her apron and took it off. "I'm going to need a horse and wagon to get our stuff out there. Ma'll be happy as a cat knee-deep in cream." She paused and looked at him for a moment. "Get over to Patience and Ginger. Ask them what you asked me. You know Patience can put Yellow Leaf back on her feet if anyone can, and Ginger can help me with the cooking and Ma with the housework. Patience has got to handle the books. I can't take that on."

"All right, I'll talk to them." He had a flash of fear she wasn't being serious. "Are you sure you want to do this?"

"Idiot, of course I do. Are you willing to take on more help? We're going to need it."

"All you need," he said and finished the thought in silence: *as long as the money holds out.* He had begun to worry some about that. But the truth was, he had very little to worry about where money was concerned and, anyway, was too tired by nightfall to do anything but sleep.

He went from the Rio Grande's bar to the boardinghouse where Patience and Ginger were staying. "Patience," he said, "it will be all right to decline, should you choose to, but Yellow Leaf is very ill, and I need help in looking after her. The ranch house is very large, and, should you decide to come out, you and Ginger could live there. Of course, I will pay you whatever you and she think is appropriate and provide board. Jane has committed to move in tomorrow and bring her family."

That might have been the longest speech he had made since leaving Harvard. He felt extremely self-conscious and sure they would turn him down.

The two women stood looking at him as if they were seeing him for the first time. The silence stretched out, and Jonathan felt certain he was sunk. Then Ginger rushed forward and grasped his right arm.

"Dr. Wainwright, you look exhausted. Come over here and sit down." She pulled him toward a small table and two wooden chairs. "Patience, is there any coffee left in that pot? What were we thinking, letting you go on that way?"

By the time Ginger had folded Jonathan into one of the chairs, Patience had a white china mug of steaming black coffee of the table in front of him. One hand on his shoulder, she said, "Of course we'll go to the ranch, and we do not want to hear anything about paying us. There's a few of Ginger's donuts left. I think they're fit to eat."

Ginger set a small, cracked, white plate in front of him. Patience put two brown donuts on it. It came to Jonathan that they were both thin as saplings and there was nothing in the room aside from the aged table and chairs but the potbellied stove. The table's surface was scoured down to the bare wood. The room's only window was missing one of its panes, the hole covered with a square of white butcher's paper. Belatedly, it occurred to him that the two donuts might be all the food they had.

He sipped coffee for politeness's sake and stood. "Do you still have your mules and the wagon?"

"We have the buggy," Patience said.

"As soon as I reach the ranch, I'll send

Horn in with Sam all harnessed. You can hitch him to the buggy."

Ginger glanced at Patience. "The buggy's in the livery stable, and we owe rent on it."

"And we don't have any money," Patience said.

Anger stung Jonathan, that these two were in such a situation. "I'll soon take care of that. Ginger, can you come along with me?"

Patience was white as a sheet. "From this moment on," he said to her, "things are going to be much better for you and Ginger. Can you believe that?"

After a moment, Patience nodded. "Yes, Jonathan, but I am so ashamed."

"You listen to me, Patience Stockbridge." He stepped toward her. "You're living in a world full of idiots who are not fit to walk in your wake. Believe me, you have nothing to be ashamed of."

With that, he and Ginger went out the door. "Is it all right if I call you Jonathan?" she asked.

"Yes. And don't you worry. Very soon, things are going to be better for you and Patience."

By dinner time the next day, the smell of cooking beans, corn, squash, and beef steaks hung heavy in the air around the cookhouse.

Morgan, having taken over Yellow Leaf's hunting chore, flushed two rogue steers out of a gully near the spring and shot the one that charged him, then threw a loop of rope over the beast's horns and dragged the carcass into camp. Isaac True and Merced Kinsell gutted and quartered the big steer and cut the steaks out of its loin and upper midsection. Jane, shirt rolled to her elbows and a calico apron tied around her waist, grilled the steaks over red-hot coals, turning and moving the meat with a long-handled fork. A stack of steaks was piled on the table behind her.

"We've got to heaven without the cost and trouble of dying, and you're my first angel," Ephron Watson told Jane as she dropped a steak onto his plate. He was a long, lanky man who had gathered some years and lost a front tooth in the process, but he could smile with the best, and Jane smiled back.

"Why, thank you, Ephron," she said, wiping the sweat off her face with a ripped strip from a blue towel she had slung over one shoulder. "Go put some beans and squash on that plate before the meat chills."

"Looks like you struck gold, Colonel," Jubal said, standing beside Jonathan. They were in front of the cook shack, watching the men filing past Jane, most of them not daring even to look at her, shy and self-conscious as twelve-year-olds.

"We have," Jonathan said, "but she's going to need help. Patience and Ginger can't do it. They're both busy as one-armed paper hangers. I didn't realize what a mess the house was in."

"How is Yellow Leaf?" Jubal asked. "The men will want to know. I'm really surprised they've taken to her the way they have."

"She's something special, that's for sure. Right now, she seems to be stable. The test will be whether or not we can keep her from developing infections in the fissures made when she was assaulted." His jaw tightened. "She finally passed out but can recall four men. I think there were more."

"It's beyond my understanding how anyone could do it," Jubal's voice was sharp with anger. "Well, we took care of some of them. I wish we'd gotten them all."

"I'm surprised they didn't kill her," Jonathan said.

"You two going to eat or stand here and jaw?" Jane asked, one fist planted on her hip, her other hand brandishing the long-handled fork in a way that suggested she might at any minute spear one of them.

"We're going to eat," Jubal said, quickly and loudly.

Jonathan was caught up looking at her. She was flushed from the heat, her hair plaited and wound around her head. He thought that with a sword in her hand, she would look like the Norse goddess Freya.

"Jonathan!" Jubal shouted, having started off and found himself alone. "Come along, before she sticks you."

"What are you thinking about now?" Jane asked as Jonathan reached her, a smile playing around her lips.

"You, but I'll eat if you don't stick me."

"Come along." She tucked her arm through his as he passed her. "You need looking after."

"And you need help." He took her hand. "You're going to have it as soon as I can find a way to get it."

Three weeks later the cook shack had a large room added, outfitted with a long table and benches and a black potbellied stove installed at the center of the north-facing wall with a huge wood box beside it, facing the entrance door. The second door opened into the cook shack proper, a sturdy building with a huge stove, three work tables, and a second enormous wood box beside the stove that was kept filled, or someone lost skin at the hands of Jane

Howard.

Yellow Leaf's worsening condition had cast a cloud over everyone on the ranch. Despite close attention from Jonathan and Patience, she was not healing, and having to remain in bed had drained her strength.

"We're losing her," Patience finally told Jonathan. They had just come from Yellow Leaf's room and were standing in front of the fireplace. The evenings were dipping toward frost now, and fires were being lit in the bunkhouse stoves and in the ranch house fireplaces.

"Her temperature is rising, and that means there's infection, despite our efforts," she continued, a slight frown of concern wrinkling her brow. "Do you agree?"

"Reluctantly, yes. We have to stop the infection from spreading, give her body a chance to fight off what's there now."

"This is beyond my capacity. Suggestions?"

"Our best chance," Jonathan said, "is to wash the area in a solution of carbolic acid and accompany that by boiling everything that touches her and washing our hands and arms to the elbows in chlorinated lime. Finally, we swab the affected area with resorcinol and camphor liquefied in alcohol."

"It's worth a try. What about Morgan?"

"I'll tell him, but let's talk with Yellow Leaf first."

They went back into the sickroom. Yellow Leaf lay with her eyes closed in her pale face, her black hair spread around her on the pillow. Before Jonathan could speak, she said, "Whatever you're going to do to me, do it. Not talk to me about it."

"All right," he said. "You'll be sore for a few days. The good news is that, if this works, your fever will go away, and you'll begin to feel better very soon."

She opened her eyes and fixed him with one of her looks. "If not, maybe die," she said.

"I'll do all I can." Jonathan bent down and clasped one of her hands. "And with Patience and Ginger's help, I'll make sure you *don't* die."

She closed her eyes again. The following morning, he found her awake and sitting up, the bedcovers pulled to her waist. She had plaited her hair in two braids that lay against a fresh white doeskin shirt. "Nothing down there where you will be," she told him.

"Fine," Jonathan said. "Your shirt is very nice. I don't think I've seen it before."

"No more talk. Go to work," she said.

Before he could come up with a response,

Patience and Ginger came in, carrying a small table between them, covered with the things Jonathan had requested.

"We're going to put you to sleep and give you a little bath, Yellow Leaf," he said, taking her hand as he had done the day before.

"Someone not has to say anything, Jonathan Wainwright," she said quietly, fixing him with her intense gaze. "You already know."

"Yes," he said, "and Yellow Leaf also knows."

Patience and Ginger laid her back down on the bed.

Yes, she knows, he thought. *It is a good day to die, but not if I can help it.*

Twenty minutes later, Jonathan and the two women dropped the cloths and syringe they had been using into the pail beside the bed. "We've done what we can," he said, painfully aware of the limits of his doctoring abilities.

"I think we've all done a good job," Ginger said with a wide smile. "Now, what she's got to do is heal."

"Let's hope so, Ginger."

"Morgan is waiting outside," Patience said. "Do you want to speak to him or shall I?"

"I will. I'll also tell Jane. She and Yellow

Leaf were very close on the trail, and she finds it difficult to deal with her emotions in this kind of situation."

He left but couldn't help overhearing Ginger's quiet remark to Patience: "Talk about the pot calling the kettle black."

CHAPTER 35

Within a week, Yellow Leaf was out of bed and walking, and the bunkhouse was filled with laughter at the very loud battle she and Jonathan had a day later over whether or not she could ride her pinto. Isaac True was a born mimic and was called on repeatedly to imitate Yellow Leaf's detailed description in her version of English, vanishing at the highest moments into Osage, of the colonel's shortcomings as man, doctor, and human being. Then he would shift voices and say, in an uncanny semblance of Jonathan, "All right, all right, if you want to bleed to death, get on that damned horse. Go right ahead and undo all the work I will have wasted on you."

Yellow Leaf didn't get on her pinto, but, for the next couple of days, everyone who came near her lost some hide, except for Patience and Ginger. Morgan rode into the ranch yard at the height of her war dance, took one look at Yellow Leaf, spun his horse, and fled, not returning until supper time. Once back, he fed his horse in the barn and brushed him, ate with the hands, and disappeared for the night. It was rumored he slept in one of the hay mows.

Jonathan began his new treatment of Yellow Leaf the second week of August, a week before the second mowing of the hay fields that summer. When it was done, the barn haymows were stuffed to the roof, all the hay dry and safely stored. By then, the cows were being milked twice a day by two dark-haired, short, broad-shouldered men Jubal had identified as Genizaros.

"Probably killed somebody," he said, "and decided to take a trip for their health. I'll keep an eye on them, but I doubt they'll give us any trouble. If they had problems with *gringos,* they wouldn't have showed up here."

"Where did they come from?" Jonathan asked.

"Fairplay, Colorado. Said they were working in the gold mines. That's where they learned their English, such as it is. I know what you're thinking. Somebody in the Ring sent them here."

"What are the chances?"

"I think very slim. They've been working

their way south for two months."

"Are they heading for Mexico?"

"Not right away. They say they're sick of moving. Apparently, they went to Colorado to make their fortunes. That didn't happen."

"What are their names? I guess we're going to keep them."

"Good. The taller one is Jose Luger. The other one is Angel Santiago."

"Tell them they're going to take care of the cows, the hens, and whatever else goes on in the barn and around it, and give them all the help they need with learning whatever they don't know."

Jonathan and Jubal were coming out of the barn when they saw Yellow Leaf striding toward them, gripping something in her right hand. The two men stopped to watch her approach, and, as she drew nearer, Jonathan saw she was carrying Patience's buggy whip.

"Lord a' mighty," Jubal muttered. "We're in for it."

"Jubal Smith," she said, closing on them. "Go away."

"Good luck," he said to Jonathan out of the side of his mouth. "Shoot her if you have to."

Jubal moved off, and Yellow Leaf thrust the butt of the whip into Jonathan's stomach. "Take," she said.

He grabbed it to keep it from falling to the ground.

"Now you will beat me," she said. "So I will feel better. Start now."

Her last words were muffled because she had dropped to sit on her heels, with her hands folded across the back of her neck.

"What are you talking about?" Jonathan demanded, badly shaken. He glanced around to see who was watching. Fortunately, no one was. The two new men were behind the barn, building a board fence for the sheep Jonathan had bought. "Yellow Leaf, get up," he went on, beginning to feel desperate.

"No," she said. "You must beat me."

Jonathan feared her mind had slipped. Casting the whip aside, he bent down, slipped his arms around her and, with some effort, straightened up and carried her into the barn in a shuffling run. Once inside the doors, he sank to the floor still holding her.

"What in God's name do you think you're doing?" he gasped.

She'd kept her hands folded behind her head, with her elbows pressed against the sides of her face. Now, she lifted one elbow and turned her head just enough to peer at him with one eye. "Where is whip?" she demanded.

"I don't know," he said, still short of breath.

"Put me down. I will find it. Then you beat me."

"No, I will not."

She tightened herself into a ball, gave a long cry of misery, and broke into tears just as his ability to hold her gave out. He tried to lay her down and get up at the same time but failed. Yellow Leaf rolled out of his arms and thudded to the floor. Jonathan lost his balance and landed on his back.

Jubal, with Jacob Drew in tow, came into the barn then and found them.

"There's got to be some reason this is happening," Jacob said drily, "but it escapes me."

"It's not funny." Jonathan struggled to his feet.

"I saw that from the start," Jacob said, scratching his beard.

"Why is Yellow Leaf crying?" Jubal asked.

Jonathan glared at him. Jacob said, "Why not ask her? Though you better hope she ain't carrying a knife."

Jubal walked over to her and squatted down near her head. "Yellow Leaf, why are you crying?"

She made no answer, only cried harder.

Thoroughly disgusted with himself, and more concerned than he wanted to be, Jonathan strode around Jubal, reached down, wrapped his arms around Yellow Leaf, and lifted her off the floor.

"Come over here, Jacob," he said. "Help me unfold her."

"Somebody will stand herself," Yellow Leaf barked. "I must go away. Jonathan Wainwright will not forgive me."

"Did she ask you to beat her?" Jacob said, suddenly serious.

"Yes," Jonathan said. "She's either ill or something's disturbed her mind."

"And you refused, Colonel?"

"Of course I did."

"She is saying she is sorry for something, and if you beat her, she knows you forgive her," Jacob explained. "If you don't, she'll know you haven't forgiven her."

Jubal stared at him. "How did you know that?"

"I lived with the Pawnee a while back, right after I left Vermont. I took to one of their young women. Then she died of the pox, and I left and joined the army. They're an interesting people, the Pawnee. I reckon they growed me up."

Jonathan sat on his heels beside Yellow Leaf. "Is this true, what Jacob says?"

She wouldn't look at him. "Someone knows it is and is still angry with me."

Jacob and Jubal, apparently thinking their work was done, walked off talking about living with the Indians. Jonathan stayed where he was. "I am not angry with you, Yellow Leaf," he said. "I'm sorry I quarreled with you. You just wanted not to be sick anymore and to get your old life back. I was angry because I knew, if you did ride your paint, something very bad would happen to you."

She turned her head and met his gaze. "You were worry about me?"

"Of course."

"Why I not know that?" Her face, which had begun to brighten, fell again.

"Do you read minds?"

"I don't read anything," she snapped, showing a hint of spirit.

"Patience or Ginger would teach you to read if you asked one of them."

"What would I read?"

"If you learn to read, I will give you so many books and newspapers that you will read all day long, every day."

She looked at him for a full minute before speaking. "I will stand up. Perhaps, if someone will not beat me, he would put his arms around me."

"Let's find out."

She stood, and Jonathan pulled her against him. It felt good to hold her, and he had a fleeting thought that he should do more of this. He realized he would like to go right on hugging this woman and reluctantly released her. "Seems he would," he said.

She clung to him for a moment longer before stepping back.

"We have work for ranch," she said.

"And lives we're committed to," he added, taking one of her hands.

They walked out of the shadowed peace of the barn together into the bright light of the day.

Gradually, all that needed doing regularly on the ranch developed a rhythm, and all the people knew what they were to do and when it was to be done. Jonathan, freed of any tasks concerning the ranch house, spent most of his days riding with Jubal. Jubal made it a rule to be wherever a cow was calving, or Morgan was beginning the task of training the two-year-old horses to tolerate saddle blankets and saddles on their backs.

"Can't rush this," Morgan told Jonathan. "Cow horses have to strengthen muscles in legs and back to carry a man. Spoils a horse to ride it too soon. Breaks down later on."

"How long does the training last?" Jonathan asked, somewhat surprised.

"A year. A two-year-old has more growing to do."

"He won't break them by riding them to a standstill if they buck," Jubal told Jonathan later. "He says it ruins the relationship between horse and man to do that to it, and there's no need. He says he 'eases them into accepting a rider.' "

"And all that's in Morgan's head," Jonathan said, surprised even more. "He's a remarkable man."

"I believe you could say that," Jubal replied. "I think he talks to the critters."

Jonathan had some additional surprises to absorb — this time from Patience, who had quietly but effectively, enlisting Yellow Leaf's help, managed to persuade Morgan to train one of his three-year-old fillies. She was Ginger's pick, a reddish-brown sorrel with flaxen tail and mane, named Rosebud because of a small daub of white on her forehead. Rosebud was taught to wear a harness and pull Patience's buggy.

Once Patience had mastered harnessing Rosebud and driven her in the buggy back and forth on the ranch road a dozen times, she and Ginger made several trips to town. That done, they set up a room, wrangled from Jane, as the ranch office. It was a large corner room at a distance from the kitchen and busier parts of the house, with two windows and a view of the mountains. Patience had also talked Jubal into lending her two men to move a twelve-foot red, black, and beige wool rug into the room, and over the next week a large rolltop desk and chair, two wooden filing cabinets, and a dark wooden table with four straight-backed chairs.

"There," she said to Ginger when the black iron potbellied stove was installed and its metal piping fitted into the fireplace chimney. She set a brass reading lamp on the desk and placed two metal-nibbed pens and an ink well at the corner of the green writing square. "Let's get to work. Straightening out this man's finances will be as difficult as cleaning out the Augean Stables."

"The what?"

"I'll explain later."

As the weeks passed, Jonathan came to dread one thing and look forward to another. Being called to the office made him feel like a boy being told to report to the headmaster. Invariably, he was obliged to sit and have the meaning of *bankruptcy* explained to him and how close he was to

511

experiencing it. He never did find the courage to tell Patience he was heir to a fortune he had left in Boston untouched. He had promised himself he would make the ranch a successful business but obviously had miscalculated how long it would take.

What he increasingly looked forward to was having dinner with Jane and her mother and the three younger Howard children. At first, Jane had tried to dissuade him. "Those young ones are rackety and have more to say than a flock of crows. Shutting them up is harder than stopping water from running downhill."

"No use, Jane," he said. "You, your mother, the children, Patience, Ginger, Horn, and I are eating together."

He failed to drag Yellow Leaf and Morgan into the group and lost Jubal to the cook shack. "Better I eat with them, Colonel," Jubal had said. "I will hear of everything leading to trouble before it gets dug in."

The clear, crisp days of autumn brought the mountains so close, as Jane said, "Why, when I step out of the house, I feel I can reach out and touch them."

Quite suddenly in September, the aspen leaves turned color, and great swatches of yellow, gold, orange, and red spread across the mountainsides. Snow began to show on the tips of the highest peaks, and, when the nights dipped below the frost line, high on their mountain pastures the ranch's flock of a hundred Churro sheep — an old and hardy breed in New Mexico — followed the elk, led by Bidzil, their young Navajo shepherd. Bidzil packed up his wagon hut, which had been his home for over a month, harnessed his horse, and, followed by his flock and the old belled ewe, moved slowly down the mountain to where he could see the smoke from the ranch house, only to find the elk were there before him. Elk and sheep alike left the ranch's heights and northern boundary to the eagles, the frost, and the knife-sharp wind.

The fall had brought a sense of tranquility to the ranch, shared by Jonathan and all the others. The days were filled with a warm instead of a flaming sunshine, stars blazed in the sky on the cold, clear nights, and the moon was made of silver.

September was running out of days when the tranquility was shattered by rustlers. They hit half an hour before daybreak on a full moon and stampeded more than half the cattle west around the mountain.

"They're turning the cattle north," Jubal told Jonathan, "and, by the looks, headed for the Pecos Wilderness."

"How far will they run before they stop?" Jonathan asked.

"I've known them to run twenty miles. The shooting started them off, but they ain't scared enough to run that far. Also, the going between here and the Wilderness is mighty rough. If the rustlers try to keep them running, the herd will break and scatter."

"Do we saddle up and begin the chase?"

In the time it had taken Jonathan to get outside and find Jubal, all the hands from the bunkhouse had poured out into the ranch yard, followed shortly by the women. Morgan and Yellow Leaf, mounted and armed, arrived last.

Shouts from the men urged action, but Jubal waited until the shouting stopped and then said, loud enough for all to hear, "Colonel, once the cattle stop running, the rustlers won't be able to walk them much more than fifteen miles a day, with a noonday rest to graze and a full halt at dark. My advice is, we hang here 'til breakfast, gather our gear, take pack animals with what we'll need for, say, five days. Check our guns, take plenty of ammunition, then go after them."

"I don't think we'll need more than a day

to overtake them," Jonathan said, "but I take your point. Some of us will have to stay with the cattle to bring them home."

"Take Bidzil for scout," Yellow Leaf said. "He can see better and knows when bush moves if wind or person."

"Bidzil!" Jonathan called. "Will you scout for us?"

"Sure," the young Indian said, "but lion and young one making ready to kill sheep. Someone better watch."

"Someone will watch," Yellow Leaf said.

Jonathan turned toward her. In the first light breaking over the mountains, she sat on her brown and white pinto as if she were part of it, her back straight, her rifle resting in the crook of her left arm. Beautiful in a way entirely her own, the picture of unyielding courage.

"Can you and Morgan stay with the sheep until we return?" he asked her. "Two or three of the men will attend to the rest of the cattle and the horses here. Jose and Angel will take care of the milk cows and barn animals and give Jane and Patience and Ginger whatever help they need. Have you seen Jane?"

His question was answered when Jane, rallying her crew, called out, "We better start the cookhouse fires for breakfast."

He caught up with her, hurrying toward the cookhouse, and stopped her long enough to tell her who would stay to look after the ranch.

"Are you worried about the Ring?" she asked, frowning slightly as if anticipating his answer. "If you are, don't be. We have enough guns here to hold off the whole town. You just concentrate on getting those cattle and coming back in one piece." She gripped his shoulder firmly. "I've gotten used to eating my suppers with you at the table."

"I find it the best part of my day," he told her and realized it was true.

They looked at one another for a long moment. Then she snapped out of it and gave him a shake. "Get on," she said. "Sooner you start, sooner you'll get back."

Jubal was waiting when Jonathan returned. "I'll have three of the older men keep watch here," he said. "I'm thinking this cattle raid may be the opening of something. It's got the smell of the Ring about it."

"I agree," Jonathan said. "Add two of our best gunmen to the three older men you've chosen. Looking ahead that way makes me think that, as soon as we've recovered the cattle, we had better get back here, and fast."

CHAPTER 36

Midmorning on the second day, Bidzil, riding one of the fastest horses in the remuda, burst up out of a valley, his black hair flaring out behind him, and pulled up in a clatter of stones beside Jonathan.

"They come!" Bidzil shouted. "One see me."

They were crossing a stretch of rocky table land, strewn with broken ledges and clumps of dense spruce brush. "Rifles out," Jonathan shouted to his men. "Scatter and take cover. Fire at my word." Turning back to Bidzil, he said, "Ride on until you hear shooting. Go!"

Bidzil put his heels into the roan gelding and raced away. In less than a minute, Jonathan, Jubal, and all the rest had dismounted and vanished behind cover. A moment later four horsemen came into sight, riding hard. All were bare to the waist, with feathers in their hair. They had nearly reached the first riderless horse, browsing on a clump of wire grass, when the lead rustler appeared to guess what Jonathan and his men had done. He reined in his horse and began shouting. His companions yanked their animals into a turn.

"Fire!" Jonathan shouted. The four riders went down in the first barrage.

As the echo of gunfire faded, Jonathan reached the first of the fallen men. "Indians," he said. "Anyone know what tribe they belong to?"

"Here's Bidzil," one of the men called out.

Jonathan turned to the Navajo boy as he rode up. "What are they, Bidzil?"

"Comanche!" Bidzil said with alarm in his voice. "These ones bad."

"I didn't know the Comanche were still raiding here."

"They do this for someone else now," Bidzil answered. "Anyone who will pay them. Kill everybody. Bad ones. If they catch me, I am dead with" — he used two Navajo words that everyone understood when he went on — "stuffed in mouth. Guts spilled."

"We've lost the advantage of surprise," Jubal said, "but there's four we won't have to deal with."

Jonathan and his men mounted up. "Let's get this over with," Jonathan said. "Bidzil, when did you see the cattle?"

"Follow them one night," the young Navajo said. "Not go fast. Men push but animals tired."

"Are they all Comanches?"

"No, men I saw white and Mexicans."

"How far ahead of us are they?" Jubal asked.

"Not far. Will hear shooting."

"You stay with me, Bidzil, and be my eyes," Jonathan said. "The rest of you, follow close enough to hear me call. Stay as spread out as possible but within sight and hearing."

They dropped down off the ridge into a grassy valley and soon came on the tracks of the cattle, along with evidence of their having slowed to graze at intervals. The small, shallow valley soon gave way to rocky, brush-dotted hills.

"Smell them?" Bidzil asked Jonathan in a low voice. "Close. Over next hill maybe."

When they were partway up that hill, Jonathan stopped them. To Bidzil, he said, "Go up the rest of the way on foot and take a look, and keep your head down. Crawl the last few yards."

The Navajo boy slid off his horse and raced up the hill, toward a small stand of spruce. He dropped to his stomach and went the rest of the way on his elbows and knees, then halted and stared through a clump of brush. After a few moments, he crawled back below the crest of the hill.

"They are there," he told Jonathan. "Must cross open place to reach them. They will see us."

"How many are they?"

"I count six. They are trying to push cattle, but very rocky. Lots of trees. Not much grass."

Jonathan looked up, thinking over what Bidzil had told him. He saw they were hemmed in on both sides and further in the front by mountains.

"Does this trail run all the way to the Wilderness?" he asked Jubal, who had joined them.

"I believe so. The Pecos River is out there somewhere."

"We will get this done as quickly as possible." Jonathan swung back up on Sam. "Bidzil, you stay back, away from the shooting. Thank you for your good work. I'm proud of you, and I don't want you getting shot. Get behind us."

"They much spread out," Bidzil told him. "Maybe I should come and tell you where."

"On your horse, Bidzil," Jonathan said with a smile. "We'll find them as soon as they start shooting at us."

With Jonathan on the right wing of the line, and Jubal on the left, the ranch riders went over the crest of the hill. Once below the point where they were silhouetted against the sky, Jonathan signaled a pause. Below them, less than a quarter of a mile ahead, the herd was moving slowly along the side of a ledge and a rock- and spruce brush-strewn hill.

Bidzil had been right about the rustlers being spread out along the edges of the cattle. As far as Jonathan could tell, none had seen them come over the hill. *Too occupied,* he thought, turning Sam toward Jubal. "Who is the best rifle shot among us?" he asked.

"Orrington, I would say," Jubal answered.

Orrington listened carefully to Jonathan's instructions, nodded, and moved away down the hill, taking advantage of all the cover the spruce growth could give him.

"Now, we wait for the crack of Orrington's rifle," Jonathan told the men. "Then we break cover and move down as quickly as we can. Start shooting as far back of the herd as possible so as not to spook them. Stay in sight of one another. I don't want any mistakes."

A minute crawled by. Then a rifle shot

rang out, and Jonathan saw one of the rustlers knocked off his horse.

"Our turn," Jubal said. The men spread out and drove toward the cattle, riding as fast as the ground would let them.

Jonathan counted five rustlers, but only one pulled his rifle free and stood in his stirrups to fire. He was too late. Jonathan and his men were in firing distance, and the man was killed instantly. The rest of the rustlers made no effort to draw their weapons and spurred their horses in a full retreat.

"Hold your fire!" Jonathan shouted, reining in Sam.

The men also pulled in and for a few moments sat in silence, watching the rustlers racing off. Jubal called to Isaac True, "Find the lead cow. Turn her. Put a rope on her if necessary. The others will follow her. The rest of you, drive in the stragglers."

"We're going home, gentlemen!" Isaac shouted, bringing cheers from the men as they set off to gather the herd.

"Let's you and I take a look at that downed man," Jonathan said to Jubal.

The man lay on his side, his bloody hands pressed against his rib cage. Seeing them approach, he struggled to draw his revolver.

"Don't be a fool," Jonathan told him, peeling the fellow's hand off the gun butt and shoving it back into its holster. "I'm a doctor. Let me have a look at that wound." He ripped open the man's shirt and carefully lifted his other hand off the bleeding injury. Looking up at Jubal, he said, "We're going to need the pack horse. It's carrying the medical supplies and my bag."

"Maybe we should just shoot him," Jubal said flatly.

"Let's try something first," Jonathan answered calmly. "Fetch the pack horse carrying the medical bags."

With a grunt of disapproval, Jubal mounted and heeled his brown quarter horse into a run.

"What's your name," Jonathan asked the wounded rustler, proceeding to tear the man's shirt off. He folded the torn cloth and pressed it against the wound.

"What difference does it make? You're going to kill me."

"No, I'm going to save your life if things go well. What's your name?" He had taken a good long look at the man, trying to draw conclusions about him. He judged the rustler to be in his forties. The man was sweating from his pain, his thick dark hair plastered to his head.

"Hodge Walker," the man said, trying to stifle a groan.

"You native to these parts?" Jonathan asked, trying to talk him through his jolts of pain until Jubal returned.

"Kansas," the man gasped. "Chose the wrong side. Lost farm, wife, kids."

His voice grew weaker between the words. Moments later, Jubal arrived with the piebald pack horse. The animal shied, snorting and rolling its eyes at the smell of blood. Jubal slid to the ground and grasped the animal's bridle, quieting it by backing it away a few yards.

Meanwhile, Jonathan unstrapped one of the sacks and unpacked his bag, instruments, ether, and a roll of boiled cloth. He set them all within reach and knelt again beside the wounded man. Around them, nervous from being turned, cattle were crashing through the scrub brush and bellowing. Despite the herd's efforts not to cooperate, the men were slowly pressing them together and driving them toward Morgan and the lead cow.

"Who hired you to steal these cattle?" Jonathan asked.

"Was I to tell you, I'd be dead within the week," the man said between gasps.

"I'm going to give you a choice, Mr. Walker. If you refuse to answer my question, I'll leave you here to bleed to death. It will take about an hour." He felt severe jolts of conscience for making such a threat, but he would treat the man whether he answered or not. That knowledge took some of the sting out of having said such a thing — but not much.

"Now, if you tell me who hired you, I'm going to take that bullet out of you, clean the wound, tie off the severed blood vessels, sew you up, bandage the wound, give you water and four days of grub, hobble your horse here where he can graze, give you back your rifle and sidearm, and wait until you regain consciousness. By tomorrow, you can mount and ride. It won't be comfortable, but you will manage."

The man drew a hissing breath. "I don't have anyone's name, but I was told it's the Ring that's paying me."

He'd thought as much. "One more thing, Mr. Walker," Jonathan said. "Don't ever go back to Santa Fe."

"Deal," Walker said and fainted.

"Good." Jonathan grabbed the ether. "He's making it easy for us."

Half an hour later, Jonathan tied the last bandage around Walker's middle and got to his feet. Over the next half hour, he and Jubal made the man as comfortable as possible. Jubal started a small fire, circled with rocks, with a supply of wood close by. Food and water lay within the man's reach, and his horse was hobbled and tied.

"Just in case," Jubal said, after watering the animal in a nearby stream. He eyed the unconscious rustler doubtfully. "Will he be able to stand by tomorrow?"

"I think so. The bullet missed the vital organs and didn't do much collateral damage," Jonathan said, pulling Sam's head up. "He'll be sore, but he should be on his horse by tomorrow afternoon."

CHAPTER 37

Once turned toward the ranch, the herd, at ease with their lead cow in front of them, needed no prodding.

"They know where they're going," Jubal said, "and are in a hurry to get there."

Jonathan was pleased with the cattle's eagerness. He sent Bidzil ahead to tell Jane and the others they would be at the ranch sooner than expected. "Be sure to tell her we have not lost anyone, and make a point of telling Yellow Leaf as well."

At day's end, Jonathan sat in his saddle, watching the herd stream past him into the shallow canyon Jubal had chosen for the night's bedding ground. There was plenty of grass, and the lead cow had gone straight to the creek running the length of the valley, followed by the rest of the herd. Night was climbing in the eastern sky, and, behind him in the west, the colors were fading from the clouds over the mountains. The temperature had slid during the day, and Jonathan felt the chill enough to make him shiver.

As he lifted his coat from his bedroll, he experienced a sudden drop in his spirits. The last of the herd had trotted down the slope toward the water, and the cattle that had slaked their thirst were grazing. A few of the leaders were already lying down, chewing their cuds. Looking over the sea of brown backs and breathing the sharply cold air, redolent with the herd's pungent smell, he suddenly realized he was intensely lonely.

At first, he thought it was just the flushing out of adrenalin after recovering the cattle and driving away the remaining rustlers. But that proved an inadequate explanation, although in the past he would have forced himself to believe it.

No, he admitted. *I'm lonely, and from my own choosing. I'm lonely because I have repeatedly told myself I'm not fit to care for a woman. Well, I'm not.* The old excuse sounded suddenly hollow. "No, cowardly," he said, loudly enough to startle a dozing Sam awake.

"Whoa," Jonathan said. "Easy, Sam. Settle down and eat some grass."

Sam was always comfortable with eating. Jonathan dropped the reins over the horse's neck and went back to thinking about his situation. He thought so long, the red in the sky had faded to pink and then purple along the tops of the eastern mountains, and cooking fires bloomed below him on the bank of the creek.

"Colonel, you planning to eat tonight?" Jubal asked, walking up to him. "The meat will be a burnt offering if you don't come along."

"I lost track of the time," Jonathan said. "Thank you, Jubal, for calling it to my attention. I can certainly eat."

"You've had a load on your shoulders lately, Colonel. I guess you're entitled to watch the sunset."

They both knew that was not what he had been doing, but Jubal could usually be counted on to find a way out of an awkward moment. Jubal had not wanted to pry, and Jonathan ate his supper with no idea where his revelation was going to take him.

From the place where they reversed direction to where they were in the high country, the temperatures had been dipping to the thirties at night and rising into the seventies during the day. The skies were clear, and the cattle were up and eager to go by daylight. Their advance had not been hindered by weather or bear or wolf attacks, and the steers did a minimum amount of damage to one another or the other cattle. The men had learned very early that, in responding to a call of nature, it was essential to keep one's horse within reach throughout the ceremony, however absorbing. Even the herd bull kept his distance from the older longhorns.

"Well, Colonel, there she is," Jubal said cheerfully when their mountain came into view.

"A welcome sight," Jonathan agreed. "I think we'll sleep in a bed tonight."

And they did.

The next morning, over breakfast, he gave Jane, Patience, and Ginger an account of Hodge Walker and the flight of his fellow rustlers. "What are you going to do about the Ring?" Jane asked him.

"Might it not be wise to do nothing?" Patience suggested. "They've been beaten twice. I would think they have learned their lesson."

The others stopped eating at that and stared at Jonathan. He set his coffee mug back on the table, not in order to answer Patience, but to shake off the flicker of battle scenes that began running through his head.

"I'm not sure," he said, struggling to

extract himself from the unwelcome images that had flooded his mind. "I'm not sure men learn from experience — especially when their pride and their money are threatened."

"You're thinking of the war," Patience said. "In those events, I would find your assertion undeniable, but we're speaking here of a group of unscrupulous thieves, motivated chiefly by greed."

"I say they should be hanged and get it over with," Jane said. "Too much talk makes my head go round." She grinned suddenly and added, "I like the Yellow Leaf solution: 'Put knife in them. Talk later.' "

Patience groaned, but Ginger laughed. So did Jonathan and took the opportunity to end the discussion. "Perhaps Patience is right. Perhaps we won't have to do anything. We have the cattle back. There's plenty of grass on the lower pastures. The barn's full of hay. The grain room's chock-a-block, the chickens are laying eggs enough to feed us, the cows are giving milk and cream from which Jane is churning butter. By March, we will double, minus one, our sheep numbers, and Ginger has stopped burning the bacon."

"Oh! You!" Ginger threw her napkin at him.

Later in the morning, he rode out to speak with Morgan about how they should handle the horses with the cold weather coming on. It was the wrangler's opinion that they should be brought well below the tree line so they could graze without contending with the snow, and where there were pines enough to give some protection from the wind. "I'll watch the mares that are pregnant. You can take them down when the time comes and let them foal in the stables."

"How do you tell?"

"When her udders start leaking milk, usually. Sometimes they fool you."

And that was all Morgan had to say on those subjects.

Riding back down the mountain, Jonathan met Yellow Leaf.

"Someone has to speak. It will not be easy," she said, swinging down from her pinto.

Her words, and the serious look on her face, gave him pause. "All right," he said, dismounting and dropping his reins as she had done, letting Sam graze.

She didn't start talking right away. Then: "Horn needs to find out who he is. I will take care of him."

She had difficulty saying the words, caus-ing Jonathan to suspect that she had something much more important to say and was finding it hard to continue.

"He is a good boy. I think it is very good of you and Morgan to take him into your family."

"He is Indian, but he has always lived among those who did not know who they were."

He felt a chill. "Yellow Leaf, what are you trying to tell me?"

"With the next full moon, I will go away with Horn."

That floored him. "Where will you go?"

"Back to my people. Horn will become Osage and have real name. He will talk with the old ones and learn who he is."

"Has he agreed to this?"

"Yes."

"What does Morgan say? Will he go with you?"

"He may go. Not know."

He floundered, having run out of objections. "Why are you doing this?"

"You do not say, 'Don't go.' " She paused briefly, then said, "Jonathan Wainwright knows why I go."

"If I said, 'don't go'?"

"You don't say." Her answer had the ring of finality. He found he could not respond.

"I will go back to what is left of my

people," she continued, "and give Horn a life. He will marry and have children. His life will have meaning."

"You said you left because the day of the Indian nations was drawing to a close."

"And I spoke wisely, but some of that world remains. Enough, I think, to save Horn."

She paused again and held Jonathan's gaze for a long moment. "He will be child we never had."

"Yellow Leaf . . ." Jonathan couldn't go on. The stinging behind his eyes was too intense, a sensation that startled him and knotted his stomach. He had not wept since he was a child, but her words went through his heart like the thrust of a knife, and he dared not speak for fear of breaking down.

"Jonathan!" she cried. "Not have to speak. We both know."

"We know," he admitted. Then, his voice cracking despite his best efforts, he asked, "Why the full moon?"

"We will travel at night, sleep in day. More safe," she said.

"Where will you go?"

"West of where trail started, but all the bands will move soon, I think. Buy land to make permanent home in Oklahoma. You know place?"

"Yes, it will become a state soon. Is that where you were going when you found Morgan?"

"No, had been west in mountains. Not sure where to go. Thought Morgan was place to rest."

Jonathan managed to laugh. "You have not had much rest."

"Found you and Jane and Patience. Almost enough to start a village."

She got back on her paint. Looking down at Jonathan, she said quietly, "I will leave with Horn in ten suns."

Not giving him time to reply, she swung her mare away from him and rode up the mountain toward her camp, disappearing at last into the trees. For several minutes he continued to stare at the place where she had slipped from sight. When he finally turned to Sam, he was still struggling with the pain of her going, with no cessation in sight.

Over dinner, Jonathan told Ginger, Patience, and Jane what Yellow Leaf intended to do. Their responses were varied. Ginger was sure she was leaving because of what happened when the slavers abducted her. "No one could get over that," she said with a shudder. "There's too much around here to remind her of it. When she sees one of us, she has to think of it."

Patience agreed in part with Ginger, but she thought Yellow Leaf was missing her people. "We've never learned why, exactly, she went off by herself. Whatever it was, I wonder if she decided to go back and deal with it among her own kind."

Ginger shook her head. "You're always telling me that certainty comes from facts, and what you've told us doesn't have any."

Patience made no response to that, save for a good-natured smile. She returned to eating, forcing Ginger to abandon her argument. Throughout the exchange, Jane watched Jonathan.

"What do you think, Jane?" he asked, then instantly wished he hadn't.

"How do you feel?" she asked quietly.

That was just what he did *not* want to talk about.

"Well," he said, bracing himself, "she's a valued member of our group, and I hate the idea of losing Morgan. I doubt we'll ever find someone who knows horses the way he does."

"You didn't answer Jane's question," Ginger said sharply.

"How do you feel?" Jane repeated.

"Is this a group interrogation?" he demanded, trying to sound jocular.

"I think you two had the makings of a pair," Ginger said, blundering forward. "What do you think, Jane?"

Jonathan needed to end this.

"If you remember," he said, "Yellow Leaf and I spent a lot of time together, riding point for the train. I found her to be an intelligent and complex person. It was never easy to understand her. She hasn't had an easy life, and she often found me wanting, especially about the world around us. She thought I needed looking after. She was particularly impatient with my inability to see things she saw even when she pointed them out."

"Like what?"

"If a deer was running, it was probably being chased. If buffalo are stampeding, you must run sideways to escape the herd, never try outrun it."

"I think you've answered me," Jane said coldly and picked up her knife and fork.

Jonathan went back to eating, though the food tasted like sand to him. He had not escaped unscathed, but he had lived to maneuver for another day.

The following day, news arrived that turned attention away from Yellow Leaf's departure. Half a dozen of the ranch men had decided to spend some time in town. They had agreed in advance that the beer was better in the hotel bar than anywhere else and settled on going there. The evening grew cheerful, and the six ranch hands decided to sing. The attempt wasn't entirely successful. People sitting at the tables eating and playing cards shouted and threw bread at them. So, they gave up on that and agreed to confine themselves to arguing and drinking beer.

Another group at the bar had taken umbrage at having men from the Wainwright ranch in their bar. They were men who worked for the bank, the lawyers, the stores and stables, providing the muscle when someone got out of line. Their leader, a tall, bearded, ape-armed man missing a front tooth, stepped away from his group and sucker-punched the ranch hand closest to him. He stepped over his victim and started to say something, but the next two Wainwright men threw their beer in his face, picked him up, and heaved him headfirst over the bar.

By then the first ranch hand was on his feet, aggravated by what had happened. When another of the town gang took a swing at him, he dropped the man in his tracks. For the next few minutes, the bar was filled with flying punches, tables overturned, drinks spilled, and one or two men thrown through the windows and into the street. When the dust settled, the six Wainwright men were the last ones standing.

"You are dead men," the ape-man said, staggering to his feet behind the bar, blood running down his face from the gash in his head. "Before this week is out, we're coming for you Yankee bastards."

Harland Boone reached across the bar and gave the fellow a shove. "I came from Kentucky," he said. Unsteady as he was, the ape-man fell back, crashed into a shelf lined with bottles, and went down in a splintering of glass and the strong smell of Whistlepig Whiskey.

"I believe it's time we went home," Boone said, "before one of those fellas remembers he's got a gun."

Harland Boone was out of his bunk before the sun was up, and, when Jonathan came out on the porch shortly after, he found Harland waiting for him.

"Colonel," Harland said, "I'm sorry to be bothering you with this so early in the day, but I couldn't go on sleeping for fear I'd forget it. Me and some of the others went into town and overheard something I think you should know." He went through the bar fight, ending with the ape-man's threat. "Fella said, 'Before the week is out, we're coming after you Yankee bastards.' I'm sorry about the strong language."

"Were you at the hotel bar?"

"Yes, and there were some pretty hard cases in there."

"Ring men?"

"Couldn't say, but I didn't see no Sunday school teachers among them, and many of them weren't men any of us had seen before."

"Why am I not surprised? Thank you, Harland. I'll get us together at midmorning. Would you get word to those up on the mountain?"

"I'll go myself."

"After breakfast will be soon enough. Have you spoken to Jubal?"

"No, Colonel, I ain't seen anyone but you since leaving the bunkhouse."

"I'll speak to Jubal."

He did so at the first opportunity. When Jonathan and Jubal came out of the ranch house after their brief conference, everyone, including the house staff, had gathered in front of the bunkhouse, in a grassy space as close to being flat as anywhere on the ranch lands. Jonathan saw at once that Yellow Leaf was there, sitting on her paint, her rifle cradled in her left arm. Seeing her jarred him and made him slightly angry.

He stepped up onto a low outcropping of granite that gave him a view of everyone. The women had gone to some trouble to dress well and stood together quietly, avoiding the banter with the men that usually sprang up when they were together.

"Thank you for being here," Jonathan began. "We may be in danger, and, while I have no proof of it, beyond a report Harland Boone gave me, I feel it necessary to make the same preparations I would take if it were a certainty."

He paused, noting the restlessness in the people before him. He realized he was only delaying what he had brought them together to say.

"The Ring may be planning another attack on us. They have probably brought in new gunmen to replace those they lost in the last encounter. Jubal and I have agreed on a plan that should tell us when they are coming. If they're coming, it will probably be soon, possibly within the week."

He stopped again. This time there was no restlessness. The group's attention was riveted on him.

The hardest part of his task lay before him now. "I want to tell you all how sorry I am that what I have done since coming to Santa Fe has repeatedly put you in danger. None of you is obliged to stay here and risk your life. I will think of you just as highly and fully understand should you decide to leave. No explanation will be needed."

He stopped talking, finding it difficult to continue. Then Yellow Leaf broke the silence. "Someone thinks Jonathan Wainwright should get on with it, not waste time. Anybody who wants to leave didn't come here anyway."

That produced laughter and broke the tension. Jonathan said, "Jubal and I agree that, when they come, they will not approach up the road but from the mountain, along the old Pecos Wilderness trail they used to drive off the cattle and we used to bring them back."

"You going to set a watch on the road anyway, Colonel?" someone asked.

"Yes, indeed. We'll do just what we did before, only add watches on the mountain as well. There's going to be some sleep lost, but I see no way to avoid it."

"Keep Bill Johnson out there as much as you can, Colonel," Burchard Harley said. "He snores something awful."

More laughter.

"If any of you have any ideas how best to

go about this, talk to me or Jubal. We've drawn up some plans, but we're ready to improve them. Roughly speaking, I'd like to catch the Ring men before they get down here."

"Where do you want us?" Jane asked. "Wherever that is, we will need to be armed."

"Where do you want to be?" Jubal asked.

"Wherever the men are," Patience said. "If there's someone hurt, we need to be, as Jane said, armed and close by."

Her words sobered the group again.

"You and Jane take charge of that," Jonathan said. "If we are short of anything, let Jubal know before the day is out. One thing more. I have to talk to the commanding officer at Fort Marcy. I expect to be back late this afternoon. Any questions?"

The fort was nearly abandoned, and the small detachment of men remaining, under the command of Captain John Sparing, did not occupy the fort but lived in barracks outside the nine-foot-high adobe walls.

"You have built a reputation in the short time you have been in Santa Fe," Captain Sparing said, leaning back in his swivel chair and eyeing his visitor with indifference. "Who are you, anyway?"

Sparing was short and heavily built, his dark hair thickly laced with white. Jonathan guessed he was a man approaching retirement who had lived his entire adult life in the army and had been sent here to sit out the last few years of his service, a man who had done nothing wrong but who had simply filled a space in advancement to advancement from enlistment to the present.

Jonathan decided to lean in heavily. "I am Colonel Jonathan Wainwright, retired, General Philip Sheridan's cavalry. I rode with the general from the Shenandoah campaign to Appomattox."

Sparing shot out of his chair and saluted. "Colonel, I am sorry. I did not associate your name with the achievements of General Sheridan."

"No reason why you should, Captain. The honor of those campaigns belongs to General Sheridan. I just happened to be one of his officers."

"More than that, sir. Your achievements go before you and are not forgotten. How can I be of help?"

"You are familiar with my encounters with the Ring?"

"I could pretend not to know what you meant by the *Ring,* but I will not insult your intelligence. There are rumors that they are planning another assault on you, and there's nothing I can do about it."

"Do you know who the head of the Ring is?"

"Let me digress a moment. One of the few assignments given to this posting is to keep as close track as possible of the criminal activities of the Ring. I have, however, the strictest orders not to intervene." Sparing tugged at the bottom of his not-too-clean jacket and stared at his boots, which needed polishing.

"What else are you supposed to do?" Jonathan asked.

"Protect Santa Fe and surrounding areas from Indian raids, especially from the Comanches, who haven't raided this area for several years."

"And you've got what? Seventy men?"

"Sixty."

"Well, I suspect the army will close you down before long."

"You're probably right."

The captain sighed, glanced out the window with a spider web in the top right corner, and said as if unloading a burden, "Elwood Chandler, owner of the biggest realty company and the big General Store in the town center, where his office is, and enough other property, most of it stolen, to start a town of his own. A mouse doesn't fart in Santa Fe without his permission. If anyone is coming after you, he will have sent them."

"If anything were to happen to him, is there someone who could step into his shoes?"

"No. He didn't allow anyone to gain that much leverage. There are half a dozen men, mostly lawyers and a couple of judges, who would have to fight for a while before someone came out on top."

"If I were to shoot him, who would come after me?"

"Not I, nor anyone else. Everyone would be too busy making sure they weren't getting their throats cut."

Jonathan put out his hand. "Thank you, Captain Sparing, for your time and your help. Good luck with the remainder of your assignment."

"My pleasure, Colonel, and we never had this conversation. We had another one, reminiscing about old army days. Do you wish you were still with the cavalry?"

"Whenever I begin to feel that way, I know I'm coming down with something and look for a pink pill."

Sparing grinned. "I can't imagine not being in the army. Been in it my whole adult life. Never known anything else. Didn't even marry."

"Not too late," Jonathan said and took that thought with him out the door, wondering which of them he was saying that to.

Once on the dusty street, filled with creaking and rumbling wagons, drawn by teams of horses and head-swinging oxen, he paused in the shade of a warehouse and asked himself whether he was going back to the ranch or if he should try to talk with Elwood Chandler . . . make an effort to reach some sort of settlement with the Ring that didn't involve shooting one another.

Quite aware that he might come out of such an effort feet first, he decided to talk with Chandler anyway, because he owed it to all the people on the ranch. As he crossed the street and strode off toward the General Store, his mind suddenly conjured a picture of Yellow Leaf, sitting on her pinto. She could not be kept out of the shooting, and the thought filled him with dread. He would do this for her as well as the rest.

The General Store was bigger than his barn, and every square inch, except for the aisles, was covered with merchandise ranging from barrels of molasses to arms and ammunition. The aisles were crowded with men and women waiting to speak with the clerks. The smell in the place was a heady mixture of clothing, leather, spices, and kegs of liquor. Over it all was the hum of voices rising and falling but never ceasing.

Jonathan was directed to Chandler's office, located in a walled-off section of the store at the rear of the building. Two large men with holstered guns got up from chairs at each side of the office door at his approach.

"Stop right there," the one with the turned eye said. He and his partner moved toward Jonathan.

"That's close enough," Jonathan said, stepping back a pace.

The second man began to draw his gun. Jonathan drew quicker and shot it out of his hand. The man howled with pain. The first guard tried to draw but found Jonathan's gun pointed at his head.

"Drop it," Jonathan said.

The guard's gun banged to the floor, breaking the silence that had fallen over the back part of the store. At the same moment, the office door swung open. A tall, grizzle-haired man in a gray cutaway coat stepped through it, holding a revolver. Taking in the scene in a glance, he cursed Jonathan and raised his gun, but, before he could fire,

Jonathan shot him through the heart.

"You've killed Mr. Chandler," the man with the turned eye said in an awed voice.

"It looks that way," Jonathan said. "Now, were I you, I would take your friend to the hospital and get that hand seen to. Then the two of you should put as much distance between you and Santa Fe as you can. I believe a war is about to break out, and you're likely to be the first casualties."

CHAPTER 38

"I went into the store to talk to him," Jonathan told Jubal when he was back at the ranch, "but things got out of control. It was my intention to try to find a way to stop any more bloodshed."

"And Captain Sparing thinks that with Chandler gone, there'll be a struggle for control of the Ring?" Jubal asked.

"Yes," Jonathan said, "but I'm not ready to stop our preparations for defense."

Which was just as well, because two mornings later at first light, the watch came racing back from the road, shouting that there were attackers on his heels. This was a slight exaggeration, but Duncan Harley had spotted a posse of armed men turning onto the ranch road. Jubal was out of bed in seconds and ringing the warning bell in front of the bunkhouse. Within three minutes, the women were running for the barn, carrying their rifles, and hands were boiling out of the bunkhouse and running for their positions. They were only partway to their stations when Yellow Leaf burst out of the woods from the mountain, calling out, "They come! They come!"

She sprang off her pinto to the ground and ran towards Jonathan, who stood with Jubal in the gathering place, making sure the men were moving into position. She had her rifle in one hand, and two belts of ammunition crisscrossed her breasts.

"How many?" he asked.

She opened and closed her free hand three times.

"There's at least a dozen coming from the road," he said. "Make for the barn."

"More use up there," she said. "I will shoot from trees."

"Where's Morgan and Horn?"

"I hide Horn. Morgan waits for me."

"Go," Jonathan said, "and for God's sake, Yellow Leaf, be careful."

She turned and made a running leap onto her paint. Standing still on horseback for a moment, she shook her rifle over her head, shouted, "Jonathan Wainwright! It is a good day to die!" and raced away up the mountain.

"God only made one of her, Jonathan," Jubal said, watching her go.

"I agree, and then He threw away the plans," Jonathan added, feeling a rush of joy from her arrival.

The two groups of attackers rode from opposite directions, shouting and shooting, into the defense Jonathan's people had thrown up. Not a person was in sight, but the ranch people were there, firing from behind brush and trees and rock outcroppings, from the doors and windows of the barn and every other building except the ranch house. Their attackers were shot out of their saddles, with nothing to shoot back at. Then an extraordinary thing occurred. The two groups of raiders saw one another, spread out as best they could, and began firing at each other.

"Lord, Lord," Jubal said, lying with Jonathan behind a granite outcrop. "What is this?"

"This part is probably the war Captain Sparing told me would break out as soon as Elwood Chandler was out of the way. Let's help both sides while we have the chance. They had us in a vise, had they chosen to fall back, dismount, and then press us."

But the raiders hadn't fallen back and soon the situation became too hot for both factions. In ones and twos, the contenders backed away from the fray and then scattered in the general directions from which they had come. For a few minutes a strange silence fell over the ranch. Then, her paint advancing at a leisurely walk, came Yellow Leaf, her rifle cradled in her left arm.

"Rifle got too hot. Had to stop shooting those ones," she said, sounding offended.

Jonathan got to his feet. "Bad luck," he told her, trying to cover his strong rush of relief at seeing her unhurt. "Jubal, have the team harnessed and hooked to the wagon. Throw some bedding in. Yellow Leaf, will you tell Jane and Patience to fix up a couple of rooms in the house for the wounded? Then lead the men with the wagon to where the fallen are?"

"Yes, but not good to mix them," she said. "Bullets coming from two ways."

"Right," Jonathan said. "Tell Patience to keep them in separate rooms."

Just then Bill Johnson joined them. His left sleeve was torn off and tied around a bloody forearm.

"Let me have a look at that," Jonathan said.

"Colonel, it ain't nothing but a scratch from a ricochet."

"You go along with Yellow Leaf and let Patience dress it. I don't want to chance an infection that might cost you the arm. Then, when the wagon comes, separate the wounded raiders into two groups."

"Will do, Colonel. What about our people?"

"I'll take care of them," Jubal said.

"You want to ride, and I lead horse?" Yellow Leaf asked, immediately riling Johnson. They went off together, trading insults.

Jubal chuckled. "Had I not seen it, I would never have believed that Osage woman could have won the hearts of this bunch of roughnecks you've got working for you. They would walk through fire for her."

"She's leaving us, Jubal," Jonathan said, his throat tightening. "She and Morgan are taking Horn to live with her band of Osages, in Kansas or Oklahoma. I hate like fury to see her go."

"I suppose you can't persuade her to stay."

"No, her mind is made up, more's the pity."

It took the men nearly an hour to locate all the wounded and get them into the ranch house. Five of the injured were ranch men, but none was hurt seriously enough to require Jonathan's attention. As for the remaining dozen, over the next two hours Jonathan, Patience, Jane, and Ginger saved all but four.

"What now?" Jane asked when she and

Patience and Ginger had finished bandaging the last man, cleaned up, and joined Jonathan and Jubal in the living room, where the house staff had laid out cups and saucers, glasses, a tall pot of coffee, and a bottle of whiskey, along with a large block of cheese, newly baked bread, and thick slices of ham.

"Anyone hungry?" Jonathan asked.

"I'll stick to the coffee," Ginger said. "I'm afraid whatever I ate would come back up."

Her comment broke the tension in the room and produced some subdued laughter, and the group turned to the coffee.

"As soon as you tell me I can move them," Jonathan said to Patience, "the men you've been working on are going to the town hospital."

"They won't be comfortable," she replied, "but most have flesh wounds, and none of them is in danger of dying."

"Then I'll have them loaded into the wagon. Ten of our men will go with me. Jubal will mount a guard here until our return, although I don't think you're in any danger."

"Yellow Leaf left to go back up on the mountain," Ginger said in a serious voice. "She's a small army all by herself. Several of the mountain attackers said some Indian woman on a paint horse shot them."

"The men have had no breakfast," Jane said, breaking up the gathering. "I had better round up my crew and get started."

At noontime, with Jonathan leading, the wagon carrying the wounded men from both sides, lying on piled hay and blankets, moved at a trot through the town to the hospital, followed by a growing parade of children, men and women, and dogs. The men in the wagon who could sit up shouted to the people they knew. To Jonathan's surprise, both groups of injured raiders got along together surprisingly well during the journey.

After the raiders were in hospital beds, and Jonathan and his men were mounted and preparing to take the bodies of the dead to the undertaker's, Governor Oroño appeared, riding a large palomino stallion and accompanied by three armed riders.

"Colonel Wainwright," he called out, trying to force his horse to stand, "please excuse me. There may be a mare somewhere near coming into season. I see you are making deliveries again. Had they paid you a visit?"

"They had, Governor."

"Elwood Chandler was beyond the skill of our physicians, as I recall."

"He was. We have four more of his gun-fighters in the wagon. You might want to have a look at them. We had a visit from two groups. They began shooting at us and ended by shooting one another. As one of our people said, 'They were shooting two ways.' "

"The struggle over leadership of the Ring appears to have begun on your ranch," the governor said. "Your resulting visits are a mixed blessing."

"My apologies, Governor. We seem to have a hard time living peacefully. People are either stealing our cattle or shooting at us. Do you think this visitation is the last?"

"I'd like to think so. You talked with Captain Sparing."

"Yes. It was a satisfactory conversation."

"I hope he did not tell you to go on shooting the town's citizens."

"Where your citizens are concerned, he advised discretion."

"Oh, Colonel, please! In the name of the Holy Mother! They are not *my* citizens."

"Governor, would you take a look at the dead men in our wagon and say whether or not you recognize them?"

Just then the stallion reared up on his hind legs. Oroño brought the big horse down and dropped from the saddle, passed the reins

557

to one of his men, and walked briskly to the wagon. One of the men gave him a hand up, and he made a quick survey of the corpses.

"Well, well, Colonel," he said, after his escort handed him down from the wagon. "Two of them are important figures in Santa Fe's legal community. One of them, Dirksen Wallows, is — was — the most powerful judge in the county. The other, Samuel Burns, was a criminal lawyer and one of the wealthiest men in town. His wealth is chiefly in property, and how he got it is best answered by explaining why he lies dead in your wagon."

"A Ring member competing with another member for control," Jonathan replied.

"That's three, and a good start," the governor said, remounting. "I hope you will stop the next time you're in town — say, to buy a pair of boots. We should talk. *Vaya usted con Dios, mi amigo.*"

He raised his hand to Jonathan and let the stallion run, which it had clearly been itching to do, with his guard scrambling to catch up.

Jubal watched the governor race away. "This is a strange place, with some mighty strange people in it, Colonel."

"It will take some taming," Jonathan agreed.

The first night of the full moon, and before the moon had risen, Yellow Leaf and Horn, mounted and leading two pack horses, stopped in front of the ranch house porch. Having been forewarned of their coming, Jonathan was on the steps, waiting for her. He walked to the side of her paint and stood with his hand on the animal's neck. Looking up at her, he asked quietly, "You're sure about this?"

"We will go, yes. Morgan will stay."

He did not have to say he was sorry. Both of them had expected it.

"Will you try to find a way to let me know when you reach your people?"

"I will try."

She leaned forward and pressed her hand on his. "Perhaps we will meet again when we reach the place where no one is ill or cold or hungry."

"Perhaps we will meet again sooner."

"Jonathan Wainwright, you are a child still, and I will never forget."

"Nor will I," he answered. "Ever."

He spoke briefly to Horn, wishing the boy well in his new life, and returned to Yellow Leaf, but neither spoke. After a moment of looking at one another, he stepped back and nodded in response to her silent question. She touched her paint with her heels. Jonathan watched her pass the ranch house and realized that Jane, Patience, and Ginger had come out on the steps to wave to her. Horn waved back, and then she and Horn were lost in the trees.

"Are you in love with Yellow Leaf?" Jane asked him when he stepped onto the porch. The others had gone inside.

Jonathan was taken aback and had no answer to give. After a brief hesitation, he said, "I don't know, Jane. She and I spent a lot of time together on the trail. We told one another a lot about our lives, and her accounts of Indian life fascinated me. I have never known anyone remotely like her."

Jane's voice turned frosty. "So you don't know whether or not you love her."

"Yes, I love her, but that's not what you asked me. You asked if I was in love with her."

"When you figure it out, Jonathan, let me know," she told him and went inside, slamming the door behind her.

Jonathan remained on the porch for a while, feeling very uncomfortable and unsure what, if anything, he was supposed to do about Jane's anger. He had thought of saying he also loved *her* but guessed that might not be the right thing to do just then. *Was* he in love with Yellow Leaf? He lingered outside, clearing away a lot of the uncompleted thoughts cluttering his mind and in the resulting clarity said to the chicken hawk circling over the vacated chicken run, "Probably, but to what end? How likely is it we will ever meet again? And what would be the point of my telling Jane that?"

Four days later, eight men rode into the ranch yard and dismounted at the hitching rail. Rifles nestled in their saddle scabbards, and, although they were dressed in business suits, they also wore gun belts. As soon as they had gathered in front of the porch steps, Jonathan came out and said, "Gentlemen, before you take another step, look around you."

They did and found they were looking into the barrels of a dozen rifles at a distance of only a few yards. That didn't seem to bother them, though. The oldest of the visitors mounted the first step and said, "Impressive, Colonel Wainwright. Very impressive. May we come in? We have business to discuss."

"And the nature of the business?" Jonathan asked.

"We represent most of the small businesses in Santa Fe, and we've been robbed blind by the Ring. We're fed up and want to rid the town of it. You've made a good start, and we would like to ask how we can help you finish the job."

He thought he knew where this was going. "I don't much like the idea of becoming sheriff, if that's what you're proposing, but I would be glad to give you something to take the road dust out of your throats and listen to what you have to say."

He waved to the men holding rifles on the visitors and took everyone inside. The meeting lasted for nearly an hour, and, when the visitors left, they all shook Jonathan's hand and expressed their satisfaction with his responses.

Jubal had been lurking near the porch and came to stand beside Jonathan as he watched the men disappear around the corner of the house. "Are we going to war, Colonel?" he asked.

"I hope not, but I think we can help those people do what they want to do."

"Which is to clear Santa Fe of all remnants of the Ring."

Jonathan nodded.

"Did you add your name to the list?"

"Yes."

"Good, Colonel. Good."

He felt himself smiling. "I could be wrong, Jubal, but it's my conviction that if these men hang together and we add a little heft, they won't have to fire a shot."

CHAPTER 39

And he was right. The small farmers joined them and forced the remaining members of the Ring out of Santa Fe. As for Jonathan, the ranch flourished. Over time, as the hands married, Jonathan built houses for them.

Farms, invited to come in, covered much of the lower land, and cattle grazed the rest, but the best grazing had been fenced off for the quarter horses Jonathan had been breeding intensively since the year Yellow Leaf left. He had sent Morgan in search of the best Indian mares on sale whenever one of the tribes brought a herd into Santa Fe to sell. Using his own contacts in Santa Fe, he sought the black thoroughbred that had come with one of the wagon train remudas, and he finally found the animal, thin and neglected in a pasture full of tumbleweed. After Morgan had gone over the big stallion and declared him underfed but sound,

Jonathan bought him.

Under Morgan's care, the thoroughbred quickly recovered his condition and began attending to the needs of the Indian mares. Within the year there were fifteen sons and daughters of the thoroughbred bouncing around their mothers, all of whom were pregnant again. In the next year, he sold all but two — one of each sex, chosen by Morgan for strength and intelligence — to the farmers on the ranch and around Santa Fe. The male yearlings he sold were all geldings. In that year he laid the groundwork for a type of quarter horse, slightly larger than the average, that grew up to be worked during the week and often raced on the weekends.

Eight months after leaving, Yellow Leaf sent Jonathan a letter. She had printed the message, which read, *Colonel Jonathan Wainwright, Someone and Horn got here.*

Jonathan stared at the stained scrap of paper. The finality of the message made all the strength go out of his legs. He sank down on the porch steps and stared at the grass at the bottom of them.

"You all right, Colonel?" The question came from the young, dark-haired maid who had been sent from the house with the letter. She looked frightened, likely after

565

seeing him drop down so heavily.

He forced a smile. "Fit as a fiddle, Theresa," he said.

She nodded uncertainly. "I should get back."

He nodded in turn but scarcely noticed when she left at a run. Not wanting to be troubled by other company, he got to his feet and walked to the back pasture, where he climbed through the rail fence and walked out into the dozen or so mares, who snorted and pretended to be alarmed by his arrival. But all of them were too close to delivering their colts to do more than toss their heads a little and then go back to grazing.

Moving among the large, warm bodies, placing his hands on their backs or stroking their heads when one stopped grazing to press her nose against his chest, quieted the pain the letter had brought him. After a struggle, he stroked the nose of the silent gray mare having her first foal and said to her what he could not say to himself. "She's not coming back, girl. She's never coming back."

For a moment, he pressed his forehead against the animal's, his eyes squeezed shut. The tears leaked through anyway onto the mare's head. Then it ended. He straightened up, blinked away the last of the tears, stroked the mare's neck a final time, and strode out of the pasture.

By the time he was climbing the steps to the ranch house porch, he had decided he was now free to ask Jane to marry him.

Jonathan found it much easier to think that — and he kept the assertion very much to himself — than to act on it. In fact, it was a full month before he made any effort in that direction. The cool days of September were on them. Higher above the ranch, the aspens were turning yellow, red, and gold. The temperature at night was growing sharp, and soon frost was on the grass in the morning, and the squash and pumpkin vines were wilting under the assault. But the air was clear and the sun warming, not scorching. The brave still slept with their bedroom windows open.

Patience and Ginger appeared at the ranch house one evening without prior warning and asked if they could talk with him. Worried by their formal behavior and fearing there had been trouble of some sort, he settled with them in the living room and asked if they'd had any dinner.

"Thanks, but we've eaten," Patience said.

"What it is," Ginger said, not waiting for Patience to get there gradually, "we're concerned about Jane."

"You talk with her more than most of us do," Patience put in. "Have you noticed how silent she's become?"

"I don't think I've seen her to talk to this week," Jonathan said, not adding that, since the arrival of Yellow Leaf's letter, he had carefully avoided her.

"You didn't tell her about Yellow Leaf writing that she and Horn had gotten to wherever they were going?" Ginger said, not trying to cover her astonishment.

"Well, no," Jonathan said, prepared to be angry on that subject. "How do you come to know what's in that letter? I'm the only one who's seen it."

The two women smiled at him as they might have smiled at an innocent child.

"I'm afraid not," Patience said. "Theresa read it over your shoulder. Everyone out of the crib knows what's in the letter. Jane was among the first."

"Jonathan," Ginger said. That brought home their seriousness more than anything else — she almost never called him anything but "Colonel." "You've got to talk to her. Your not telling her about the letter has hurt her deeply."

"You do know she loves you, don't you, Jonathan?" Patience said. "We thought it likely you would marry her once Yellow Leaf was gone."

"I was not . . ." he began, but Ginger shook her head and waved her hand at him to stop.

"Everybody south of the Canadian River knew about you and Yellow Leaf," she said. "After she left, every ranch bunkhouse had a wager on whether or not you would marry Jane. They're laying down money yet, saying you're both still above ground."

"Don't let this linger," Patience insisted, frowning slightly. "Talk to Jane. Don't leave her hanging any longer. It's not what a gentleman would do, and you are, if nothing else, a gentleman."

With that directive, the two women rose as one and left, leaving Jonathan with several open wounds.

A while later, after he had hogtied his anger with them both, he began to recognize the truth in what they had told him, and their insolence transformed miraculously into valid advice. The "if nothing else" continued to sting, but, otherwise, what they said had him on his feet.

On the third morning following his verbal comeuppance, and two troubled nights as further warnings, Jonathan took particular care shaving and brushing his hair, dressed in clean clothes, and ate a scanty breakfast. When he knew Jane would be in her office, he gathered his courage and walked briskly along the hall to her door. He rapped on it, waited for a "Come in," and paused to check that Yellow Leaf's letter was in his shirt pocket before stepping into the room, his stomach in knots.

Despite the fire crackling cheerfully in the fireplace, the room still held some of the night's chill. Jane was dressed for it, in a long-sleeved dress of dark-blue wool and a heavy, dark-green wool sweater over her shoulders. She stood up behind her desk and gave him a thin-lipped smile. "Jonathan. To what do I owe this honor."

He came forward as far as the desk and held out Yellow Leaf's letter. "I believe I owe you an apology, Jane," he said. "I've had this for a month."

She took the letter and dropped it on the desk without looking at it. "Yes, I know. 'Someone and Horn got here.' Not very enlightening."

Determined not to be distracted, Jonathan said, "Scanty English vocabulary. There is something . . ."

"As I recall, that was the only *scanty* feature of Yellow Leaf. All her other features were generously on display. But I suppose you would know more about that than I do."

"Jane," Jonathan began again, "I'm very sorry I didn't come to you at once with the letter, but I had something to discuss with you, and I have had a lot of trouble finding an appropriate way to approach the subject." He heard himself going on and desperately wanted to stop talking.

Jane's cold blue eyes narrowed slightly. "What is it you want to discuss?"

Jonathan increasingly felt the cat was in the cellar, and he was the no-hole mouse. "I wanted to talk about getting married," he said, groaning inside.

"To whom?" she demanded, her eyes widening as she leaned forward, her hands pressed flat against the desk top.

"Well . . ." This wasn't going at all as he had hoped. He cleared his throat. "I had thought to ask you to marry me."

Jane fell back into her chair as if she had been struck in the chest.

"No!" she shouted. "No! Go away! Leave!"

Her fury stunned him into frozen stillness for half a second. Then he strode out of the room, slamming the door behind him. He stood for a while with his eyes shut, pressing his back against the door as if he feared what was on the other side of it might rush out and kill him.

"And serve me right," he muttered, collecting the scattered pieces of himself and striding away down the hall.

Word of the explosion leaked swiftly, through two of the maids who had been working in an adjoining room, and that evening Jonathan had a second visit from Patience and Ginger. After prying all the details from him, the two women sat back and stared at him in silence.

He felt his face reddening as he filled the quiet. "I am fully aware that events got seriously and destructively ahead of me. I would not be surprised if Jane never spoke to me again. I am profoundly ashamed of myself — really, I have no idea how to go about correcting what I have done."

"The thing is, Jonathan," Patience began, speaking softly, "Jane has lived a hard life. I can't betray her confidence, but she's been hurt badly, especially by men, so she avoids close relationships for fear of being hurt again."

He knew that — Jane herself had told him, one long-ago day on the Santa Fe Trail — and he cursed himself for not remembering the likely consequences. He said nothing to Patience of this, merely waited for whatever else she wished to tell him.

It wasn't long in coming. "When you went into her office with Yellow Leaf's letter in your pocket, and *then* proposed, it was clear as water to Jane that you'd decided to settle for second best, since you were never going to see Yellow Leaf again."

"And you didn't even tell her you love her," Ginger put in, not masking her disgust. "What the hell were you thinking?"

"I wasn't," Jonathan said, "and I don't know why."

"Do you love Jane?" Patience asked gently.

He sighed. "Yes . . . though it's true, if Yellow Leaf had not left, I doubt I would have seriously considered marrying Jane."

"That is neither here nor there. Yellow Leaf is no longer in the picture." Patience tilted her head. "Ginger and I have offered you our help, but what do *you* want to do about the situation?"

"I'm going to apologize to her at once and do what I can to restore our friendship. After that . . ." He shrugged. "It depends on how things go. I'll try not to make them worse again, I can promise that much."

And that's what he did. Patience and Ginger played their part once Jane's blood had stopped boiling, carefully exploring with her the possibility that she and Jonathan might become more than friends. It took the better part of a year, but, in the end, Jonathan convinced Jane that he did love her. At that point he proposed properly, and she accepted.

Unfortunately, they would not live happily ever after.

A year after that, Jonathan built an elementary school in town, over the vigorous resistance of the De La Salle Christian Brothers, who had built the Academy of Our Lady of Light adjacent to the San Miguel Chapel in 1859. There had been a time before the war when there were six thousand Catholics in Santa Fe and a mere six hundred Americans, or so the bishop of the region had written to his superiors when appealing for teachers. In 1852, the Sisters of Loretto had responded to the call and came to teach in the Brothers' academy.

There were many more "Americans" in Santa Fe by the time Jonathan built his school. Patience and Ginger soon filled the two-room building with eager young students, and over time the city built its own schools. The Catholic school continued to flourish.

As the years passed, the Wainwright ranch grew ever larger. Jonathan gave his school to the town and built another elementary school on the ranch, to lessen the strain of getting the ranch children into town and back five days a week through all sorts of weather. Ginger taught the first three grades, while Patience took grades five through eight and taught Latin to those with the courage and desire to tackle its six cases of nouns, pronouns, and adjectives. He'd long since hired a full-time accountant as well as an assistant, to deal with the financial side of the ranch. If Patience regretted giving up her father's cause of cleansing slavery from Santa Fe, she didn't show it. Time itself, Jonathan reckoned, had done that job better than anyone could. The Genizaros had their own communities now, and those few who stayed with the wealthy Mexican families did so because they wished to.

One afternoon in late summer, Patience walked over to the ranch house and met Jonathan coming down the porch steps. Between her teaching responsibilities and the demands the ranch made on him, they seldom encountered one another, and Patience paused to talk with him. Watching her as she came towards him, Jonathan thought time had been kind to her. Aside from the graying of her hair, she was little changed in appearance from the young woman who, with her father, had joined the wagon train in Kansas. Ginger, he supposed, deserved much of the credit for that. She had kept Patience too busy living to grow old. He liked that idea enough to make him smile.

They had been talking only a short time when Patience suddenly said, "This morning I saw some yellow leaves on the aspens behind the house, and I thought at once of Yellow Leaf. Do you ever wonder what has become of her and Horn?"

"He'll be a man now," Jonathan said with a twinge of pain, "and, yes, I guess she is never far from my mind. Do you remember the letter she sent a year after leaving here? All it said was, 'Jonathan Wainwright, Someone and Horn got here.' "

The old tightening in his throat stopped him from saying anything more. With her quiet laugh, Patience bailed him out.

"It sounds like her," she said. "Yellow Leaf was a remarkable woman, but there were times when she turned those black eyes on me, that it would have been easy to be frightened."

"I remember them well," he said. "She and Horn may be living in or near the Oklahoma Territory by now. She told me shortly before leaving that her tribe, after negotiating with the government, was going to purchase land in the adjacent Indian territory."

"Ginger and I both feel we lost a friend when she left." Patience hesitated, then said, "Do you miss her?"

"Yes, but time has lessened the pain." It surprised him that the lie came so quickly, and he was sorry he'd said what he had but left it. "How are your children? I haven't had time to visit them for a while. Perhaps when winter comes and our world slows, I will make time."

A few years earlier, Patience and Ginger had adopted the two grandchildren of Jonathan's Mexican housekeeper, who had died of heart failure, leaving them with no place to go. "They're well. Rosa will be twelve in November. Pablo is eight. Neither Ginger nor I see as much of them as we would like, but Abril has taken wonderful care of them and us." Abril kept house for them, and the two women had grown to love her dearly.

A little silence fell between them. Then Patience gave him a somber look. "Speaking of children . . . how is Jane? I actually came to see her today, but I'm a little uneasy about raising the miscarriage with her. It's the third, isn't it?"

He looked down at the steps beneath his

feet. "Yes. I'm afraid she's not doing very well. She blames herself, and it's not her fault."

"No, of course it's not." Patience fell silent again, as if waiting for him to go on. When he didn't, she said quietly, "I recall she took her mother's death very hard, and her brother and sisters' growing up and leaving home was difficult for her also. Well before their last years as youngsters, she was the only mother they had. I suppose she hoped having a child would be a way to replace them."

"It seems pure cruelty of some sort," Jonathan said, bitterness creeping into his voice, "that she was ever able to become pregnant. I'd be angry if I knew who to be angry with."

Patience laid her hand on Jonathan's arm. "When I was a girl, I remember some of the old people saying of similar situations, 'There's no contending.' I suppose they meant there are situations in which one can do nothing but endure."

He sighed. "Perhaps that's wisdom speaking, but sometimes I wonder if the struggle is worth the candle."

"How would Yellow Leaf have responded to that remark?" Patience asked with a smile.

" 'Someone needs head held under water until bubbles come up,' " Jonathan said and managed a laugh. Patience laughed with him.

"Goodbye, Patience. Say hello to Ginger for me," he said and turned away with Yellow Leaf's voice in his head.

CHAPTER 40

Eight years after the shooting stopped and a lot of grueling labor, the ranch became a money-making enterprise. Jubal, forming a cabal with Jane, Patience, and Ginger, began to lean on Jonathan to give the ranch a name. Before long, the wrangling became so intense that Jonathan threw open the choice to everyone on the ranch. His purchase of the black stallion, and the subsequent spread of its offspring among the surrounding farmers, ranchers, and horse dealers, made the words *black horse* and *mountain* so frequently used in referring to the ranch that it seemed destined to be named *Black Horse Mountain.* After a certain amount of arguing and one fistfight, an arch shaped from aspen logs sawn in the ranch mill went up over the entrance to the spread, wearing the name *Black Horse Mountain Ranch,* in black letters.

There was a barbeque and a dance and a

certain amount of drinking following the raising of the arch, in early September following the first frost. Jonathan had persuaded Jane to dance, and, as the yard in front of the ranch house was the nearest thing on the ranch to a level piece of ground, it became the dance floor. Two fiddlers and an accordion provided the music. Jane joined in one of the dances but soon tired.

"There are at least fifty people here," Jonathan said to her as they sat together on a short bench near one of the four fires lighting the dance ground, "and that's not counting the children." Hearing that last word escape his mouth, he could have kicked himself.

"Where are my children?" she asked bitterly.

He put his arm around her shoulders. Not for the first time, he worried about how thin she was. "Try not to dwell on it, Jane. It only makes you feel worse."

"I have every right to feel bad, Jonathan," she said, her voice rising. "I have lost three children!"

His face flushed. "I'm sorry. I'm sorry, Jane."

He drew breath to suggest that perhaps the time had come to adopt a child, then stopped himself, knowing it would further upset her.

"Help me into the house, Jonathan," she said. "I don't think I can get there alone."

They made the walk in stony silence. Jonathan settled her in a comfortable corner of the parlor, with a blanket tucked around her knees and a hot cup of tea within reach. She managed a thin smile and shooed him back outside. "Go rejoin the fun. Dance if you want to. I'll be all right."

He kissed the top of her head and wandered back out onto the porch. Beneath a clear sky pinpricked with stars and a sickle moon riding herd on them, the men and women danced while the children raced and shouted. No sooner had a woman stopped dancing with one man than another whirled her away until they were nearly danced into the ground. Finally, the fires burned down to coals, dimming their light. At a word from Jubal, the musicians broke into "Goodnight, Ladies." All the men began singing the words, bringing the celebration to an off-key end while Jonathan watched.

A year later he lost Sam to old age and what appeared at first to be a cold. Sam had been put out to pasture two years earlier, but Jonathan visited him nearly every day, carrying apples or striped candy. Despite Morgan's efforts, the cold deepened. Sam's breathing grew more labored, and he went off his feed and soon stood, head sunk, under his favorite aspen tree.

"Nothing to do," Morgan said finally, shaking his head. "He'll choke soon. Best put him down. Want me to do it?"

"No," Jonathan said. "You go along. I'll spend a few minutes with him."

Wordless, Morgan pressed his shoulder and then left him to it.

Jonathan stroked Sam's neck. The horse tried to lift his head but couldn't, needing all his strength to breathe. Jonathan stood for a while, recalling some of the things they had done together over the years, especially in those long days they had spent with Yellow Leaf and her pinto. Having put it off as long as he could, Jonathan pulled off his neck cloth and tied it gently over Sam's eyes. That done, he stood for another moment, gathering his own strength. Then he stepped back two paces, drew his revolver, and shot Sam in the center of the forehead, halfway between his eyes and his ears. Sam plunged forward, dead before he collapsed onto the ground.

Word had travelled swiftly, and, at the sound of the shot, those near enough to hear it stopped what they were doing. Some spoke or exchanged looks, but most simply stood for a moment, keeping death company, before bending again to their work.

Jubal hurried up to where Jonathan was, but he moved less quickly these days and reached Jonathan somewhat winded. Noting his friend's concern, Jonathan laid a hand on Jubal's shoulder. "We'll bury him right here," Jonathan said.

"How old was he?" Jubal asked.

"A little over twenty."

"He would follow you around like a dog," Jubal said, running a hand through his white hair. The sight of it reminded Jonathan of the silver in his own. "The men claimed you two talked to one another."

"I wish," Jonathan said. "Let's get this over with. Round up a few of the men. Bring me a shovel. I want to do some of the digging."

"You mostly do the heavy looking on, Colonel. I don't want them to have to dig two holes."

"Get on with it, Jubal." Jonathan looked past him, seeing in his mind's eye faithful Sam falling out of life.

In the following years, the ranch continued to thrive. The railroad came within easy reach of Santa Fe, and Jonathan was soon shipping his quarter horses to Texas and every other state where herding cattle on open ranges was an important part of the economy. Black Horse Mountain quarter horses contributed substantially to the establishment of the quarter horse as a breed.

Much of the credit for this success went to Morgan, and Jonathan often told him so. He seemed to appreciate the praise but resented having to share the task of caring for the growing herd and the paperwork mounting as the breeding gained speed and the black stallion was replaced by others. One morning, the ranch woke to find Morgan gone. A piece of paper, discovered by Jubal, was shoved under the bunkhouse door, bearing the message, *Gone to Texas.*

As well as losing Morgan, Jonathan lost Jane. She never had found a way to make peace with herself or with Jonathan over her inability to carry a child long enough to live on its own. Her miscarriages not only damaged her emotional stability, they ruined her health. In 1889, following a trip to Albuquerque to visit one of her sisters and her family, Jane contracted cholera. She refused to see a doctor on the first day, and, when her sister and brother-in-law took her to the hospital over her protests, she died within hours of being admitted.

In keeping with her wishes, Jonathan arranged for Jane's burial on the mountain in a small, grassy clearing partially surrounded by a grove of aspens that opened to the south, providing a view of the ranch house half a mile below and the rugged country beyond. "It's one of the few places that seemed to give her peace," Jonathan told Patience and Ginger, standing with them in the ranch house parlor the day Jane's body arrived from Albuquerque. "She said the sun always shone more brightly there."

"It is a beautiful place." Ginger stared at the sealed coffin, laid on a table in front of the fireplace. "I hope she *will* find peace there."

" 'The peace that passeth all understanding.' " Patience stroked the casket, then turned to Jonathan. "I wish we had found a way to ease her grief. You must feel that yourself."

"I do," Jonathan answered. "I'm afraid I didn't try hard enough."

"You did, Jonathan," Ginger said. "I don't think the Angel Gabriel could have shifted the weight burdening her."

"But that's not to say she was in any way to blame," Patience put in quickly, shooting

Ginger a warning glance.

Jonathan saw it and said, "I'm sure Ginger didn't mean it that way. I'm grateful for the effort you both made to ease her pain. I've moved up the burial to tomorrow, at ten in the morning. There's some weather coming, and I know she would have wanted to be buried in the sunshine."

The day broke cloudy, but by midmorning the sun was out and taking the chill from the air. Most of the people from the ranch came on horseback. Only the hardiest and youngest of the adults climbed the half mile. Those of Jane's brothers and sisters who could make the trip, along with various nieces and nephews, stood among the mourners as well. Thomas Winthrop, the Presbyterian minister from Santa Fe, conducted the burial service, and, between the people and their horses, the clearing was nearly filled. In an arc behind them, the aspens were alight with red, yellow, and orange, their leaves rustling in the early wind.

The minister was a tall, rangy man with a lined face stamped with sadness. *Not unlike Lincoln's face,* Jonathan thought. Winthrop stood at the head of the open grave, bowed his head in silence for a moment, then raised his head and said, "We are gathered here in the sight of God to bury our sister Jane Wainwright, wife of Jonathan Wainwright and dear friend to many and loved one to several of you."

He paused again and opened the Bible he held. " 'Let not your heart be troubled,' " he began without glancing at the page, his voice rising slightly in the wind that had begun to blow, his attention on the bowed heads before him. " 'If ye believe in God, believe also in me. In my Father's house are many mansions: if it were not so I would have told you. I go to prepare a place for you. And if I go and prepare a place for you' " — the wind rattled the pages, and Winthrop closed the book — " 'I will come again and receive you unto myself; that where I am, there ye may be also. And whither I go, ye know and the way ye know.'

"Let us pray. 'Our Father . . .' "

Their voices rose to recite *The Lord's Prayer,* and the children there recited it with them, their high, clear voices rising in the wind. At the end, Winthrop said, "Let us sing together," and the assembled throng sang *Rock of Ages* and *Abide with Me.* Winthrop had a powerful baritone, and the hymns were familiar to all save the Mexicans. The clearing rang with the voices, bringing water to Jonathan's eyes for the first time since Jane's death.

By the time he was obliged to drop the first handful of dirt onto the lowered coffin, he was once again master of himself, and he did not break down, but many did, remembering other burials in other places and the awful finality of death. From some corner of Jonathan's mind, fragments of a piece of prose, read many years ago, drifted into his awareness as he stood looking down into Jane's grave.

"No man is an island, entire of itself; every man is a piece of the continent . . ." There was a gap in his memory, and then the lines, *"Any man's death diminishes me because I am involved in mankind, and therefore, never send to know for whom the bell tolls; it tolls for thee."*

For an instant, Jonathan's hands felt cold. The temperature had fallen, and heavy clouds were scudding over the mountain as the ceremony came to an end. Jonathan took Winthrop by the arm and gave him a fat envelope Patience had prepared for the occasion. "Reverend, we are going to have some snow, and I want you down off the mountain before it gets ahead of us. I had planned some refreshments to prepare you for the ride home, but I think it would be best if you were well on your way before this thing breaks."

Winthrop nodded. "I trust we will see one another again soon, under less stressful circumstances. It is not often I get to talk with a man of your training and experience."

"I would be honored."

Jonathan passed the minister to two of his men, who bundled Winthrop onto his horse, then mounted their own animals and took Winthrop at a smart trot down the mountain, past the ranch house, and on to the road to Santa Fe. They got the minister home at the outset of a roaring blizzard and holed up in a hotel, and didn't get back to the ranch for two days.

The winter was the longest and harshest Jonathan had experienced since joining Sheridan's cavalry. There was no retreating to his fireplace and letting the wind howl around the eaves. The horses and cattle on the high pastures had to be brought down, the snow having grown so deep they could not scrape it away to feed. A herd of elk came down with them and ate hay along with the cows and horses. The barn was full of sheep, along with pregnant cows and mares, and was the one place the elk weren't welcomed.

"I figure with a little effort we could tame

them elk down," Bill Johnson told Jonathan one day, when the temperature hovered near zero and they were pitching hay out of the hayrick onto the snow for the hungry animals. "We could eat elk meat all year round and never have to go hunting them."

"You can't eat no deer or elk meat in the spring," Burchard Harley put in. "The meat's slippery and stays that way 'til summer."

"I've heard that," Johnson replied, "but I reckon was I hungry enough, I could force it down."

"Yes, you could," Burchard agreed, "but you wouldn't want to get too far away from the backhouse."

That produced a rattle of laughter from the men near enough to overhear the conversation. Jonathan laughed along with the others and thought, as he had so many times, how men in hard places who had never had much space between them and nothing could find occasions to tell stories and laugh, often at themselves.

Jonathan did not laugh very often that winter. The loss of Jane weighed heavily on him. He not only missed her company, difficult as it had become just before her death, but also found it hard to discern where his life was going. Although he was surrounded most days with the men and women living on the ranch, and although he worked among them, in part to take his mind off himself, he was alone at night when there was little but whiskey for company, and he found it an unsatisfactory companion that only darkened his thoughts.

By spring, he found he had lost most of his interest in the ranch. Once the snow melted, the world around him burst into green grass, wildflowers, birdsong, and a rush of new life that transformed the mountain into a constant celebration of renewal. Jonathan, for all his sense of being withdrawn, did not go untouched. A restlessness was growing in him, and he increasingly found himself wanting something, but he couldn't put a name on it.

Jubal, who walked with a cane now and tended to doze off if he sat down in the sun to talk with anyone, saw more clearly than Jonathan what was gnawing at him. In the latter part of April, after the frost went out of the roads and the snow melt dried, making the roads passable again, he caught Jonathan alone near the bunkhouse. "Colonel, you've had a long spell of work and little rest. Maybe you should think of changing the scenery for a while."

"I'm all right, Jubal. There's nowhere I

want to go."

"I'm not much in favor of travelling myself. It's hard work, and, when you get there, it ain't often any better than where you left. You ever hear from that Indian woman who came here with us? Went off with that Horn boy, as I recollect."

"Yellow Leaf," Jonathan said, feeling his stomach twist.

"Quite a woman. Left Morgan, didn't she?"

He wandered on a bit longer about Morgan and Yellow Leaf. Jonathan had stopped listening and found himself thinking about Yellow Leaf with a mixture of pain and pleasure. Since Jane's death, he had kept Yellow Leaf locked away in a dark corner of his mind and had not allowed himself to visit it.

"No, Morgan left her," he said abruptly. "That is, she asked him if he wanted to go with her and Horn, and he said no."

Jubal laughed. "Thought more of the horses."

"Possibly."

"Jessup and the others filled his place better than I expected, but I still miss him."

"We're not likely to find another like him," Jonathan agreed.

He didn't get much sleep that night. His

windows were open and without screens, and he lay listening to the night sounds, coyotes serenading the moon, night birds' occasional calls, the rustling of small creatures scuttling past, intent on their own affairs. He heard all of these intermittently, his mind occupied with his own thoughts. He slept briefly before first light, then was up and dressed well ahead of the sun.

He startled Isabel, his cook, who was up early as usual, still wearing her nightdress and a blue woolen cardigan as she fired up the stove.

"Dr. Wainwright," she said, turning to face him in alarm. "Is something wrong?"

"No, Isabel. I'm sorry if I frightened you. When you can, give me some coffee and one of your apple muffins. I'm going into town. If anyone asks, I'll be back by the middle of the afternoon."

"Mr. Wainwright, you are not making that long, cold ride on a near-empty stomach. An apple muffin is not enough. Come back here in fifteen minutes or when you have saddled that roan of yours and sorted your gear. I will have your breakfast ready."

Isabel McCafferty was five feet tall, but it was best not to argue with her, as Jonathan had learned. "Fifteen then, Isabel, and I thank you."

She folded her arms. "The nosey Parkers, meaning everyone on the ranch, will be asking why you are going to town. What shall I tell them?"

"Tell them I'll be speaking with my lawyer and Mr. Carmichael at the bank. That should hold them until I get back."

"They will build a castle of nonsense from that information and have you in bankruptcy, but it will take their minds off the north wind."

"I haven't heard the wind," he said in surprise.

"Nor have I, but dress warm and wear a scarf. You'll need it coming home."

He left her breaking eggs and slicing bacon and dropping a steak into an iron frying pan between pauses to stuff the stove with kindling wood for quick heat.

Once in town, Jonathan spent two hours with his lawyer, leaving the man shaking his head when their work was done. After eating at the hotel where Jane had worked years ago, he went to see John Carmichael, the bank president, and left him equally shaken. "Are you dead certain you want to do this, Dr. Wainwright?" Carmichael asked. "It's highly irregular."

"I am never certain of the outcome of most things I do, Mr. Carmichael," Jonathan replied. "So, let's do it, and let time take care of the rest."

The afternoon was waning, the late sunlight turning the cliffs and ledges pink, when Jonathan returned to the ranch house bearing a leather case filled with papers, typed, signed, stamped, initialed, and dated. Once there and with the roan unsaddled, rubbed down, watered, and fed, he sent Juanita, one of the housemaids, in search of Patience and Ginger. "Tell them to plan to have dinner here," he told the girl.

They arrived soon after Jonathan had washed and changed to remove the dust from the ride and spread the papers from his briefcase on the table in his office. Shortly afterward, Isabel and one of her girls brought coffee in along with cups and saucers, and plates stacked with sandwiches and cookies.

"It is still an hour to dinner," Isabel said firmly, brushing aside Jonathan's concern they would spoil their appetites. "Eat."

Before sitting down, Jonathan stood looking at the two women whom he had known for twenty years. He wondered how they would respond to what he had to tell them.

"First," he said, once they had settled into chairs with the papers arranged in front of him, "what I'm going to ask is an enormous favor. So, brace yourselves." He spent most of the "hour before dinner" talking while Patience and Ginger listened, one or the other of the women asking the occasional question. Dinner was nearly ready by the time they came to the end of their conversation.

Patience settled back in her chair. "Are you sure you want to do this, Jonathan?"

Jonathan smiled. "That's just what John Carmichael asked me. Having you two take over the running of this ranch, it's exactly what I want you to do. What do you say?"

"Well," Ginger said, "if you're willing to risk us reducing this place to economic ruin, I'm in. What about you, Pace?"

Patience gave Jonathan a sharp look. "You're not going to tell us where you're going."

"No."

"Will you tell us when you get there?"

"I'm not sure I'll be where there's any means of communication."

Patience shook her head but returned Jonathan's smile. "Taking over the running of this ranch is even more ridiculous than our coming here in the first place, but I'm in, and the consequences are on your shoulders."

"I don't know any prayer that fits this occasion," Ginger said, "but, Lord, if You're listening, I want You to know Pace and I are going to need all the help You can give us."

"A little less august but possibly more dependable are the men and women working this ranch," Jonathan said. "Keep Jubal near you, but start looking tomorrow for someone to become his second in command. Do it without making him think you're replacing him. I suspect within the year he'll step aside without being asked, but keep him on the ranch. He has a house and a housekeeper" — mentioning the housekeeper made the women laugh — "so just make sure he's cared for, and when there's something you can't seem to get a hold on, talk to Jubal."

"Are you coming back?" Patience asked quietly.

"Maybe." He rose to his feet. "But something I know for sure is that dinner's ready, and Isabel does not like it if I'm late. Remember that when you eat here, which I hope you'll do a lot with the top hands and the children, along with the string of people buying and selling that you'll have to deal with. Listen to your top hands, and you'll learn more about the ranch than you ever could alone."

■ ■ ■ ■

A week later, Jonathan rose before daylight, ate breakfast with Isabel, saddled the roan, and put the pack harness on a handsome pinto mare with the closest to equal body coloration of any horse in the stud. Once his gear was strapped to the mare, he mounted the roan and, leading the pinto, rode away. Only a barn owl that had been hunting mice saw him leave. A few days later, word reached the ranch that he had been seen in the town of Lamy, loading his horses onto an eastbound train.

EPILOGUE

A midsummer morning, breaking with calves bawling for their mothers in their pasture and Jessup and his men herding a dozen two-year-old quarter horses past the ranch house, on the way to town and the train junction. The aspens on the mountain were heavy with leaves, and the cattle and horses grazing on the open pastures were knee high in grass. Further up the mountain, the ranch's flock of sheep and their lambs grazed among the ledges and rock outcroppings. Above them, a pair of golden eagles climbed on the updrafts of warmed air.

Beneath all this, Ginger and Patience had come out of the ranch house to walk in the sun for a bit before beginning their day's work. They had walked out far enough to look down the ranch road when Ginger, who had been reading English poetry for, as she said, mental improvement, threw wide her arms, spun around, and cried, "God's in his heaven, all's right with the world."

After months of managing the ranch, Patience had begun to take a somewhat less ebullient view of life. She made no response, merely turned to go back inside, when Ginger suddenly called out, "Pace!"

She was staring down the road. Patience turned and came to stand beside her.

Ginger squinted into the sun. "Is that who I think it is?"

They saw two riders and two pack horses following, perhaps three-quarters of a mile away. Patience pushed her glasses up onto her forehead. "Let's go in. They'll get here soon enough."

She turned to re-enter the ranch house. After staring for a few more moments, Ginger caught up with her. "Odd," Ginger said. "I thought something looked familiar about them, but you're probably right. It's just two more people looking for work or wanting to sell us something."

"Yellow Leaf, who was that?" Jonathan asked. He'd seen the two figures beside the ranch house and reined in his roan and pulled off his hat to shade his eyes better from the morning sun.

"Patience Stockbridge and Ginger Stearns," Yellow Leaf said, moving her pinto closer to him. Like Jonathan, she wore deerskin leggings and a jacket, though her jacket was elk hide trimmed with wolfskin. Her heavy black braids trailed over her breasts. "Why they go back?"

Jonathan looked at her and smiled. "They don't have your eyes." He enjoyed looking at her, especially at her eyes, which were deep, dark, and changeable as the weather. They sat together at ease, their affection for one another evident in their voices.

"Are you worried we won't be welcome?" he asked.

She stared at him, not smiling, but her eyes gave her away. They softened when she was amused, as she was now.

"Someone will be," she said. "Maybe not you."

He laughed and said, "Let's go and find out," happier than he had ever hoped to be.

ABOUT THE AUTHOR

Kinley Roby lives in southwest Florida with his wife, Mary Linn Roby, author and editor.

The employees of Thorndike Press hope you have enjoyed this Large Print book. All our Thorndike, Wheeler, and Kennebec Large Print titles are designed for easy reading, and all our books are made to last. Other Thorndike Press Large Print books are available at your library, through selected bookstores, or directly from us.

For information about titles, please call:
  (800) 223-1244

or visit our website at:
  gale.com/thorndike

To share your comments, please write:
  Publisher
  Thorndike Press
  10 Water St., Suite 310
  Waterville, ME 04901

Printed in the USA
CPSIA information can be obtained
at www.ICGtesting.com
JSHW022145280424
61956JS00001BA/1

9 781432 887254